SHADOWS ON THE MOUNTAIN

Diana Wallis Taylor

TotalRecall Publications, Inc.

TotalRecall Publications, Inc.
1103 Middlecreek
Friendswood, Texas 77546
281-992-3131 281-482-5390 Fax
www.totalrecallpress.com

ISBN: 978-1-59095-078-4
UPC: 6-43977-40780-1

Library of Congress Control Number: 2013953126

Printed in the United States of America with simultaneous printings in Australia, Canada, and United Kingdom.

FIRST EDITION
1 2 3 4 5 6 7 8 9 10

To the prodigal sons who returned from the far country and the women who waited for them.

"...for this my son was dead and is alive again. He was lost and is found."

Gospel of Luke 15:24

Author

The author is a former teacher, and served as Director of Conference Services for a private Christian college. She is the author of five books of Biblical Fiction, three other books of Christian Fiction, a book of poetry and has completed an Easter Cantata with her musical collaborator, Carolyn Prentice. She serves on the Board of the San Diego Christian Writer's Guild. She and her husband live in San Diego, California.

Acknowledgment

With grateful thanks to Major Zippo Smith who first told me the stories of these forgotten men and the organization that is dedicated to bringing home as many as they can find.

Preface

MIA's in Vietnam were all declared dead by President Carter. This is a fictional story of one who returns after 25 years, based on an organization operating in Thailand who helps MIA's return via their underground church.

Introduction

Oliver Thornwell leaves for Vietnam thinking that Kathryn, his young wife of five days, has taken a check from his wealthy father and agreed to an annulment. Kathryn, horrified at the hard-heartedness of Oliver's parents, throws the check away and returns to the home of her god-parents. When Oliver's helicopter goes down, he is presumed dead by his family. Nine months later Kathryn gives birth to a daughter and raises her in secrecy, fearing her father-in-law. When Oliver returns home after 25 years, with the help of the underground church, he faces not only a reconciled family, and a daughter he doesn't know he has, but brings a half-Vietnamese daughter he cannot leave behind.

Oliver Thornwell, only son of a wealthy society couple in San Francisco. Tall, auburn hair and eyes that crinkle when he smiles. Wants to be an architect, but is pressed by his father to enter law school to one day join his father's firm.

Kathryn Hilliard, reddish auburn hair, green eyes, art student, orphaned at 3, she and her sister Ruth, 5, were raised by Alma and Edwin Miller, a missionary couple who knew her parents.

Gordon Thornwell, head of a prestigious law firm in San Francisco. Ruthless, with many contacts he has power over, he sets the course of Oliver's life. Offers Kathryn a large check to file for an annulment and then uses those contacts to keep Oliver and Kathryn apart when Oliver goes to basic training with the Army.

Thea Thornwell, short in stature and haughty in nature, she wants only someone well-bred and of social standing for Oliver.

Edward (Corny) & Martha Culpepper, butler and cook for the Thornwells. Devoted Christians, they feel it has been their mission to stay with the Thornwells under adverse circumstances. Helped raise Oliver.

Noreen Simons, housekeeper to the Thornwells for many years, who carries a secret that almost tears the family apart.

Ralph Jensen, missionary doctor with a traveling medical team, who discovers Oliver in a small village in the mountains of Northern Vietnam and helps arrange the escape of Oliver and his 15 year old daughter, Kim Ahn.

Allison Thornwell Carradine, Kathryn and Oliver's daughter who learns at last of her paternal grandparents and contacts them, starting a chain of events she couldn't imagine.

Jason Carradine, Allison's husband and the catalyst for the reconciling of a fractured family.

Joshua CarradinE, Allison and Jason's small son.

ONE

Northern California, April 1997

Kathryn gave the painting a last couple of strokes and laid down her brush. She stood up, stretched, and strolled over to the window to stare at the river that ran past her mountain home.

Tell her.

She sighed. Perhaps it was time. Allison was grown now; the danger was over. Had she been silent too long?

When the thoughts pressed in on her that morning, Kathryn felt herself balking. She didn't want to open up old wounds.

She needs to know.

How should she go about telling her daughter about her grandparents? After all these years she still battled with the old resentment that threatened to rise like bile in her throat. Once again she gave those feelings over to the Lord. She knew she was not to carry those things any longer.

Kathryn sighed and returned to her painting. The whimsical rabbit stared back at her with his lopsided smile. At least her gift of artistry had provided a home and paid the bills over the years as she raised her daughter alone.

She bowed her head. "All right, Lord, I'll tell her, but it won't be easy. What happens from there on is up to You."

Just then the tires of a car made a crunching sound on the gravel driveway, and her heart lifted as she hurried down the stairs to greet her family.

Her daughter, Allison, stepped into the hall, holding her small son, Joshua and Kathryn hurried towards her.

"Honey, it's so good to see you." She hugged Allison with one arm and then reached for her three-month old grandson. She tucked him gently into the crook of her arm, marveling again at the wonder this precious new life had brought their family. She reached out and touched Allison on the cheek. "How are you feeling?"

"Great, except for little or no sleep. I'll sure be glad when he's sleeping through the night."

Jason stood grinning at his mother-in-law. "He's a pretty big eater, Mom, almost every two hours."

Kathryn beamed at her handsome son-in-law. His dark, almost black hair and brows framed incredible blue eyes. As she glanced down at her grandson, it was obvious that Joshua was the spitting image of his father.

She led them into the dining room where she'd placed a vase of summer daffodils on a table spread with a soft green tablecloth and green and white striped napkins. She enjoyed making every part of her home look like a still life painting.

They sat down to lasagna, salad and garlic bread and Kathryn nodded to Jason to ask the blessing. During dinner he regaled them with stories from his recent stint at summer camp with the junior high school kids from their church.

Kathryn shook her head. "How in the world did you manage them all?"

He grinned and waggled his fork. "I kept them very busy."

"Oh," Allison turned to Kathryn, "By the way, Mom, Jason's parents are having their annual barbeque on the 4th of July."

Jason reached for another piece of garlic bread. "And if there isn't anyone in Lewiston who hasn't seen pictures of my folk's first grandchild, I'm sure they'll get the opportunity."

When there was a pause in the conversation and Kathryn looked at her daughter. "Darling, there's something I want to talk to you about."

Allison looked up, quizzically. "What is it?"

Kathryn gave her a wistful smile. "Why don't you come up to my studio after dinner and we'll talk."

Allison glanced at Jason. "Okay, Mom. I'll be up after Joshua is settled."

Kathryn started up the stairs to her studio, gathering her thoughts. What should she tell Allison? The Thornwells were her grandparents. How much of what they did should she share? How should she begin her story? Thoughts spun in her mind like a hamster in a spinning wheel. She finally took some quiet moments to pray for wisdom, then waited for Allison's footsteps. They weren't long in coming.

"Mom?"

"Come in Allison. Is Joshua asleep?"

"Yes, I fed him and he's out for the time being."

"Is Jason coming?"

"He said he'd stay with the baby. I think he felt you and I needed to talk alone."

"That's very thoughtful of him, honey. You can share what you want to with him later."

Allison sat down on the edge of the small settee and waited expectantly.

Kathryn turned and stared out the window a moment, thinking back.

"I think it's time I told you about your paternal grandparents."

"The Thornwells? I thought they were dead."

Kathryn shook her head slowly. "I'm afraid I gave you that impression. I didn't want you to contact them."

"But why?"

I didn't know what they would do. There is more to the story of the loss of your father --"

TWO

"It was spring, 1972. I couldn't put my finger on when I knew. Maybe it was the way he strode next to George as they crossed the lawn. I was standing in the rose garden at the home of my roommate, Gloria Horton, as I watched him approach. Gloria was going on about her mother's prize roses..."

"Your brother George is coming with someone."

Gloria turned to look and her face lit up.

"Kathryn, he's invited Oliver Thornwell! We can be a foursome. Ollie's not only handsome, he's fun. His father owns a huge law firm."

As Oliver came towards her with George, they seemed to move in slow motion.

George spread his arms expansively. "Hey sis, look who's here."

Oliver nodded to Gloria. "It's nice to see you again."

"You too, Ollie."

Kathryn felt a nudge at her back. "This is my roommate, Kathryn Hilliard. Kathryn, this is Oliver Thornwell, Ollie to most of his friends."

She looked up at his six feet two frame and his reddish auburn hair seemed to pick up flecks of sunshine as he acknowledged her. Gloria was right. He was handsome.

"I'm glad to meet you, Oliver."

He took her outstretched hand in his and smiled. It was a warm smile that made crinkles at the corners of his eyes.

"Kathryn." He drew her name out. "I'm delighted to meet you."

He didn't let go of her hand.

George interrupted the moment. "Say, you two, we just came down to tell you lunch is ready. I'm starved." He took Oliver's arm. "Lunch, old man, lunch. The girls are joining us, so you can let go of her."

Embarrassed, Kathryn withdrew her hand. George steered Oliver towards the house as Kathryn and Gloria hurried behind them.

"Well you certainly made an impression on Ollie," Gloria whispered. "I've never seen him look at a girl that way." She gave Kathryn a sideways glance. "Hey, you like him don't you?"

"Yes." The word was woefully inadequate.

"Well don't go getting too serious. You haven't met his parents. From what George tells me, they're pretty controlling. I mean, they have his whole life planned, the girl too, if you know what I mean."

Kathryn, still mentally processing her reaction to Oliver, just nodded.

During lunch, Kathryn glanced at Oliver's profile when he turned to speak to someone else at the table. It was a good thing Mrs. Horton loved to talk, for the conversation seemed to flow over and around them.

"--and this war, well, you know, they call it a police action or some silly thing like that. Can you imagine all those boys going over there when there isn't really a war? She turned to her son. "Now George, I don't want you mixed up in all this business in Asia."

"Vietnam, Mother. And you don't have to worry, I'm still in school." George turned to Oliver while his mother was distracted passing a bowl of salad.

"Did you know two of my fraternity brothers are going over? Sam was flunking out anyway and Ed just decided to sign up. I guess they wanted to see some action, though I wouldn't choose to be in their shoes for a million dollars."

Mrs. Horton's' ears were sharper than they gave her credit for. She gave her son a baleful look. "George dear, people are getting killed over there Those boys could get hurt. Now promise me you won't do anything foolish like that."

Mr. Horton chuckled. "Mable, don't get all worked up. The boy will finish school and this thing will be over by the time he graduates. No need to worry."

Mrs. Horton peered at her husband over her glasses and gave a slight shake of her head, then, remembering her duties as hostess, turned to Kathryn. "How are your art classes coming, dear?"

"Fine, thank you. One of my instructors actually wants me to submit some of my watercolors to an editor she knows who's looking for an illustrator."

Mrs. Horton beamed and waved a hand to include all at the table. "You should see the darling creatures she paints. She reminds me of Beatrix Potter."

Not wanting to keep the attention on herself, Kathryn turned to Gloria. "You got high marks on your fashion sketches. Mr. Zumwalt was very impressed."

Gloria struck a pose. "Of course, dahling, you must all come to my next showing"

As usual Gloria's effervescence brought laughter, and the conversation began to flow in several directions. Kathryn learned Oliver was in his senior year at Stanford and headed for Stanford School of Law the next year. George would do the same.

As Kathryn listened to the banter among the family, she realized how much she enjoyed coming here. There was such genuine warmth among the family.

She sensed Oliver's eyes on her, and was puzzled by the turmoil in her feelings. She had never been subtle and if she looked at him her face would tell him everything she felt. She glanced at each one of the family as they spoke, but avoided looking at Oliver.

As the meal was ending, George turned to his friend with a slight grin. "The initials of my grandparents are carved into the trunk of the old oak tree. Kathryn might like to see it. How about it, Ollie? I have to take care of a few things. I'll join you later."

"Be glad to," smiled Oliver. Gloria looked at Kathryn and with a wink not seen by her parents, added gaily, "We'll meet you down there in a little while, okay?"

Kathryn accepted the plan as casually as possible and made herself turn to Oliver. "I would love to see the tree, Oliver, that is, if you would like to show it to me."

"Can't think of anything I'd rather do at this moment." He turned to Mr. and Mrs. Horton, "Will you excuse us?"

They walked casually until they were out of sight of the house, then Oliver impulsively took her hand and they began to run.

THREE

"Come on, the tree is this way."

Laughing and out of breath, they leaned against the gnarled old tree. Their eyes met and he bent his head to one side, looking at her face a long moment. Distracted, Kathryn looked down at the ground. Oliver took her hand and pulled her down to sit on the soft grass, facing each other.

He grinned, "So, tell me about yourself, Kathryn Hilliard, where you grew up."

She sighed and wondered where to begin. "Well, my sister, Ruth, and I were raised in Marysville by my godparents, Alma and Edwin Miller."

"Godparents? What happened to your parents?"

"They served with a mission in China. Traveling down a river to one of the villages, the boat they were riding in was fired on by Chinese bandits. It sank and they were both drowned."

"Whoa, that's pretty traumatic. How old were you when it happened?"

"I was three and Ruth was five."

"Are you related to the Millers?"

"No, Alma was a dear friend of my mother's. They met in missionary training camp. The Millers were on furlough in the States from Guatemala when they received the telegram from my father's office telling them about the tragedy. My father evidently left their names on file with the main office to be notified in the event of an emergency. The Millers flew to Asia to the mission family that had taken us in and got us. They've been our family ever since."

"You have no other family?"

"No. If it hadn't been for the Millers we'd have been placed in an orphanage."

"They sound like wonderful people. I hope I'll have the

opportunity to meet them someday."

Kathryn just smiled up at him.

He rested his elbows on his knees. "So you're attending the Academy of Art University with Gloria. What's your goal?"

"I want to do illustrations for children's books."

"Sounds like you might get that opportunity. I'd love to see your work sometime."

She shrugged. "If you'd like to, I don't know how good it is right now."

"Well, I'd still like to see it." His eyes twinkled. "Perhaps the next time we meet."

She felt her face redden. She did want to see him again, more than she realized. She covered her embarrassment quickly.

"Tell me about your family, Oliver."

He looked off into space, his expression unreadable. Then, after a moment, his ready grin reappeared. "I'm an only child, a mid-life surprise, I believe. My parents thought they couldn't have any children. Sometimes I've heartily wished for brothers and sisters, to take the heat off, so to speak."

She laughed softly. "Gloria said they were strict. Are they?"

He made a face. "I guess that's as good a description as any. Oh, I'm sure they love me, and mean well, but every aspect of my life has been planned from the moment I was born, the right playmates, the right schools, the right everything."

"The right girl?" she ventured.

He smiled that slow warm smile and his eyes twinkled. "That privilege I believe I will reserve for myself, in spite of their good intentions."

Distracted by his smile, she struggled to gather her thoughts. "You're going to be an attorney, Oliver?"

He tilted his head to one side. "You know I'd have you call me Ollie like everyone else does, but somehow I like the way you draw out my name. Say 'Oliver'."

She obliged, and he grinned with approval.

"How do you think you'll like law school?"

He looked off in the distance. "If you want to know the truth, I hate law. There just doesn't seem to be any way out. The slightest resistance to their wishes and I get major recriminations for all their efforts on my behalf. It hasn't been worth the battle."

She studied his long fingers.

"If you could choose any vocation you wanted, what would you like to do?"

He stretched out on the grass and stared up at the leaves above him. "I want to be an architect. To design homes that fit in with the terrain around them, homes with light and space." He had been toying with a small twig and suddenly snapped it in two. "I might just as well wish for the moon."

She put her hand gently on his arm, "Oliver, you can be anything you want to be. Maybe you could finish college, get your law degree, and work for your father a couple of years, then go to night school to become an architect."

He gave her a searching look and chuckled, "Where in the world did you come from? I like your way of thinking." Then he frowned and sighed heavily. "A junior law assistant is kept pretty busy. I think my father would make sure I didn't have any free time. He plans on having me take over the firm some day." He chewed on his lower lip and stared off in to space.

Hearing the voices of George and Gloria approaching, Kathryn and Oliver jumped up, brushing the leaves from their clothes.

George grinned knowingly and Gloria put her hands on her hips, pretending to look stern. "And what do we have going on here?"

Oliver started to protest, but George waved a hand, "Don't worry old man, our lips are sealed."

Oliver looked relieved and the four of them walked back towards the house. Gloria turned to Kathryn when the men were far enough ahead and whispered, "Oliver's mother monitors all his relationships, if you know what I mean."

Kathryn frowned but didn't respond.

When the girls caught up to them, George elbowed Ollie and grinned. "How about a little tennis, old man? You beat me two sets out of three last time. I need to get even."

Oliver grinned. "You're on." He turned back to Kathryn. "Do you play?"

She gave him an impudent smile. "I can hold my own."

They changed clothes and met back on the tennis court. Kathryn kept up her end of the team, but at the same time watched Oliver, who was not only lithe, but obviously a strong player. They switched sides but no matter whom Oliver had for a partner, his team won.

The shadows lengthened, and before they realized, it was time to change for dinner.

As Kathryn turned towards the house, Oliver waited for her.

"You play a mean game of tennis, Ms. Hilliard."

"You did pretty well yourself, Mr. Thornwell."

He walked her to the stairs and with a tip of his fingers to his forehead and a smile, followed George.

FOUR

As the girls got dressed in Gloria's room, Kathryn asked about Oliver's mother.

"The girls at Radcliff, including my mother, were in awe of Thea. Mom says she was very smart and could pin you to the wall with a few well-chosen words." Gloria paused to pull a fine gray wool dress over her head.

Kathryn slipped on her one good dress of soft green jersey. With a sigh she looked in the mirror and examined her complexion, marred, she felt, by the parade of freckles that marched across her nose. They seemed impervious to all the creams she tried. She gave her thick strawberry blond hair a vigorous brushing, but it seemed, as usual, to have a mind of its own.

As she and Gloria started down the stairs, arm in arm, Gloria continued talking about Oliver's mother.

"Her father was extremely wealthy; the head of the law firm and Thea was his only child. When she married Gordon Thornwell, he was just a struggling young attorney. He sure had everyone's undying sympathy! Because of Thea's money, Gordon took over the reins of the law firm when his father-in-law died. They moved into the family mansion and Thea became the reigning society queen."

"Oliver told me he was an only child, born later in the marriage."

Gloria laughed. "I think Oliver's mother went into shock when, after twelve years of marriage, she learned she was pregnant. Maybe she thought people couldn't, you know, get pregnant any more at her age. Anyway, Oliver was born by caesarian section, and it seems there were all kinds of complications. The doctor basically said there would be no more children."

"I take it his mother doted on him," Kathryn mentioned casually, savoring any information she could glean on Oliver.

"Well, my mother said that she felt the Thornwells were a little overbearing, but in a loving way of course."

"Your mother doesn't have a mean bone in her body, Gloria."

They entered the dining room and Kathryn was once again seated across from Oliver. This time she didn't look away from him.

George maneuvered them into a game of Monopoly after dinner and while Oliver stayed neck in neck with him, George rapidly advanced, making himself a property mogul and finally crowing in triumph over them all.

As they conceded defeat and parted for the night, Kathryn felt a warm hand on her arm.

"Good night, Kathryn Hilliard," Ollie whispered, but the way he said it was enough to keep her awake half the night.

The next morning after breakfast, as the Hortons prepared for church, Kathryn dressed carefully, looking forward to the possibility of sitting near Oliver. Her disappointment was tangible when she came down the stairs and saw George kiss his mother, shake hands with his father and announce that Oliver had a paper to finish and he needed to drive him back to school. Their bags were already by the front door.

Oliver looked up and saw Kathryn standing at the bottom of the stairs and came to face her, his eyes searching her face as if to memorize every contour. "Will you write to me, Kathryn?"

"Yes, if you'd like me to." *Don't leave, Oliver, not yet.*

He took down her address and the phone numbers for her residence hall and the Miller's home.

"I'll call you," he whispered.

"All right," she whispered back. He and George gathered their bags and left the house. The click of the front door seemed to echo in the silence. She walked slowly to the window and touched her lips wistfully as George's car turned out of the driveway and the sound of the engine faded into the distance.

FIVE

Oliver's first letter arrived in the mail and Kathryn could hardly contain her euphoria. She wrote back right away. Then Oliver called her. He would be in San Francisco on Saturday and asked her to meet in Ghirardelli Square.

When she got off the trolley, he was standing by the chocolate shop, leaning up against the building. He came forward with that wonderful smile and tucked her hand over his arm.

"I'm glad you could come. How about lunch? I know of this little café that serves great sandwiches."

"I'd like that." She didn't care where they went, it was just so wonderful to be with him again.

They sat and talked over pastrami sandwiches and cokes for two hours. The waitress came by several times and refilled their glasses, but finally, with a knowing smile, left them alone.

Finally they walked along the waterfront and sat on a bench, feeding the seagulls some bread scraps Oliver had wrapped in a napkin from their sandwiches.

"I'd like to see you again, Kathryn. With our class schedules it may be a little hard."

"I'd like to see you again, too."

He gave her a wry smile. "That's great. I hope you won't take this wrong, Kathryn, but from now on I need to stay away from public places. There's always a chance someone my parent's know will see us."

Since he'd explained how things were with his parents, she nodded but felt a small sense of apprehension.

"Where did you want to meet then?" Did it matter as long as she could see him again?

Oliver thought a moment. "There's a small state park about halfway between Palo Alto and San Francisco where we could meet.

If you could get to the bus station near there, I can pick you up. I'll call you with the directions." He chuckled. "I figured that no one in my parent's circle of friends would be caught riding a bus."

She had to laugh too. He was right.

Halfway sounded fair. It would be about an hour's bus ride, but she realized it was also a long drive from Stanford in Palo Alto.

As they walked, hand in hand, Oliver spotted a small alcove between the buildings and drew her into the shadows. He took her upturned face in his hands and slowly leaned down. The kiss was all she'd longed for. They stood for a long moment with their arms around each other.

"I've been wanting to do that ever since the day I met you, Kathryn. I've never felt like this about a girl."

"It's been so different for me too. I feel like I've known you for always."

He kissed her again and they reluctantly returned to his car. He dropped her off and drove away ~~so~~ quickly, without even a backward glance. She entered the residency hall, her feelings tumbling in confusion.

SIX

Kathryn sat quietly in the waiting room of the bus station, her eyes riveted on the main entrance. People went in and out and she shivered in the draft from the open door. Each time some men entered, she looked up, her shoulders sagging in disappointment when it wasn't Oliver.

She glanced at the big clock again. *One fifteen.* He promised to be there by one o'clock. Maybe he'd changed his mind. He wouldn't stand her up, would he? She read the note with Oliver's instructions for the tenth time to be sure she was at the right place. Then she got out a small map she'd purchased and traced the route from Palo Alto with her finger. Well, it was a long drive. Kathryn sighed deeply. She'd brought a book to read on the bus and tried to concentrate on the story but her eyes would wander up to the big clock on the station wall. *One thirty.* She jumped up and hurried to the entrance to look up and down the street. Maybe she could spot his car. After a while she wandered back inside and plunked herself down on the bench again. *One forty-five.* Was he going to be there or not? Had he just been stringing her along? Was there another girl? Had he met someone else? Impatiently she opened her book again and forced herself to read. After a couple of pages she looked up at the clock again. *Two o'clock.* Tears stung her eyes. Perhaps she should find something to eat. Her bus back to San Francisco didn't leave for four hours. It was going to be a long afternoon. She wiped her eyes with a tissue and stood up, not sure which direction to go for a restaurant.

"Kathryn!" She whirled around and Oliver was there. He gathered her in his arms. "I got caught in a traffic jam. A big semi overturned on the freeway. I took the first exit I could and came through some residential areas. I was afraid you would be gone!"

She leaned against him in relief. "Oh Oliver, I thought you'd changed your mind."

He chuckled as he led her out to his car. "I would have come if I had to walk. It's almost a two-hour drive. And, I had to cover my bases. That is, if anyone called."

She sighed heavily. "Your mother."

He nodded. .

They found a local hamburger stand, ordered cheeseburgers and shakes and drove to the nearby state park. They ate their lunch at a stone picnic table and tossed some crumbs to the ever-present sparrows.

"How was your bus trip?"

"The bus was crowded. A Hispanic man gave me his seat."

"That was kind of him. I'm glad to hear courtesy isn't dead yet."

The conversation bordered on the mundane and Kathryn felt neither of them were talking about what was foremost on her mind. *What's to become of us?*

They disposed of the trash and then Oliver took her hand. They strolled deeper into the park. Full with the leaves of summer, the huge trees offered shade and privacy. They stopped in a secluded place in the shadows under a spreading oak tree. He took her in his arms, kissing her tenderly, then hungrily.

"Oh Oliver, I've missed you. I can't seem to concentrate on any of my classes."

He laughed, looking down at her. "I'm supposed to be studying but all I can think of is running my hands through that beautiful thick hair of yours."

She lifted herself up for his kiss again.

They strolled under the trees with their arms around each other and spoke of the future. Somehow they had to find a way to be together. Finally, as the shadows lengthened, Oliver checked his watch and shook his head.

"We'd better get back to the bus station. You've got a long ride and it's a long drive back for me too. My mother feels the need to call more often. George covers for me, but she's a stickler for explanations."

Kathryn caught her breath. "You don't suppose she knows about us? The Hortons wouldn't tell, would they?"

"George and Gloria will keep our secret. I doubt their parents know."

A sigh came from her soul. "When can we see each other again?"

He chewed on his lip. "I don't know, sweetheart. Finals are coming up and next weekend George and I are invited for dinner at the home of some family friends. If I don't show up I'll get the third degree. It will have to be two weeks from today. Same time?"

She nodded, but felt miserable. *Two weeks.*

They returned to Oliver's car and he drove her back to the bus station. They held hands until the very last moment when she had to board the bus. She gave him a small wave from the window. He held up one hand in response, then turned back to his car.

The summer break arrived too soon. Most of the students were staying for summer school, but Gloria was going home. It didn't matter if Kathryn stayed at school or went home, for she and Oliver would not be able to see one another for the entire summer. As Gloria packed her suitcases, she tried to cheer Kathryn up. Yet even Gloria's natural buoyancy didn't dent the heaviness in Kathryn's heart. She could still feel Oliver's hand as he brushed her hair back and explained that when he returned home it meant many social engagements his mother had planned along with working in his father's legal office.

"It's not a good idea for you to write to me at home," he cautioned. "At least for now. I'll just have to call every chance I get." When he held her the last time, she could feel his heart beating and she didn't want him to let go.

Since she thought Oliver wasn't leaving Stanford for another week. She poured her heart into one last letter and sent it to his fraternity house as usual. At least he'd have that before he went home.

SEVEN

Thea Thornwell glanced at the envelope their butler, Mr. Culpepper, placed in the tray on the hall table. It had a woman's name in the upper left hand corner and was addressed to Oliver. Her eyes narrowed. She didn't recognize the name from any of the families they knew. It had been forwarded from his fraternity house. She picked it up, caught a whiff of a flowery fragrance and frowned. Turning the letter over, she saw a tiny sketch of a tree. Her lips tightened as she grabbed her paper knife, slit the envelope open and scanned the contents.

It was a love note, from a girl named Kathryn. She quickly read the contents. How dare this girl be so familiar with their son? Thea slammed the envelope down on the desk, then rose and hurried into the library where her husband was reading the paper.

"Gordon, you must read this letter that just came."

He looked at her face and reluctantly laid the paper down. He reached for the letter and as he read, his eyes narrowed. "Call Oliver in here, now," he growled.

When Oliver answered the summons and strolled into the room, his mother held up the letter.

"Oliver! Who is this Kathryn Hilliard? And where did you meet this girl? We've never heard of her."

He stared at the paper in her hand, and when he realized what it was and that they'd both read it, he felt the blood rush to his face. He reached out and snatched the letter.

"You had no right to open mail addressed to me! That's my private business!"

Gordon Thornwell fixed his son with a hard look. "Nonsense. You come from an influential family. We have the right to know if some female has set her sights on you. Obviously the girl is infatuated."

"We're in love if that's what you mean, and Kathryn is a

wonderful girl. She's beautiful and sweet." He hesitated. He couldn't tell his parents they met at the Horton's. It would just cause more trouble. "We, ah, met at a school dance, several months ago."

His mother was unperturbed. "And what kind of a girl would you meet at a school dance? This is unacceptable, Oliver. We know nothing of her background. You need to concentrate on your studies. You graduate this next year and you still have law school ahead of you."

Gordon rose, smiled benevolently at Oliver and patted Thea on the shoulder. "Now, Mother, boys will be boys. He's just having a little fling." He turned to Oliver. "Perhaps it's time to call off this relationship, son, before you get carried away. You know, complications. Why don't you just tell this girl you can't see her anymore, hmmm?"

Oliver looked from one to the other, "You don't understand. This isn't some passing fling. I love Kathryn. She loves me. I don't intend to give her up."

"May we remind you that your father is paying for your college and furnishing your allowance?"

"Planning my life you mean!" He shouted at them. "Look, I didn't plan this, but it happened. Kathryn is the girl I love and no one is going to tell me who I can and cannot see. Here's another fact. I never wanted to be an attorney or establish myself in the firm. My dream has always been to be an architect. You knew that, but you've never been interested in what I wanted to do. You think only of yourselves!"

Thea drew herself up. "Oliver, control yourself, you are in no position to choose anyone right now. There will be no more of that sort of talk. Now if you will not write to this girl and end this, then I will."

His mother could be bluffing, for he knew they thought he would give in to their wishes, he always had. But then again, his mother was capable of doing just what she said. He stared at them both for a moment, not sure what to do.

His father's eyes were hard as he gripped his son's shoulder. "I suggest you think things over before you make any irrevocable decisions."

"I think I have made an irrevocable decision. If you will excuse me--" He jerked away from his father's hand and strode out of the library.

His mother started to protest, and he heard his father calming her down. "Now Thea, just give the boy a little time, he'll come around."

Oliver paused a moment, then rushed up to his room, taking the stairs two at a time. He grabbed his suitcase out of the closet and threw in underwear, shirts, his toiletry bag and anything else he thought he would need. He couldn't take a chance on using the phone in the hall. A pay phone would have to do. The address of the residency hall was on the envelope. He knew he had to get to Kathryn before his parents did. He loved her and this was one relationship they were not going to spoil. He paused, taking out a picture she'd given him.

"I won't lose you, Kathryn," he murmured as she smiled up at him from the photograph.

He stalked back down the stairs with his suitcase and noted his parents had returned to the library. They were talking and didn't look up. That was fine as far as he was concerned. They wouldn't see him leave, but he made sure they heard the front door as he slammed it behind him.

EIGHT

Oliver waited impatiently as the phone rang and was about to give up when Kathryn answered.

"I can't believe my luck, Kathryn. You're back in the city. I need to see you right away." He gave her the name of the hotel where he'd registered under the name of John Newman. "I'll be in the restaurant." Something has come up. Can you meet me right away?"

"Oliver, you sound like something terrible has happened.

"I'll explain when you get here."

"All right. I'll be there as soon as I can. I'll have to take the trolley."

"Thanks, sweetheart, I'll be waiting."

Fortunately the hotel was only a mile or so away and within a half hour, Kathryn hurried into restaurant and spotted Oliver in a booth at the far corner.

"Kathryn." He jumped up to enfold her in his arms for a quick hug before they both slid into the booth.

"Oliver, what happened? You sounded as though it was urgent."

He related the incident with his parents, how her letter had somehow come to the house, that his mother had opened her last letter and the ultimatum they'd given him.

"Oh Oliver. I thought you would still be there another week. I'm so sorry. What happened?"

"Your letter was forwarded to the house."

"I can't believe your parents reacted that way. Why do they hate me?" Then as realization set in, she looked at him wide-eyed. "You told them you were going to marry me?"

He grinned, "Well, I was going to get around to asking you after the holidays." He looked down at her tenderly. "Will you marry me, Kathryn?"

She touched his face. "Of course I will. I want to spend the rest of my life with you, but what about law school, and your parents?"

"Well, there is something else I need to tell you." He took her hand, rubbing it softly with his thumb. "I won't be going back to school, at least not just yet. I've done something I guess I shouldn't have. I was so angry at my parents I joined the Army."

She jerked back as if someone slammed her in the chest. "The Army? Oliver, why in the world did you do that? They'll send you to Vietnam."

"I know. I just wanted to do something that would shock them. To tell them I was tired of all the plans they've made for me, plans I never had any part in. And there is another benefit. The army will pay for my schooling in architecture after I've finished my commitment. I don't have to depend on my folks."

"Oliver, I understand, truly, but the Army? What can we do? I mean what can we do right now?"

"I have to leave for basic training in five days." We could get married. Will you marry me, Kathryn, today?"

She put her hand to her face. The Millers had always been loving and supportive. They would understand. And she was of age. She nodded slowly. "Yes."

"We have to be careful, Darling. If I know my father, he'll put out feelers to find me. He has many influential friends in high places. I'm sorry you had to take the trolley, but I wouldn't put it past him to claim my car was stolen just so the police would look for me. My car's out of sight in the hotel parking garage."

He took her hand again. "Kathryn, I talked to the recruiter after I signed up and he gave me the name and phone number of the military chaplain at the Presidio. He can marry us. It's the last place my folks would look for me."

Kathryn looked bewildered. "We have to get a license, don't we?"

"Yes, and that means going down to City Hall. It's closest and we don't have time to get to another courthouse. We'll have to take the chance that no one from my father's office is around. It's four-thirty. Most courtrooms have adjourned for the day."

Oliver called the number the recruiter had given him, and told Kathryn the chaplain agreed to meet them at the chapel at six, so they'd have to hurry.

In a small jewelry store near the hotel they found a delicate gold band, simple, and inexpensive. Oliver had gone directly to the bank after leaving his home, and drawn out all his savings before checking in the hotel.

He left his car in the hotel basement garage since it was still daylight, and looking at his watch decided it was better to grab a taxi to city hall. They slipped into the building from opposite doors in case anyone recognized him, and met in the clerk's office ten minutes before closing time. To their relief, there were few people on the floor and no one Oliver recognized. The clerk that waited on them was new and appeared to be touched by the young couple's urgency. She agreed to stay and process their license as quickly as she could.

At ten after five they hugged each other in relief. With the precious paper in hand, dashed back to the hotel to get Oliver's suitcase and his recruitment papers; this would get him on base.

He cautiously retrieved his car and drove her to the student residence building, circling the block slowly several times while she dashed up to her apartment to pack her suitcase. The building was quiet with most of the students gone for the summer.

Kathryn hurried out the entrance twenty minutes later wearing a blue silk dress. He stared at her. "You look beautiful."

She blushed and he could see she was nervous, she kept touching her hair.

"I tried to call my godparents but they didn't answer the phone. I wanted to at least tell them."

"We'll try them again later, sweetheart. But it will have to be after the fact."

Glancing around he moved quickly into traffic and headed for the Precidio.

Once on the base, they found the old mission chapel and as they stepped inside the cool shadowed foyer, a portly man wearing an

Army uniform with a cross on each side of his collar met them. He reached out and shook Oliver's hand. "Captain Kirby Anderson, current chaplain here. You must be Oliver Thornwell. I got the call. Do you have the marriage license?

"Yes, Sir." Oliver handed the chaplain the document and watched as the chaplain glanced over the paper and nodded. "All seems to be in order."

Kathryn's eyes went to the collar. "What denomination are you?"

When he smiled, his eyes crinkled at the corners. "I'm Baptist, but I represent all the Protestant faiths. Do you attend a church?"

"A Community Church, non-denominational"

"And you, son?"

Oliver hesitated. "My parents are Episcopal."

The chaplain had not missed the emphasis on the word parents. "How about you, Oliver?"

He glanced at Kathryn and shrugged. "I'm afraid church hasn't figured into my schedule too much during college." He felt a moment of panic. Maybe he wasn't going to marry them!

"Well, son, looks like you've been busy, what with joining the Army and taking on a new bride." He looked at Kathryn and asked solemnly, "Do you love this young man?"

She nodded vigorously. "Yes, sir, with all my heart and soul."

Reverend Anderson turned to Oliver. "And you love this young woman with all your heart and soul?"

Oliver reached for Kathryn's hand. "Yes, sir," he answered firmly. "I do."

The chaplain studied them a moment and nodded. "Well then, since you have the license, I suggest we make you two husband and wife."

They entered the chapel and to the astonishment of Kathryn and Oliver, it was decorated in red, white and blue. There were white lilies and red roses with baby's breath adorning the altar and small bouquets of red roses and blue bachelor buttons were attached to every other pew. Red and white candles in candelabras graced either side of the altar. It was a beautiful sight.

Kathryn turned to the chaplain. "Has there been a wedding here?"

"Well, we're having another wedding, but it isn't until eight o'clock this evening. The florist had two weddings and had to decorate early for this one. Red, white and blue for a July wedding. I'd say the Lord was helping you young folks out." He glanced at the candelabras and winked at them "Of course you know we can't light the candles."

Kathryn had tears in herr eyes as she looked around the lovely old chapel. She sighed with relief. It would seem like a real wedding.

They approached the altar and Father Anderson reached behind a panel and pressed a switch. A familiar melody began to play.

"Oh Oliver. It's my favorite piece. *Panis Angelicus."*

Oliver took her hand in his.

"In the sight of God as our witness, we gather here to unite Kathryn Hilliard and Oliver Thornwell, as husband and wife…"

And with the scent of roses all around them and sacred music playing in the background, they were married.

"You may kiss that pretty bride of yours, son."

Oliver took her in his arms and kissed her gently.

The chaplain cleared his throat. "If you'll just step into my office, we'll sign the marriage certificate."

As they were getting ready to leave a few minutes later, Oliver turned to the chaplain.

"Sir, do you know of a quiet place we could honeymoon? We only have a few days until I have to report to basic training."

Father Anderson thought a moment, wrinkling his brow. "Well…I just might have a place for you two young folks." He reached for the phone.

NINE

"Margaret? This is Kirby. Is that little guest house on the back of your property vacant? Ah, wonderful. Would you mind if I send a young couple there for a few days? I just married them and he's leaving shortly for basic training." The chaplain paused, listened and then winked at Oliver and Kathryn. "I knew I could count on you, Margaret. May the Lord bless you abundantly for your kind heart."

He hung up the phone and reached for a piece of paper. "Margaret is a widow who lives in Sausalito; her house is kind of tucked away, but people from all over the world visit her at various times and she keeps the guest house for them. She just got back from Italy and would be delighted to have you come."

Kathryn was overjoyed. "That is so kind of you. How did you know about her?"

He shrugged. "Her husband Mac and I were in the service together. I've known Margaret for almost thirty years."

Oliver hesitated. "Do you know how much she charges?"

Captain Anderson put a hand on Oliver's shoulder, and his eyes twinkled. "I don't think you have to worry, son, it'll be well within your budget."

The newlyweds left the Presidio and wended their way through the traffic over the Golden Gate Bridge to Sausalito. Following the directions they finally found a stone marker at the beginning of a gravel driveway with the address and turned down towards a country craftsman home. The view of Richardson Bay was spectacular with city lights blinking in the distance.

A tall woman with her salt and pepper gray hair wound back in a bun, came out on the porch. Her smile made them feel instantly welcome.

"You must be the Thornwells." She enfolded each of them in a warm hug. "Welcome to Seaside, I'm Margaret Osborne. Have you had any dinner?"

They looked at each other and shook their heads. There had been no time to think of dinner but Kathryn realized she was quite hungry.

"I didn't think so. We can get better acquainted tomorrow, but for now, let me show you to the guest house. I put some things in the refrigerator. Didn't know if you drank wine, but there's also some sparkling cider."

They followed her down a flagstone path. The guesthouse was a charming white cottage with tiny pink Cecil Brunner climbing roses covering the lattice over the door.

The floors were polished oak, the walls and furniture white. Various pillows in bright blues, greens and coral added a bright splash of color. The queen-sized bed was of polished oak with a white canopy and being summer, the stone fireplace was filled with a pot of greenery. Across the room sliding glass doors opened onto a small deck with a Chinese Elm hanging over the railing and beyond that, a view of the bay.

A delightful smell greeted their noses and they turned towards a tiny kitchenette at one side. A table was set for two with Italian hand-painted plates and crystal wine glasses.

"My special chicken marinated in olive oil, butter and garlic and baked with bread crumbs and parmesan cheese. I had a casserole in the freezer. There's a salad in the fridge."

Kathryn turned to their hostess. "You didn't know us and you went to all this trouble? I don't know what to say. We could have gone into town to a restaurant."

She eyed them over her half-glasses. "Nonsense, my dears, it's late and you're tired. This has been a special day for you both. I had four sons, and I was fortunate enough that when my third son found his bride in Italy and was married far from home, a kind couple did the same for him. I'm just passing on a good deed. Now you stop protesting and enjoy the food. I'll see you both tomorrow." With a wave of her hand, she stepped out the door and closed it behind her.

Oliver stood there a moment scratching his head. "I'd better get our things. You stay here, Darling, I'll be right back."

Kathryn looked around the cottage and quietly thanked God for His provision for them. She wanted to pinch herself to see if this was a dream. Then, seeing the telephone by the side of the bed, she took a deep breath and called her godparents, collect. Edwin answered and Kathryn blurted out what she'd done, and that she was all right and would call them again as soon as she could. Alma came on the phone, flustered at first, but then gave her blessing and told her they loved her and would pray for her and Oliver and hoped to meet him soon. She gave them her love back and hung up the phone just as Oliver tapped on the door with his shoe. She hurried to open it as he burst in with their luggage.

"Oh, Oliver, this is all so wonderful. Such nice people, I can hardly believe it."

"Well, the chaplain said it would be within our budget, but he didn't ask me what our budget was. I only hope I have enough money with me to pay for it."

She told him she'd called her godparents and what they'd said and Oliver looked relieved. "They sound like really special people. I'll look forward to meeting them too."

When Kathryn opened the refrigerator for the salad, she found a small cake with sugar wedding bells on it and felt her eyes well up at Mrs. Osborne's thoughtfulness. How had she managed to do it all in such a short time? She'd only had about an hour and a half.

Oliver deferred saying the blessing over their food to Kathryn, and they polished off the chicken and salad and toasted each other with red wine for Oliver and sparkling cider for her.

The dishes were placed in the sink and they went to stand by the sliding glass doors. With their arms around each other they took in the view.

"Oliver, this has all happened so fast. I hope you won't be sorry."

He turned to her, taking her chin in his hand and looking down into her eyes. "My beautiful girl, my wife, I'll never be sorry. You've made me very happy today."

He leaned down and kissed her, tenderly and then passionately. She leaned against him, returning his kiss as he lifted her in his arms.

TEN

The morning sun streamed in the window as Oliver and Kathryn shared their first morning as man and wife. They sipped steaming cups of coffee and talked about their future; architectural school when he returned from the war; the houses Oliver would build one day; and children.

"How about four Mrs. Thornwell?" He grinned broadly.

"You are very ambitious, Mr. Thornwell but I'll see what I can do." She nestled closer to him and put her head on his shoulder.

Mrs. Osborne was nowhere in sight and the front house was quiet. They drove into town briefly to get a couple of steaks and salad makings. With so little time together, they wanted to be alone in their little hidden away cottage. The sun which had been glorious in the morning, was hidden behind dense clouds that had rolled in ominously. The rain came sporadically leaving pools of water in small puddles in the streets.

When they returned to the cottage, a car was in the driveway so they knocked on the front door. Margaret Osborne opened the door and waved them in.

The living room's wall to wall glass windows took advantage of the magnificent panoramic view of the bay. Kathryn looked around and appreciated the tasteful variety of eclectic furnishings; paintings from a multitude of artists, bookcases full of interesting titles. Figurines and artifacts were everywhere. Obviously the Osborne's had traveled all over the world. As Kathryn admired the thick Persian rugs, she remembered a line from one of her favorite poems, *Vagabond House,* by Don Blanding.

They were old, old rugs, from far Chow wan,
that a Chinese princess once walked on.

"So nice to see you, did you find everything you needed?" Their hostess indicated the large sectional couch. "Do sit down."

Kathryn sat back but Oliver perched on the edge, his long legs crossed in front of him. Hesitantly he reached for his wallet. "We wanted to make whatever arrangements we need to make with you, Mrs. Osborne. What do you charge?"

Margaret chuckled and waved a hand at them. "I don't plan on charging you dear children anything. I had a marvelous time preparing for you and I knew that anyone Kirby Anderson sent my way was all right. As I said, someone did this for my son and I was eternally grateful. He was a pilot and they too had just a few days before he had to get back to his ship." She looked away out the window, her face somber.

Sensing some deep emotion, Kathryn asked quietly, "Where is he now, Mrs. Osborne?"

She faced them then with a trace of tears in her eyes. "His plane was shot down three months later. Barry knew the Savior, and right now he is in heaven. I'll see him again one day."

At the slightly puzzled frown on Oliver's face, she reached out and laid her hand on his. "I believe that when we know Christ as our Savior, Oliver, we have eternal life. The Bible says that to be absent from the body is to be present with the Lord."

Kathryn glanced sideways at Oliver. His expression was not pessimistic but thoughtful. "I'm sure that is a comfort to you, Mrs. Osborne." he said finally.

"I've got coffee brewing. How about a cup? And please call me Margaret. Mrs. Osborne makes me feel ninety."

With the gift of the guest cottage, Oliver could hardly say no. He raised his eyebrows. "Kathryn?"

"I'd love some."

He nodded at their hostess who disappeared into the kitchen to return with a tray laden with three mugs of coffee and some oatmeal raisin cookies.

Margaret watched Oliver down a second cookie. "Are you two working or going to school?"

"I just graduated from Stanford. I was to attend the Stanford

School of Law in Palo Alto."

"You'll be a lawyer then, any particular field?"

Oliver glanced at Kathryn. "I haven't really decided yet."

"Well, it's a very good school." She turned to Kathryn, "And you, dear?"

"I attend the Academy of Art University, in San Francisco." Foreseeing the next question, Kathryn added, "I'd like to illustrate children's books."

Margaret sipped her coffee and peered over her glasses.

"Do your parents attend a church, Oliver?"

Oliver raised his eyebrows at the sudden shift in conversation, but the expression on Margaret's face was casual.

"They are Episcopalians. It seemed pretty rigid to me and I found it an ordeal growing up. I'm afraid that other than when I'm home, I don't attend church."

"Oh I do understand, dear, school can keep one very busy."

Kathryn decided to volunteer her information. "My mother and aunt go to a small community church. I grew up in Northern California."

Their hostess was silent for a moment, then, "You know of course that you will go to Vietnam, Oliver?"

Oliver sighed deeply. "Yes, ma' am. I imagine that's where I'll end up."

"I hope that through what you have to face, you will find the Savior there, Oliver. He says in His word, He'll never leave you nor forsake you when you belong to Him. I hope you'll give that some thought."

Oliver didn't answer, he merely nodded. Margaret looked at him thoughtfully but didn't say any more.

Kathryn felt her heart wrench. She didn't want to think about Oliver going so far away from her. Margaret leaned over and patted her on the arm. "Pray for him, Kathryn, every day. It will be the strength that will keep you through the coming months."

"I will, Margaret, I will."

Oliver stood up. "Thank you for the coffee."

"Oh, I've kept you honeymooners too long. Of course you want to be alone."

Kathryn put out her hand. "Thank you so much, the cookies were delicious."

The time went far too quickly and the last evening they turned the radio to a classical music station and Kathryn lay curled up against him on the sofa. They didn't talk as much, knowing it was their last evening before facing his parents. While he spoke encouragingly about the meeting, she felt he was as apprehensive as she was.

On the fourth day they straightened up the cottage, and bade Margaret farewell, thanking her profusely for her kindness and hospitality. She'd left them alone for the duration of their short honeymoon and they were grateful for the privacy.

Then they drove to Oliver's home.

ELEVEN

Oliver was determined to make sure his parents knew they were married before he left for basic training.

As they approached a set of wrought iron gates, Kathryn glimpsed a huge two-story cinnamon-colored house with white balustrades and side porches. It sat like a slumbering giant that had occupied its space for dozens of years. The yard was perfectly manicured with well-trimmed hedges and trees. Kathryn noted the absence of flowers and wondered if there was a garden in the rear of the house. The front door was black with a large wrought iron knocker. On either side of the main porch a pair of stone lions sat poised on their concrete pads.

A sense of dread filled Kathryn as they approached the mansion that Oliver called home. Oliver stopped in the circular driveway and came around to help her out. She was trembling and he gave her shoulders a quick squeeze.

"Buck up, Darling. Wait until you meet the Culpeppers. You'll love them."

"The Culpeppers?"

"Our butler and cook. They practically raised me while my parents were busy with the social whirl"

She nodded and gave him a wan smile. A butler and live-in cook?

"It will be all right, Darling. Once my parents meet you, they'll love you just like I do."

A gentleman in a dark gray suit answered the door.

"Master Oliver! It is good to see you." He leaned over and whispered. "The two of them have been beside themselves. Shall I tell your parents you are home?"

Oliver grinned. "Not on your life, Cully. I'd like to announce our arrival myself. Kathryn, this is Edward Culpepper. He's been with us for as long as I can remember. His wife, Martha, is the best cook in the county and she's a treasure." He turned back to the butler. "Cully, I'd like you to meet my wife, Kathryn."

The butler's face registered astonishment, but he regained his composure quickly.

"An excellent choice, Master Oliver, if I may say so. May the missus and I extend our congratulations?" The English accent was unmistakable.

"I'm happy to meet you, Mr. Culpepper." She wasn't sure if she was to shake his hand.

"How do you do, Madam." As he inclined his head towards her, she could have sworn he winked at Oliver. Mr. Culpepper approved of her! He nodded towards the library. "They are in there, Master Oliver. They have been most unhappy over your absence, especially since they couldn't find you."

"Taking it out on the staff, eh, Cully?"

"A bit difficult, sir, but not unbearable. You know, sir, they are not going to take this well." The butler looked at Kathryn's ring.

"Well, make yourself scarce and you can miss the fireworks."

"An excellent idea, and for what it is worth, I'll be rooting for you."

He gave them a brief smile and hurried away towards the kitchen, no doubt to fill Mrs. Culpepper in on the coming explosion. Well, Oliver seemed to be on good terms with at least one member of the staff.

Oliver took her hand and headed towards the double doors of the study. Kathryn's heart pounded as he opened the doors and they strode into the room to face his startled parents.

"Mother, Father, I would like you to meet my wife, Kathryn. Kathryn-- my parents, Gordon and Thea Thornwell."

"My God, Oliver, what have you done?" His father nearly exploded out of his chair, his voice harsh.

His mother opened her mouth to speak but no words came out. She stood almost bewildered, staring at them.

Kathryn wanted to sink through the floor, but Oliver was

determined. "Joined the army and married the girl I love"

"The army? Married?" His mother echoed.

Gordon Thornwell's face got so red Kathryn thought he would have a stroke and Oliver's mother who'd risen from her chair when they entered, suddenly sat down. They just stared at Kathryn and Oliver. When his father got over his shock, he walked over to Kathryn, looking her up and down like a mannequin on display.

"Well, you have good taste in women, son. Kathryn is it?"

"Yes, Sir."

"I wanted you to meet her before I leave tomorrow for Fort Ord," Oliver said.

"Fort Ord? Tomorrow?" His father's cigar paused in mid-air.

"Oliver! You didn't have to do that." It was one of the few times in his life he'd seen his mother near tears.

Kathryn realized Oliver was counting on the fact that he didn't think his father could do much about the army in spite of his influence.

"Well, son, it seems that when you make a decision, you do carry it through. This is pretty final?" Gordon Thornwell paused, sighed heavily and appeared to be resigned to the idea, and then with a meaningful look at his wife, put his hand out to Oliver.

"It would appear that we need to make the best of it, my dear. Oliver has brought his bride home to us. If he has to go off to the Army tomorrow, we can at least make his last night with us a friendly one. We'll have time after he leaves to get better acquainted with our new daughter-in-law."

"Gordon?" Thea Thornwell looked at her husband who had turned so his back was to Oliver and Kathryn. She suddenly regained her composure. "Yes, of course. You are right, dear. If Oliver is happy, we should be happy too, should we not?" She rose and put out her hand to Kathryn.

His father smiled broadly. "I suggest we have a drink, son, to mark this occasion, our capitulation and your celebration." turning to his wife, "You might enjoy a chat with our young lady."

Oliver gave her a wink and a smile. He was elated at how things had turned out. Kathryn's intuition told her something different.

"Welcome to the family," Thea's smile was like ice.

TWELVE

The men retired to the study. Kathryn, left with Oliver's mother, suddenly felt she knew how a soldier must feel facing a major battle. She was terrified. Well, she would show them that she had poise and would be a credit to Oliver.

"Ah, sit down won't you? Now, tell me about yourself. You met Oliver at a dance?"

So that is what he told them. She didn't want to lie, "I was with friends from school when we met. We were just drawn to each other right away." She looked earnestly at her new mother-in-law. "I do want Oliver to finish college. I didn't know he'd joined the army until he told me."

"Yes, well we'll see what we can do about that. Now, tell me about your parents. What does your father do?"

She told Thea about the boating incident, the loss of her parents and how the Miller's raised her and Ruth. "My godparents are retired missionaries."

"Missionaries?" Thea made it sound like she'd found a dead mouse behind the chair.

Kathryn told her new mother-in-law, she was in her second year of college as an art major, and that her sister Ruth had already graduated and married a young dentist. Kathryn had been raised by her godparents with good manners and good taste and she knew she must somehow convince Oliver's mother of this.

Oliver's mother continued with elaborate politeness, asking about her home and family, nodding with her tight smile as Kathryn answered. "And your roommate at school, my dear, is she compatible with you?" The question was so subtle Kathryn answered before she thought of the consequences.

"Oh Gloria is lovely. We're best friends."

"Gloria?" Thea's eyes narrowed. "Gloria who?"

"Gloria Horton." Kathryn realized her mistake. Now Thea would find out how and where she and Oliver really met. The thought crossed her mind that she should feel sorry for Mable Horton.

Thea was gracious, in a cool manner. Kathryn couldn't know at the time that she was just setting the stage.

Since they were legally married, and Oliver was leaving the next morning, his parents insisted that their home was Kathryn's home. The least they could do, to make things up to Oliver, was to watch over his wife while he was away.

His parents were the epitome of graciousness and hospitality at dinner. They seemed to bend over backwards for Oliver's sake to make Kathryn feel at home. They drew Kathryn out, asking about her art and her plans for after she finished college.

Even so, Kathryn felt an undercurrent of strain and was relieved when Oliver asked his parents to excuse them to retire for the night.

"We'll make sure Kathryn is taken care of, son." Gordon said, putting an arm around his wife. They stood smiling up at them from the bottom of the stairs.

Oliver closed the door to his room and took her in his arms. He was grinning.

"I told you they wouldn't be able to resist you. You can get better acquainted before you return to your residence hall, but our home is your home now. There are still a few more days before your college starts again. I'll get leave at the end of basic training. It's only six weeks. We'll have some time together again then."

Kathryn knew Oliver wished he hadn't joined the army, and was beginning to regret his hasty decision, but Uncle Sam had his name on the dotted line and he was classified One A.

They had one last wonderful night in each other's arms.

The next morning, convinced his parents had accepted Kathryn as his wife, Oliver prepared to leave. He took a picture of himself out of a small frame on his desk and gave it to Kathryn. His friend, George, had taken it one weekend. It was a good picture. Oliver was laughing and looking back at the camera.

She was tearful when Oliver got into the taxi the next morning. The Culpeppers came out to see him off. Oliver said goodbye to his mother and father and everyone went back into the house, to give them some final moments alone. It was hard for Kathryn to see him go and she was terrified of his parents. If she could have gotten into the taxi with him and driven off too, it would have been easier, but she had promised Oliver she would stay, at least a few days to get better acquainted before returning to school.

When Kathryn walked back up the steps into the house she had a feeling that the walls were going to come down around her ears and the Thornwells didn't disappoint her. They were waiting in the library like a couple of vultures. They had worked it all out and knowing Oliver would be gone for only six weeks, didn't waste any time.

"Will you step in here a moment, my dear?"

She held her head up and walked slowly into the library.

THIRTEEN

Thea Thornwell stood by the fireplace, her face like chiseled granite. She inclined her head towards her husband who evidently was going to speak for both of them.

"We understand your attraction for a young man like Oliver. He comes from a good family and has the social background that might appeal to a girl like you. It is a natural thing for two young people to be attracted in the atmosphere of a dance, however, Oliver is not in a position to take a wife at this time. He has law school to finish and will be entering my firm upon graduation. He does not at this time have an income of his own, which you need to understand, certainly not any funds to support a wife."

Kathryn's chin went up. "What are you trying to tell me?"

"We want you to break off this untimely liaison with our son. My firm will make the necessary arrangements for an annulment to dissolve the marriage. You will find in time that it's for the best."

The silence was deadly. She wanted to say something harsh to these two terrible people but though she opened her mouth, no sound came out. Her face flushed with embarrassment and shame.

Finally she stammered, "But I love Oliver. I don't want to leave him."

"We've called a taxi for you. You will receive the paperwork from our firm shortly."

She had no more words. It was so unreal. Feeling like a cornered animal, she stood there for a moment and then turned,and ran up the stairs to Oliver's room. She threw her things in the suitcase, sobbing as she did so.

There was a knock on the door and Gordon Thornwell entered. He saw she was packing and smiled benevolently. "There's a good girl,"

He pulled a piece of paper out of his pocket and handed it to her.

It was a check. "We anticipated that this would be difficult for you and wish to make it a little easier. Her mouth opened and closed in silent astonishment.

"Yes, my dear. As you can see the sum is sizable. Ten thousand dollars should help a great deal towards your college. We felt this would be enough to convince you that we are serious. As we said, our only stipulation is that you agree to the matter of the annulment, and never see our son, Oliver, again."

She wanted to throw the check in his smug face. How could a man like Oliver come from such monstrous people?

Apparently anticipating that her lack of words meant consent, Gordon patted her on the shoulder. "You will see this is for the best, Kathryn. You'll find yourself a nice young man more suited to you. Believe me, in time you'll get over Oliver, and Oliver can get on with what he has to do."

He turned and left the room. She stood looking after him with tears streaming down her cheeks. The check fluttered to the floor as she threw herself on the bed to cry out her frustration.

Finally after pulling herself together, she picked up her suitcase, gave one last look at the bed she'd shared with Oliver and left. Her foot pressed the check into the carpet on the way out.

She walked down the stairs, head held high. Mr. Culpepper appeared out of nowhere with her coat and scarf and took her bag. "The missus and I are terribly sorry. Good luck to you," he whispered as he put the bag in the taxi. Without a word to the Thornwells, she climbed in and looked straight ahead, holding her tears until the taxi turned out of their driveway and bore her away.

"Where do you live, Miss?"

"Marysville." She answered without thinking, her mind whirling with the events that had just occurred. It wasn't until they were on Interstate 80 passing through Napa that she realized she should have had the cab take her back to the residence hall. She started to lean forward to tell him, when the bitterness of her experience rose up. They wanted to send her home? Then home she'd go and it would cost them. Cost? She panicked suddenly and leaned towards the driver.

"Who is paying for this taxi?"

"Those folks you just left. Gave me a credit number and told me to take you wherever you needed to go. You seem pretty upset, you okay?"

She took a deep breath, "I'll be all right. I just received some bad news. Thank you for asking." She sat back against the seat. "I just need to go home."

The driver hummed to himself. Probably anticipating the juicy fare he was going to pick up for this trip. He tried a few more times to start a conversation but seeing she wasn't up to talking much, settled down for the long drive and turned on the radio to a music station that played golden oldies.

Alma Miller came out of the house to see who'd arrived in the taxi, and when she saw Kathryn's face put an arm around her shoulders and led her into the house, Edwin went out to get her suitcase from the porch.

When she tearfully told her godparents the whole story, Alma pursed her lips.

"I can't imagine people doing this kind of thing to their son."

She gathered Kathryn in her arms. "Oh child, I'm sure Oliver is a wonderful man if you love him. While you only mentioned him a few times, Edwin and I will just look forward to meeting him when he gets out of his training camp. And if you don't have any place to go, you bring him here, understand? He's welcome. "

Comforted and reassured, she finally went to her room and with determination, picked up the phone and called the number of the base that Oliver left for her.

FOURTEEN

Allison interrupted. "So you told my father what really happened?"

"Well, no. I didn't realize how far Gordon Thornwell's sphere of influence went."

><>

"Yes, Ma'am," the clerk responded with a sigh, "I'll do the best I can." It was the same clerk and the same response. She returned to the college but called every day and there was always a reason that Oliver couldn't return her call, he was out on maneuvers, he was in class, or it was past hours. They seemed like flimsy excuses to Kathryn, but then she didn't know anything about the Army and what happened during basic training. She called her godparents again when the clerk finally told her that Oliver could call her at the end of the six weeks of training. She waited as patiently as she could , but when the six weeks were up she still had not been able to contact Oliver, nor had she heard from him. She fought down the panic that was gradually rising. The letters she wrote him didn't come back, and there were none from Oliver.

"Alma, what should I do?" She wailed into the receiver.

Edwin came on the phone. "Let me call the base, love. Something is wrong here and I'm going to get to the bottom of it. I'll call you back shortly."

Kathryn paced the floor waiting for the phone to ring and when it finally did, she grabbed it, hoping to hear Oliver's voice.

It was Alma.

"Kathryn dear, I told Edwin I'd call you. He did get through to the base and spoke to the commander. At least someone else other than the clerk you mentioned. I believe they were a little chagrinned when, in no uncertain terms, he told them just what had been going on."

"Then where is Oliver? Why haven't I heard from him?"

"Dear, his unit left yesterday. He's on his way to Vietnam."

Kathryn burst into tears, bordering on hysterics. "What shall I do?"

"Kathryn, get hold of yourself, honey, there's a letter from Oliver."

She sniffed. "A letter?"

"Yes, it just came in today's mail. Shall I send it to you?"

Oh Oliver. Her heart soared. "No, no, open it now. Tell me what it says."

"We don't want to pry--"

"It's all right, please open it." Kathryn sat down suddenly on a chair and held her breath as Alma began to read."

My Darling Kathryn,

This letter will be the last letter I'll be able to write to you before I leave. They have stepped up our date to ship out. We leave tomorrow. I wrote you at my parent's home before I got their phone call. My father told me you had accepted a large check from them and agreed to an annulment. I don't want to believe this, and yet there's no word from you. No letters, no phone calls. Where are you, my Darling? I tried calling your home for three days but no one was there. I left a message at your residence hall but you didn't call. There's been no word from you these past six weeks and my only conclusion is that my parents were telling me the truth. It's a bitter pill to swallow. I love you still, and will until the day I die. That may be sooner than I think. My father has tried to get me out of the army but I refused. The word is that it is pretty rough over there, but without you, nothing matters anymore. Take care of yourself, I hope you will remember me a little. You carry my heart.

Oliver.

There was a long silence and Alma spoke softly. "I'm so sorry Kathryn, he must have called when Edwin's sister was so sick and we drove to Oregon for a few days to help them out."

Kathryn fought for control. "But he says he left a message here at the residence hall. No one's given me a message."

"Check with the office, dear, I'm sure there is some explanation. In the meantime, Edwin got Oliver's overseas address."

Her heart leaped. "His address? If I write to him right away will he get the letter?"

"I don't believe anyone overseas will tamper with Oliver's mail."

"Tamper? What are you saying?"

"Dear, I think someone has deliberately been keeping your letters from Oliver, and his from you."

"Oh Alma—"

"Well, that is what Edwin thinks. I believe it too. The officer he talked with said the mail is not kept from the recruits and they are allowed to make phone calls."

"The Thornwells." She gritted her teeth. "Alma, it had to be Oliver's parents. His mother said something about getting him out of the Army. His father has a lot of influence."

Her godmother huffed indignantly into the phone. "Well in that case, I think that clerk you talked to is in trouble. Tampering with the mail is a federal offence. I'll forward Oliver's letter. Here is his overseas address. Be brave, honey, this will work out. Put it in God's hands."

Kathryn sat for a moment after she hung up the phone and tried to assimilate all the information of the last five minutes. Finally, with determination, she hurried to her desk and took out some stationary. She poured her heart into the letter, telling Oliver how many times she had tried to get through to him and that she loved him with all her heart, that she didn't take the check and would never leave him. She told him to take care of himself, stay alive and come back to her, that the Millers had offered their home for them. Then, hand trembling, she told Oliver the one thing that she had not yet shared with her godparents. She was going to have his child.

She took the letter directly to the post office to be sure she mailed it with the correct postage. Then she marched into the office in the residence hall.

"Someone said they left a message for me several weeks ago. I never got it."

The girl at the desk frowned and looked in Kathryn's box. "There's no message." She put a finger on her lips and studied the boxes. "You know, that girl that helped out this summer got a few things mixed up." She put her hand in another box down in the corner and pulled out some pieces of paper. "There was another Kathryn. Her last name was Dorsey or something like that. She had to go home for some family emergency so her messages were just left there. Here, take a look."

Kathryn pulled the folded note out from the stack. Tucked back in the wrong box it had laid there for weeks without her knowing it was there.

The girl looked at up at Kathryn with sympathy, noting a tear rolling slowly down Kathryn's cheek. "I'm really sorry."

Kathryn nodded and went up to her room. She read the note over several times and then quietly slipped it into her Bible along with Oliver's picture.

Waiting for a reply from Oliver seemed an eternity as the weeks went by. Then one day, as she picked up her mail, she recognized a large envelope. The letter she'd written to Oliver. She turned it over and read in large letters, "DECEASED, RETURN TO SENDER."

She stared at the words and as comprehension dawned, collapsed on the floor. When she revived, there was a pillow under her head, and the dorm manager, Mrs. Tibbets, was bending over her. then Gloria appeared and knelt by her side.

"Kathryn, I was just starting up to our room when Mrs. Tibbets saw me. What happened?"

Mrs. Tibbets handed Gloria the envelope. "This was in her hand when she fainted."

Kathryn looked up at her roommate, her eyes filled with tears. "He's dead, Gloria, Oliver is dead."

Gloria looked at the letter wide-eyed and shook her head. "Oh Kathryn, no, not Oliver." She looked at the letter again and cried, "That's no way to notify you. They're supposed to send someone to tell you in person or at the least, a telegram. This is horrible."

Kathryn closed her eyes as the tears poured down her cheeks. "He's dead, Gloria."

Gloria turned to Mrs. Tibbets. "Stay with her. I'm going to get my car. She needs to go home and I'm going to drive her."

Mrs. Tibbets clucked her tongue sympathetically. "Who is Oliver?"

"Her husband. They were married just a little over three months ago."

Mrs. Tibbets gasped. "Dear God."

FIFTEEN

Kathryn stared unseeing out the window of Gloria's small sports car. Her roommate had thrown some necessary things into Kathryn's suitcase and tucked her dazed friend in her car.

"I don't understand this," Gloria was saying. "It's a pretty rotten way of notifying you."

"The Army wouldn't officially notify me," Kathryn murmured. "They may not even know about me. Oliver probably gave them his parent's home address, so I imagine his final effects were sent to them."

Gloria reached over and gave Kathryn's hand a squeeze. "Well, I'm going to get you home. That's where you need to be at this time. I notified the college and they said they'll get word to your instructors. You can make up the work when you get back but they insisted you take the time you need. I called the Millers too. They are expecting us."

Kathryn just nodded her head and closed her eyes, leaning back against the head rest."

They drove on in silence for a while and then Gloria began to talk about some of the good times they'd had with Oliver and how she and George kept the secret from their parents.

Kathryn let Gloria's words flow over her, hardly hearing. All she could think about was the face with laughing hazel eyes that danced in her mind.

As they approached Marysville, Kathryn sighed and turned to Gloria. "There's something I haven't told anyone, not even my godparents. I'm pregnant."

Gloria turned to stare at her and the car briefly swerved. Gloria jerked it back on track. "Oh Kathryn, you poor kid. I was wondering if you had anything of Oliver's to remember him by. That's something all right."

Kathryn turned to watch the scenery again. "I have the letters he wrote this past spring from college, and the picture George took that Oliver had in his room at home." Kathryn fingered the chain around her neck that held the slim gold band. "I have my wedding ring and the marriage certificate." She leaned back on the seat and closed her eyes again. She didn't want to talk anymore.

SIXTEEN

Alma had been watching out the window for the last hour and as Gloria's car turned in the driveway, she hurried down the steps followed by Edwin and her friend Doris, who was a nurse at the nearby hospital. The women helped Kathryn from the car and led her to her room. They settled her down on her bed and Alma removed Kathryn's shoes.

Doris checked the girl over and took a packet out of her pocket. "Dr. Jergenson prescribed these. It's a sedative. He said it was safe for her to take."

Alma quickly got a glass of water and Doris held the pills out to Kathryn "These will help you sleep, dear." Alma murmured. She wasn't fond of taking medicines, having been mostly healthy all her life, but in this case she'd agree to anything to help her precious goddaughter slip into oblivion and away from the reality she couldn't face right now. The medication was strong and in moments, Kathryn drifted off into a deep sleep.

Alma covered Kathryn with a quilt and the two women returned to the living room where Edwin and Gloria waited anxiously.

Doris gathered her bag. "She'll sleep quite a while. The sedative will let her body rest from the trauma. Keep an eye on her, Alma, you don't know how she is going to react when she wakes up." She turned to Gloria. "Can you tell us what happened?"

Gloria went to Kathryn's purse and pulled out the letter. "I think this will explain everything."

Alma took the letter, a puzzled frown on her face. Then she saw the printed letters on the envelope. "Oh, my dear. Oh Kathryn," With tears she turned to Edwin and he put his arms around her. "The letter she wrote to Oliver in Vietnam came back."

Gloria shrugged. "Someone, an officer or something must have written that on the envelope. She read that and I guess she fainted.

The dorm manager, Mrs. Tibbets, spotted me coming in just then and called out."

Doris shook her head slowly. "What a horrible way to find out about her husband's death."

"That's what I thought," Gloria fumed, "I'd like to tell that commanding officer a thing or two."

Edwin rubbed his chin. "That isn't how they usually notify the widow. Perhaps they didn't realize it was his wife."

Gloria snorted. "The envelope says, Mrs Oliver Thornwell, right in the upper left hand corner. That's pretty plain."

"That's true, my dear, but in the heat of battle or jungle circumstances, sometimes there isn't a lot of time to think about things."

"In any case, "Doris said, "Keep an eye on her. I'll stop by tomorrow to see how she's doing."

Gloria hesitated. "I know I shouldn't be the one to tell you, she just told me on our way here, but in her condition, you need to know. She's pregnant with Oliver's child."

Alma gasped and glanced up at her husband. "Bless her heart. Oh, Edwin. He never knew. She's going to have to go it on her own."

"Not alone, honey, we'll be there for her and help her in every way we can. And we can pray."

Doris put a hand on Alma's arm. "Stay with her tonight, Alma. This is a crucial trimester. She could lose the baby. I'll be back to check on her tomorrow. If there are any problems, call the hospital."

"We will, Doris, and thank you for coming so promptly."

Gloria gave the Millers each a hug and they thanked her for bringing Kathryn home.

"We'll drive her back when she's ready to return to college."

Gloria sighed. "I hope she won't give it up. She's really a talented artist."

After Gloria had driven away, Alma turned to her husband. "I'm going to sit with our girl. I want to be there for her when she wakes up. Would you call Ruth?"

Edwin squeezed her hand. "I was just thinking of that. They're pretty close. She'll want her sister through this."

Alma walked in quietly and gazed down at the sleeping form. Tears had dried on Kathryn's cheeks.

"You rest, child, and when you wake up, we'll be here for you, just as we always have," she murmured. Then, sitting down in a nearby armchair, Alma opened her Bible and bowed her head in prayer.

SEVENTEEN

It was a long night. Kathryn woke fitfully from time to time, sobbing and crying out Oliver's name. Alma talked to her soothingly, wiping away the tears and holding her hand. When at last the first light of dawn crept into the room, Kathryn opened her eyes and looked around slowly.

"I'm home?"

"Yes, child, Gloria brought you yesterday."

"Then it wasn't a dream?"

"No dear, it was not a dream."

Kathryn was silent. The weight of sorrow pressed her chest until she felt she couldn't breathe. "Oh Alma, I don't want to live without him."

Alma's voice was gentle but stern. "Is that what you think Oliver would want? What about the child? You carry a part of him within you. You'll get through this. God will give you strength. Now no more talk like that."

The baby. Kathryn had forgotten about the baby. "Gloria told you?"

"Yes, she felt we needed to know because of the state you were in. You must take care of yourself, Kathryn, this is a crucial time. You're carrying Oliver's child. A precious part of the man you loved."

"Oh Alma, how could God let a man like Oliver die? What kind of a God would do that?"

"It wasn't God who killed Oliver, Kathryn. Men fight wars, and in war men get killed. It was a bullet from the enemy, an enemy that doesn't answer to God or know Him, that struck Oliver." She paused. "Speaking of God, was Oliver a believer?"

Kathryn's voice sounded small as she looked up at her godmother. "I don't think so. I loved him so much I thought I could share Christ with him when the time was right."

Alma's face had always been an open book to her thoughts. Kathryn knew what her godmother was thinking. In all the years in church, and knowing 2 Corinthians 6:14, she'd married an unbeliever. *Be not unequally yoked—*

Finally Alma sat down on the side of the bed and stroked Kathryn's face gently. "God knows Oliver's heart, dear. We don't know what transaction took place between the Lord and Oliver in his final moments. We think in finite time, but there is no time with Him. A moment of our time can be enough for our Savior to reveal Himself."

It was a thread, but Kathryn clutched it in her mind. It was true. She'd heard that many men in battle reached out to God in their last moments. She would hold the thought that she would see Oliver again one day, in heaven, for now, it was all she had.

Edwin appeared in the doorway. "How's my girl this morning?" He came over and leaned down to kiss her on the cheek. "Don't you worry, love, we're here and you're going to be all right." He stood up slowly. "How about a bowl of oatmeal with brown sugar and raisins?"

It was her favorite but she had no appetite. "Thank you, but I'm not very hungry."

Alma helped her sit up. "Nonsense, child, you're eating for two now. Let's get your face washed." She turned to her husband and stated firmly, "We'll be in shortly, dear."

The days moved slowly as Kathryn struggled to contain her emotions. Doris had come again and brought more medication, but was pleased when Kathryn refused. It was better for the baby's sake. Sleep was elusive and nights were long and wakeful. She hadn't felt the nausea she knew other women dealt with and was glad for that. Her sister Ruth called and offered her love and prayers. They talked a long time. Ruth was ready to drop everything and come to Marysville, but Kathryn declined gently.

"Oh Ruth, I knew you would come, but really, there's no need. For once I have to be the practical one. I need to get back to school or

I'll lose a whole semester's work"

"That's' true. I'm glad you are going to be able to return. Matt and I will keep you in our prayers, and you know, if you need anything at all, just call me, okay?"

"Thanks, Ruth, just knowing you and Matt are praying helps a lot."

Kathryn took long walks and poured through some of her favorite psalms. She knelt in prayer and poured her heart out to God, the Abba Father, that He had been all her life.

Finally, by the end of the week, she stopped struggling. She knew what she had to do. As the moonlight poured in her window, she knelt at the side of her bed and with tears, at last gave her burden over to God, trusting in His plan for her. Her head rested on her arms a long time, but when she finally crawled into bed, she felt the whisper of a breeze brush her face and for the first time since she learned of Oliver's death, she sank into a restful sleep.

EIGHTEEN

Allison shook her head slowly, trying to digest the story she had just heard. Kathryn had gotten up and stood looking out the window, lost in thought. Allison got up and laid her head against her mother's back and wrapped her arms around her.

"Oh, Mom, I had no idea you went through something like that. I can't believe my grandparents offered you ten thousand dollars to leave my father. That was so cruel. You loved each other."

Kathryn nodded.

They stood quietly for a few minutes and then Kathryn turned and put her arm around her daughter's shoulders. Tears streamed down Allison's face and Kathryn handed her a tissue.

"That's why we live here in this mountain community. You see, after their scheming to get rid of me and annul the marriage, I certainly didn't feel I could trust them. With their only son dead, they could accuse me of trying to extort money from them on the pretext that you were their grandchild, which I couldn't face."

Kathryn took Allison's hand. "Or, accepting you as their grandchild, the child of their only child, they could try to get custody. Oliver's father owned a prominent law firm. He had influence in high places. I couldn't take the chance of losing you. You are all I had left from your father."

"So you brought me here."

"Yes, when you were three. I continued my college and had you in a small county hospital. Alma was there with me. I brought you back to their home and they helped me take care of you until I finished my last year of college and graduated. One of my sketches caught the attention of a man who published children's books and I was offered my first illustrating job. The success of that one led to others."

"I was little but I remember when the Millers died. Everyone was so sad and I missed my granny Alma. You were crying and people were coming and going and bringing things. You said it was only a month after your graduation. They were on their way home from a meeting at the church when a drunk driver veered over and struck them head on."

Kathryn looked down at the floor, remembering. "They were killed instantly. Their will left what little they had to Ruth and me, which included their home in Marysville. Ruth was married to your Uncle Matt and had their house in Porterville. I was so afraid the Thornwells would find out about you, we sold the Miller's house and Ruth gave me her share to come up here and buy a home. For my illustrations and artwork, I chose the name Longwood from a street sign and shortened my first name. No one would know me by Kate Longwood, especially your grandparents."

Allison smiled. "That sounds like Aunt Ruth, putting her own needs aside to help her widowed sister and niece." She paused. "Mother, I'm twenty-four. Why haven't you told me all this before now. I would have understood."

"Perhaps, dear, but there were so many years of feeling like I had to hide you—worrying that someone would find out who you were. I would read about children kidnapped from school by an estranged parent and I had visions of someone hired by your grandfather, taking you away. And, I'm ashamed to say, there was another reason, my hardened heart. I couldn't forgive Oliver's parents for what they did. I believed that by telling him those terrible things, they brought about his death. I was wrong, but I felt justified in keeping you from them."

"I'm glad you changed your mind and told me about them. I've often wondered what my father's parents were like."

Kathryn took her hand again., "Dear, the reason I told you all of this was, yes, because it was time, but mostly because I realized that I'd never be free of guilt until I'd forgiven the Thornwells. I couldn't ask God to forgive me for things in my life if I wasn't willing to forgive those who'd hurt me." She looked earnestly at her daughter.

"I've found my faith in Christ again. I've seemed to lose it sometimes through the years. I was so busy running and hiding, immersed in my work, living in this community where no one knew my past. I feel like a great burden's been lifted from me. For the first time in a long time, I feel at peace with myself, and with God."

Allison acknowledged her mother's words and smiled, but appeared thoughtful.

"So my legal name on my birth certificate is --?"

"It's Allison Marie Thornwell." I told the school that I was a widow and I was going to take my former name, Hilliard. You were to be known by that name even though your birth certificate was different. I told them that it was for your safety. The secretary was new and inexperienced and didn't ask questions."

Kathryn straightened up and patted Allison's shoulder.

"Tell Jason I'll be down in just a little while. I have some things to finish."

Allison hugged her mother again. "Thank you," she whispered, "for telling me all this."

Kathryn watched her daughter leave the room and felt she could almost see the Lord smiling in approval. She took Oliver's picture from the pocket of her Bible and studied it a few moments.

"Well, Oliver, I've told her about your parents and what happened. What she does with it is up to her." She hugged the picture to her for a moment and then, slipping it back in her Bible, went downstairs to hold her small grandson again before Allison and Jason left.

Jason looked at his watch. "Its six thirty already. This day's sure flown by. Honey, we need to get going. I've got to collect some tools to help repair the Morrison's dock. Some guy who'd had a few too many beers clobbered it with his party boat."

Kathryn smiled fondly at her son-in-law. Jason could fix anything it seemed, and had no lack of odd jobs to see them through the summer until school started again.

She glanced at her daughter and noticed the look on Allison's face. She'd seen that look before and the thought crossed her mind that she knew what Allison was planning to do.

NINETEEN

"Mother, the Thornwell's are still alive. I wrote to them." Allison's voice on the phone sounded eager. "I've prayed about it and I feel it's only right that they know about me. I don't want anything from them, but I really felt they should know my father left them a grandchild."

Kathryn considered her words a moment. "I'm not sure what kind of reaction you'll get, but if you feel that God is leading you, I suppose you needed to do it. How did you get their address?"

"The internet is a marvel, Mom. They are still listed. I checked the bureau of records and there is no death certificate in either Gordon or Thea Thornwell, so I'm sure they're still alive."

"Oh." Kathryn regrouped and tried to sound cheerful. "I'm coming into town this afternoon. I've got some banking to do and some more illustrations to mail off, would you like me to stop by?"

"That would be great, Mom."

An hour later Kathryn drove up to her daughter's small house on a hill. She hugged Allison and Jason and planted a kiss on Joshua's forehead as he looked up at her, wide eyed from his infant seat.

"I can't stay long, darling."

"How about a cup of tea?" Allison put the teakettle on and Kathryn joined them at the small table in the kitchen.

"I hope you don't mind, Mother, but I really needed to contact the Thornwells. If they chose to ignore me I'd like to at least say I tried. Maybe they've changed after all these years."

"I wish I could be sure of that."

Jason, who had been listening to this exchange, spoke up. "I don't want to see Allison get hurt any more than you do, but I told her that if she wants to pursue this, I'll help her any way I can. I think this is something she has to settle for herself, however it turns out."

Kathryn played with a teaspoon, moving it around the tablecloth.

"I know, Jason, I knew this time would come someday. I do pray it will go well for Allison's sake."

"Prayers are certainly what I'm going to need. I can't do this without the Lord's help."

Allison handed her mother a copy of the letter she'd sent the Thornwells. Kathryn read it and quietly laid it on the table.

"Well, it seems a fairly unobtrusive way to start." Her voice trailed off.

Jason chuckled. "It is about as unobtrusive as she can get considering she's dropping a major bombshell on their household."

Kathryn nodded. "It should pique Thea Thornwell's curiosity if nothing else. I'm thinking that she will want to see you, even if just to make sure you're a fraud."

Allison took her mother's hand and looked earnestly into her face. "If she'll see me, Mother, I know she'll believe me."

"I can't imagine they would want to recognize you as their granddaughter when they did everything in their power to keep your father and me apart."

Jason leaned forward. "Perhaps because their son is dead and she's a part of him. He lives on in the child he fathered. They have lived alone in that big house all these years, perhaps nursing their bitterness over the death of their only son. I would say that Allison could bring them hope."

"Hope? Yes, I suppose that's true. They could refuse to believe you for the simple reason that they would then have to recognize me as Oliver's wife and the mother of his child."

"But Mother, there's the matter of the check. If they destroyed it, wouldn't you want to know? I don't think I can rest until that is resolved."

"There's no need to vindicate me, Allison, God already did that. Whatever happened to the check is past history."

Jason leaned back and folded his arms, his brow furrowed in thought. "Allison told me what happened. It was pretty underhanded. Were annulment papers filed?"

"I received papers from Gordon Thornwell's firm, and threw them in the trash, as well as all the other correspondence from them. When Oliver died I guess it became a moot point."

Allison's mind seemed to be turning with ideas. "Mother, would you give me a copy of my birth certificate? I'll need it to prove who I am."

Kathryn sighed. "Yes, of course. I'll get you a copy."

Allison put her hand over her mother's. "It will be all right, I just know it will be."

Kathryn smiled lovingly at her daughter, but an infinite sadness filled her heart. "If anyone can bring this off, you can." She pushed her teacup aside. "I need to get on with my errands. I'll stop in the bank and get the documents. Maybe it would be best if I made a couple of certified copies."

Jason gave her a hug and kissed Allison on the cheek. "Bye Sweetheart, I better get back to work on that boat dock. We'll probably be through early this afternoon."

Kathryn watched him go and turned back to let Joshua grasp her finger.

"We talked about having at least four children." She murmured.

"You and my father wanted four?"

Kathryn sighed. "Yes, as an only child with his whole life regimented, he decided that he wanted to be a different kind of father, one who enjoyed his children and spent time with them. He wanted to be everything his own father wasn't."

"I wish I could have known him."

"I do too. When he was killed in Vietnam, I thought I would die too. The only thing that kept me going was the thought of having you."

"Did you ever want to marry again?"

"Oh, there has been a gentleman or two interested through the years, but no, I just never found anyone who could measure up to your father. I loved him with all my soul. That's been enough for a lifetime."

Kathryn wiped her eyes with the back of her hand and touching Allison on the cheek, hurried out to her car.

She got the documents, copied them and dropped them off. She knew the letter would stir things up, and was afraid the Thornwell's reaction would devastate her daughter. When she was driving home, she was aware of a sense of things put in motion that were to affect the rest of their lives. Allison had taken the first irrevocable step.

TWENTY

Thea stood at the window of the library, fingering the strand of pearls around her neck and observing the heavy rain. There was a quick flash of lightning followed by the roll of thunder as the fury of the unexpected spring storm shook the house. She impulsively shuddered, hating storms and anything else that disturbed her ordered world.

"Mail come?"

At the sound of his voice she turned and regarded her husband who was sitting quietly by the fireplace in his wheelchair, watching her. Sometimes it still seemed strange to her to see him so incapacitated. In the two years since his devastating stroke, she'd learned to understand his garbled words.

"I'm sure it has. Edward will bring it."

She gave him a half-smile and went to dutifully tuck the lap robe closer around his legs. The stroke paralyzed his right side and turned the muscles on that side of his mouth into a perpetual frown. In a day he'd gone from being the powerful and ruthless head of a large law firm to a helpless old man in a wheelchair. A lion to a lamb, someone had commented after the stroke. His auburn hair, brushed with gray had turned white almost overnight.

She endeavored in many ways to help him keep his dignity and involved him in the decisions of the household. It was neither love nor pity, for Thea rarely felt her heart touched by the needs of others. She'd closed off those emotions years ago.

The door of the library opened and Edward entered.

"The mail has come, Madam." As she sat, he laid the pile in her lap, a daily ritual. Thea would read each piece to Gordon and discuss any necessary details.

"Thank you, Edward."

"You're welcome, Madam."

Thea watched him leave knowing he was headed for the kitchen and a cup of tea with Martha, for she would be finished with the breakfast clean-up by now. It was a routine that rarely changed over the years. With breakfast over, Mr. Thornwell fed and the mail seen to, Thea knew the Culpeppers looked forward to a discussion of the coming day's affairs.

Thea dispensed the usual bills quickly with the exception of the heating bill. Gordon adamantly wanted to conserve more heat and Thea, who liked comfort, sighed and suggested closing off more rooms in the large house. Built shortly after the great earthquake of 1907, each bedroom had its own heater and fireplace. They seldom had company anymore and the large dining room, as well as the three guest rooms stood empty.

She pulled a letter off the pile and stared at it a moment.

"Do we know anyone named Carradine, Gordon?"

He frowned, considering the question, and then slowly moved his head from side to side. "Nooooh."

She shrugged, slit the letter open and began to read.

Dear Mr. And Mrs. Thornwell,

It seems strange to address you this way, considering what I am about to tell you, but since we have never met, perhaps it is appropriate.

My mother is Kathryn Hilliard. Her legal name was, and still is, Mrs. Oliver Thornwell. She was married to my father before he was sent to Vietnam. I have a birth certificate showing Oliver Thornwell as my father, which makes me your granddaughter.

Please understand that I am not writing this to ask anything of you. I'm married and have a beautiful little boy, Joshua. He will be raised with the benefit of knowing his grandparents, something I did not have. I wish only to get to know you.

Obviously you are wondering why I am revealing myself at this late date. I only recently learned of your existence and have been wondering how to go about this.

I would be most happy if you would be willing to at least meet and talk with me. I will await your reply.

Sincerely,

Allison Thornwell Carradine

Thea clutched her heart, the color draining from her face. "Good heavens, Oh Gordon--"

He reached out his good hand, which shook slightly. "What's iss?"

Thea gathered herself together, her shock tempered by anger. "This young woman claims to be our granddaughter! She says her mother was Kathryn Hilliard, that woman Oliver was briefly married to." She read him the letter.

He clenched his good fist. "Impossible."

"Yes, of course, Gordon, but what kind of a young woman would write us a letter like this after all these years?"

"Office, Jacob." He spit the words out harshly.

Jacob Tingley took over Oliver's position as head of the law firm after Gordon's stroke and was a trusted friend. Thea nodded.

"Yes, the office. I'll call right now. Surely Jacob will know of someone who can look into this."

She made the call quickly and spoke with their attorney. After a few moments she hung up the phone and turned to her husband, a satisfied smile on her face.

"He has a young man in the office he will send to check into who this young woman is. He'll get back to us as quickly as he can."

Gordon pounded his good left fist on the arm of the wheelchair. "Now!"

"Gordon, calm yourself, Jacob will do what he says as soon as they can. We both need to move carefully in this matter."

Thea sat down again, staring at the letter. A child? Their son Oliver and the young woman, Kathryn, were only married five days but Thea realized the possibility existed. It wouldn't be the first time a child had made its way into the world nine months after the wedding. Her mind turned with thoughts she could not even begin to speak. Had Oliver known? If he'd known, would he have put himself in harm's way? After all, the young woman had indeed taken their check, her silence agreeing to an annulment and it wasn't difficult with Gordon's contacts to make sure they had no further contact with each other. The Army clerk was given specific instructions. She and Gordon never anticipated that their actions would cause Oliver's estrangement from them. Oliver had taken his young wife's desertion hard and blamed them for his loss.

How long had she carried that burden in her heart? If she only had a few moments to turn back the clock and undo what they did. He was so young and died so far away from them. The ache in Thea's heart over her son had been her cross to bear for twenty- five years.

Not a woman given to weeping, Thea steeled herself to keep her emotions in check. She took a deep breath and when she felt she had herself under control again, picked up another envelope. "Shall we continue with the mail, Gordon?"

His expression was unreadable, neither angry nor sympathetic.

For a moment he just stared at her and in his face she saw something she hadn't seen in a long while, pity.

"Oliver--would'nt--lissen"

"No. We saved that cancelled check to show him when he came home, but what difference does it make now."

Gordon hung his head, shaking it slowly back and forth. "Never—came--home."

Gordon stared into the fire and Thea stood up and quickly returned to the window to look out at the rain. She knew what he was thinking. There was nothing to prove and no one to prove it to, for in a fiery helicopter crash in Vietnam, Oliver was lost to them forever.

The wind whipped a branch steadily against the house and with each sound, she felt she could feel the beat of her heart.

"Oh Oliver," she put a hand over her mouth to stifle a sob and hurried from the room.

TWENTY-ONE

The phone had an insistent ring to it and Kathryn hurried to answer it.

"Mother, you won't believe what just happened. I'm still shaken up."

Kathryn's heart began to pound. "Are you all right?"

"Oh yes, I'm fine. It was this man."

"What man?"

She listened intently almost holding her breath as Allison related what had occurred.

"This morning I heard a car coming slowly up the driveway and looked out the window. It was a sleek, black sports model. No one we know drives a car like that. I called the hardware store but Hannah said Jason had already left. She said Ted was going to the bank to make a deposit for the store and would look for Jason's truck. "

"Oh, dear. Who was it?"

"A man in a suit, mid-thirties, dark glasses, he looked the house over as though he were making mental notes. He pulled a briefcase out of the car and when he took off his sunglasses, I'm sure he'd come to do business, and I knew he had something to do with my grandparents. Oh, mom, I was terrified. I just started praying for Jason to come straight home!"

"And this man came to the door?"

"Yes, I opened it pretty reluctantly, and he asked if it was the Carradine residence. Then I knew for sure he was from my grandparents."

"Was he from the Thornwell's law firm?"

"I think so. He gave me a card from that said he was Gerald Monroe of Erickson, Hammond and Tingley, Attorneys at Law."

"Well, you've been anxious for a response from your grandparents. Looks like you got one."

Allison went on to relate what happened—

>◇

The young man at the door frowned, waiting for Allison to speak. While he was dressed neatly in a dark suit and tie, his face had a pinched look and his eyes studied her like she was barely worth his time.

She stepped aside, "I suppose you'd better come in. My husband will be home shortly. He just went to the hardware store." She prayed again for Jason to come home soon. She gave one last desperate glance down the driveway to see if she could see Jason's truck. It was nowhere in sight.

Gerald Monroe was looking around the house. "You own this place?"

She didn't like his superior attitude. "No, we are renting. If you would like to sit down, as I said, my husband will be home soon."

"My business isn't with your husband, Mrs. Carradine, it's with you."

"What exactly is your business, Mr. Monroe?" She had a knot in her stomach.

He pulled a paper out of his briefcase. It was a copy of her letter to her grandparents. "I believe you sent a letter to Mr. and Mrs. Gordon Thornwell suggesting that you are the daughter of their deceased son, Oliver Thornwell…"

She interrupted him, "I did not suggest it, Mr. Monroe, I am the daughter of Oliver Thornwell."

"Yes, well we will discuss the allegation in a moment. Now I—"

She glanced towards the window and to her immense relief, she heard the sound of Jason's truck coming up the driveway, and jumped up.

"Excuse me; I believe my husband has returned." She hurriedly opened the door and saw Jason hop out of his truck and head for the house with a determined look on his face.

"Honey, I'm so glad you are home. This is Mr. Monroe from Erickson, Hammond and Tingley, a law firm."

"I suspected as much. Evidently Mr. Monroe here has been asking about us around town. Glenn Evans told me at the bank. I thought I'd better hurry home."

"What can we do for you, Mr. Monroe?" He held out a hand and Monroe took it with a perfunctory shake.

"As I told your wife here, my business is with her. I assume you are aware of a certain letter written to our clients, Gordon and Thea Thornwell?"

"Yes, I'm aware of the letter, and contents."

"Mrs. Carradine claims to be the long lost granddaughter of the Thornwells and as you can imagine, after all these years since their son's death, this has caused my client's extreme concern and distress. A claim of this sort cannot be taken lightly."

Allison felt her blood pressure rising, but strove to remain calm. They had not underestimated Thea Thornwell after all. "My only 'claim' as you put it, was that I was their granddaughter and wanted to meet them. As I stated in my letter, I want nothing from them other than that."

"That is what you state now, Mrs. Carradine, but as we have experienced, once identification has been accepted, there is usually a change in the direction of the claim.

"You know, Mr. Monroe, the position you are taking on behalf of my grandparents only shows me that my mother had good reason to keep me from them! If I weren't a Christian, I would not have contacted them at all."

Gerald Monroe looked pained. "Please, Mrs. Carradine, let us keep religious issues out of this. The bottom line is; how much do you want to relinquish any claim against the Thornwells? I am prepared--and he reached into his briefcase again, "to offer you a check."

Jason had been sitting quietly and to all intents and purposes, he appeared calm. Allison knew when he was agitated a muscle in his neck twitched. It was doing so now. Jason rose from the couch and taking the man's elbow, gently but firmly assisted Gerald Monroe from his chair.

"We understand you are just doing the job you have been hired to do, Mr. Monroe, but my wife is not interested in your check. Not now, and not ever."

Allison looked the attorney in the eye. "My mother didn't take a check from the Thornwells years ago and I have no intention of being bought off either. What kind of people are they anyway, that this is their only response?"

The attorney studied them both for a moment and took another tack. "Do you have any proof that you are who you say you are?"

"I have a copy of my birth certificate, and my parent's marriage certificate." Allison went into the bedroom and got the papers from their file box. They'd been right to have certified copies made.

She came back and handed a copy of each certificate to the attorney who studied them carefully.

"I will have to take this information to my clients. Are these your only copies?"

"No," Jason answered evenly, "we have others."

Gerald Monroe got out a small notebook and jotted a few things in it. He reached in his pocket for something, but evidently didn't need it for he took his hand out again.

"Let me see if I understand you correctly, Mrs. Carradine. You claim that your mother was married, however briefly, to Oliver Thornwell, and you were born after he left for Vietnam?"

"My mother was married to Oliver Thornwell until he died. She is his widow."

"Yes, he was killed in a helicopter crash, a deep tragedy for my clients."

"And for my mother, Mr. Monroe, they loved each other very much."

"Hmmm, as you say."

He had seated himself again and now rose, gathering his papers and putting the small notebook in his pocket.

"I will present the information you have given me to my clients. If they choose to pursue this matter, you will hear from us."

Jason opened the door, and as the attorney stepped out, he turned to Allison with a bit of a smirk. "There is one point on which your information is inaccurate, Mrs. Carradine."

"And that is--?"

"Your mother did take the check. Good afternoon, Mrs. Carradine, Mr. Carradine."

TWENTY-TWO

Kathryn had listened in stunned silence. "He said I took the check? How in the world did he come to that conclusion?"

"I don't know, Mother. What an insufferable man. And to insinuate, to say so confidently—"

"It's all right, Allison, we have to just let it go. It's enough that I know the truth."

"Jason told me Mr. Monroe was doing the job they sent him to do. He was giving me a rough time, but only so he could determine a couple of things for the Thornwell's information. He saw what he was up to right away."

Allison's voice quavered. "Mother, we barely made expenses when I was little. If you had money you would have spent it on us. We almost lost our house once and if you hadn't gotten a really good illustrating job at that time--."

There was a pause as she sniffed and Kathryn heard Jason murmuring in the background. Allison blew her nose.

"What did Jason mean when he said Mr. Monroe was doing what he was sent here to do? He tried to pay you to stop trying to meet your grandparents!"

"Jason said he was deliberately baiting me to see what kind of a response he would get. Our whole conversation will be run past the Thornwells."

"How could he remember your whole conversation from a few notes?"

"Jason said he had a tape recorder in his pocket. He reached in to make sure it was on before he continued with his questions. He said they make some pretty small tape recorders these days."

"You mean he was asking those questions to see what you would say and how you would react to the offer of the check, and recording it all for your grandparents?"

"That's the general idea."

Kathryn fumed. "That's pretty underhanded."

"Actually, Jason seemed to think it was a pretty smart move. If you were the Thornwells, and had a lot of money, and someone appeared on the scene out of nowhere claiming to be your granddaughter--."

"Which could make you a possible heir," Kathryn offered.

"Jason is right. I guess I'd be cautious how I approached the situation too."

Kathryn hurt for her daughter. "Allison, you didn't really think they would get your letter and call to welcome you with open arms, did you?"

Allison's voice sounded small. "Something like that, I guess."

There was a murmur of voices and then Jason came on the line.

"Mom, Allison and I were talking afterward and we were puzzled as to why this Mr. Monroe seemed so sure you took the check. It wouldn't have been cashed under the circumstances, unless—"

Kathryn felt a jolt in her midsection. "Unless someone took the check and cashed it. Is that what you're saying?"

"Yeah, I guess it is. Allison said you left the check lying on the floor."

She interrupted him. "Jason, my head is spinning right now. I think we just need to wait to see what Allison's grandparents are going to do. If they don't respond, there's no point in pursuing this."

"You're right, mom, I guess the ball is in their court. We'll let you know if we hear anything else."

Kathryn placed the phone back in the cradle and shook her head slowly. What sort of Pandora's box had Allison opened?

TWENTY-THREE

The following week Thea Thornwell served her opening volley. Allison called Kathryn in high excitement. "Mother, my grandmother called!"

Kathryn gasped. "She did? What did she say?

She said, "This is Thea Thornwell. I wish to speak to Allison Carradine" and I said, "This is she." Then she said she wanted to see me next week on Thursday afternoon at one o'clock sharp. She said not to bring you, and I was to come alone."

Kathryn's heart was beating erratically. She put a hand to her chest. "Well, I don't think I'd want to go anyway."

"Mom, I was tongue-tied, and when I didn't answer, she spoke again, this time she sounded really irritated and asked if I was still there. I found my voice finally, and answered, "yes."

"You're going then?"

"She said she'd send directions, and I just said, 'yes', again. Then she hung up. I felt like an idiot."

"She has that affect on people."

"Well, Mom, this definitely isn't going to be a cakewalk."

"She knows you'll come, Allison, and she's setting her own boundaries."

Allison clicked her tongue. "That was really great, Mom, the first time speaking to my grandmother and all I can come up with are one syllable words!"

"I hope Jason is going with you. I wouldn't walk into that place alone."

"Jason already told me he was going to go no matter what she said. He'll help with Joshua. We have to take him since I'm still nursing."

Kathryn thought for a moment. "What did Thea sound like on the phone?"

"About as warm as an ice cube."

"Will you be all right with this? They're a tough pair."

"I'll be all right, Mother."

"I hope so, dear. I didn't mean to sound negative. It was just the way they treated me. I didn't want you to be subject to that."

"It was kind of funny if you think about it, you know, "Allison imitated the voice. "My place, one o'clock Thursday. Be there! Oh, Mom, will you please pray? I'm excited, but I'm scared too."

"Your Aunt Ruth and I have been praying ever since you told us about writing to her. I hope you don't mind but I called her. I know God will go before you."

"I'd like to take a copy of the letter you wrote to my father in Vietnam, that is if that's all right with you."

Kathryn hesitated. It had been a long time, what did it matter. "Of course, I'll make a copy for you."

When she hung up the phone, Kathryn thought again of Mr. Culpepper and how nice he'd been to her. She couldn't imagine him taking the check. She'd never really met his wife Martha, the cook, or the housekeeper, so she didn't have any impression of what kind of people they were. The housekeeper had to have found the check on the floor and taken it. Yet, if she did take it, how in the world could she have cashed it? They wouldn't have had her signature. Were any of those people still with the Thornwells after all these years? Surely they'd all found better employment by now. Her questions led to more questions. Perhaps at the Thornwells, Allison and Jason would find the answers.

TWENTY-FOUR

The car entered the driveway and came to a stop. Rigid in her chair as she waited next to Gordon, Thea's thoughts flew from one end of the spectrum to another. Could Oliver have fathered a child? Had he known he was to be a father? If the girl was an imposter, would it be possible to tell? Thea would have to rely on intuition alone, unless the girl brought some sort of proof.

Gordon continuously cleared his throat indicating he was just as anxious to see this young woman. Gathering all the strength she possessed, Thea steeled herself to face the scene to come.

Edward was greeting someone and a man's voice replied. Thea pursed her lips. She'd told the girl to come alone, but she'd brought someone with her. An attorney? Well, we'll make short work of any agenda they had.

The doors to the library opened and the butler came in followed by a young couple.

"Madam, may I present Mr. and Mrs. Jason Carradine, Mr. and Mrs. Carradine, Mr. and Mrs. Gordon Thornwell."

As the two couples faced each other, the butler seemed reluctant to leave.

"You may go now, Edward, and close the door as you leave." Thea rose and drew herself up to her full five feet two inches.

The girl turned and smiled at the butler as he left. She was young, mid-twenties perhaps. Well-dressed and not coarse-looking.

When the young woman stepped forward and faced her, Thea felt her heart begin to pound. The hazel eyes, the auburn hair. She put a hand to her heart and struggled to remain in control of the situation.

The girl appeared shocked and sad at the same time as she became aware of Gordon's condition.

"I asked you to come alone."

The young man answered for the girl, courteously but firmly. "I didn't feel it appropriate for her to make the long drive by herself, Mrs. Thornwell."

"Yes, well you're here, so you might as well be seated. What is your name again?" There was no graciousness in her tone as she indicated a settee across from her.

"Jason. I'm Allison's husband."

Thea nodded and then seated herself again on the Victorian chair, keeping herself rigid as she sought how to proceed.

"I cannot understand this charade," she began, facing the girl. "Why would your mother hide you from us all these years, if indeed you are our granddaughter?"

"As I said in my letter, Mrs. Thornwell, under the circumstances, it seemed to be the only thing she could do. You didn't want my mother to be married to my father, and she assumed you wouldn't want me. If you did, you had the means to take me away. I was all she had of my father so that wasn't an option." Allison lifted her chin defiantly as she spoke and Thea's hand went to her breast for a brief moment. The familiarity of her gesture was unmistakable. Oliver. She took a deep breath before she returned the hand to her lap. She observed Jason covertly squeezing his wife's hand.

"We didn't know anything about your mother. For all we know she was after his money."

"It didn't sound as if you wanted to get to know her. She said you made it clear that Oliver had no money, at least of his own. My mother is a wonderful person, kind, gentle, artistic--"

"She could have come to the house and been introduced to us sooner, given us a chance to learn about her character."

Allison did not appear to be intimidated by Thea's manner. "You confronted my father over one of my mother's letters and told him he needed to get rid of her. You never invited her to the house. It was why he left and joined the Army. Then you managed to keep them apart in the last weeks before my father went overseas. It doesn't appear to me that you wanted to know my mother's character."

"Don't be impertinent! We did what we thought was best for our son."

At the mention of the army, Gordon's shoulders slumped. He looked up at Allison and there were tears in his eyes. He spoke slowly, out of one side of his mouth. They were almost unintelligible. Allison looked at her husband and back to Gordon, then she leaned forward, concentrating on understanding the words.

Thea put her hand on his arm. "My dear, we couldn't be sure. We just have to be certain. We don't want to make any hasty decisions, do we?"

Gordon's eyes flashed. "Nohh--" he answered, and shook his head. He looked back at Allison and lifted his left hand slightly, crooking his finger at her.

"He wants you to come closer."

The young woman knelt down in front of her grandfather and looked earnestly into his face. He in turn studied hers. After a moment his eyes softened and he nodded.

Thea couldn't deny his words. "She's the spitting image of Oliver."

TWENTY-FIVE

Her stern facade crumpling, Thea put her hands over her face for a moment and then reached out to grip her husband's shoulder again. "Yes, Gordon, I know."

Her hand trembled slightly as she stood up and took a framed photograph from the nearby piano. As she looked at the photograph, once again anguish filled her heart. As Allison also stood up, Thea wordlessly handed it to her.

The young woman studied the picture and her face took on a soft, gentle look. The eyes and face looking back at her mirrored her own. Thea knew what she had seen as soon as the girl had entered the room. It wasn't documents Thea needed. Seeing her in person verified beyond a shadow of a doubt that she was Oliver's child.

Thea sat straighter to regain her composure and attempted once again to take charge of the situation. "Tell me about your mother. As I recall, she told me her parents died when she was young and she and her sister were raised by their godparents."

Jason came to stand behind Allison, his hand on her shoulder. She impulsively put her hand on her grandfather's paralyzed right hand and he,, with great effort, covered it with his left hand. Now, hearing Thea's request, she removed her hand gently, patted his arm, and she and Jason sat back on the settee.

"My mother went to an art university in San Francisco and planned to do illustrations. A publisher saw her work at an exhibit and offered her a contract to illustrate a couple of children's books. That led to other offers. She uses the name of Kate Longwell."

"Kate Longwell?" Thea stared at her.. "That is your mother? I purchased two books with her illustrations for a friend's grandson. She is well known in the art world."

"It was that income that supported us all these years."

Thea's eyes narrowed. "Well, I imagine that ten thousand dollars helped considerably also."

Jason, who had remained remarkably quiet through this conversation, looked Thea in the eye. "She didn't have the benefit of that check, Mrs. Thornwell. She left it lying on the floor in Oliver's room. I know Allison's mother well. If she said she didn't take it, she didn't."

Thea drew herself up. "We'll just see about that." She reached for a small series of buttons on a mahogany base next to her chair. Edward opened the door of the library so quickly that she saw Allison suppress a smile. He'd been listening as usual.

"You rang, madam?"

"Edward, would you please bring me the metal box from Mr. Thornwell's office?"

He raised one eyebrow in question, then nodded and left the room. They waited in awkward silence until he returned.

He handed Thea the box and stood waiting as she opened it, taking out a manila envelope. She drew a paper out of the envelope and handed it to Allison. It was a cancelled check for ten thousand dollars, with her mother's name endorsed on the back.

Allison gasped. "You actually kept it all these years?" she handed the check to Jason to examine. He studied the check. The writing was precise and the signature clear.

Thea clasped her hands together and with knowing glance at her husband, waited to see what Allison would do.

Suddenly Jason spoke up. "Sweetheart, let me see that copy of the letter your mother wrote to your father in Vietnam, the one that was returned."

Allison opened her purse and got out the copy of the letter, handing it to him.

Jason shuffled through to the last page, looking at the check and then the signature on the letter. He handed the page and the check to Thea. "Take a look at the handwriting, Mrs. Thornwell. The signatures aren't close to similar."

The butler couldn't help himself. "I always thought that nice young woman couldn't have done that, madam. She loved young Oliver, I could see that … "

She gave a small snort of annoyance. "That will be all, Edward. Surely you have other duties to attend to?" She waved him off with one hand.

"Very good, madam," he said stiffly, but as he left the room she noted a pleased smile on his face.

Thea frowned as she studied the letter and the signatures. Bewildered but not convinced, she looked up at Allison. "If your mother did not sign and cash this check, then who in the name of heaven did? One needs identification. This is very upsetting We believed--"

"That Kathryn had cashed the check and was the type of person you thought she was?" Jason said.

Thea still stared at the signature on the letter. "Yes, but someone signed this check and cashed it. Who else would have done such a thing?"

"That, among other things, is what we'd like to find out," said Jason..

TWENTY-SIX

Thea shook her head slowly. "This is most distressing. Someone, possibly here in my own house is or was a thief."

Jason leaned forward. "Mrs. Thornwell, I realize this is a shock, but can you tell me who was here at the time the check was written?"

"Twenty-five years ago?" She sighed. "Well, the Culpeppers, who have been with us for years. Edward's wife is our cook. The Culpeppers would never do such a thing."

"So Mr. Culpepper was here at the time my mother and father were married."

"Yes."

Jason glanced at Allison. "Was there anyone else?"

"Ms. Simons, the housekeeper. She has also been with us many years." Thea narrowed her eyes. "All of our employees are trustworthy, I can assure you."

Jason smiled. "I'm sure you're right, Mrs. Thornwell. It doesn't make sense for someone to take a check of that size and then stay around all these years. They wouldn't want to take a chance on being discovered."

"Gordon, do you think," but he had dozed off in his wheelchair and his head was nodding to one side. She studied him for a moment and rang for the butler who wheeled her husband back to his room.

"I will need to give this matter some thought and discuss it with my husband. It has been many years. I will see what he wishes to do." She raised her eyebrows. "Perhaps a handwriting analysis would clarify things."

Jason shrugged. "Whatever you think best."

Allison looked earnestly at Thea's face. "Mrs. Thornwell, do you believe I am your granddaughter?"

Thea studied her and after a long moment sighed heavily. "It is uncanny. You have Oliver's eyes and hair, many facial features. Even his mannerisms, the way you lift your chin and run your hand through your hair. Either you are a very good actress, or you are Oliver's daughter."

Returning the portrait to the piano, Thea turned back to Allison. "We wanted so much for Oliver. He was our only child. We should have considered his feelings more than we did. We were so sure your mother was after his money and to us he was too young. Not old enough for marriage. We thought we were protecting him. Yet, and her voice broke as she fought for control, "yet, we lost him anyway."

Thea picked up the box again and took out a yellowed envelope. "This was his last letter, written the day before he was killed. He loved your mother and believed he had lost her. He didn't want to admit she had taken our money and left him. He was devastated. He didn't care to live. I often wondered if he--"

Allison gently put her hand on her grandmother's arm. "If he volunteered for some dangerous assignment or something that resulted in his death?"

She looked down at Allison's hand and slowly covered it with her own. "All these years, we thought there was nothing to remember him but our memories. He left us a legacy, but we didn't know--" She held out the letter.

As Allison read the letter from her father, a tear trickled slowly down one cheek.

Thea waited until Allison had finished, took it gently, folded it and put it back in the box. Allison wiped her cheek with one hand.

"He was angry with us and would not forgive what we did."

Obviously touched by the anguish of her father's letter, Allison sat quietly for a moment, as did Thea.

"I wish I could have known him. From my mother's description he sounded like a wonderful man."

Thea nodded. "He was everything we hoped for in a son." Her voice broke. "He wouldn't let Gordon use his influence to keep him from going overseas. He was as stubborn as his father. When we received that last letter I had a premonition. I wanted to reach him somehow in that horrible war-torn country and bring him home. There was no hope of that. Gordon even tried to contact people he knew to do something, but it was too late. Then we received the telegram." She bowed her head.

"My mother said they probably sent his personal effects home."

Thea looked up and frowned. "That was the most unusual thing. There were no personal effects. Most of his unit was killed. The helicopter they were being transported in exploded, shot down by the enemy. We were told that there was nothing left to send us."

Allison gasped, "How terrible. That will be a hard thing to share with my mother when I get home." She glanced at her husband and then turned to Thea again. "I can't bring your son, my father, back, but you are right. He did leave a legacy for you. You not only have a granddaughter but also a small great-grandson."

Thea's eyes grew wide. "A great grandson? Yes, now I remember. You mentioned him in your letter. Where is he now?"

Allison shrugged self-consciously. "He's only four months old and I'm still nursing. I had to bring him. He's with Mr. Culpepper's wife in the kitchen."

This time Thea's finger laid on the buzzer and when the butler appeared, his face was bland. "Yes madam?"

"Edward! Bring me my great-grandson!"

His mouth twitched as he sought to suppress a smile. "Ah, yes, Madam."

Edward brought the still sleeping baby quickly. Thea's face softened as she looked down at him. "He's a handsome child. You said you were nursing?"

"Yes. He'll probably be waking up in a little while. He can be pretty noisy when he's hungry."

Thea shook her head, feeling bewildered. "A grandmother and a great-grandmother. I must get used to the idea."

"What would you like me to call you? It seems strange to call you Mrs. Thornwell."

"You may call me, "and she paused, considering, "Grandmother. I abhor granny or grandma."

"Grandmother." Allison repeated the word reverently.

TWENTY-SEVEN

Jason had been listening without comment and finally spoke up quietly. "I'm happy you and Allison have finally found one another."

Thea looked at Jason as if really seeing him for the first time. A very handsome young man, obviously devoted to Allison. She extended her hand. "You may call me Thea, Jason."

She turned to her butler. "My husband?"

"He is resting, madam."

"We will have tea now, Edward." She assumed a familiar role, the gracious hostess. "Do you drink coffee or tea?"

"Coffee is fine for me. I believe Allison would like tea."

"Very good, Madam." He hurried out, returning almost momentarily with a large ornate tea tray and silver tea service. He brought coffee, tea, cream, lemon slices, small triangular crustless sandwiches, petite fours, and slices of lemon cake. Mrs. Culpepper had been busy. Allison's eyes lit up.

The china cups were obviously fine china, for they had a fragile, transparent look-- white with hand-painted red roses tipped in gold.

Jason smiled at Thea. "This is nice of you. It has been a while since lunch." He and Allison helped themselves, politely but with relish.

"When did my grandfather have his stroke?"

"Two years ago. We were playing bridge at the home of friends and suddenly he dropped his cards, almost in slow motion and slumped against his chair. It was so unexpected." Thea became somber, recalling the moment.

"Did you know what was happening?"

"We weren't sure. We called the ambulance and he was taken to the hospital. He was speaking strange words and I couldn't understand him. When they got him into the emergency room, they almost lost him twice. They managed to save his life, but the remains of the stroke are as you see. He will not recover the use of his right side."

"That's sad. He couldn't continue in the law firm, could he?" Jason asked.

"No. His partners took over and he remains at home."

Thea studied her new granddaughter. What had happened in Gordon's office after the stroke still galled her, but now was not the time to speak of it.

She poured coffee into a cup and handed it to Jason, then poured the tea for Allison and herself. Holding her cup she sat back, watching them with curiosity as she sipped the steaming liquid.

"Tell me about this mountain community where you were raised, Allison."

"Well, Lewiston has about sixteen hundred people. We like to say that includes kids and dogs." She smiled ruefully as Thea cocked one eyebrow.

"I attended the elementary school from kindergarten through the eighth grade..."

Thea interrupted, "It wasn't one of those one-room schoolhouses was it?" Good heavens, where was this child educated?

Jason appeared amused but remained quiet.

"Oh no, it had separate classrooms for each grade. The seventh and eighth graders changed classrooms depending on what subject was being taught, just like any other junior high school. Many children were bused in from smaller outlying communities. We had a multi-purpose room and a gymnasium."

Thea sniffed. "I assume it must have been adequate. What about the stores and shops in the community?"

"Let's see. We had a small historic district that had a general store, a bed and breakfast, an old hotel that serves the greatest prime rib. Oh, and a combination bookshop and coffeehouse, an antique store and a small craft shop. Then up on the main road there was a convenience store, a motel and the one gas station. On another road was the post office, another convenience store and a pizza shop. There was another small mall that had a market, a Laundromat, and a combination snack shop and video store." She thought a moment and turned to Jason.

"Did I forget anything?"

"Looks like you covered most of the bases, sweetheart. I think you might have left out the churches."

"Oh yes. There was a Catholic and Seventh Day Adventist church and then the Community Church, where my family went."

Thea set her tea cup down and was silent for a moment, pondering her next question.

"I take it you attended Trinity High School." The young attorney who reported to her had done his homework. "What accomplishments can you attribute to your high school years? Did you hold any class offices?"

Allison looked down at her hands. "I was a little shy to run for any offices."

At Thea's frown, Jason broke in. "What Allison has neglected to mention, Thea, is that because of her high grade point, she was selected Valedictorian for her class and received a teaching scholarship.

She perked up. This information was more of what she could identify with and share with her bridge group.

"Your grandfather will be most happy to hear that, Allison." She took another tack. "I understand your mother never married again. As I recall, she was attractive."

"She loved my father, Grandmother. She said she just never met anyone else who measured up to him. After he was, well, after he died, she said that for some people one love is enough for a lifetime."

Thea looked away, staring out the window for a long moment. "Yes," she murmured quietly, "I suppose that is to her credit."

She summoned Edward.

"Mr. Thornwell?"

"Still resting, madam, most likely until dinner time."

The mention of dinner brought Thea to her feet. "I have been remiss in my duties as hostess. You will join us for dinner?" She would brook no dissention at this point.

Allison smiled happily at Jason and he nodded.

"We'd be honored to join you, but we do need to start home before it gets too late."

Thea waved a hand at them. "Nonsense, you must be our guests tonight. That is too many hours of driving in one day for Allison and the baby. We'll prepare a room for you."

When Jason started to protest, she arched her brows and gave him a knowing look. "I've just met my granddaughter and I believe we have matters to discuss."

Jason looked at Allison's eager face and smiled. "You're right. I know you and Allison want to get better acquainted."

"Then it is settled. Edward, please call Noreen and tell her that we need a guest room prepared."

"If you will forgive me, madam, I have already taken the liberty of informing her. She is preparing a room now."

Thea raised her eyebrows at his boldness, but was not surprised. "What room have you prepared?"

"I had thought Master Oliver's room."

"Oliver's room? But it hasn't been--I mean--" She put a hand to her breast. "No, not yet, put them in the blue room." Composing herself quickly, she was embarrassed at her sudden display of emotion. She turned to Allison. "Do you have any overnight things?"

"Actually we do. We were planning on staying at a motel if it was too late when we started home."

"Good. Dinner is at five o'clock. We eat early. Do be prompt. You have about two hours to rest." She picked up the check and studied it thoughtfully. We'll look into this."

TWENTY-EIGHT

Jason picked up the baby. Joshua was waking up and beginning to fuss. They quickly followed Mr. Culpepper out of the library where they met a rather dour faced woman. She glanced at the baby carrier and her eyes widened.

"Ms. Simons, may I present Mr. and Mrs. Thornwell's granddaughter, Allison Carradine, her husband, Jason and their son Joshua. We are instructed to show them to the blue room instead."

The housekeeper acknowledged them with a curt nod. She glanced at Allison and for a moment Allison saw something in the woman's eyes. Fear? Ms. Simons pursed her lips and started up the stairs.

As they climbed the great staircase Allison couldn't help but think of her mother and father ascending these stairs the night they came here to announce their marriage. She was anxious to see the room her father grew up in, but realized it would have been awkward for her grandmother. Was it still the same as it was when he was alive? She'd heard of bereaved parents who kept a child's room as a memorial for years.

Allison was pleasantly surprised. With the age of the house, she'd imagined the Blue Room to be dark. Yet the drapes and coverlet on the large queen-sized bed were soft blue sateen with tiny white roses. The room and furniture, in white and different shades of blue was, all in all, quite comfortable. The housekeeper moved through the room and opened a door.

"The bathroom is here." They glimpsed a large white tub with blue towels laid out on its side.

Allison turned to the housekeeper. "Did my grandparents build this house, Ms. Simons?"

"I don't believe so, ma'am. Mrs. Thornwell can tell you better than me. If you have need of anything else, please let me know."

Just as Allison was about to ask how they were to do that, the housekeeper pointed to a buzzer by the door, "If you push that, I'll come." She frowned and looked at them over the glasses that were perched on her nose. "It's a long way up the stairs, so give me time."

"We'll be fine." Jason gave her his warmest smile and Allison could see Noreen Simons softening under its glow, which not many people could resist.

When the housekeeper left, Jason pulled Allison into his arms and kissed her.

"Your grandmother is quite a woman, sweetheart. I thought the meeting went better than we expected. You know, looking at that photograph, your resemblance to your father is uncanny. She had to see it the moment you entered the room."

"Oh Jason, isn't it exciting? I have grandparents. They believe me." She kept her arms around his waist. "My poor grandfather, he wants so much to talk, and with that stroke you have to listen so carefully to his words to understand them.

"From what your mother told us, it is quite a change from the man he used to be. He is dependent on others to help him. Not the man firmly in charge of a busy law office."

She was about to sink down on the edge of the bed when a loud cry came from the carrier. Allison sighed. Her small charge wanted his dinner.

When the baby was satiated and dozing again, Jason made a makeshift crib out of the bottom drawer of the big dresser for Joshua.

"You're tired, aren't you sweetheart? Would you like to take a rest before dinner? I can just sit in that chair and read while you nap. If Josh wakes up I'll take him for a walk."

She nodded gratefully, lay back, closed her eyes and was asleep in a moment.

Allison had been dreaming something, but couldn't put it together in her mind as she slowly awoke. Jason was leaning over her, shaking her gently by the arm.

TWENTY-NINE

"Is it time to get up already? I just went to sleep."

"You've been sleeping over an hour and a half. I thought you might want to freshen up before dinner."

There was a knock and Noreen stood at the door looking a little uncomfortable.

"Mrs. Thornwell has asked us to watch the baby for you while you have dinner with your grandparents. Do you have any, ah, other means of feeding him?"

"How very kind of you." Allison got a bottle of breast milk out of the cooling compartment of the diaper bag and handed the bag to Noreen. Joshua was carefully moved, still sleeping, into the baby carrier and the housekeeper carried him gingerly downstairs.

As Allison and Jason descended the staircase a little while later, they were aware of voices at the back of the entry. Ms. Simons and Edward were talking quietly. "...after all these years," Noreen was saying.

Jason coughed and the conversation ceased abruptly. The butler came forward with a smile to escort them to the dining room. Noreen slipped out through a door cut in the paneling at the back of the hall. Jason eyed the panel a moment, and then followed the butler to the dining room.

Bay windows in the large dining room overlooked the garden. Soft green damask draperies complemented the pale green velveteen on the chairs. The furniture was Queen Anne and Allison was sure the table at its fullest could seat sixteen people. obviously some leaves had been taken out. After the butler seated them, Allison glanced at her grandfather's empty chair. Thea merely murmured, "He will join us after dinner. Meals are difficult for him."

When the first course of French Onion soup was placed in front of him, Jason turned to Thea.

"Allison and I are accustomed to asking a blessing on our meals. May I?" He gave her a warm smile.

Thea gave a heavy sigh. "It's been a long time since grace was said at our table. My husband--" then, as Jason continued to smile at her, "Yes, if you wish."

Jason thanked the Lord for the safe trip, for bringing Allison and her grandmother together, and blessed the food and the hands that prepared it. Thea listened thoughtfully and contemplated Jason for a moment before picking up a spoon and eating her soup.

They waited on her to begin the conversation, but it was Allison who broke the silence.

"Is there any hope of recovery for my grandfather?

Thea looked down at her napkin. "No, he will remain as he is. There have been several more minor strokes, each one seeming to take away more of his abilities. I'm sorry you couldn't have known him before. He was a brilliant man."

When Edward served the salads, Thea glanced at Jason.

"And what is your occupation, Jason?"

"A high school teacher, history, mostly. I also coach the football team."

"Have you considered a more lucrative field?"

"I guess it depends on why you do what you do. I enjoy teaching and working with kids."

"But you live in a rented house. Wouldn't you prefer a home of your own?"

"Of course, Allison and I have talked a lot about a home of our own. We are saving up to build as soon as we can. I figure in about three years."

"Build one? You have property?"

"Actually we do. About six acres near my parent's land with pine and oak trees. It's a good place for a family."

"Surely you'd have more advantages with a teaching job in the city. Your child would attend better schools--."

Allison broke in. "Our elementary school received the Governor's commendation for high marks in math, science and reading. We have good teachers."

"If all you have ever known is a small town, you cannot imagine the importance of the right social circles, my dear. You both grew up there, did you not? And in spite of both of you going to college, you're still living in a small community."

"We are very happy in the small town where we live now."

Thea gave an exasperated sigh.

A dinner of fresh string beans, stuffed potatoes, and lamb chops with a wonderful sauce over them was served. No wonder her grandmother kept her cook, thought Allison, she was a treasure. The Thornwells ate simply, but well.

They retired to the library after dinner where Edward brought Gordon to join them. He seemed eager to see Allison again and his eyes lit up when she came over to him and gave him a gentle smile. Perhaps Gordon's vulnerability made him more receptive now.

Jason smiled good-naturedly. As he leaned back against the couch, Thea was struck again at how handsome he was; and he reminded her of someone.... She shook off the memory and studied Jason. With one leg crossed over the other, he was totally at ease, just listening, content to let Allison take the spotlight.

Thea glanced at Gordon, who nodded his assent. "While Allison was resting, Gordon and I discussed the check. There is someone who can examine it, to put all our minds to rest."

Gordon nodded his head emphatically.

Allison shrugged. "As long as I know my mother is innocent and her signature isn't on the check, it doesn't matter."

Allison looked thoughtful for a moment and then spoke tentatively. "It seems strange to me that the check could disappear but no one knew anything about it. According to my mother, it should have been found on the floor of my father's room, where she left it."

Thea sighed. "As I said, I trust my employees implicitly. I'm sure none of them were involved."

Allison and Jason exchanged glances again and he gave an

imperceptible shrug.

He addressed both the Thornwells. "I'd like to pursue this if I may. I have some ideas that might prove helpful. Let me think about it tonight."

They talked about Joshua, and Allison produced a picture of him to leave with her grandparents.

As it drew late, Allison smiled. "It has been a wonderful day, not only meeting you, finally, but knowing that my mother is exonerated after all these years." She took a step towards her grandfather and kissed him on the forehead. He was startled but didn't seem to object. She turned towards her grandmother. Thea, anticipating her intent, put her hands on Allison's arms and kissed the air by her left ear, a social gesture. However, judging from her grandmother's nature, Allison knew that even that gesture was a big step. She just smiled and wished them both good night.

"Allison, Jason, breakfast is at eight a.m."

"Yes, Grandmother."

Noreen brought the baby carrier in and her face was somewhat softer as she looked down at the baby. "He's been no trouble." She turned and hurried out.

THIRTY

Up in their room with the door closed, Jason put the baby carrier gently down and took her in his arms. "How do you feel, sweetheart?"

"Excited, tired. It's been an emotional day."

He kissed her but she knew his mind was turning. "Where are you, Jason? I can hear the wheels going around."

He laughed. "That noticeable huh?"

Joshua was awake so they place him in the middle of the bed where he could wave his arms and legs and Allison sat down on the edge, watching him. "Do you think someone in the household here did something with that check?"

"I'm not sure what to think, sweetheart, but my gut feeling is that Mr. Culpepper is a decent man." He rubbed his chin with his hand. "Yet, even decent men get themselves into situations that cause them to make wrong decisions."

"How could he or his wife or the housekeeper have cashed the check?" Someone had to have identification to cash the check, or know someone dishonest at a bank.

Jason sat next to her on the bed and chewed on his lower lip as he absentmindedly rubbed her back with his hand. "We keep coming back to the identification. No, I don't think Mr. Culpepper could have participated. It would take someone at the bank, maybe someone who could bypass the rules."

Allison frowned. How would they do that?"

"I'm not sure, but we can sure find out."

Allison picked Joshua up and took her time feeding him until his eyes grew heavy with sleep. When he was done she got ready for bed, but when she came back into the bedroom, Jason was still dressed.

"Aren't you going to bed, Honey?"

He was sitting in the overstuffed chair with his notes. "Hmmm?

Oh, no, not right now sweetheart. It's a little early for me. I've got some thinking to do. I may read a little while."

He got up and put his arms around her. When he kissed her, she clung to him. He seemed to arouse her deepest feelings just by being near. "Jason…" she whispered. There was a short pause and he kissed her eyelids and her mouth again.

"On second thought, sweetheart, maybe it's time to turn in." he murmured softly, and began unbuttoning his shirt as he reached for the light.

Later, as Allison was softly snoring, Jason lay next to her and watched her sleep.

He curled a strand of her hair around his finger and then kissed her on the cheek. "Sleep well, love," he whispered.

Dressing again Jason checked on his small son to make sure he was still asleep, slipped out the door and closed it quietly behind him. He tiptoed down the stairwell and looked through the dining room towards the kitchen. A soft light showed under the door.

THIRTY-ONE

Jason felt like a small boy entering forbidden territory. He heard a man's voice, probably Mr. Culpepper. A woman's voice answered softly. Was it the housekeeper again or the cook he hadn't met yet? He didn't want them to think he'd been spying on them, although he knew that was exactly what he was doing by listening. Then he had an idea. He backed up, coughed, and strode boldly towards the door, pushing it open.

"Oh, excuse me. I saw the light. Hope I'm not bothering you."

"Can we help you, Mr. Carradine?"

Jason shrugged self-consciously. "I couldn't sleep. You wouldn't happen to have some hot chocolate around would you?"

The woman had a kind face and didn't appear to be ruffled by his intrusion. Mr. Culpepper stood quickly. "Allow me to introduce you to my wife, Martha."

"Glad to meet you, Mrs. Culpepper."

She stood up also. A woman in her mid-sixties, wearing metal-rimmed glasses on her nose, and a white apron. Her reddish brown hair was streaked of gray at the temples. As she smiled at him, Jason noted she was still a handsome woman.

"Call me Martha. Now you just sit right down and I'll have a cup of hot chocolate ready directly, Sir. How about the missus? Is she all right?"

"Oh, she's fine. Sleep seems to come easily to her these days."

"And that precious little boy?"

"He's sleeping too, at least for now. Thanks for watching him."

Martha beamed.

If Jason had interrupted a clandestine conversation there was no evidence of it, just a husband and wife having a cup of tea and wrapping up their day. He felt guilty intruding.

Mr. Culpepper had taken off his jacket and tie. His shirt was open and he had rolled up his cuffs. As he reached for his jacket and attempted to put himself to rights, Jason waved a hand and grinned.

"Hey, I promise not to tell the boss if you don't."

Somewhat relieved, Mr. Culpepper indicated a chair. "Very good of you, Sir. Ah, won't you join us?" He looked down at his mug of tea for a moment, still a little uneasy.

"Do you believe Oliver's wife took the check, Mr. Culpepper?"

The butler looked up, startled that Jason had seemingly read his thoughts. "No, Sir, it was obvious that she worshipped the ground young master Oliver walked on. It was indeed a love match. She wouldn't have taken that check and left him."

"From what I have heard, it certainly was that. She's never remarried." Jason eyed the cup of hot chocolate placed in front of him and gave Martha a warm smile. "You're terrific. Thanks!"

She beamed at him. "I added a little cinnamon and of course, the marshmallows, just like young Oliver liked it, when he was here. He was my boy, you know. His parents were always so busy with social activities. He used to sit right where you are. Nearly did me in when he was killed over in that terrible war."

Sensing friendly ground, Jason acknowledged her feelings with a sympathetic nod.

"Do you remember anything about the day Kathryn Thornwell was here, after Oliver left for basic training?"

A glance passed between husband and wife and Jason waited.

"I think it is all right, Edward. This is a puzzle to all of us. If we can help right a wrong, it's our duty."

"When I opened the door that day, I was indeed most happy to see young Oliver. He had his girl with him, pretty thing, not blousy or coarse. She had a lovely face. I liked her right away. Master Oliver introduced her as his wife and it nearly bowled me over. He took her hand and strode towards the library where Mr. and Mrs. Thornwell were and I could tell it would be the devil to pay when they walked in."

He shook his head slowly. "I expected them to have me show her to the door, but after a while things were quiet, and then Mrs. Thornwell informs me as calm as you please, that young Master Oliver and his bride would be joining them for dinner and to see that his room is properly prepared for them for the night."

"What was Noreen's reaction?"

"Noreen? It was her day off." Martha's eyes widened. "You could have knocked her over when I told her what had happened. She'd come back just that morning, but didn't appear until after breakfast. Don't think she ever got a chance to meet the young missus before the Thornwells hustled her off in a cab!"

"Were you aware of the check, Mr. Culpepper?" Jason looked directly at the butler over the top of his cup.

The butler looked a little uncomfortable. "Well, Sir. When you work in a house as long as the missus and I have, you know things. Staff always does, but we keep it amongst ourselves."

Jason waited, and Martha waved a hand at her husband, encouraging him to continue.

"Well, as the missus says, we want to clear ourselves and Noreen of any wrong doing too." He cleared his throat and with a glance toward the kitchen door, continued.

"Mr. Thornwell called Oliver's wife into the library after Master Oliver had gone away in the cab. If ever I saw a look of terror on a girl's face it was then. She knew she was in for it. Next thing I know, the library doors opened suddenly."

The butler gave a slight shrug. "I just happened to be standing in the hall, and the girl came out. She looked a little dazed. She ran past me and up the stairs to Master Oliver's room. Then Mr. Thornwell came out of the library and went upstairs. In a few moments he came back down looking a rather pleased. About five minutes later the girl appeared and came down. She'd gotten herself together and had her suitcase. I took it from her to put into the taxi that was waiting outside. She held her head high she did, and didn't even look at Mr. or Mrs. Thornwell, but marched right out, popped in the taxi and left.

"Then what happened?"

"Mr. Thornwell got on the phone. You have to understand, sir, he was a stern man in his day, formidable, even, before the stroke. He made several phone calls. I didn't hear the words but the sound of his voice carried from his den.

Jason stared thoughtfully at the table. "Kathryn, Allison's mother, said she left the check lying on the floor. The check was never found?"

The butler shook his head and looked at his wife. She shrugged and shook her head too.

Martha stood and reached for Jason's now empty cup. "Noreen never mentioned it, and she would have found it when she cleaned Master Oliver's room. The Thornwells were silent about the whole matter, at least where the staff was concerned."

Edward broke in. "They were silent until the monthly statement envelope came from the bank. Then I remember at dinner Mr. Thornwell pounding his fist in his hand. He said something like, "'By Jove I was right all along!'"

The butler leaned forward with a confidential air. "He had the signed check in his hand. I was serving the salad and saw it plain as day."

"What did Mrs. Thornwell say?"

"She just looked a bit smug and answered, "You were absolutely right, Gordon. She opted for the money after all."

Suddenly the butler looked embarrassed. He had been free with information about the family he worked for. Jason knew he'd better tread carefully.

"Mr. Culpepper, the Thornwells are most fortunate to have such fine people working for them. I know you've told me these things because you believe a wrong has been done to your employers. You haven't betrayed any unknown confidences. We're just trying to get at the bottom of the matter and find out what we can for Allison's mother."

He took a different tack. "Could you tell me a little about Noreen?"

Mr. Culpepper studied Jason a moment, and then lowered his

voice to a conspiratorial whisper. "Well, sir, since we're going to be collaborators, why don't you call me "Cully."

Jason gave him a thumbs up.

Cully smiled ruefully and then regarded Jason's question, scratching his head. "As I said, Noreen couldn't have had anything to do with this since it was her day off. She wasn't even in the house when this whole bloody mess went on."

Martha took a sip of her tea. "I must tell you, Jason, Noreen doesn't talk much, even to us."

Jason nodded. "Anything else you can tell me that would help?"

She glanced at her husband, "Not really, except, well, there was her brother. Noreen was always worrying about him. He was older than she and always borrowing money from her. She'd save up a little and he'd sneak in the back way, more than once and put the bite on her, always promising to pay it back. I doubt if he ever did."

Jason was intrigued. "The back way?"

Edward sat back, "There is a little used entrance that opens to the garden. In an earlier day the tradesmen used it when they brought groceries to the cook."

"What was Noreen's brother's name? Do you remember?"

Martha wrinkled her brow. "Wasn't it William, Edward? I assume it was William Simons, since he was her brother."

Edward regarded Jason for a moment and chewed on his lip. "I do feel a bit flummoxed over all this, Sir. It makes me a little nervous. Rather a cloak and dagger affair, if I do say so myself."

Jason gave the older man a disarming grin. "You must admit, Cully, that this has all been intriguing."

"It has been a puzzle and Martha and I would certainly like to see it settled, in a right way, of course."

"We all do. That's why I'm here."

Cully continued, "We didn't see Noreen's brother often. He didn't appear to wish to see the Thornwells, or us. We didn't mention him to the Thornwells as we assumed Noreen had told them about him."

"He just came to borrow money then?"

"That is what Noreen finally confided in you, didn't she Edward?" Martha asked.

At his emphatic nod, Martha continued, "I'm sure she felt she must help him if he needed it."

"Yes, I guess family is family. Martha, does Noreen usually join you in the evening? I half expected to find her in here too."

"No, she usually visits with me in the morning. She has dinner with us here in the kitchen when she is on duty but usually goes to bed early. Mrs. Thornwell is an early riser and expects Noreen to be ready for her. She also acts as Mrs. Thornwell's secretary upon occasion.

"I told her about the check and the signatures not matching and she was as startled as we were. Upset she was." Martha shook her head. "She's very protective of Mrs. Thornwell. Left her dinner and hurried right off."

Jason digested that bit of information and tucked it away for future reference. He decided to get to the point.

"I wonder if Noreen's brother was here on the day Allison's mother left the check in the envelope on the desk of Oliver's room."

Cully pounded a fist in his palm, startling his wife and Jason. "By Jove, he was here that day! I remember it distinctly now. I saw the bloke just as he was starting up the back stairs. He caught my eye and I remember thinking, "all this happening and now today he's here to put the touch on Noreen for money again." His face became stern. "Didn't have much use for that fellow, even he was her brother."

Martha raised her eyebrows. "Why would he come on her day off? You don't suppose he got his days mixed up and thought she was home?" She tilted her head to one side, thinking. "You know, there was something a might strange about him. Didn't you think so, Edward? Can't say as if I can put my finger on it, just intuition. Maybe it's just that she never wanted to talk about him."

Jason started to ask another question when they all heard a sound from the entry. It was the front door opening and then closing.

Cully glanced toward the kitchen door. "Speaking of days off,

Noreen's back."

Jason leaned back in his chair with studied casualness. "Just three people having some tea and hot chocolate, Cully."

They watched the kitchen door but Noreen didn't come in. The air was heavy with unspoken thoughts.

Finally Jason turned to the butler. "Go on about seeing William Simons that particular day, Cully."

"Yes, well, I saw Noreen's brother go upstairs but I had to put young Mrs. Thornwell and her suitcase in the taxi. When I went back into the house, I saw him nipping out towards the side door as casual as you please."

"And Noreen wasn't home yet?"

"No. I didn't see her come home. Martha?"

"No, not at all."

Jason turned to Martha. "How would you say Noreen's attitude was towards her brother? You said it seemed strange to you."

She glanced at her husband, "Well, we would say things like, how is your brother doing Noreen? You know, just making conversation. She would stiffen up like a board. "Fine", she'd say. That was all, end of conversation. How would you describe it, Edward?"

The butler looked thoughtful. "She seemed, how should I put it, resigned?"

"Maybe that was because he was always tapping her for money."

"True, sir. That could be it."

Cully gave his wife an apprehensive glance. "Noreen was more inclined to be friendly towards me, in a brotherly way, of course. I remember one particular incident when William had come to see her that Noreen was most distraught. Come to think of it, it was that last time when she found he'd been here." He studied the wall, remembering back.

"Whenever he went up to Noreen's room to wait for her," He dropped his voice to a conspiratorial whisper, "I found things to do upstairs. Just to make sure he didn't go in any other room of the house you know--"

He looked toward the door again as if Noreen or Thea would enter any moment.

"When I came back in the house and saw Noreen's brother leaving I remembered it was Noreen's day off. When I reminded him, he just waved a hand, gave me a big smile. He was quite chipper. He said, "No bother, Mr. Culpepper, no bother--I'll see her another time. You don't have to mention I was here."

"And did you tell Noreen he'd been there?"

"That's the strange part. He was her brother and all. I thought she should know he'd been there. Yet when I told her he'd come, she got this rather strange expression on her face. She looked at me and just said, "I just wish he'd leave me alone'."

Martha set her cup down firmly. "'It's just as I said. Something was wrong but you couldn't put your finger on it."

"I admit it does seem a bit odd, sir. I don't know why he would go without seeing her."

"Maybe because he already had something better than what he came for."

Martha caught her breath and one hand flew to her ample bosom.

Cully pounded his fist into his palm again. "By Jove!"

THIRTY-TWO

Jason spread his hands. "It's only a theory, Cully. We have yet to prove it."

They contemplated the information for a moment or two and then a question occurred to Jason.

"Did Noreen's brother continue to visit her after the day the check disappeared?"

Husband and wife looked at each other with raised eyebrows and finally both shook their heads.

"Come to think of it, that was the last time we saw him."

"Did Noreen mention that she had heard from him?"

Cully shook his head. "She didn't mention him much. I did ask how he was once and got a very curt answer. I didn't ask again. Noreen used to receive some letters occasionally, over the years, but there was no name, and no return address."

"Do you remember where the letters came from?"

"Didn't look much at the postmark, but it occurred to me from time to time that they might be from Noreen's brother. I didn't want to pry into her affairs."

"At least he stopped coming by for money all the time like he did before," Martha said.

Cully rubbed his chin with his thumb. "Wasn't that about the time she said she had a death in her family? She was gone for three days. When she returned, we didn't speak of her brother again."

"Did the letters still come?" Something was nagging at Jason's brain, but he couldn't get it clear in his mind.

Martha sat back suddenly. "Edward. You mentioned one evening as we were talking that Noreen didn't seem to get any mail anymore."

"By Jove, you're right, Martha. There were no more letters. They had to have been from him." Cully scratched his chin. "I'm sorry it was her brother, but at least it seemed to release her from having her pocketbook nipped all the time."

Jason was puzzled. "There were no letters from any of Noreen's family either?"

"No, not a one."

"Well, it could be it was her brother that died, though I wonder why she didn't say. In any case, if the brother is dead, any lead on the check probably died with him. That is, unless Noreen knows something she is not revealing."

Martha shook her head sadly. "It's a personal matter. I don't think Noreen has had a very happy life, but I doubt she wants to talk about it to any of us."

Martha pushed her tea cup aside and looked at Jason. "I'm a God-fearing woman, Jason. There are always answers to things. There's something else I want to say. Edward has told me that you have Mrs. Thornwell saying grace at every meal and that is a wonderful step. That woman has endured a great deal. She may seem a little haughty at times, but she has a heart that needs the Lord."

"Martha, you're a treasure. You're a Believer?" When she nodded he glanced at the butler and raised his eyebrows.

"Yes, Jason. That's why we have stayed all these years. The Lord wouldn't let us go. We pray for the Thornwells every day."

Jason shook his head slowly. There was a lot of information to digest. He felt the Culpeppers had been truthful with him, he was sure of that now. He stood and stretched.

"Thank you both for your concern. Allison and I share your desire for her grandparents to know the Lord. It was the main reason we came. And thanks also for the hot chocolate; Martha, it's the best sleeping pill I know."

They rose and Jason shook Cully's hand. "I will let you know what I find out."

"Very good, Sir. You know, we British do love a good mystery."

"If you or Martha think of anything else, would you let me know?"

"Righto."

They said their goodnights, and he started up to his room. As he neared the top step, one stair creaked loudly. In the stillness it sounded like a clanging gong. He cringed and looked back at the bottom of the stairs, listening, but there was no sound.

Jasson shook his head. He was getting jumpy with all this night sleuthing.

He reached for the doorknob of their bedroom, opening it as quietly as possible. On impulse he turned and looked towards Noreen Simon's room. The door was open very slightly. As he watched, it closed with a soft click.

THIRTY-THREE

Jason and Allison started down the stairs with Joshua. He'd slept until six, and it was the first time he'd slept through the night for which Allison was deliriously grateful.

The housekeeper passed them with a tight-lipped nod. She had fresh towels on her arm.

"She's not wasting any time, is she?" Allison whispered to Jason with a grin.

He glanced up at the retreating figure. "Seems like an unhappy woman. She doesn't smile much."

"I noticed that too, such a contrast to Mr. Culpepper. At least he seems to have retained his sense of humor."

"His wife is nice too. I met her last night."

Allison gave him a puzzled glance and he hastened to add, "I couldn't sleep. I went to the kitchen and found them having a cup of tea. Martha made me some hot chocolate."

When Cully took the baby carrier from them and bore Joshua off to the kitchen, Allison decided that her grandmother preferred not to have infants in her formal dining room.

>◇

Thea had dressed meticulously for breakfast. One must keep up appearances.

She sat waiting at the head of the table for the appearance of Allison and Jason.

The ornate gold clock on the wall chimed the hour and Thea smiled to herself. They were exactly on time.

"Good morning, did you sleep well?"

"Yes, Grandmother, like a log. Joshua slept through the night for the first time."

"I'm sure that's a relief to you, my dear."

Cully appeared in a moment and poured orange juice in each of their glasses. While he was subtle, Thea caught a look between her butler and Jason, almost like a couple of conspirators. Her eyes narrowed. She'd get to the bottom of that later.

Martha outdid herself with light pecan pancakes, crisp bacon and eggs scrambled with feta cheese. Let them think she ate like this every morning, Thea thought to herself. She could return to her usual bowl of hot oatmeal after her granddaughter and family had gone.

"Do you have to return home today? I'd hoped you and Allison might stay a little longer"

Cully brought Gordon in. He had already eaten, but appeared anxious to see Allison and Jason. His eyes twinkled briefly as he looked at his granddaughter. As he started to speak, for a moment the frustration of his limited condition showed. A man who was used to being in charge, giving orders, running a large law firm, now reduced to a helpless creature in a wheelchair who could hardly make himself understood. Thea caught the look Allison gave him, not one of pity, but loving understanding. Gordon seemed to sense the difference and sat up a little straighter in his chair.

Jason turned to Thea. "I know you and Allison would like more time together. I'd like to check something out on the microfiche at the library downtown."

Gordon regarded Jason with an approving nod. "Information" he rasped.

Thea nodded. "Very well, Jason, we will trust you to inform us of anything you find."

"Fair enough."

The others went into the study, Edward mysteriously returning at that moment to wheel Gordon in with them.

They looked at some additional photographs that Thea had collected of Oliver and Allison was able to see him as a baby, a small boy, a young man and at last grown. She studied the picture of his high school graduation.

"These photos seemed to make him come alive, a real person who lived in this house at one time."

"I'm glad they help you, Allison."

"There's one thing more I'd like," she hesitated as she looked at Thea.

"Speak up, child!"

"May I see my father's room?"

Thea hesitated and looked away from them for a moment.

"Frrea?" Gordon looked at his wife and nodded.

"Yes, of course. There is no reason why you shouldn't, Allison. I will take you up."

Thea steeled herself to enter Oliver's bedroom. When she learned of his death, she had come there and wept, alone. She had not been there since. She reached for the knob of the bedroom door and then slowly opened it, stepping aside for Allison. Then she forced herself to walk in calmly and observe her granddaughter's reaction.

Noreen kept the wood on the mahogany posts and the carved headboard of the queen-sized bed polished to a soft glow. The large spread of quilted silk, in soft green, beige and white was fading as was the soft green and beige wool rug that covered the floor. It was a young man's room, hardly a boy's, yet when she looked up along with Allison she saw balsa wood model planes hanging from the ceiling. She tried to imagine Oliver as a boy, carefully gluing each piece in place.

"The whole house is lovely. I wanted to know where my father grew up. Imagine him walking through the rooms and playing in the yard. Did you build the house, Grandmother?"

"No, my parents did, shortly after the great San Francisco earthquake. They wanted something solid that looked like it would always be here. So much of the city was rubble. My father, your great-grandfather, died of a heart attack in 1947 and my mother lived here by herself for five years. Your grandfather and I came to live here due to her ill health. Oliver was born in 1953. My mother died four years later."

"Then she got to know her grandson before she died?"

"Yes, briefly. She suffered from what, at the time, we called dementia. Today they call it Alzheimer's. She needed a constant companion. In her last years she didn't know who we were."

"I'm sorry. That must have been very hard for you."

"Yes. My father and I were never close. He was very much involved in his business. He founded the law office of Erickson and Hammond along with his sister's husband, Gerald Erickson, who was often indisposed and died an alcoholic. My father became the senior partner and in time owned the firm. Jacob Tingley was made a partner in 1946. When my father died, he made arrangements for Gordon to take over his portion of the firm and his clients. Since Gordon was his son-in-law and working in the firm, it was only natural for him to take my father's place. My great-nephew, John Erickson, is also now a partner in the firm."

"So I have cousins."

"It will be of little comfort to you, Allison. We do not see that side of the family socially."

Allison nodded, but Thea could tell her mind was whirling with the information. She didn't want Allison to have a different picture than the one she was painting. It would not help her perception of her grandfather, to know before his stroke, what a ruthless man he was, who kept files on others to use for his own gain. Had Gordon truly driven his partner to drink as the rest of the firm thought?

"What of the men who now held the firm?"

Allison's question broke her reverie.

"When a partner is incapacitated, do the others usually buy him out? Is this what usually happens?"

The old anger rose up. "Sometimes that is true, Allison. But you are naïve if you believe it was for no other reason. In the field of law there is a great deal of competition. One must be strong to survive. John Erickson has always held a grudge against our family. He blamed my father for his father's alcoholism, alleging that somehow my father drove him to drink."

Thea snorted, and continued. "A preposterous idea, he was

jealous of Gordon's business ability and the fact that the most wealthy and influential clients were his. When Gordon had his stroke and it was obvious that he could no longer run the firm, the other three partners had to take over. We retained our interest in the firm. They left his name on the firm until all of Gordon's clients were apprised of his condition and all his files were transferred to the other partners. It was no more than a year and a half at best. John Erickson is now the senior partner. We have not spoken since the transaction was completed."

Allison nodded but Thea noticed a shadow cross her granddaughter's face. Was Allison beginning to glimpse the other side of her? Thea was painfully aware of the hardness in her own voice.

As if to defuse the volatile tone of the conversation, Allison smiled gently at Thea and put a hand on her arm.

"I'm sure grandfather was a fine attorney. Surely that is why clients sought him out."

Thea looked thoughtfully at Allison but did not reply.

"And I have just the one cousin, John Erickson?"

"John is married and has a daughter and a son. My niece works somewhere as a museum assistant. My nephew, Charles, is in law school. I would be extremely displeased, Allison, if you should seek them out. I have only apprised you of these matters so that you will be forewarned."

"Who is Mr. Tingley, then?"

"As I said, Jacob Tingley joined the firm in 1946 and is still a family friend. As such, he handles all our legal matters.

"So Gerald Monroe works for Mr. Tingley?"

Thea smiled sagely. "Yes, one of many able law assistants who work for the firm. Mr. Monroe is a very astute and able young man. You understand, my dear, that your letter was a great shock and we had to find out if you were legitimate. "

"Or an opportunist?"

"Just so. You were checked out more thoroughly than you

imagine. We just had to be sure. I didn't even want to let myself consider that Oliver had left us a child. It was too much to hope for at our age."

"I'm glad you believed me, Grandmother. I wanted so much to meet you and my grandfather. After mother told me her story, I felt strongly that you needed to know I existed."

Thea shook her head slowly. "I thought I had prepared myself. Yet, when you walked in the door of the library, it was as if Oliver walked into the room."

"I didn't realize how much I looked like him, even when my mother showed me a snapshot she has. It was when you handed me that picture of my father, I knew. I just wish I could have known him."

"Yes." Thea sat quietly, staring at the open closet door and Oliver's things. She put her fist to her mouth to force down the sob that rose in her throat.

Allison suddenly got up and moved towards a table by the window where she had noticed Oliver's sketchbook. Thea composed herself and went to stand at her side as Allison opened it. Sketches of animals and trees gave way to drawings of houses.

"My father was an artist."

"He liked to draw things. Gordon indulged him but discouraged his bent on making that a career."

"My mother said he wanted to be an architect."

Thea snorted. "A childish whim. He finally changed his mind and wisely decided to enter law school. He had a career waiting in his father's firm."

Allison started to say something but appeared to think better of it and closed her mouth. She looked back at the portfolio and Thea felt she wanted to look at it further. Thea was glad when the girl turned to Oliver's dresser and ran her hand over the brush and comb set that lay on a linen scarf. Oliver had used these. Thea saw tears well up in Allison's eyes and she wiped them with the back of her hand.

Thea was becoming uncomfortable. Her emotions were also too

near the surface and she struggled to keep them under control Allison turned her attention to the desk, a modest oak in contrast to the mahogany.

The notepaper, pens and pencils, a blotter and a book were still where he had left them. Noreen had obviously dusted them faithfully and left them where they were.

Thea watched her granddaughter peer in the closet that still held her father's clothes. Thea chided herself. Why had she left them there all these years? By keeping all his things somehow she felt she could keep his memory alive. It was a foolish whim.

"I imagine it's time I cleared this out. There is no comfort in living in the past."

Allison put an arm around Thea's small shoulders and while Thea stiffened for a brief second, she felt the tears sting her eyes. They stood quietly together for a moment, each with their own thoughts. Thea grieving for the son she'd lost and her grandaughter for the father she had never known.

THIRTY-FOUR

Thea wiped her cheek quickly and drew herself up. In control again, yet knowing that in deciding to remove Oliver's things, she'd taken a giant step.

Looking up at the ceiling and the model planes, Thea spoke wistfully. "Perhaps Joshua would enjoy those one day."

It was time to talk about something else. Thea regarded her granddaughter and frowned. "I noticed that Jason is rather set on saying grace before meals. Just how involved are you in your religion? I do hope you are not part of some fanatical group."

Allison appeared surprised at the sudden shift in conversation.

"We are active in our church, Grandmother, because we have both accepted Jesus Christ as our Savior. It's important that we live our lives in a way pleasing to Him. As he said, Jason leads a couples Bible study on Friday evenings."

"At the Community Church in Mountain Center?"

"No, the Baptist Church in town."

Thea sighed. "We have always been Episcopalians. I suppose when one is young religious activity is appealing. Sooner or later, Allison, one has to assume other responsibilities. I was active in our church as a young woman. I headed up the committee that gathered supplies to send to our soldiers overseas. When I married I was expected to take my place in society and uphold my husband's standing in the community."

"Don't you attend church anymore?"

"Of course, my dear, we have a family pew. I've attended as often as it is possible. One must keep up appearances. And of course there were times when other duties required my attention. Since your Grandfather has been disabled, I've remained at home. The priest, Father Devon, calls on us from time to time."

"Did Grandfather go to church with you?"

"In the beginning he did, then for some reason he didn't find it necessary. He said it was something women needed to do. He preferred a round of golf to a sermon."

"Rather a duty one has to attend to?"

"It is, isn't it?" Thea asked defensively.

"Oh no, Grandmother, we go because there we can sense His all-encompassing love and grace."

Thea thought about the times she'd gone to church, to see and be seen, in the latest fashion, and to find out the latest gossip.

Uncomfortable with emotional issues, Thea drew herself up. "I think we've talked far too long about religion, Allison." She went over and sat on the edge of Oliver's bed. "Did you teach school?"

"Yes," said Allison softly, sitting down beside her. She proceeded to share about her one year of teaching kindergarten.

Thea wanted to know many things and soon they were deep in conversation. They were startled by a knock on the door. Jason poked his head in.

"I was told where to find you," he grinned. "You two have been talking quite a while. I'm ready to go into the city."

Thea thought a moment. "It would be wiser if you took BART. You can leave your car in the parking lot. You won't have to face the traffic."

Jason rubbed his chin. "I forgot about the transit system. You're right. Where's the nearest station?"

"Come down to the library when you are ready, and I'll give you the directions."

Thea rose quickly and headed downstairs. She paused and glanced back at the room briefly. Something had occurred there and she needed to sort out what it was. She sensed more peace in her spirit.

THIRTY-FIVE

Once alone in the room, Jason gave Allison a warm hug. "How are you doing, Sweetheart? You'll have another day with your grandparents. We have to leave tomorrow though. Are you up to a long drive again?"

"I'll be fine, honey. Jason, do you realize that my father's room is just as it was when he left? All his clothes, his books, as though by leaving everything she could imagine him still there."

Jason shook his head sadly. "I have read about parents who did that when they lost a child."

"I think she let go of some things. We cried together."

Jason's arms went around her again. "How did you feel?"

"Like I could touch a part of my father by touching his things, as if he was just away and would walk in the door any minute and find us in his room. It was strange. We talked a little about church." Tears welled up in her eyes. "Oh Jason, church is just a duty for her that she fulfilled when she had time. I know if she knew Jesus He would heal the pain she's carried all these years."

"We'll pray for opportunities to share His love with both your grandmother and your grandfather."

So much had happened. Looking around the room she knew with a certainty that they would be back and there would be other chances to talk with her grandmother about the Lord. He had paved their way here and prepared the fallow ground. She could trust Him for the next step.

Jason sat down on the bed. "I got a chance to talk with the housekeeper."

Allison whirled around. "I thought that was a no-no after you mentioned her to Grandmother."

Jason shrugged elaborately. "Can I help it if I just happened to run into her?"

She grinned. "And where did you run into her?"

"My favorite interrogation room, the kitchen, she was having breakfast."

"And?"

"And-- she was about as talkative as a rock."

"Ah"

"She just repeated what Thea said. That it had been her day off and she spent the night with a relative and came back the next morning just before Oliver left in the taxi. She said she only heard what happened from Martha. Since I'm a guest she couldn't be rude, but she sure didn't want to carry on a conversation."

A thought rattled around in Allison's head. "Honey, what do you think about stopping at my grandparent's bank and seeing if there is anything the manager can tell us about someone cashing a check that size?"

"Great idea!" Jason smacked a fist into his palm. "I knew I married a smart girl."

"Maybe Grandmother would give you a letter of introduction to the manager."

"Right. I'm sure your grandparents are well known at the bank. It would help to have something authorizing me to look into the matter."

THIRTY-SIX

Jason went downstairs to the library to talk to Thea about the bank and Allison picked up their cell phone to call her mother. She knew Kathryn was anxiously waiting to hear from her. "Oh, Allison, I've been hoping you'd call. How did it go?"

"The Thornwells accepted me as their granddaughter. Thea tried to be objective and aloof but I guess I look so much like my father she said it was like having their son walk in the room. I even have his mannerisms. She just couldn't deny it."

Kathryn sighed. "That's the one thing they had to see, that I have seen over the years. You are Oliver's child in every way. I'm so glad," Kathryn paused, remembering, "And your grandfather?"

"You wouldn't recognize him from the man you met years ago. His hair is white, he's in a wheelchair all the time and he looks very frail. His whole right side is paralyzed. He has to talk out of the corner of his mouth." Allison demonstrated how he sounded. "It is so sad. If you listen really carefully, you can understand him though. He seemed pleased that I understood what he was saying."

"So one moment he was running the law firm with an iron hand and ordering people's lives and the next he was incapacitated and in a wheelchair. I suspect that with his schedule and the stress he might have brought that on himself. Still, I feel badly for anyone who has to live out his days in that condition," Kathryn said.

"It just showed me, again, how God brings good out of any situation, even a stroke. If he were not so vulnerable, perhaps they might not have received me as they did."

Kathryn broke in. "They must have loved Oliver very much to keep his room exactly as it was."

"They did love him, mother. My grandmother even admitted to me that perhaps they should have listened to him. She even intimated that perhaps because of their actions, he might have put himself in harm's way."

"Yes. I'm glad she was able to acknowledge that. It is good that they will finally clear out the closet and let Oliver go." There was a pause. "Did your grandparents by any chance mention what personal effects were sent back from Viet Nam?"

"That was the strange part, Mother. She said there were no personal effects, nothing."

Kathryn gasped as Allison shared the part she knew would be hard. "She said they were told the helicopter he was riding in crashed. There was an explosion. Nothing was found that could be identified."

"It appears that it was sudden, Mother, he didn't suffer from wounds. He was instantly with God."

Kathryn's voice sounded small. "I'm not sure where he was with God. I pray he came to know him before his final moments came. We just never talked about those things. We had so little time together, were so in love and--then he was gone."

"You don't suppose the army would have told them that maybe, if his dog tags weren't found, that maybe he--."

Kathryn moaned, "Oh Allison, I can't even begin to think like that. It's too preposterous. It's been almost twenty-five years."

"You're right, Mother. I should never have even mentioned it."

"That's all right, Dear." Kathryn changed the subject: "I'm certainly glad your trip was successful. What did you find out about the check? Who cashed it?"

"We don't know, Mother, it was a shock to the Thornwells to consider that someone in their own household might be dishonest. Jason has persuaded them to let him do a little investigating. My grandfather wants the signatures from your letter and the check analyzed by an expert. We aren't worried about it; we know you didn't sign it. I think it's the lawyer in grandfather examining all the details. Jason is going to the Thornwell's bank. We'll keep you posted on any developments. He can find out more about who cashed the check; tellers have to stamp each check when it is processed."

Kathryn sighed. "I wish they could just let the whole sorry mess go."

"Mother, they have the right to know who took ten thousand dollars of their money."

"Yes, I suppose you're right, dear." There was a pause. "How is Joshua doing? What was your grandmother's reaction?"

"They were both smitten with him and while she wouldn't admit it, I think she's going to be a doting great-grandmother.

"Well, keep me posted."

"We will, Mother."

Kathryn sent her love and hung up. Were they right in pursuing this?

THIRTY-SEVEN

Jason told Thea he wanted to talk with the bank.

She admonished him sternly. "You must kept the keep the matter strictly confidential and to only discus it in the privacy of the office of the bank president, Mr. Stockton. He'd been a friend of the family for years."

She wrote a brief note to the bank manager on their initialed stationary, introducing Jason as their granddaughter's husband and asking that Mr. Stockton help him in every way possible.

So much had happened in twenty-four hours it was overwhelming. Now, while Jason was armed with some basic information, there were questions that needed answers.

As Jason drove off he wondered if she was ready for him to find what he was looking for.

THIRTY-EIGHT

Jason located the bank building readily. It was an imposing red brick structure dedicated in 1911, according to a plaque on the outside.

Inside the bank, the plush maroon carpeting and warm rich mahogany of the woodwork spoke of tradition and opulence. He decided that this was not a place where the average working man did his business. The president's secretary looked him over in a polite but condescending manner.

"May I help you?"

Jason wasn't intimidated. "I'm here to see Mr. Stockton. My name is Carradine." He handed her the note from Thea.

"Carradine? Did you have an..."

Before she could read the note, the door of the president's office opened.

"I am expecting him, Mrs. Madison. His wife is Gordon Thornwell's granddaughter."

The eyebrows went up briefly. "Granddaughter?" Her mask of cool professionalism returned and she gave them a brief smile. "I didn't know."

"Nor did I, I'm afraid. I just received the call from Mrs. Thornwell. I will see him in my office." He indicated the doorway. "Won't you come in?"

Jason followed him inside where they shook hands. Mr. Stockton indicated a chair. "Please be seated." He let his gaze rest thoughtfully on Jason.

"What can I do for you, Mr. Carradine? Mrs. Thornwell said I might be of help to you in a personal matter. I must admit a little surprised to hear of your wife. I was under the impression that their only son, Oliver, was killed many years ago in Vietnam."

Jason leaned forward. "Allison's mother, Kathryn Hilliard, eloped with their son Oliver in July of 1972." He filled the older man in on the events leading up to the check as briefly as possible, leaving out some embarrassing details for the Thornwells.

"The check was taken by someone else and cashed. We are trying to see if we can find out who signed and cashed it in her mother's name."

Mr. Stockton's eyes widened. "And the Thornwells, do they think this person is still on their staff? Forgery is a federal crime."

Jason broke in. "We are not inclined to believe it has anything to do with the present staff, they've all been with the Thornwells too long."

Jason opened the folder Thea had given him and produced the check.

Mr. Stockton studied it carefully. "This check was deposited in another bank, but I doubt they would wish to cooperate without bringing in the federal authorities." He shook his head slowly. "Actually there is a bigger problem. It has been almost twenty-five years since this check was cashed. Records of that age are most likely destroyed by now. The statute of limitations requires seven years, though there are some banks that keep records longer. I would guess though that these records are probably non-existent, and --"

Jason broke in, "How could someone cash a check of this size without proper identification?"

"That's a good question, Mr. Carradine. A positive identification would be required to open an account, especially with a check of this size."

"Then someone had to have help, possibly on the inside--?"

Mr. Stockton frowned. "That's a possibility no bank official wants to contemplate." He studied the check again. "You've made a very interesting point though. There had to have been someone working in that bank who was involved in the crime. All the accomplice had to do was process the check as usual, possibly through a dummy account."

"Can you tell me what that is?"

"An account set up in advance with the name of the person the check was made out to. It could be opened with fifty dollars or more. When this person came in with the actual check it would not be a problem to deposit it in the existing account. The bank would assume the teller had gotten the proper ID. To make sure the check was good for that amount, the funds would have to remain in the account until the deposit check was cleared. This would be a week to ten days. Then the funds could be withdrawn. If the funds are withdrawn all at once an IRS form has to be filled out"

Jason shook his head. "I think they would want to avoid any forms like that."

"Yes, that is correct. The funds could still be withdrawn easily though. When the check cleared the bank and the funds were available, all the person had to do was withdraw in five thousand dollar increments, twenty-four hours apart."

The bank president leaned back in his chair and made a teepee of his fingers, tapping them against his chin. "If the bank is used to processing checks in large amounts, as we are, it would go virtually unnoticed."

Jason had been making more notes. "Then if we have the name of the bank where the check was cashed or deposited, would there be some form of mark to tell us who the teller was who cashed the check?"

"Yes, there would be. Nowadays the checks are encrypted with the teller code, but twenty-five years ago, there would have been the bank endorsement and the teller's stamp."

Mr. Stockton picked up the check and as he looked at the back again, frowned. "If my memory serves me correctly, I believe that the bank where this check was cashed went out of business, eight to ten years ago. I remember reading about it. Always sorry to see another bank go under. Since they are no longer in business their records have most likely been destroyed by now." He tapped the corner of the check on his desk a few times. "There is one other source that may be helpful."

"And what is that, Sir?"

"You might check with the FDIC, Mr. Carradine."

"The FDIC?"

"Federal Deposit Insurance Corporation. They take over the records of a bank when they default, or fold, as they say. You might call them and at least inquire if they have any information on the bank. I'll have my secretary give you the number."

"Thank you. I'll do that." Jason leaned back in his chair and studied the notes he had made. Then with a wry grin, he took a deep breath, letting it out slowly. "So we have a defunct bank, making it nearly impossible to find out who the teller was."

Mr. Stockton chuckled. "It would appear you have a next to impossible task."

Jason grinned at him. "We have a God who delights in making impossible things happen, Mr. Stockton. We don't know what we can do until we try, with His help."

The bank president raised his eyebrows but seemed genuinely pleased. He stood finally, handing the check back to Jason and saw him to the door.

"It was a pleasure meeting you. I'm glad that your wife and the Thornwells have found each other, Mr. Carradine. Perhaps you, and the strength of your God are just what the doctor ordered. You'll be in my prayers as you try to solve this mystery. God bless you. " He went over and spoke with his secretary who began looking in her phone directory. Returning to Jason he murmured in a low voice, "Keep me informed, will you, on all fronts?"

"Be glad to, sir."

Mr. Stockton shook hands and returned to his office, closing the door.

The secretary wrote a phone number on the bank stationary and gave it to Jason. "I hope this will be helpful, Mr. Carradine."

"I hope so too, ma'am. Thanks." He put the paper in the folder.

As he got back in the car, Jason sat and stared out the front window a moment. Then he pulled out the cell phone and called Allison.

"How are things going?"

"Josh is sleeping and I was resting. I was hoping you'd call."

He filled her in on what Mr. Stockton had told him.

"Jason, what if my grandmother could find out what happened to the records of the bank? They have the contacts. What are you going to do now?"

"I'm heading for the library. I'll see you later on this afternoon."

"She was silent a moment. "Are you going to mention the FDIC?"

"No, I'd like to just look into that myself right now."

"Don't all private detectives keep a few things to themselves? If your grandmother gets Gerald Monroe on the case I wouldn't be surprised what she can find out. He seems like a man who knows how to get answers."

Allison sighed. "He must have checked us out thoroughly. When I first saw him get out of the car he scared me to death. I was really praying that you'd come home as soon as possible."

"Well, my guess is that if anyone could find out any information about that bank, he can."

"Jason, a bank teller had to be involved."

"Possibly. As Mr. Stockton said, he, or she, could have easily processed the check. With everything stamped correctly the bank would have no idea that the proper identification had not been presented."

"What if Noreen had a beau at one time?"

"He could have to have been the teller. Then it would be easy for him to deposit the check for her. Maybe she had to agree to give him part of the money in exchange for his help."

"True, sweetheart, but the question is, if Noreen was involved, why would she stay here all these years?"

Allison signed. "I don't know. Oh Jason, she may also be innocent.

"In which case we are back to square one."

"Well, honey, let's hope God helps you find what you're looking for."

After they hung up, Jason called Thea. Allison's assumption that the bank president had called her was correct. Jason affirmed that he was heading for the library. Thea would try to track down the records for the small San Francisco Bank.

Jason thought about the FDIC. It was Friday and he didn't want to wait over the weekend to call them.

He was referred to their customer relations department and was able to ask his questions. Jason began scribbling notes furiously.

"Yes, go on, right." When he finally hung up he was smiling and shaking his head. "Amazing." He sat there studying his notes.

He called Allison back. She'd be beside herself with curiosity.

"Well, I called that number the bank gave us for the FDIC and was referred to a man named Delario. I told him what we were doing and what we needed to know and he was extremely helpful. It seems that when a bank is in trouble, say, the state bank examiner finds it is undercapitalized, the bank is ordered to infuse a set amount of capital in a specified time. Say, X million in 30 days."

"What happens if they can't come up with the capital?

"Then the bank is declared insolvent and the FDIC is appointed receiver. However, before any news leaks out, secret meetings are held with other banks in undisclosed locations. Mr. Delario says these meetings are to dispose of the assets of the bank. They divvy up the accounts like cutting up a pie. It depends on who wants a piece of the action."

"Like selling off your household goods in a foreclosure?"

"Something like that. The banks perform what is called a P and A transaction, a Purchase and Assumption Agreement. One or more banks assume the accounts. They also take the records of the failed bank that pertain to those accounts. These are kept until no longer needed and then destroyed."

"So all the records of that failed bank in San Francisco could be destroyed by now?"

Jason tapped his pen against his cheek a moment and looked at his notes again.

"Probably but not necessarily. Mr. Delario said there have been unusual cases where records have been found in basements of small banks that go back for years. He told me about a bank in Washington D.C. where Abraham Lincoln banked. It seems that when the bank closed down finally, they found records dating back to Lincoln, over a hundred years, boxes that had been put away down in the basement and forgotten."

Allison sounded hopeful. "Then there is a possibility--"

"--That this small local bank had better things to do than worry about old records."

"Maybe my grandmother can find out if there is another bank in that building, and if they have a basement."

Jason chuckled. "I wonder how Gerald Monroe feels about old basements."

"Hmmm. The smug Mr. Monroe in his impecable suit and shoes, with his sleeves rolled up, searching through musty old records. I think I rather like that picture."

"Gotta go, sweetheart. I need all the time I can get at the library."

"Bye, Sherlock."

He chuckled as he hung up.

Jason turned into the commuter parking lot. Since he was boarding after the morning rush hour traffic was over, it was an uneventful ride into the city.

When he reached the new library, he was surprised by the beautiful building with all the glass. It didn't look like a library, but more like a modern art museum.

Jason took the elevator to the fifth floor. When he saw the bank of microfiche machines and all the microfiche bins, he caught his breath. This could take days.

There were twenty machines with large gray bins of microfiche records. Looking at his notes, he anticipated scanning papers from the day of the check to the weeks following. Noting that the newspaper records went back to 1865, he was glad he didn't have that many years to search through. He was hoping to find information on when the bank folded and if another bank had taken its place, and whatever else he could find. He decided to start in on the Chronicle. If there was nothing, he'd tackle the Examiner. He found the first microfiche and got to work, plowing through issue after issue and finally when his muscles complained, got up to stretch. Checking each page of the papers for anything that might pertain to their search was tedious work.

He rubbed his temples and rotated his shoulders in circles. "I wish I knew what I'm looking for," he muttered to no one in particular.

Three hours into the search, he heard his stomach growl and decided to take a break. He'd start in on the Examiner after lunch.

Returning from the small sandwich shop he'd located, he felt a sense of anticipation. God was leading him somewhere and he knew beyond the shadow of a doubt that something was "out there."

He hadn't gone more than three days into the Examiner when a sidebar caught his attention, causing him to almost leap out of his chair.

After printing off the article, he read it over again, then on a sudden inspiration, turned to the obituaries for that week. As he searched each write-up, he moved the pointer slowly. Finally, there it was. He read the notice carefully, and shaking his head slowly from side to side, murmured, "Bingo."

THIRTY-NINE

BART was crowded and he had to stand. A drunk leaned against him and his breath smelled like dead fish. Fortunately, it wasn't far to the commuter lot and Jason was glad to get to the car. If he hurried, he could get out of the congested area to Piedmont without getting in heavy traffic.

He'd no sooner driven up to the house when Allison hurried down to the car.

"Oh Jason, I'm so glad you're back. It's Noreen. The paramedics were here. I think she's had a heart attack. they took her to the hospital."

Thea met him in the entry, obviously distraught. "Oh, Jason, I prayed you'd come home early. Please, take me to the hospital. Noreen collapsed at my desk where she was working. Edward went to run some errands and has the car. Allison called the ambulance and they just left with her. They've taken her to the Alameda Medical Center. We need to hurry, now. Allison has the baby to take care of and Martha has to stay with Gordon."

Jason assisted Thea into the car and dashed back to the driver's seat. Allison could only watch from the porch as they drove away.

Following Thea's directions, Jason sped down one street and another.

"Turn here, on Coolidge—" Thea ordered, "then go left on Foothill Blvd. Oh, hurry, Jason!"

"Doing the best I can, but I have to stay under the speed limit. We don't want to waste precious time being stopped for a speeding ticket, do we?"

Thea watched the street ahead in silence.

"Turn here--there's the medical center."

Jason pulled up in front of the building. "Go ahead, Thea, I'll park the car and come and find you."

She hurried into the foyer of the medical center.

Jason found a parking place and went to join her. They were directed to the ICU.

Thea drew herself up and with all the authority she could muster, asked how to find Noreen.

"What was she admitted for?"

"A heart attack, not more than an hour or so ago."

The nurse checked the computer. "She hasn't come up from emergency yet. Are you family?"

"My name is Theodora Thornwell. I'm the only family she has. She works for me."

"I'll check and see what is happening." The nurse checked her computer, then picked up the phone.

"You have a Noreen Simons down there? Yes, heart ... I see. Yes. Her employer is here at my station. Says Ms. Simons has no other family. Yes. All right. I'll tell her."

"What did they say?"

"Ms. Simons has been stabilized. They will bring her to the ICU shortly but you cannot see her just yet. Depending on what procedures were necessary, she may or may not be conscious."

Thea slumped visibly. "Thank God she is still alive."

The nurse's attitude softened a bit and she pointed down the hall. "There is a waiting room for family members around the corner. We will let you know as soon as we have any news."

Thea nodded and Jason put an arm around her shoulders, leading her down the hall to the waiting room.

She sat with her hands in her lap. "I should have known Noreen was ill. She has been acting strangely ever since you and Allison arrived. I tried to ask if I could help but she didn't want to talk about it. Noreen usually confides in me. I don't know what is wrong."

Jason reached over and covered Thea's finely veined hands with one of his own. "Thea, you said you prayed I would come in time for you and I did. You also thanked God when you found Noreen hadn't died. Would you like to pray for Noreen now?"

Thea sighed and looked straight ahead of her. "I don't know why God should answer my prayers. I haven't had much time for him over the years. I've railed at Him for many things in my life. He's probably thoroughly disgusted with me at this point. I'm just a cranky old woman."

Jason was startled. In his brief experience with Allison's grandmother, he couldn't imagine her saying something like this.

He spoke softly. "Just when we are at the point where we recognize our limitations and weaknesses, God steps in. He loves you, Thea. He always has. He's seen everything you've ever done, and heard every word you've ever spoken. He knows every thought, yet He loves you with an everlasting love."

"I have nothing to offer Him, Jason. I've been headstrong and selfish. Why should God love me?" The tears threatened to escape her eyes again, and she held herself rigidly.

Jason chuckled. "Thea, you don't have anything in this world He wants, except your heart."

She gave him a skeptical glance. "My heart?"

"Jesus died on the cross for this moment, Thea, so that you could bring Him all the heartache and troubles of your life and lay them before Him. All He wants of us is all of us. Lay all the burdens you've been carrying on your own shoulders on His. The Bible says that 'whosoever believes in Him shall not perish but have everlasting life.' It also says that 'if we confess our sins, He is faithful and just to forgive us our sins and cleanse us from all unrighteousness'. When He says all, He means all."

Thea listened quietly.

Jason smiled gently and waited until Thea looked at him.

"Would you like to give your life to Jesus, Thea? Would you like to let Him have all these things you've been carrying for so long?"

Thea's struggle showed in her face. Jason prayed silently, willing her to make the right decision. Finally she sighed. "Yes, I think I would."

Jason's heart lifted with joy as he anticipated what this would mean to Allison. As he led Thea in prayer, and she repeated the age old words of eternal life, God poured the Living Water into her soul.

Thea, who had bowed her head to pray, looked up at him and her face radiated what she felt inside. The pinched look she carried so much of the time was gone.

"I had no idea it would feel like this. It's like someone did take a great weight off my shoulders."

"Someone did, Thea. Your Savior did that for you."

"Jason, how can I ever thank you, for the courage and grace you and my precious granddaughter have shown me with all I've said and done?"

Jason gave her a warm hug and for the first time, Thea hugged him back.

"You know, Thea, Allison has loved you ever since she first saw you and maybe even before that. I think God had his hand in this all along."

She nodded, "Perhaps He did, Jason, perhaps He did."

There was the sound of footsteps and they looked up to see a doctor standing in front of them.

"I'm Dr. Pierce." He looked at Thea. "Are you her employer?"

"Yes." Thea stood anxiously, "How is she, Doctor? Will she be all right?"

"She is stable and I believe will make a good recovery. It was fortunate that the ambulance was able to get her here in time."

"Doctor, how soon can I see her?"

"Well," he said, indicating the doorway with his hand, "There's no time like the present. I can only give you five minutes. She's gone through a severe trauma, but she's awake and is asking for you."

When she had gone down the hall, Jason picked up his cell phone and heard the gasp and happy tears in Allison's voice as he shared the wonder of her grandmother's step of faith.

"Oh, Jason, I can hardly believe it actually happened."

"We serve a big God, Sweetheart. He knew what it would take to soften your Grandmother's heart. I can't help but feel that this is the tip of the iceberg. There is more to come."

"Well, there's still my grandfather. I wonder how he will take the news."

"We'll find out soon enough." Jason tucked the clipping back in his pocket. There would be time for that when Noreen was well enough to tell them what she'd been carrying all those years.

"Did you find anything, honey?"

"Yes, but I can't tell you about it right now, and I don't want you to ask about it in front of Thea. I'll explain when we're alone."

"Oh Jason, I'll be beside myself until you get here!"

"I know, sweetheart, but hang in there."

After he hung up he pulled the copy of the newspaper clipping from his pocket and chuckled to himself. "God, You sure have Your timing for everything. If I'd rushed in with this clipping I might have spoiled Your plan."

FORTY

Jason showed the clippings to Allison and as she read them she gasped.

"Oh dear, this is terrible."

She called her mother and told her about Noreen.

Kathryn was speechless for a moment. ""I don't know how any heart attack could be classified as mild, Allison, and I can hardly believe Thea's transformation. It's a lot to take in."

"And Mother, you cannot believe what Jason found at the library." She shared with Kathryn what Jason had found.

"Has he shown them to Thea?"

"He's waiting for a better time. She's too distraught over Noreen."

"Well, he's very wise. There will be a right time."

They talked a little longer about Joshua and what was happening back at home and Allison finally flipped the cell phone closed. She wasn't anxious to get that bill at the end of the month. They'd never used their cell phone so much.

Allison and Jason canceled their plans to return home right away. Jason drove Thea to the hospital each day to visit Noreen. Each evening, after Gordon retired for the night, Allison and Jason read the Bible with her grandmother and answered questions. They started with the Book of John and discussed each passage with her. It was a delight to Allison to see the austere woman who had first met them become almost childlike in her eagerness to learn, yet Thea retained her dignity and Jason was careful to let Thea move at her own pace.

With the stress level of the household, Jason kept the newspaper clipping to himself and waited until the Lord showed him it was the right time. He, Allison and Thea prayed for Noreen and now for Gordon, and his reaction to the change in his wife. .

Finally, after four days, Noreen was allowed to come home with the promise that she'd receive complete bed rest.

When Jason and Thea returned with Noreen, the Culpeppers met them at the door and after surveying the staircase, Jason enlisted Cully's help. By interlocking their arms, they made a fireman's chair and carried Noreen upstairs. She tried to protest, but was too weak and finally allowed herself to be carried up to her room. Martha and Thea hurried up after them and after the men lowered Noreen to her bed, they were shooed out so the women could get Noreen settled. A bell was put on her nightstand so she could ring for help if she needed something.

Cully excused himself to check on Gordon who had momentarily been left alone to eat his lunch in the kitchen. Allison and Jason had been cautioned not to enter the kitchen at this time. Gordon required a bib and sometimes food was spilled. He was still a man of pride and didn't want anyone else to see him this way. Even Thea left him in Martha's capable hands.

When Martha and Thea came back downstairs, Allison had been talking quietly to Jason and turned expectantly.

"How is she doing?"

"She's asleep already. Probably from the medication the doctor gave her." Thea led the way into the library and they sat down.

"Dr. Pierce told me she was very fortunate, this time. She has evidently had a heart murmur for years. No angioplasty was necessary and he feels that with proper rest she will recover her strength."

Allison put her arm around her grandmother's shoulders. "Did the doctor say what caused the heart attack?"

"Yes, he felt she was laboring under a great deal of stress. He wanted to know if anything unusual had happened to her in the last few weeks. I told him about your coming here but somehow I don't think that is the cause." She sighed and shook her head. "There just has to be more to it than that."

Jason glanced at Allison and tried to choose his words carefully. "It does and it doesn't, Thea. Allison's appearance after all these years just started a chain reaction. It goes back to the missing check."

Thea's eyes widened. "What in the world could Noreen have to do with that check? I'm sure she didn't take it, Jason." Allison sat back on the couch, her hand on her grandmother's arm.

"No, I don't believe she did. I think it has to do with her brother, William."

"Her brother? Noreen has a brother?"

"He was in the house the day the check disappeared, Grandmother."

"How do you know this?"

"I asked Mr. Culpepper if there was anyone else around the house the day Allison's mother left. He remembered seeing him."

"What in the world was he doing here that day? I've never seen him."

"I think that's something Noreen needs to tell you about."

Thea looked up at Jason, bewildered. "Why would Noreen keep the knowledge of her brother from me? I thought we were friends."

"Grandmother, it's possible that Noreen was ashamed of her brother. Maybe he was in trouble and she didn't want anyone to know. After all, he seemed to be her only family. perhaps he was an embarrassment to her."

Jason had been praying silently and finally spoke up. "Thea, the only way we can get to the bottom of this is to talk to Noreen." When she started to protest he raised his hand, "I know. This isn't the time but sooner or later we have to talk to her." He reached in his pocket and quietly handed Thea the copy of the newspaper article and the obituary notice.

Puzzled, Thea unfolded the clippings and as she began to read her eyes widened.

"Oh dear God…" She looked at Jason, her eyes watering…"You found this at the library in your search?"

"Yes, ma'am. It explains a few things, but Noreen will have to fill in the pieces when she's ready. I was going to show it to you several days ago, but when I got back from the library Noreen had just been taken to the hospital."

"I appreciate your keeping this for a later time, Jason. You are a very compassionate young man."

At that moment, Edward entered the room. "Mr. Thornwell has already eaten but wishes to join us in the dining room, madam. Lunch is ready."

"Thank you Edward. We will be right along." Thea waited until the butler had left the room and then handed the newspaper clipping back to Jason. "We will talk about this as soon as Noreen is well enough. In the meantime, I would appreciate it if you would keep this to yourselves, at least for a little while longer. I wish to speak to Gordon in my own time, you understand?"

Jason nodded and Allison smiled at Thea. "We understand, Grandmother, we'll wait until you are ready."

"I'm happy to leave that to your discretion, Thea, however, Allison and I must be getting back to Weaverville tomorrow. Some people are waiting on me to do some work for them."

Thea appeared distressed. "Surely they can wait just a little longer Jason? I have so many questions about our study. I'm not sure where to start."

"Why don't you speak with the priest at your church? I'm sure he would be happy to share this step of faith with you, Thea. How would you describe him, as a minister?"

Thea thought for a moment and smiled ruefully. "He has talked to me about God, but I wasn't ready to listen. I let him pray for Gordon and me when he came on occasional visits. I believe he is a good man, and a good priest. I'm sure he will be shocked at my news."

Jason laughed. "Pleasantly so, I'm sure."

Allison checked on Joshua who was in his infant seat being entertained by Martha. She smiled and waved that everything was all right. Joshua seemed to love watching her move around the kitchen. As they entered the dining room, Thea smiled at her husband. There was something in her smile that caused him to look at her more closely.

Jason sat down and turned to his hostess. "Would you like to say grace?"

There was a moment's hesitation but Thea straightened her shoulders and just before bowing her head, glanced at her astonished husband. "I believe I will," she said.

FORTY-ONE

The next morning, Thea met them in the hall just as they were coming out of their room with Joshua to go down to breakfast.

"Noreen wants to speak with the three of us. She seemed very agitated and said it was important. I told her we knew about her having a brother. Perhaps she thinks Edward told us. She knows you went to the bank about the check, but something else is bothering her. I thought she should rest, but she was most insistent."

"I'll join you in a moment." Allison hurried downstairs, handed the baby to Martha, and went quickly back up to Noreen's room.

Jason and Thea were standing by the side of the bed. Noreen's face was drawn and she looked much older than her years. Her eyes were dark pools in her face, like the eyes of the frightened doe Allison had come upon once in the woods.

Jason smiled down at her. "You wanted to talk to us, Noreen?"

She seemed encouraged somehow by his smile and raised a hand slightly. "You might as well know the story too. I knew what you were doing, and I figured you'd find out something sooner or later. I've kept it to myself for too long, and this is where it has gotten me."

Thea touched Noreen's arm. "Are you sure you are up to this right now?"

Noreen nodded. "I'll feel better for the telling of it. Maybe it will bring me the peace I've sought for so long."

Looking up at the ceiling and gathering her strength, Noreen began…

"I do have a brother, but I didn't want you to know about him, so I kept him to myself. My brother William spent ten years in prison for robbery and attempted murder."

There was a gasp from Thea. "Your brother was in prison?"

Noreen closed her eyes a moment and then continued. "I wasn't visiting my parents on my day off like you thought, I was visiting William. My parents died when I was fourteen. Since William was over eighteen, we were able to stay together. He provided for us the best he could. He worked down on the docks, unloading cargo. He was good to me, but when he was drinking he had a tendency to get into trouble."

Thea was hesitant. "What sort of trouble, Noreen?"

"Brawls, mostly, but he also liked to play cards. William sometimes lost a lot of money. I got what small jobs I could, but William always needed money to pay back his losses. One day I was in the car with him and he'd been drinking. He parked in front of a liquor store and told me to stay put. I didn't understand why he left the motor running but he said he was just going to just buy a six-pack of beer and come back to the car. In a few moments I heard a popping sound and he ran back to the car and jumped in. He tried to drive away quickly but evidently the storekeeper had pressed an alarm and the police soon chased us down. A police car pulled in front of our car and the officers leaped out with their guns drawn."

"Guns? What did you do?" Thea put one hand on her heart.

"They made me get out of the car. William was down on the ground with his hands cuffed behind his back. I was terrified. I kept asking the officers what happened."

Jason shook his head. "It looks like he tried to rob the store. Was the storekeeper shot?" When Noreen nodded, he added, "fatally?"

"No, and he was lucky. The bullet just grazed the man's shoulder. It's a good thing my brother was so frightened his shot went wild."

"What happened then?" Allison was listening intently, and praying for strength for Noreen to finally get this ordeal off her chest.

"Even though William was my brother and my only relative, he still had to go to jail. They took me to Juvenile Hall and I was booked as an accomplice."

Thea waved a hand impatiently. "An accomplice? But you didn't know anything about what he was going to do."

Noreen sighed. "No, and they finally believed that. William told them I had nothing to do with it and he didn't mean to get me involved. There was a trial and William confessed to firing the gun. He was sentenced to fifteen years."

Noreen looked at the face of her employer hesitantly, but there was no anger or distaste. Thea was thoughtful.

"Go on, Noreen," she finally murmured.

Noreen appeared puzzled by Thea's response, but went on with her story.

"I was sent to various foster homes until I was eighteen. Since I had been a minor when the robbery occurred, my records were sealed and I didn't have to divulge anything about it on an employment application. I worked for the Metzers for two years and when they moved they recommended me to you and Mr. Thornwell."

Thea drew herself up. "I understand your brother came to the house to see you, uninvited."

"He was paroled after ten years and I helped him get a small studio apartment. He got a couple of jobs but they didn't last long and his health was bad. Soon he was gambling again. One day he showed up in my room. He said he'd found the back entry and broken the lock. He used that entrance to sneak in." She glanced at Thea's face and faltered. "I didn't want anyone to know about him because I'd have to explain."

She sighed and closed her eyes for a moment, then continued. "Every time I saved up a little bit of money, he'd come around and take it. When I said I couldn't help him anymore he threatened to tell you about his prison record."

Thea shook her head. "Tell us about what happened to William, Noreen."

The housekeeper gave her a puzzled look but continued.

"He was in debt to someone. It was a rough crowd. They played serious poker. I don't know how many thousands of dollars he owed. He called me a few days after you sent Oliver's wife off in the taxi. He'd registered in a hotel under a different name. He was desperate and needed money."

Jason frowned. "He thought you could pay his gambling debts?"

"I was so upset I almost hung up on him, but he begged me to listen. He said that the check only bought him a little time..."

Thea's eyes widened and she leaned forward, "He mentioned the check?" She glanced up at Allison and Jason.

Noreen closed her eyes for a moment and nodded slowly. "I asked him, what check? And he said, "The one the Thornwells gave the girl. She didn't want it, left it on the floor. I needed the money."

"I was horrified that he'd come into the house and taken the check from Mr. Oliver's room," She gave Thea an agonized glance, "and I didn't know, really I didn't. We all thought the daughter-in-law took it."

Allison put a hand on her grandmother's shoulder. "We believe you, don't we Grandmother?" Thea was silent. Allison nodded to the housekeeper. "Go on..."

"He told me he heard the girl crying her heart out so he went through the closet between the rooms and peeked into Oliver's room. He saw what looked like a check lying on the floor. When young Mrs. Thornwell left the room with her suitcase, he went in to investigate and picked it up."

Jason rubbed his thumb on his chin. "I still don't see how he could have cashed a check of that size."

"That's what I wanted to know. How he cashed it. He said that the people he owned money to had connections. They took the check and said that if it cleared they'd accept it as a down payment on what he owed."

Thea looked down intently at her employee. "So you've known about the check all these years? Why didn't you come to us at the beginning, Noreen? Letting your brother sneak into the house and then covering up for him, was wrong. We would have helped you if you'd only let us know about William. How could you let us think Kathryn had taken the check?"

A large tear rolled down Noreen's face. "I know I'm at fault. I thought I could save up the money and pay you back somehow."

Jason shook his head slowly. "Well, at least that solves one mystery." He pulled out the clipping. "We know about William's death, Noreen. Do you want to tell us how it happened?"

Noreen looked at them hesitantly, "Well, he was talking in a low voice in the phone. Guess he didn't want anyone to hear him. He told me the check had gone through but by the next day he had to come up with the rest of the money."

Thea broke in, "How much money?"

Noreen waved a hand. "Somewhere around twenty-five thousand dollars, I almost shouted the amount at him, it was so preposterous. It was a good thing you and Mr. Thornwell were at the doctor's office and it was the Culpepper's day off. At least no one could hear my conversation. William begged me to help him. He said those men played for keeps." She looked imploringly at Thea. "I was afraid of what that meant."

"Evidently that wasn't an idle threat," Jason muttered.

"I told him I didn't have that kind of money, that I had no way to get it." She looked imploringly at Thea. "He begged me to go to you and Mr. Thornwell and give you some kind of a hard luck story, thinking you might give me the money."

Thea's face was stern. "Gordon would have checked your story to the letter and that would have been the end of that, and your employment."

"That's what I told William. I didn't know what to do so I told him I'd try to come up with something and would call him the next day. Maybe I could get a loan on my car. It was old but maybe I could get enough to buy him some time. He was going to try to sneak out of town, take a bus or something."

Allison clicked her tongue. "He was certainly desperate, wasn't he?"

"Yes. I hardly slept that night. I was frantic, thinking of some way to help him. Because he'd taken my extra cash I never had a chance to save any money. I called the next morning and the clerk said he wasn't answering his phone. I waited for him to call me back and then," her voice quavered, "and then, the next day I saw the picture and the article in the paper, his body was dumped in that vacant lot. They'd found him."

Noreen's shoulders shook as she sobbed out her pent up grief. Thea reached out her hand tentatively and finally patted Noreen on the shoulder.

Tears coursed down Noreen's cheeks. "I nearly fainted from the shock, Mrs. Thornwell. I knew you wouldn't recognize him since you didn't know about him, but Cully had seen him several times. When you and Mr. Thornwell were through with the paper, I took that page and put it in the trash. No one commented and I just went about my work as usual."

Noreen looked at Thea sadly. "I'm sorry for the trouble I've put you and Mr. Thornwell through. I'll be leaving, just as soon as I can make arrangements."

Thea hesitated, but only for a moment. "Where would you go at your age, with no family, Noreen? I understand what you have gone through and from what you've told us, you never meant to deceive us, you just tried to help your brother, but this is going to be difficult to explain to my husband."

"I know. You were out that money. I really was saving up to pay you back. I had saved almost enough to come and tell you the story, but then I had to pay for William's burial. I had a small service for him. Some ladies from a local church came. They do that for people that have no family. Then my car broke down and it just seemed there was something that needed money. I didn't know what to do."

She looked up at Thea, her eyes imploring, "Please, will you forgive me?"

Thea sighed. "Noreen, we've done without that money all these years. You cannot make up for the act of someone else, even though he was your brother." Her gaze softened, "And yes, you are forgiven for I've found I was in need of forgiveness myself. God has forgiven me from so much more."

Thea looked up at Jason. "With the help of my granddaughter's dear husband, I've found my Savior."

Noreen's eyes widened. "I knew there was something changed about you but I didn't know what it was. You looked a lot more peaceful and you were acting so different." She looked away towards the window again, as two large tears rolled down her cheeks. Her eyes started to close as her body gave in to the weariness and trauma it had been through.

Thea put a hand on her shoulder as Noreen drifted off. "Rest, Noreen. We want you to recover. You're welcome to stay. This is your home."

Noreen's eyes widened as she realized what Thea was saying. "Ohhhh, Thank you," she whispered.

Thea stepped back from the bed. "I think we have taken a great deal of Noreen's energy." Then, to Noreen, "Get some rest now, Martha will bring your breakfast up later."

As they left the room and started towards the stairs Allison finally spoke up.

"How will my grandfather take this? Will he be angry with Noreen?"

Thea drew herself up and looked at them thoughtfully for a moment. "I will speak with your grandfather when the time is right, if I choose to share this at all. I don't know what purpose it would serve and Noreen has certainly suffered enough by keeping this to herself all these years." She sighed. "I'm still trying to find a way to tell him what has changed in my own life."

Jason put a hand on her shoulder. "God has His own good time for everything."

Cully met them at the foot of the stairs. "I was just going to call, madam, breakfast is getting cold and Mr. Thornwell is getting a bit impatient." He looked at the three of them curiously. "Is everything all right, madam? Is Ms. Simons all right?" He raised his eyebrows briefly at Jason who gave him a wink...a signal that meant one of their late evening kitchen talks. Jason had filled them in on the moment in the hospital and they had rejoiced with him over Thea's decision.

Allison beamed at him. 'Everything is just fine, Cully."

Jason offered an arm to each lady, and with their arms in his, took them in to breakfast.

FORTY-TWO

Father Devon sat in the Thornwells' living room and held the delicate cup of hot tea gingerly. He had been up to see Noreen and prayed with her for a few moments, promising to come again soon.

"I'm glad to see Noreen is looking stronger. I'm sure she'll be up and around in no time."

Thea nodded graciously, holding her own cup of tea. The reason for the stress is gone. I don't think she will have to worry about any more heart troubles."

With Jason's urging, Thea had called her Church and talked with Father Devon. Not only had he been delighted with Thea's call and what she shared, but he had come that same day to call on her.

Now the four of them sat facing each other in the Thornwells' formal living room. Father Devon smiled benevolently at his prodigal parishioner.

"We have a new Bible study class starting next week, as a matter of fact, one o'clock Tuesday afternoon."

Thea was still treading on new territory. "What do I have to do?"

"Just show up. Counting yourself, there will be six. If Noreen would like to come, that will make seven."

"I don't know if she's ready for that,"

Allison leaned forward and gave her grandmother an encouraging smile. "I'm sure if you go, Noreen will go with you. I think she's looking for answers too. The church isn't that far away. After all, the doctor did say that Noreen should be walking about soon and getting some exercise."

"Allison could drive us," Thea answered quickly, raising one eyebrow and cocking her head.

Jason caught the implication. "If you're trying to steal my wife again, I'm on to you." There was a twinkle in his eyes. "I think I'll just take her home with me as planned." He nodded toward the priest with a grin, "Besides, I think you are in good hands now."

Thea, who in the last days seemed to find her sense of humor, threw up one hand in mock disgust. "You can't blame me for trying, Jason."

Allison felt as if her heart could burst out of her chest. The events of the last few days were overwhelming. She had met her grandparents and they had accepted her. She and Jason had solved the mystery of the check and cleared her mother's name. Her grandmother accepted the Lord and the whole tenet of that household changed. Her musings were broken by a startling exclamation.

"Wha's all theesh tak aphout Shurrsh!" Allison's grand-father had just been wheeled into the room.

Gordon had been watching Thea intently for several days with an unreadable expression on his face. He had endeavored to have Cully place him in the middle of every gathering and every meal. Now, evidently he had come to join them again as they talked with Father Devon.

Both Jason and the Father Devon rose as the old man spoke and Gordon shook the priest's proffered hand with his one good one.

"Glad to see you, Mr. Thornwell. you're looking very well. I believe you had a cold the last time I was here."

Gordon fixed him with a stern eye. Even in his garbled way, the question was clear. "Here for a check, Father?"

Father Devon returned Gordon's glare with a steady gaze. "No, Sir, I'm here to share in the joy of your wife's decision to follow Christ."

Thea's eyes widened but she kept her composure. Jason and Allison looked at each other and waited for his response.

Gordon lifted his eyes to those of his wife and studied her a moment. There was no anger in his look. "I thought it was something like that," he rasped. He gave her a lopsided smile and lifted his left hand towards her. "Waited almost fifty years to see that girl I saw, a long time ago."

Tears began to roll down Thea's cheeks as she went slowly and stood by her husband's wheelchair. "You knew, didn't you, Gordon?"

He nodded, still looking at Thea. This time it was a look of love.

Thea sat down on a footrest by Gordon and looked up at the three of them. "When Gordon and I married, I was in love with someone else. Someone my family didn't approve of. I had to let him go." She turned to her husband. "I tried to be a good wife, Gordon, I tried." She took his hand and held it to her cheek. "I didn't want to love you. I was rebellious and angry with my family for ruining my life. I didn't know until these last few days, Gordon, how much I do care for you. That I have indeed, loved you."

Allison's eyes pooled with tears and Jason put his arm around her shoulders. Father Devon came and put his hands on Thea and Gordon's shoulders.

"God is able to restore the years the locust has eaten. Love is the same, whether we are young or in our golden years. Hearts don't change even though our outside appearance does. God has given you a gift in your later years that perhaps you can appreciate more than you would have if you were young."

Gordon lifted his left arm slowly and reached out to touch Thea's face gently with one finger. "My girrrll."

Thea looked up at him with tears that trickled down her cheeks. "I've wasted so many years, Gordon, so many years."

Gordon just shook his head slowly and patted her hand. Its alright, it's alright now." He shook his head slowly. "Lost sight of things. Business, making money, no time for God."

Father Devon put a hand on his shoulder. "There's time now, my friend. There is time now."

After Father Devon had gone, Cully returned to take Gordon down to his room for a nap. Gordon shook his head. He looked at his wife as she nodded mutely and then looked up.

"We'll stay here a while, Edward."

"A jolly good idea, Madam."

As he hurried out, Thea sighed. Martha was going to get an earful.

It was a time for privacy. Allison kissed her grandfather on the top of his head and gave her grandmother a quick squeeze before she and Jason left the room.

Joshua was asleep when they checked on him in the kitchen. Jason picked up the carrier and followed Allison upstairs. He gently laid Joshua in the drawer they'd made into a bed and Allison decided to rest and read for a while.

Jason gave her a hug. "I thought I saw a copy of a book I've been looking for in the library on the Dead Sea Scrolls. Think I'll browse a while."

"All right, honey. I'll be down in an hour or so.

Settling down on their bed, Allison looked up at the ceiling, contemplating the events of the afternoon. How could she have imagined the events as they transpired? She and Jason had no idea what God had in mind when she first contacted her grandparents. It was as if the joy inside of her was spilling out of every pore. She lay the book down and after making sure Joshua was sound asleep, went down the back stairs to find the door that Noreen's brother had used. It was locked up but opened easily at her touch. As she went out into the back garden she watched the afternoon breeze rustle the leaves in the tall willow tree. There was a sound and turning, she saw a man in his late fifties at work pulling out a rather tired-looking rose bush from a shady area of the garden.

"I wondered who tended my grandmother's garden and made it look so nice."

The man glanced up and nodded pleasantly. "Well now, you must be the long lost granddaughter, are ye?"

She laughed. "Yes, I guess that's me. I'm Allison Carradine." She offered her hand and after wiping his hand on his workpants, he shook it gingerly.

"Angus McPhee."

"Nice to meet you, Mr. McPhee. Have you worked for the Thornwells very long?"

"Oh, just a wee time. Their previous gardener retired a couple of months ago."

Allison loved the soft burr she heard in his voice. She contemplated the rose bush. "That didn't grow much, did it?"

Mr. McPhee shook his head. "They don't do well in the shade. Roses like sun and fresh air. This one was in the wrong place."

"Is there any hope for it or are you going to have to throw it away?"

"Aye, there is always hope, Lass. When you bring a rose bush out of the shadows into the sun, with a little nourishment and good soil, well there is no telling what the good Lord can do with it."

Allison thought of her grandparents and Noreen...people who were living in the shadows, needing the Son to warm their hearts. They had been planted in solid ground now and they would have a chance to grow.

"You're absolutely right, Mr. McPhee. I can see my grandmother has just the right person to tend her garden. I'm sure you'll be making some wonderful changes here."

"I'll be doing my best." He turned back to wrap burlap around the newly exposed roots of the rose bush.

Allison stood for a moment with her arms wrapped around herself and her face turned up to the warm sunshine. With a sigh she went back into the house. Tomorrow they were going back to their own home. They had accomplished what God had intended here, and though she knew they would be back for visits, it would be good to be back among her own things. Maybe she'd plant a rose bush. The thought pleased her and still thinking about the rose bush, she went to find Jason.

FORTY-THREE

Vietnam, October, 1997

Anh Cao leaned his tall frame against the doorway of the house in the gathering dusk and watched the sun go down over the beautiful dark green mountains of Sa Pa. The shadows were gradually claiming the terraced fields and the mist moved rapidly across the skyline with almost a physical force. Though the temperatures in the mountains of Northern Vietnam were unpredictable and could change in moments, the chill he felt did not come from the weather.

The colors of the sunset came suddenly, expanding into a breathtaking panorama. Many times he had enjoyed the sunset's short beauty, but today the sunset only heralded the coming night and he dreaded the darkness. His wife, Thuan, seemed to suffer most during the night hours. The sickness that invaded her frail body was like a rampaging lion, striking as it chose.

He also suffered in the night hours. The headaches and chills came more frequently. he symptoms of malaria started a few weeks before and a friend obtained some quinine on the black market for him. The quinine helped, but supply could be a problem.

In the shadows the dreams came also. Thuan once told him that he called a woman's name from time to time. She didn't ask about the woman, it was not her way.

He shivered a little as the mist rolled into the mountains and the dampness seeped into his bones. He had gotten used to the sudden changes in the weather over the years. The *Nguoi Thuong*, People of the Hills, were grateful for the mists. During the war, the clouds hid Sa Pa from the enemy planes. They had not been bombed as had other villages.

"Where did you find me?" he asked haltingly one day, when he'd learned some of the language of Thuan's people and she'd learned enough English.

"Just over border in Laos. We carry many supplies. One man hear you moan. If you Viet Cong, he kill you."

"You took me to a cave, somewhere in the mountains."

"We hide you. Viet Cong search villages for prisoners." She smiled her shy smile. "I do not wish you taken away."

Under Thuan's gentle care, his body healed and he regained his strength. She'd taken him back to her family in Sa Pa, for the war had ended and the American troops had pulled out. With the helicopter explosion, he would be considered dead and he realized no one would look for him. He was on his own.

Now he fingered the rough bump of cartilage on the back of his head from the shrapnel wound years before. As long as it didn't affect his movements or thinking, it seemed best to just ignore it. While he carried the visible scars of his wounds, the invisible scars on his heart were another matter.

Though he was fearful of capture at first, he submitted to a Communist "re-education program" and pretended to listen with great interest. It didn't matter. He had no religious convictions.

Life in Sa Pa was simple, working in the fields with Thuan at first, and then helping with construction work in the village. Eventually he'd acquired a jeep damaged in the war. With the help of Thu Mang Thi, a man in the village who had a talent for mechanical things, he was able to get it running. Now Anh Cao earned part of their income driving occasional European tourists around the area, for after the war was over, the tourists began to come again.

Life was peaceful in Sa Pa, but Vietnam was still a communist country, and although European tourists were allowed, the bureaucracy could make travel confusing and tedious. Anh Cao knew that to travel by himself outside of Sa Pa could be dangerous.

He dressed in the simple clothing of his wife's tribe, the Hmong, one of the many ethnic hill tribes that inhabited the mountains, Dao,

Tai, Muong, Hmong, Giay and the Montagnards. He had high regard for the Montagnards, fierce fighters who fought in Laos and Cambodia with the Special Forces teams from the United States and other European countries. The American soldiers called them 'yards' for short. Many had been killed in the war, but others had lived to tell their stories in Sa Pa and the other villages.

Thuan's stepson, Chau, was another matter. Anh Cao frowned. Only five years old when they married, the boy had been sullen and unresponsive. He'd seen too much death and war.

As the shadows lengthened, Anh Cao considered his wife's illness. There was no one in the village to help her. Hanoi was not only many kilometers away, but she would never survive the ten-hour trip over the crushed marble road.

His daughter, Kim-Anh, appeared at his side soundlessly. He was used to the girl's quiet movements and accepted her presence companionably. After the loss of three babies, he was especially grateful that Kim-Anh had survived. Now fifteen, she would be the only child of their union. The midwives of the village had used their ancient arts to save Thuan's life then, but there could be no more children. The women of the village shook their heads at him. He understood what they did not say.

Her voice was soft and she bowed her head. "My Father, she calls for you."

He acknowledged the statement with a slight nod and rose quickly following her into the house. Thuan lay quietly on the bed, a light blanket covering her thin frame. Her skin had taken on a yellowish tinge and was almost translucent. Large luminous eyes were held captive in dark sockets. The once luxurious hair had lost its luster and lay spread out on the pillow. As he listened, her breathing was so shallow she appeared to not breathe at all.

He squatted slowly next to the bed and took her hand, more bone than flesh, in his own. Thuan opened her eyes.

He spoke quietly in the tongue of her people. "Dear one, how is it with you?"

"The shadows draw closer. God calls for me."

"I don't want to let you go."

Kim-Anh came and knelt on Thuan's other side. She laid her head on her mother's shoulder, not wanting to hurt her, but needing to be close.

"You will take care of your father for me?" She slowly reached up to stroke Kim-Anh's head.

The girl's response was muffled, and Thuan continued to stroke her hair. Her voice grew stronger in her love for her child.

"I will always be with you, my dear one, in the sunset you watch, in the mountains around you. I will be as near as your breath. I will be there in the eyes of your father when he looks at you, for together we gave you life. You must be strong for him, and for your brother, Chau. Will you do this for me?"

Kim-Anh nodded, struggling to be brave, yet torn between the emotions of a child and the young woman she was becoming.

As she looked up at him, he saw the anguish in his daughter's eyes.

"You must call your brother. It is time."

Anh Cao considered his stepson and the hardness in his face in recent months. He'd sought over the years to reach Chau, but always his stepson maintained a polite distance. Chau was active in the Communist government and became a soldier in the Communist army; eventually assuming a position of authority in Sa Pa. Now when Anh Cao looked at his stepson's face, he wondered what was behind the dark, brooding eyes. He almost had the feeling that Chau was waiting for something, like the hunter waits patiently for the right moment to seize his prey.

Suddenly Chau burst into the room, an uncharacteristic intrusion, and spoke in a fierce whisper,

"There is an American doctor and his team in the village."

Anh Cao stood up. "A doctor? When did they come?" He glanced at Thuan and hope rose within like the wings of a fragile butterfly, fluttering in his chest.

"Within the last hour. You must speak with him. They have been given a building to set up their clinic. It is by the hotel."

"Thank you, Chau, I will go at once."

It was the most compassionate speech he'd heard from Chau.

Leaving Thuan in Kim-Anh's care, he and Chau climbed in the jeep and drove through Sa Pa to the hotel.

The village marketplace was busy as usual. Children ran here and there and the smell of many foods being cooked over small braziers wafted through the town. Women sat on blankets, sewing. A panorama of ethnic clothes, rich in bright colors and embroidery were spread out on the blankets. Each tribe was represented. Traditional silver jewelry, vegetables, sugarcane, and fruits from the hillside fields were in abundance. Newer items from Europe filled wooden bins.

People paused for a moment to watch the jeep pass. Word had gone through the village like wildfire of the medical team that had arrived.

He was not surprised the innkeeper had offered the building next to his hotel. The innkeeper was a good-hearted man and had become a friend, allowing Anh Cao the use of his extensive library and several hundred books that brought hours of pleasure. The innkeeper was generous for Anh Cao always carefully returned the books he borrowed.

A few Europeans, sitting in front of the hotel looked curiously at the jeep as it approached, but soon returned to their conversations. It didn't concern them.

Three vehicles, an ancient Land Rover and two equally ancient trucks, were parked by the hotel. As the jeep approached the makeshift clinic two men came over to meet them. One was Vietnamese, an interpreter, no doubt sent by the government to report on the medical team's actions. The other man was tall with a shock of blond hair and piercing blue eyes. His beard was the same color as his hair, yet with a few touches of gray. He wore a khaki shirt and pants. European? Somehow he didn't look European. The interpreter greeted Anh Cao in Vietnamese but peered closely as he approached.

"You not Vietnamese. You speak English?"

Anh Cao nodded. "Where are you from?"

The other gentleman seemed relieved that someone spoke English.

"Our medical team has received permission to call on some of the mountain villages and treat the sick. I'm Ralph Jensen, one of the doctors." He turned to his colleagues who had also come out of the makeshift clinic. "This is Dr. Mendoza, these ladies are Sarah Martin and Ann Suzio, our nurses."

"I am called Anh Cao," and he smiled, "It means "tall one." This is my stepson, Chau."

The doctor nodded at Chau and looked quizzically at the tall man looking down at him. "I'm happy to make your acquaintance, ah, Anh Cao."

The doctor put out his hand and he gripped it briefly. It seemed strange to shake hands with another man after all these years. "How can I help you?"

"My wife is very ill."

"I'd be happy to take a look at her. Can you bring her to the clinic?"

He shook his head. "She cannot be moved. Many times she spits up blood. I will take you to her."

"I'll be right with you." In a few moments he'd gotten his medical bag and had climbed into the jeep. Chau sat silently in the back seat.

When they reached the house, he spoke quietly to Thuan, quieting her fears and assuring her the doctor was just going to look at her for a moment.

Dr. Jensen stooped down by the side of the bed.

Thuan looked frightened but Dr. Jensen just smiled at her and glanced at the bloody cloths in a bucket nearby.

"How long has she been coughing up blood?"

"Over a week, now."

"What other symptoms?"

"Great pain, in her stomach."

"Any blackouts, fainting spells?"

"Yes, she fell a couple of times and told me she did not remember falling. Then the pain began to increase and when she complained of her stomach hurting, we thought she had eaten something that didn't agree with her."

The doctor's skillful hands moved over her stomach with practiced gentleness.

"There is a large mass here."

"What does that mean?"

"More than likely a tumor, very large."

He studied Thuan for a moment and then faced Anh Cao. "From her appearance, the blood, the other symptoms and the pain in her stomach, I can pretty much tell you what you are facing here. I have seen this before."

Realizing what the doctor was saying, he clenched his fists and willed himself to keep his emotions under control.

The doctor stepped into the other room and Anh Cao and Chau followed.

Dr. Jensen turned to them, his practiced eyes going over Anh Cao's face.

"You are also ill. Are you on any medication?"

"Malaria. A friend got me some quinine. It helps"

"We have some new drugs from the States that can treat malaria at the clinic. I'll bring it by."

Ignoring his stepfather, Chau interrupted, holding himself stiffly. "We are prepared for your diagnosis, doctor. What can you do for my mother?"

"My professional opinion is that it is cancer. From what you have told me, it has advanced rapidly. It has probably metastasized."

Anh Cao began to grasp what the doctor was saying. "Metastasized?"

"That means that it has spread to other parts of the body, possibly the brain. That would cause the blackouts."

"You can remove it with surgery?" From Chau it seemed more a command than a question.

Dr. Jensen looked grim, "I want to be honest with you. I'd say it's probably too late for surgery. We can give her morphine to help with the pain, but other than that there is little we can do for her." He looked steadily at Anh Cao. "Her feet and hands are cold, indicating the extremities shutting down. I'm so sorry, my friend, but I believe that your wife is dying."

He heard Chau's sudden gasp of breath and wanted to comfort him but knew his stepson would not suffer his touch or his sympathy.

Chau's voice took on an unfamiliar desperation. "You are a doctor. You cannot help her?"

"Yes, I'm a doctor, and I'm dedicated to saving lives, not losing them. At this stage it would take a miracle. There is only One who can do such a miracle, and for that we can only pray."

Anh Cao gave the doctor a wary look. He had prayed for many things when he was growing up, but this so-called benevolent God had been too busy to hear or answer his prayers. He had gone to mass with Thuan several times just to please her, but found the rituals as rigid and unmoving as his own upbringing. They confused and bothered him. It was better to find other things to do, so most of the time Thuan went with Kim-Anh. When he declined to go with her she would look at him sadly, but made no comment. He knew she prayed for him. It occurred to him one day that Chau was not a regular attendee at mass either.

Dr. Jensen's eyes were compassionate. "You do not pray, Sir?"

Aware of Chau's cold, searching gaze, his response was flat. "I've found it a futile gesture, Doctor, but I will accept anything that will help my wife."

"I see." Dr. Jensen reached for a syringe and filled it from a small bottle. He approached Thuan who watched him with wide eyes.

"You are a brave woman. You have done well. This will ease your pain." He turned to Anh Cao.

"I have seen patients suffer like this and the pain is great. She does not want to let go."

Taking his wife's hand, he looked into her face and his eyes misted. "You have been brave for me, haven't you?"

Her words were breathy, forced. "I do--not wish to--leave you, my husband."

"I don't want to let you go. We must do all we can. You must get well."

"No, dear one, I will not--get well."

Dr. Jensen waited with the syringe.

Anh Cao eyed the needle. "Is that morphine?"

"Yes."

"How long will it help the pain?"

"Three to four hours. I'll come here and check on her later. In the meantime I can give you the supplies for another shot later this evening."

He sensed the doctor's kindness and regretted his attitude. "Thank you. I didn't know how to help her. I just wish there was something else I could do."

"Stay with her and give her the comfort of your love. That is a great deal, my friend."

"How much time does she have?"

Dr. Jensen glanced at Chau and shook his head very slightly.

"A short time, but her will is strong."

The doctor left them to return to the clinic and Chau spoke quietly with his mother for a few moments and lest his emotions get out of hand, turned and left the house quickly to share with his wife, Toan, what the doctor had told them, and to prepare the children for the death of their grandmother.

As Anh Cao stepped outside, the familiar mists moved over the mountains, covering the town like a benevolent blanket. Beauty and ugliness alike were hidden, like the mists he allowed to cover his memory.

He'd asked Kim Anh to sit near her mother and let him know if she awakened. With a heavy heart he sat on a small wooden bench and leaned against the side of the house.

He considered the doctor, Ralph Jensen. The man was obviously curious and would ask more questions. Did he wish to reveal any more information about himself? If they were seen talking together too much, would the officials take notice? He could take the doctor on a tour of the town as he'd done for many European tourists, and talk, but this was different. He had not talked to an American in almost twenty-five years. The emotional strain of the last few weeks, the doctor's diagnosis and his concern for Chau took its toll. He leaned against the house, lost in thought.

"Mother calls for you. She wishes to speak with you alone."

Her eyes were cast downward as she spoke, but he heard the urgency in her voice.

The house was still. The candles had burned down and the room was in shadows.

He sat down gingerly near Thuan for she appeared to be sleeping again. As he watched her sleep, he thought of their years together. It had been a good life. She had given him a daughter who was a treasure to his heart.

Finally he put his head on his arms and waited. He wasn't aware at first that Thuan had spoken. He looked up suddenly and saw her watching him. She spoke again, "Husband…"

He moved closer and leaned down to hear her better. "I am here."

"You must return."

"Return? Return where, dear one?"

"To your people, your country. It is time."

"I have no one to return to, Thuan. Here are my people and my country."

"You have family."

He shook his head. "My parents are probably gone by now. They were not young when I was born. If they still live, they believe I am dead. It is best to leave it at that after all these years."

He sensed that she was gathering her strength as she spoke again. The morphine was wearing off and he knew the pain could strike without mercy at any moment.

"God has spoken to my heart. I will leave you soon. When I am gone you must find a way to go home. Promise me you will do this, and you will take our daughter. I fear for her. There is no future for her here." Her eyes beseeched him. "Promise me--"

Kim-Anh's future? He pictured his daughter, who had her mother's dark eyes but her father's long legs and fair skin. Her hair was auburn, which surprisingly, was a product of both of them. The women of the hill tribes did not have the black ebony hair of the rest of the women of Vietnam. Kim-Anh's mixed heritage had caused her a few problems growing up. In Viet Nam she would always be an outcast. Thuan was right. Only in America, where many races blended, could she have the freedom to get the education she should have.

Thuan gave a sharp intake of breath and he knew the pain had returned.

He reached for the syringe. The doctor had shown him how to administer the morphine.

She shook her head. "Not yet. I must hear your answer. Do—not--refuse me."

"I don't know if there is a way for me to leave. The government makes it difficult. And too, I don't know if my government will let me come back. There are many questions that need answers."

"There is a way. You will know. You will try, for my sake, and our child's?"

He could not resist her plea for he loved her. "I can only promise that I will try, dear one, I will try."

She gave him a weak smile and lay her head back down on the pillow. As she closed her eyes a slight sob escaped her lips. "Thank you."

He gave her the shot and watched as the morphine did its work.

The faint light of dawn crept in the window banishing the shadows. His mind tumbled with many thoughts. Return home? How can I do that? I promised Thuan I would try, but what do I return home for? I have no family to return to. He sighed.

Thuan was right. There was little hope for his daughter here. She was half Hmong and half American. Now that she'd finished the village school here in Sa Pa what other schooling was available to her? Chau had once let slip that he had plans for her, and he realized Chau was jealous of her. Whatever plans he had didn't bode well for Kim-Anh.

He looked up at the ceiling. *She believed in you, God. If you won't hear or answer my prayers, do it for her. If you are there and real, make a way for me to take Kim-Anh to the States, and please, let my parents still be alive.*

As he bowed his head, he felt something soft brush his cheek, like the touch of a feather. He looked around and saw nothing, yet there was the distinct sense of a presence nearby. For some reason he didn't understand, he felt peace settle in the room.

FORTY-FOUR

An insistent knocking on the door startled him. Anh Cao glanced at Thuan, but her eyes were closed. When he opened the door, he faced the local priest, Father Mang Thi, on his doorstep.

"I have received word that Thuan's time is near. I came to give her the last rites of the church."

Anh Cao held his tongue. He didn't want to recognize what giving her the last rights meant. He stepped back from the doorway. "Come in."

Thuan was awake. She saw the things the priest had brought and her eyes told them it was all right. The priest pushed aside part of the mosquito netting and squatted by the bed.

As he watched the priest go through the rituals of the last rites, he didn't feel the sense of apathy he'd felt in prior contacts with her religion. If it gave Thuan comfort in these last hours, where was the harm?

The priest bent over Thuan. "I will hear your last confession."

Though he didn't like the tone of voice the priest used, Liam was puzzled by her silence. She opened her mouth as if to speak and then slowly closed her eyes and appeared to doze.

"I'm sorry, Father, she is still under the effects of the morphine. She has gone to sleep again."

The priest frowned as he looked down at Thuan, but reluctantly continued with the ritual of the last rites.

Anh Cao helped the priest up, thanked him, and prepared to walk him to the door. Father Mang Thi paused and looked expectantly at him, clearing his throat several times and rocking back on his heels.

"I will pray for your wife, for her soul," he murmured, looking around the room and back at Anh Cao. When the old priest didn't make a move towards the door, he suddenly understood and turned away so that the greedy priest couldn't see his expression. At that moment he wanted to smash the man's smug face. He stuffed down his outrage and opened a small box on a shelf. Taking out a few coins, he kept his face bland as he placed them in the priest's outstretched hand. The priest smiled, put the coins in a deep pocket in his robe, and left.

When the priest was gone and the door was closed, Anh Cao kicked over a small stool, breaking one of the three legs.

He went back to Thuan who was watching him with a slight smile on her lips.

"Is there something you want to tell me," he said, squatting down by her bed.

"Since when have you not made confession?"

"I speak to God for myself now," she murmured softly.

He adjusted the covers over her and as she touched his hand, he brushed her forehead with his lips. Suddenly he put his arm around her head on the pillow and lay his face near hers. She clung to his other hand.

After a long silence, she whispered his name.

"Yes?"

"Call Le Nam for me."

"Le Nam?"

"He will know what words to say with me."

"But the priest..."

"Please, call Le Nam." She closed her eyes again.

He rose and went to Kim-Anh in the small lean-to room adjoining the main house. She was instantly awake, wary, "My mother?"

"She lives still, daughter. She has asked for Le Nam. I don't know why."

Kim-Anh put on her sandals. "I understand. I will get him for her, Father." In an instant she was gone.

It seemed only moments until she returned with the man who had a small farm outside the village.

Anh Cao was startled. "How did you get here so fast?"

Le Nam smiled gently, "I had word earlier to come. May I speak with Thuan? We are old friends. We grew up together as children. May I say goodbye, alone?" At Anh Cao's reluctant nod, he entered the room and closed the door behind him.

Puzzled, he sank down cross-legged on a cushion and waited. Perhaps there were things her people spoke of in these last hours that he didn't understand. Le Nam was of her tribe.

Chau and Toan came with the children and when Chau learned of his mother's visitor, he scowled. "The door should not be closed to the family."

The old aunt and uncle came again, moving slowly up the hill. Neighbors also gathered by twos and threes from their homes. How did they seem to know?

At last Le Nam came to the doorway and thanked him for allowing him to speak to Thuan. He stepped outside ignoring a glare from Chau who hurried to his mother's bedside.

Dr. Jensen came also, bringing another dose of morphine for Thuan, but when he entered and saw her, he shook his head.

"I don't think she will need this, my friend."

Thuan opened her eyes and looked at her family gathered around her bed. Chau knelt by her and she put a hand softly on his cheek. He bowed his head over her hand, his body rigid with suppressed emotion, then stood up quickly and stepped back.

Toan and the children bid her a tearful goodbye and she touched each one lovingly as they knelt by her bed.

Kim-Anh in turn knelt and wept. Thuan touched her cheek and murmured something softly to her, taking her hand, and then turned her face toward her husband. There was no sign of pain, only peace. He knelt across from Kim-Anh and took her other hand. Just then Thuan looked up at the corner of the room and her face was lit with a radiant smile. He followed her gaze but saw nothing. When he turned back to Thuan, her eyes were closed. Dr. Jensen stepped forward and touched him on the shoulder.

"She has gone."

The old aunt took a cloth out of her pocket and placed it on

Thuan's face. She then beckoned to Chau's wife, Toan and Kim-Anh to help her wash the body. The men were ushered out of the room. Thuan would be prepared for burial and they would let the men know when they were ready. Thuan's casket had been purchased a year before against his wishes, but he bowed to the customs of her people and it had served as a bench in the corner of the house.

Thuan's body was prepared with heavily scented lotion and wrapped with strips of cloth and a white silk shroud. Reed branches, paper and other objects were placed in the coffin, which was then sealed and a bowl of uncooked rice was placed on top of it, for the villagers believed it would keep the body from rising. A special altar was erected for he wanted to follow the customs of his neighbors and not offend. Three bowls of rice, three cups of tea and a bundle of joss sticks in the bowl of uncooked rice were surrounded by lighted candles. This was to continue for 100 days. Anh Cao knew the mourning period acceptable for him was a year. He had no interest in prolonging the ceremonies, but knew Kim-Anh and the rest of the family would be offended. He wore a black band on his arm and a piece of black material was attached to Kim-Anh's clothing.

When Chau presented his stepfather and his half-sister with the mourning garb of white gauze, and he thanked Chau for it, he couldn't see himself walking about for a year with white gauze wrapped around him and leaning on a stick to proclaim his grief.

Dressed in an army uniform, Chau only used a small piece of gauze for his head, yet seeing his stepfather's careless attitude towards the mourning garb Chau's eyes grew dark with anger. He turned and left without a word.

Many of the villagers came to offer their condolences, bringing money and food. Those that seemed particular friends of Thuan's puzzled him. They knelt silently and he knew they were praying but it was their faces he watched. It was as if they were lit from within.

When it was time for the funeral procession, Chau, as the oldest son, had to borrow a large ten-foot red hearse, painted with dragons, for the coffin and led the procession with most of the village following. Thuan's coffin was at last placed in a grave with food and offerings. The wailing and crying nearly caused Anh Cao to cry out. He would have liked a small, quiet burial with only the family but forced himself to adhere to Chau's wishes and customs.

He returned to the house and after the last of the mourners had gone, he and Kim-Anh were alone. When she went to her small room, he sat on a stool, his mind whirling with many thoughts. Chau's eyes held a look that was chilling and he knew Chau was spending a lot of time in town with the Communist officer in charge of the barracks there. Was Thuan trying to warn him about Chau? Did he have some plans for his stepfather and half-sister?

He listened to the sounds of the village. Life went on as usual in Sa Pa, but the light had gone out of his house. He got up and went to a storage chest, retrieving a small black lacquered box. Opening it slowly, he studied the contents and held up the chain. The metal had not rusted and the imprints were still readable. He slowly dropped the tags and chain back into the box.

FORTY-FIVE

He stood quietly in the small house, remembering the promise he'd given Thuan, but how and where did he begin? He didn't even know who to contact. When there was a sudden knock on the door, he frowned. He didn't want to see anyone right now, but also didn't want to offend one of the neighbors. Hoping it was not the wily old priest again he opened the door and was surprised to see Dr. Jensen standing there, holding a small cardboard box.

"May I come in?"

As the doctor entered, Anh Cao quietly closed the door. For some reason he couldn't explain, he had been expecting the doctor and he was apprehensive yet anxious to talk about the States.

The doctor set the box down on the floor and extended his hand. "I wanted to tell you how sorry I am that we were unable to do anything for Thuan. It's the bane of a doctor's life to find he is too late and all his practical skills can do nothing."

Shaking the doctor's hand, a Western custom, seemed strange. Anh Cao rubbed his forehead with one hand keeping his emotions in check.

"I understand. At least you made her final hours easier to bear." He indicated a rounded low chair and the doctor gingerly sat down, crossing his legs in front of him.

"What will you do now?"

He sank down on a cushion and stared at the floor, then looked up at the doctor. "I'm not sure. I made Thuan a promise before she died, but I don't know how I can keep it.'

"Is it that difficult?"

He knew his face reflected the despair he felt. "I promised I'd take Kim-Anh, and go home."

"The States?"

He sighed heavily. "Yes."

"I know Anh Cao, *tall one,* isn't your real name, though I can see how it fits. Do you feel comfortable telling me your American name?"

"I don't know if I deserve to claim it." With a shrug he gave the doctor a rueful smile. "It's Oliver. Oliver Thornwell."

"Oliver. Do you mind if I call you that?"

Oliver took a deep breath and nodded. "It's kind of nice to hear it after all these years, Dr. Jensen."

"Well, it's good to know you, Oliver. Where was your home town?"

"Bay area, Piedmont, near Oakland."

The doctor's eyebrows went up. "I'll be in the Bay area for Thanksgiving. My daughter and son-in-law live there. Do you still have family there?"

"I'm not sure. I was a mid-life baby. I don't even know if they're alive."

"How would you feel about my checking out your folks, maybe talk to them?"

Rubbing the back of his neck with one hand, Oliver winced.

"It's been twenty-five years. Even if they are alive, I don't know how receptive they'd be. They think I'm dead. To find out I'm alive and haven't contacted them in all this time, they'd probably wash their hands of me."

The doctor leaned forward, his elbows on his knees. "You may be surprised, my friend."

"You don't know my parents."

"Why don't you call me Ralph. You know, I guess I'm wondering why you stayed in Vietnam. You weren't a prisoner of war."

Oliver rubbed the back of his neck again and grimaced slightly. "It's a long story."

"Well, I'm a pretty good listener." The doctor leaned back in his chair, crossed his arms and waited.

"Maybe it would help to talk about it." Oliver filled the doctor in on how he and Kathryn met, their elopement, short honeymoon in Sausalito, and his parent's reception of Kathryn.

"I figured, we were married and there wasn't anything my parents could do about it. I'd never deliberately defied them before. Yet, surprisingly, they seemed to accept Kathryn. Reluctant, mind you, but it seemed like acceptance. They promised to take good care of her while I was at Fort Ord in Basic Training."

Oliver gave a derisive laugh then continued, "They took care of her all right."

"What happened?"

"I'd no sooner left in the taxi than my parents handed Kathryn a check for ten thousand dollars."

Dr. Jensen's eyebrows went up. "Ten thousand?"

"Yeah, to file for an annulment."

"She didn't take it?"

"Oh yeah, she took it, so much for love and forever after."

Oliver was surprised at how much bitterness still spilled out when he thought of it.

"That must have been quite a blow. I take it your folks told you she'd accepted the check?"

"My father called me. He was almost gloating. He didn't say 'I told you so', but it came across loud and clear."

"That's a considerable bribe. I'm sorry, Oliver."

"I guess it was enough. I left for Vietnam shortly after that. I was here four months and then the chopper I was riding in crashed."

"Any other survivors?"

"No, just me." Oliver put his head in his hands, remembering his own cowardice.

"I don't deserve any sympathy. When the helicopter crashed, I deserted my buddy. I should have helped him and I didn't, I ran."

"What happened?"

Oliver shrugged. "It's not a pretty story."

The doctor's manner was non-judgmental. His eyes as he studied Oliver were kind. Oliver looked up at the window a long moment, remembering.

FORTY-SIX

"We were on our way from our base camp to a demarcation zone. We had word that troops were going to be pulled out and sent home. I was scheduled to go on a later flight but I'd become buddies with another fellow in my unit, Jake Peterson. Jake knew the pilot. He got him to let me trade places with another soldier so we could ride together. Everyone was feeling pretty good. We'd missed the worst part of the war. We were about half-way to our destination when there was a burst of enemy fire and the chopper's rotor blade was hit. We went down.

"Most of the guys, including the pilot, were killed instantly. I had a head wound and shrapnel had creased my arm but I managed to crawl out of the chopper with my rifle and part of my pack. Jake had one leg severed at the knee, and shrapnel had pretty well chewed up the other one. I was dizzy from the wound in my head but figured I could carry Jake out and somehow get us back to safety. A dozen Viet Cong were coming out of the trees on the other side of the chopper. They couldn't see us. Jake begged me to get away while I still could. He said he'd be all right. He had his rifle and some rounds. He kept yelling for me to go, to get away and get help. He'd cover for me. I almost passed out but I staggered into some trees and hid where I could see the chopper. Jake was a pretty good shot. He was picking them off and got about five or six."

Oliver paused and his face was contorted with pain. "Then I heard Jake scream. I came out of the trees like a mad man, spraying them with bullets. I didn't care if I got shot, I had to get to Jake. I got the rest of the detail…killed them all…guess they weren't expecting me."

"And Jake?"

"They'd killed him, with a bayonet. I was sick, literally. Then I looked up and from under the chopper saw more Viet Cong coming down the mountain towards me. I managed to get back into the trees and hide again. Just as I got into cover, the chopper exploded. Jake and the other guys were cremated."

"I assume the Viet Cong didn't see you."

"I hoped they thought the chopper explosion killed all the survivors but I didn't have time to find out. I kept pushing through the trees and brush trying to put as much distance as I could between us."

"Did they come after you?"

"I heard them yelling at one another. I guess they wanted to be sure there were no others left alive. I…" Oliver looked at the doctor and bit his lip. "I should have stayed with Jake. He was my friend."

"How'd you get away?"

"Well, I just kept going and came to a river. When I stopped moving and listened, there were no more shouts or sounds of pursuit. I guess they decided we'd all been killed at the crash site and they'd gone."

"So you were wounded in the head and on the arm? Forgive me, as a doctor I just wanted to know how you managed."

"I found a wound in my side too. Didn't realize I'd been hit by one of the bullets. It went through, left a clean wound. I stopped the bleeding with grass and wrapped my shirt around my middle. Then I tore up my undershirt to bandage my arm and head. A bullet had torn away part of the pack with my rations in it, but I still had a small first aid kit."

The doctor nodded approvingly. "Amazing, the one thing you really needed was still there. Sounds like you handled the wounds well. Then what?"

"I just kept going. I didn't want to stop, didn't want to think of those other men and Jake. I felt like such a coward. I should have done something to save him. I could have bought time, called in the rescue choppers."

"It doesn't appear that there was time to do that. Did you have a radio of any kind?"

Oliver opened his mouth and paused as he looked back. He shook his head. "No, it was in the chopper."

The doctor studied Oliver's face and asked quietly, "So how do you think you could have saved Jake, Oliver? Seems to me he saved you. If you had tried to carry him in your condition, both of you would've been killed by the Viet Cong. The leg wounds you describe meant Jake was losing a lot of blood. He wouldn't have survived very long in his condition and you couldn't have moved as well as you did, putting distance between you and the enemy. You did what you had to do. It seems to me you're carrying a heavy load of guilt for the wrong reasons."

Oliver didn't answer, but he glanced up at the doctor, considering his words.

"Who saved you, Oliver? How did you get to Sa Pa?"

Almost relieved to continue his story, Oliver took a deep breath. "The mountain resistance fighters. They were moving along a narrow trail bringing supplies to guerilla forces fighting the Viet Cong. One of them heard me moaning. I was dehydrated and hadn't eaten for several days. My water was gone and a couple of my wounds were festering. When this Vietnamese guy parted the bushes and looked at me I figured I was a dead man." Oliver closed his eyes, remembering—

Stumbling through the thick brush, he was afraid to stop and rest. God. Jake. Jake laying half in and half out of the wreck of the chopper, one leg blown off, the other in shreds. Yet he held off the Vietcong so Oliver could get away. In his head he could still hear Jake's scream as they killed him.

His head throbbed. Touching the back of his head, his hand came away bloody. Shrapnel. He listened for sounds of pursuit, stopping only long enough to stuff part of his torn undershirt against the wound in his side and held his side with his hand. He put his other hand up to protect his face as he plunged ahead through the dense jungle. He had no sense of direction, moving blindly. Several times he came close to passing out from the pain. Fear tore at his gut and drove him to keep going. His lungs cried out for rest. It began to rain lightly and with a sob he fell to his knees tearing off a large leaf to catch the precious drops of water as they fell. Waves of nausea assaulted his body.

Curling up in a fetal position, he rocked with the pain. Lost too much blood. Can't make it. At the sound of footsteps, he looked up with pain-glazed eyes. She stood before him, smiling and holding out her hand, her green eyes dancing with merriment. Her strawberry blond hair seemed to float around her face.

"Kathryn?"

He reached out to grasp her hand, blinking to clear his vision and pulled back suddenly. It wasn't Kathryn. It was a man and he was Vietnamese. What he thought was Kathryn reaching out to him was a rifle, and it was pointed at his chest.

His body was dead weight. He couldn't breathe. It was no use. He was in no shape to fight. He hated it, dying this way, a bloody mess in a foreign jungle. The pain obliterated everything else and he'd closed his eyes, surrendering to the darkness.

Oliver shook his head, willing away the cobwebs of his memory.

"Instead of shooting me, he and another man lifted me up gently like a bag of beans and took me to a cave nearby. Thuan was with them. She had lost her husband in the fighting. She nursed me and cared for my wounds. They hid me until I was well enough to travel. I don't know if it was weeks or months. For a while I was delirious. By then I think our troops had pulled out of Vietnam and our part of the war was over. I was in Northern Vietnam and it was occupied by the communists. As you know, South Vietnam was under siege. I tried to be as inconspicuous as possible. The communists left me alone after I went through their re-education program. I think it was because I pretended to buy their propaganda and didn't appear to want to run away. As far as I was concerned, there was nothing and no one to return home to. I married Thuan. It was fairly easy to settle into village life. Anyway, here I am."

"That's an amazing story, Oliver. I appreciate your sharing it with me." The doctor got up slowly. "The scriptures say, 'Greater love hath no man than he lay down his life for his friend.' Sounds like that's what Jake did for you. He knew he wasn't going to make it and held them off until you could get away."

Oliver felt his eyes pool, "Jake died to save my life."

"Yes. You know, Oliver, God's Son laid down his life for you, that if you believed in Him, you would have everlasting life and fellowship with Him. You've endured much. You've done some wrong things and hurt some people. You can make it right and God wants to help you, if you'll let Him."

He nodded warily. "I'll give it some thought."

"He's ready whenever you are. Just talk to Him. Tell Him you're sorry for what you've done and ask His forgiveness. Ask Him to come into your heart and be Lord of your life. Turn your life over to Him."

Oliver shook his head slightly. "Thanks."

Dr. Jensen didn't push. He rose slowly and picked up the box he'd brought with him.

"I have some things to give you." He pulled out some small bottles. "This is a new medication for malaria. I wish I had more to give you. You need to see a doctor as soon as you reach the States."

"Thanks but it's more like if I reach the states. I was hoping to get some more quinine through the black market."

"Make it last as long as you can." The doctor reached into his jacket and pulled out a small but well-worn black Vietnamese New Testament.

"This was Thuan's. She asked Le Nam to take it from under her bed when he came to see her. It would mark her as a member of the underground church, a believer. She knew she was dying and didn't want it found in the house by the wrong people."

"Chau?"

"Yes."

"But Thuan couldn't read."

"Kim-Anh read it to her, many times."

The surprises of the morning were not over. "Is Kim-Anh a

member of this underground church?"

"Yes." He watched Oliver carefully.

Oliver frowned. Some things now began to make sense to him and he began to understand the animosity between Kim-Anh and Chau in recent years. Chau wanted her to join the communist party. Only Thuan had intervened, saying she was still too young."

"Le Nam? Is he a member of the underground church?"

"He was her pastor. You must keep this information to yourself, Oliver, many lives rest on your silence."

"I would not risk the life of my daughter or anyone else where Chau is involved. The information is safe with me, Ralph. I give you my word." He furrowed his brow. "Why do they do it, these believers, take the chance I mean?"

"For the love of God, Oliver, just as the early apostles gave their lives in turn for the Savior. They knew what they faced and yet they continued to speak of His love and forgiveness. They continued to lead others to Christ."

Oliver rubbed his chin with his finger. "This is a lot to digest."

Ralph smiled sadly, "Oliver, did you know that more people have been martyred for Christ in the last fifty years than died in the early years of the church? Le Nam knows what he faces if the communists find out he is a believer and leading an underground church."

"Yet he continues--he has courage."

"Yes. Now, my friend, there are some things I must tell you quickly before I go, and of the reasons I came here today. In the coming weeks you will need courage of your own. There are things that Thuan knew you must hear. The communists have left you alone because Thuan was Chau's mother. Also, they didn't consider you a problem. Now that she is gone, with a daughter who is half-American, there could be danger for you both. Word has come through the grapevine that Chau has boasted of plans for Kim-Anh. There are plans for you also, though we aren't exactly sure what they are."

"You believe we are in danger?"

"Grave danger. It seems Chau was biding his time while his

mother lived. Now that barrier is gone. You are in mourning and Chau may respect that, but then again, he may decide it doesn't apply to you since you are an American. We are not sure when he plans to make his move. We also don't know what information he has about his mother and sister and the underground church."

"Being a member of the underground church appears to be dangerous. Why would Thuan involve our daughter?"

"It was Kim-Anh who led her mother to Christ. My friend, it isn't just religion. It is Christianity. They fear it for they don't understand it. The enemy wants to destroy the church."

Oliver spoke half to himself, "No wonder she wanted me to go home to America and take our daughter." He sighed heavily. "She made me promise to do that, but it's impossible. I'd never get us out of Sa Pa."

Ralph grinned. "That's where God comes in my friend. Because of Kim Ahn, the believers have agreed to smuggle you out of Vietnam."

"Smuggle us out? How does it work?"

"Are you familiar with your Civil War History, the underground railroad?"

"Yes, they smuggled slaves out of the southern states to the North."

"Yes, that's rather what it's like, Oliver. Le Nam has made the arrangements. He is making sure Chau is occupied elsewhere. One of our members works in the kitchen by the barracks. He's been keeping us posted on what he hears. We do not want Chau to become suspicious." The doctor studied Oliver's face.

"The moon is in its fourth quarter so the night is darkest now. I know this is a difficult time for you and your daughter. You are mourning a wife and mother, but you must believe me when I say that you must leave, possibly even tonight. You cannot wait for the mourning period to end. You must leave before Chau sends the soldiers. Kim Ahn knows the plan, and while it is heartbreaking for her, she understands. It's your only hope. Another day may be too late."

FORTY-SEVEN

Oliver stood for a moment, overwhelmed by the implications of the doctor's words. He and Kim Ahn would have to leave their home and never return, trusting in the believers of this underground church to get them to safety. It was a daunting prospect, but it was clear he and his daughter didn't have a chance without their help. He looked up at Ralph.

"Thank you for the warning, I wouldn't have known. I'll accept the church's help. I'll do whatever I have to do to protect Kim Ahn from Chau."

"Good." The doctor looked at his watch. "I need to get back. We are leaving today and I have to oversee packing up the gear. Why don't you give me your parent's address and I'll see what I can do there."

The doctor produced a pen and waited while Oliver found something to write on. Then, as he glanced at the address, he chuckled. "Would you believe that my daughter lives just outside of Piedmont? I know the area where your parents live."

Oliver shook his head slowly. "I wonder if they'll even believe you. It's going to be a jolt."

The doctor nodded in agreement. "You're right. Chances are they're going to think I'm a quack. Tell you what, just so they will know that it is really their son I talked to, do you have anything I could tell them that no one else would know? Sort of like proof that I didn't just make you up to get something out of them? We may need their help getting you home."

Oliver thought for a moment. When the thought came, he smiled broadly. Of course, that was perfect.

"Tell them to remember me to Mr. Salty."

"Mr. Salty?" The doctor gave him a puzzled look and then shrugged. "Okay, got it. We'll get word back to you as soon as we can."

"How will you know where we are?"

"Don't worry, we'll be tracking your progress. I'll know how to reach you. I'll let you know the results of my visit if I can set one up, and we'll go from there. Just be patient and wait until we send you word."

"I'm sorry to be the one to bring you this news, but I'll be praying for your journey, Oliver. It will be a long one and dangerous. May God go with you and your daughter."

The two men shook hands and as Oliver stood in the doorway apprehensively watching Ralph Jensen walk away, for the first time in many years hope sprang up in his heart as he realized how much he was counting on the doctor's mission on his behalf.

FORTY-EIGHT

Kim-Anh, weary from working in the fields, removed her shoes, washed her hands and began to gather their evening meal from the food the old aunt and neighbors left for them.

Oliver waited impatiently for her, to discuss the doctor's visit and what they had to do. The girl was strong, but she should be in school instead of spending the rest of her life in the fields. Thoughts of what Chau was planning hung like a weight over his head. All the more reason to get to the States any way they could.

"It has been an eventful day,"

"Dr. Jensen was here?" It was more of a statement than a question.

Word traveled fast in Sa Pa, "Yes, he brought me something that belonged to your mother." Oliver picked up the small New Testament. "I believe you're familiar with this?"

The girl became wary. "Yes, Father, it was my mother's." She watched his face carefully.

"You've read it?"

Another hesitation, "Yes, Father."

He smiled then. "It's all right, Kim Ahn, I understand. The doctor explained. He also told me other news that is not good."

"Then you know what we must do Father?"

"Yes, I know of Chau and the danger. I also know of the underground church. It appears we must leave tonight, taking nothing with us but what we can carry under our clothes."

"We wouldn't return to Sa Pa." She hung her head.

"That's true, we wouldn't see your brother Chau or the rest of the family again. How do you feel about that?"

The girl was silent a moment. I'd miss Toan and my cousins, but I won't miss Chau. He wants me to join the communists and I've refused. It makes him angry." She paused and looked up at him, her face pinched and tight.

"I understand."

"Mother kept peace between us. She told him I was too young to be involved yet. Now that she is gone I fear Chau will pressure me again."

Oliver was grim. "Hopefully we will be gone before you have to face Chau over that."

She looked up slowly, tears trickling down her cheeks. "We must leave the grave of my mother."

He drew his daughter to him and held her. "It will take great courage Kim-Anh, but we must be strong. It is the wish of your mother that I take you to my country."

She nodded, muffled against him. "Yes, Father, she has told me this. I am ready." She moved back to look up at him. "I have dreamed of going to the United States. I want to go to school and be a doctor like Dr. Jensen. One who travels and helps the poor."

She looked at him her face hopeful, "Mother said you have parents in a place called California."

"Yes. Dr. Jensen is going to try to contact them. They may not want to see us, or me."

"But why not, Father? They are family."

Oliver winced. This was going to be hard. "Because they believe I am dead." It was easier to say that than to explain how they'd feel about Kim-Anh.

His daughter nodded. "It has been many years, Father? They do not know where you are?"

"It's a long story. I'll tell you about it later. We must prepare for tonight."

She bowed her head again. "Our guides will come for us when all is clear."

"We can't say goodbye to anyone."

Kim-Anh hung her head. "Can we go to the grave of my mother one last time? I miss her very much."

Oliver sighed. "I miss her too." He looked out the window. "The sun hasn't set yet. We have a short time but we must be back here when Le Nam and the others come".

Oliver picked up the small box that contained his dog tags and his Army identification card. He took the medication Dr. Jensen had given him and put them in a small cloth bag which he placed in his wide sash. He was not sure why he felt he should do this now and not when they got back, but he shrugged and nodded to Kim Anh."

Together Father and daughter walked quietly up the mountain to the place where they had buried their loved one. Kim-Anh's shoulders shook with sobs as she looked down at the small grave, the fresh dirt a reminder of their recent loss. Oliver drew his daughter close and let his own tears run down his cheeks and drop on the ground. Finally Kim-Anh took out her mother's New Testament and read, "In My Father's house are many large houses. I go to prepare a place for you that where I am you may be also--" She looked up at her father. "I hope her house is large enough for us to come one day."

Oliver nodded. "She was a very beautiful person. I'm sure it is a very large house."

They stayed a while as Kim Ahn prayed softly. Oliver listened to her earnest prayers, and marveled at her poise for one so young. At last he noted that it was almost sunset. It would be the last time they would come here. Reluctantly they turned away and started down the mountain.

When they returned home, Chau was leaving the house with a small bag over his shoulder. He stood impatiently, waiting for them to approach.

"Where did you go?" It was more of a demand than a question.

Kim-Anh looked him in the eye. "To visit the grave of our mother."

Chau's eyes narrowed and then, seeing their faces and the evidence of weeping, he backed down. He turned to Oliver.

"We will wish to speak with you in the morning. You are to come to headquarters for some--questions. There are matters that must be settled."

"You have no term of respect for the father that raised you?"

Oliver's voice was stern. He must not let Chau know that he knew anything at all.

Chau drew himself up and smirked. "You are not Vietnamese. you did not give me life. I called you Father out of respect for my mother. Now I will call you what I wish."

"I see."

"You will report to the government office first thing tomorrow morning."

"Toan is well, and the children?"

"You think to ignore me. You do not know who you are dealing with."

Chau began to look uncomfortable under Oliver's steady gaze. "I heard you, Chau, government office, first thing tomorrow. This is important?"

The young man's eyes narrowed and he barely covered a smirk. Then his face became stern again.

"Your friend the doctor has left the village already, a day early. I have been told he was here at the house today. What did he want?"

Oliver refused to let his irritation show. There was no point in antagonizing Chau with what they had at stake. Better to patronize him. Somehow he sensed that his step-son could be dangerous if pushed.

"He was sorrowful over the fact that he was too late to help your mother. He came to bring me his regrets and to say goodbye." Oliver thought it best not to mention the medication for malaria. It would bring a good price on the black market should Chau decide to confiscate it.

"Ah..." Chau showed a moment of contriteness. "He tried to help her. For that I am grateful." Chau wheeled suddenly lest his emotions get the better of him, and began to walk away. "Tomorrow, at the government office," he called over his shoulder.

As Oliver watched him go, almost strutting with self-importance, he breathed a sigh of relief. They had tonight to get away. He glanced at Kim-Anh and saw the relief on her face also.

"Come, let's put some food in our stomachs. We must be strong for whatever is ahead."

After they had eaten, they tended to their own belongings, each choosing whatever they could carry in a pouch under their clothes. Kim-Anh packed a few small mementos, and her most precious possession, a picture of her mother that a European woman had taken with a Polaroid camera one summer day as Thuan was selling things in the market. She also took the small Vietnamese New Testament.

Oliver looked for the ivory rosary he had given to Thuan when Kim-Anh was born. It was nowhere in their room. Chau must have taken it when they were visiting Thuan's grave. It had been in the small wooden box that morning. What else had Chau put in his bag? Oliver resisted his anger. What good would it do? Then the thought occurred to him that he wouldn't need it anyway. If it would be of comfort to Chau, so be it. He was glad Kim-Anh had taken her mother's Bible when they went to the grave. Evidently his stepson did not have time before Oliver and Kim-Anh returned to search very thoroughly.

As Oliver looked around the small house he and Thuan had shared for over twenty years he felt a pang of regret. Thuan's presence had adorned their home, giving it life and beauty. She had made their home attractive until the time her sickness became too much for her. Now the house looked plain and lonely. With a growing sense of alarm, Oliver noted other things of Thuan's were missing, a favorite vase and a small rug she had made. Chau was evidently not planning on explaining to his stepfather about those things. Why would Chau feel free to take them? Oliver considered the situation a moment. He'd heard of the interrogations at the government office. He didn't know what Chau planned, but suddenly Oliver had a sickening hunch that if he went there tomorrow morning he would not return.

He looked up. "God, if you're up there and listening, for Thuan's sake, protect us and give Kim-Anh and me courage for whatever is ahead. Help us to get home."

As the sun went down and the small sliver of a moon rose, the velvety darkness settled quickly on Sa Pa. The two of them waited in the dim light of an oil lamp. At Le Nam's suggestion, Kim-Anh had bound up her hair and dressed as a boy. He felt it was safer for her. Suddenly there were three sharp knocks on the front door. Oliver felt his heart leap into his throat. Soldiers?

Kim-Anh put a hand on her father's arm. "It is the signal, my father, Le Nam is here."

Oliver opened the door and admitted Le Nam and two villagers he knew well, Nhue and Tong. They were strong men, well acquainted with the mountains.

Le Nam looked at Oliver. "It is good that you have heeded the words of the doctor. There was much activity in the soldier's quarters today."

Kim-Anh came and stood beside her father. "Chau was here. We are to report to the government office in the morning."

Le Nam nodded somberly. "We had word." His face was somber as he turned to Oliver. "There is more to it, for Chau wants to set an example in the village. We are not sure of his plans for Kim-Anh, but they are not good ones. A rumor is that he plans to send her to Hanoi with the soldiers."

As the impact of Le Nam's words struck him, Oliver felt anger rise in his heart. He knew what happened to young girls taken to the city.

Le Nam continued. "I will go with you a short ways and then must return to Sa Pa. Nhue and Tong will take you on the first portion of your journey. At each stop you will rest and then be met by others who will take you to the next meeting point. No one can be gone overnight from their village, they would be suspect."

Oliver listened carefully to the older man. "I understand. It's sort of like a relay."

"Yes."

Tong watched the street for any sign of the soldiers but Nhue told them the government house was dark. They had watched the activities of the soldiers all day and waited until the lights went out in the barracks. All was quiet. Apparently Chau was confident that his stepfather did not suspect his plans.

Looking around at the home he'd known for so many years, Oliver felt a pang of regret, yet the prospect of going home to the States buoyed his spirits. Somehow he would keep his promise to Thuan and make sure his daughter was safe if it cost him his life.

He closed the door. This chapter of his life had ended and the future was unknown. He faced Le Nam. "We are ready."

Their scouts signaled that the road was clear and Nhue acknowledged the signal with a bird call. He motioned to Oliver and Kim Ahn and one by one the five figures moved quietly into the covering darkness of the mountains.

FORTY-NINE

November, 1997

Thea surveyed her living room with the vases of cheerful yellow and orange chrysanthemums, accented by autumn leaves. This would be a Thanksgiving she'd never imagined having a year ago. Walking over to the piano she picked up a silver-framed picture of Allison, Jason and their small son, Joshua.

She looked at Allison with a tender smile. The girl in the picture smiled back at her. It was almost as if Oliver was with them again.

How Allison and her precious husband Jason had enriched their lives, bringing love and compassion into her heart and Gordon's. Because of them, she walked with her Savior.

Looking back at the bitter, resentful woman she had been, it seemed another lifetime.

Her butler stepped into the room, interrupting her reverie.

"Madam, the rooms are a veritable riot of autumn colors. A delightful choice, I must say. It's the final touch on all our preparations."

He, Martha, and Noreen, had been busy for days. The silver was polished, the furniture buffed until it shone, and the meal planned to the smallest detail.

"Thank you, Edward, it does look festive, doesn't it?" She quietly put the picture back on the piano.

"And when are they arriving, madam? I take it they will have the little one with them?"

Thea eyed him over her half glasses. "They'd better! I can hardly wait to see my great-grandson again. He was so small when they first brought him."

At ten months, Joshua was a sturdy, active child. "He took his first step!" Allison told her recently on the phone with the typical excitement of a new parent.

"Allison's mother will be joining us also."

She'd laid down her pride and called Kathryn to ask forgiveness and to invite her for Thanksgiving. She wouldn't have blamed Kathryn a bit if she had turned down the invitation, considering the circumstances of their last meeting. Yet, in the spirit of reconciliation, Kathryn agreed to come.

"That is good-hearted of you, Madam, another step, so to speak?"

She sighed wistfully. "Yes. There have been many, haven't there, Edward?"

"You have a kind heart, Madam."

She laughed then, "Ah, I'm afraid I must confess to ulterior motives."

He raised one eyebrow. "She wished to be with her daughter and grandson?"

"Guilty as charged. You've seen through me, as usual. Oh Edward, you and Martha are so good to us. I don't know what I would have done without you all these years. Why you stuck by me when I was so ungracious, I'll never know."

He smiled broadly. "We prayed and God in His mercy answered our prayers. The Lord promises to redeem the years the locust has eaten. Has He not done that, Madam?"

Thea's heart swelled with gratitude. "Indeed He has, Edward. Imagine. A family we didn't know existed a year and a half ago. A granddaughter and a great-grandson. Mr. Thornwell is so proud of him. He dotes on Allison, as you know, she's the light of his life."

Thea glanced over at the silver-framed picture of the young family. Once again her heart was filled with gratitude for what she had been given.

Cully went to find Noreen and check on arrangements. Noreen had recovered both body and spirit over the past months and had joined Thea at the Bible study when she felt strong enough to go.

Thea had gathered her courage and disposed of Oliver's clothing.

It was time to let him go. She sat down slowly on a small sofa and stared out the window, thinking again as she did almost every day of her son. *Oh Oliver, why did you have to die, and so far away?*

A buzzer sounded twice to her left and she rose quickly. Gordon wanted to see her. They had worked out the signal system so that her husband could request the person he wanted. It saved them all needless trips. Fortunately they had moved Gordon to the guest room downstairs after his stroke and it saved going up and down the stairs. With a smile of anticipation, she hurried down the hall.

Gordon was propped up in bed, the morning paper on a stand that Jason had ingeniously made for him. It swung over the bed so he could turn the pages with his good left hand and take his time reading the paper.

"Gordon?" Thea smiled at her husband.

"Ah—beautiful-- morning." Thea went over to plump up his pillow and give him a kiss on his forehead.

"Yes, dear, a lovely morning. In two days our Allison will be here with Jason and Joshua. I'm anxious to see them."

"Me too." Gordon nodded his head slowly for emphasis.

Thea reached for a book on the side table that Allison had sent them when she returned home after her grandparents had renewed their faith. It was a well-known devotional and the Thornwells had been reading from the book each morning.

Gordon slowly pushed the newspaper stand to his left and leaned back against the pillow. "Reavy..." he murmured.

Thea opened the book at the marker and read the scripture for that morning. Matthew 9:28. "Believe ye that I am able to do this?"

"God deals in impossibilities. In each life there is rebellion, unbelief, sin and disaster, but it is never too late if these things are brought to Him in faith and trust."

Gordon wagged a finger, agreeing with what she read.

"Christianity is the only thing that can deal with a man's past. The Book of Joel tells us that God restores the years the locust has eaten." Thea paused and read the words again. "Gordon, this is amazing.

Edward was just saying those very words to me this morning, not twenty minutes ago!"

He smiled his crooked smile and pointed to Thea and then slowly back at himself. "Restores the years,"

Thea put her hand on his. "Yes, Gordon, we're not young anymore, but we have found something well worth waiting for."

She read on, "He will do this when we put everything into His hands. Not because of what we are, but because of who He is. God forgives and heals and restores. He is the God of all grace.' Oh, Gordon, I could almost sing out loud when I think of what He has restored to us. It says here that we have a God Who delights in impossibilities."

Gordon's eyes were warm as he looked at his wife. "Rehhhts pray."

They bowed their heads and held hands. As Gordon silently agreed with her, Thea poured out her thanks to their loving God for all He had done in their lives. Lonely years that had loomed ahead of them, bleak and empty, were now filled with family. She also still had a daughter-in-law, but though she had been assured that Kathryn had forgiven her years before, Thea found herself apprehensive about their meeting again. This morning she laid all her fears and pride at the foot of the cross and trusted her Savior to see her through.

"Truly You are the God of the impossible, and we look to You to cover us with Your love during this Thanksgiving time. Let Kathryn feel Your love through me and let this be a time of rejoicing, I pray in Jesus' name. Amen."

"Amen," added her husband.

FIFTY

When Oliver and Kim-Anh had walked for about a half an hour, Le Nam left them to return to the village. They faced each other and bowed respectfully. Oliver thanked him, for watching over Thuan and Kim Anh and for all he'd done.

Le Nam smiled. "I wish you well, my American friend. You have a long journey, but you are in good hands. Word will come to me when you are safe, may the God Who watches over all of us, protect you and your daughter."

"I wish you well, Le Nam, and the church you shepherd and your people. I can't believe I lived here so long and never knew."

"God has His timing for everything, my friend."

Le Nam bowed again to Oliver and then nodded to Kim-Anh and with a wave of his hand, turned and disappeared into the forest.

The four continued at a steady pace on the trail and finally came to a small cave. The entrance was well hidden. Oliver realized it had probably been used many times during the war, and now for people like them. They followed their two guides inside.

Nhue gestured toward a few supplies in the back of the cave. "These are for your use. We must go. There will be others soon to take you on your journey again, but you must wait here until they come. They will not tell you their names. It is for your protection as well as theirs. If you are captured, you cannot say who helped you."

"You are from Sa Pa. I know your names."

Tong smiled ruefully. "That is true and we must trust our God protect us. We are in His hands."

Oliver bowed his head to each of the men and in a moment they were gone. Father and daughter were alone.

"I hope the others come soon, Father and we will not be a long time waiting in this cave."

"We don't seem to have a choice. I'm sure the other guides will come as soon as they can. In the meantime, we might as well make ourselves comfortable."

The bread was fresh and there was fruit and soup. Kim-Anh asked permission to say a blessing and they ate for a while in silence.

"Tell me of America, Father, what is it like? I've heard many stories. Is everyone very rich?"

Oliver chuckled. "I think I'd better straighten out a few of those myths. First of all, not everyone is wealthy. It might seem so, in that even some of the poor people have more than poor families here. There is television, movies, lots of cars and trucks. The biggest thing I remember about America, now that I look back, is freedom."

"Freedom?"

"Yes, freedom. Freedom to speak as we wish, to take the jobs we want, to worship in whatever way we want to. Mostly, we have freedom to choose our own government leaders and even to speak out against that government."

Kim-Anh shook her head. "If you do that here the soldiers will come."

"Exactly. Maybe I've not appreciated the freedom and the country I had."

"Why didn't you return home when the war was over?"

Oliver smiled at his daughter's earnest face. "Because I met your mother."

Kim-Anh sighed. "My birth was difficult for my mother. Tuan told me."

"True. But we were very glad you lived."

"The children at school made fun of me because I was half American. They said I was not Vietnamese."

Oliver pretended to study her carefully. "Let's see, brown hair, like mine, blue eyes, long legs. Nope, don't think you could pass for a Vietnamese."

"But my eyes are not like yours, Father, they are shaped like my mother's.

"If you mean that you have an Asian look to your face, yes, but you are a composite, the best of your mother and me."

Kim-Anh lowered her eyes and smiled shyly at her father's praise.

"Father, will Dr. Jensen try to contact your family?"

"He's going to look them up and see if they're still alive, and if so, he'll talk to them."

"Then I have grandparents in America?"

"If they're alive still, you have grandparents in America."

"I will pray, Father, that they are alive."

"Thank you, Kim Ahn." He pictured his parents and realized they would probably be horrified at the thought of a half-Vietnamese granddaughter. A weight settled in his chest. He'd have to decide what to do about that when the time came.

"You have other children in America?"

"Hmmm? Oh, no, no other children."

Oliver reached for the blankets and tossed one to her. "I don't know how long we'll have to wait so we had better get some sleep while we can."

He lit a small brazier and they huddled together. In moments father and daughter slept.

Oliver wasn't sure exactly what woke him, but he sat up slowly, getting his bearings. He looked over at Kim-Anh who was still sleeping. He moved to the entrance of the cave and listened. The hoot of an owl shattered the silence. The hairs on the back of his neck stood up and he remained silent, watching and listening in the darkness. In the whispy rays of the coming dawn, he sensed someone was coming towards the cave. A twig snapped and Oliver tensed as the sound of footsteps came closer.

Picking up a rock, Oliver waited. Maybe it was their new guides, but if not, he'd be ready to do what he could.

The brush parted and a large tribesman stopped and stared at Oliver.

"Friend," he said, "Hmong."

Oliver put down the rock with a sigh of relief.

"Friend," he responded.

Kim-Anh woke and rubbed her eyes. Her father was talking with a man. He was of her tribe, there was no danger. She stood up, stretched, and started to fold her blanket. Daylight was slowly streaking the sky with orange and golden light.

"We are to go with him, Father?"

"Yes. He's our next guide."

His daughter looked fearlessly at the man and raised her hand in a gesture. Oliver recognized that some signal had passed between them. He would ask her about that later. Did it signify they were both believers?

After a quick breakfast from the food that was left, they made sure the fire in the brazier was out so it was safe to leave it. He folded his blanket and they left things the way they found them.

As they followed the tribesman down the trail, their guide stopped from time to time to listen. He seemed to be aware of the droning of a plane long before Oliver and Kim-Anh and moved them into the thick forest several times to wait quietly until the planes disappeared into the horizon.

The guide turned to them. "The planes go overhead each day looking for any sign of movement or people. We must be careful."

Oliver always felt he was in pretty good shape, but with all this hiking he felt his age. The malaria weakened him. More and more he looked forward to their rest breaks but they were few and far between. They drank water and ate some of the bread they had brought with them. Kim-Anh did not complain once and Oliver was proud of her.

It was dusk by the time they reached the outskirts of a village. Oliver expected them to go around it. Instead, the guide approached the edge of the village and told them to wait in the forest until he could return and let them know it was safe. Kim-Anh sat down and leaned against a tree but Oliver found himself pacing restlessly. At last their guide returned, beckoning them. He led them stealthily to a house on the other edge of the village. He opened the front door and motioned for them to enter quickly.

A woman looked up at them from her cooking. The man told them this was his home and she was his wife. She gave them a shy smile and welcomed them then went on preparing food for their dinner.

Oliver knew the man took a great chance having them in his home but he also knew they were believers and had chosen to do this dangerous task to help others. He was overcome by their courage.

After the evening meal, their guide moved the table and a thick hand-woven mat revealing a trapdoor. A wooden ladder of branches tied together took them down to a storeroom. It was small, about eight feet by eight feet and there was a rough wooden door in one side of it. Two sleeping pads were placed against the dirt floor with a couple of pillows stuffed with grass of some kind.

"You will sleep down there tonight. In the morning you will leave by that door. It leads to a passageway. It will take you into the woods again."

Oliver nodded. "How will we know where to go when we get to the woods?"

"Follow the trail as closely as you can. When you come to the big rock that looks like a face, you must turn sharply to the left in front of the rock. Go through the trees. You will not see a trail at first, but the way leads to another cave. Wait there for the next guide."

Kim-Anh listened and voiced her concern. "Are there soldiers here in the village?"

"Yes. A small detachment arrived yesterday. We do not know why they are here, so we must be careful. If they come here they will only see a man and his wife sharing a meal."

Oliver felt uneasy. He knew they were being hunted. Chau must have been furious to find them gone. "And if the soldiers come for another reason?"

"You must remain quiet. Make no sound that will draw their attention to the room under the floor. If there is any danger, you must go through the small door and make your way through the passageway into the woods. It will be your only chance. You will have no light so we must pray that your sleep will not be disturbed."

Kim-Anh nodded, "We must pray, Father, for the safety of these friends and ours."

The four bowed their heads and she asked for heavenly protection. As Oliver listened to her prayer, he was struck again by the courage of these people. They risked their very lives to help two strangers, just because they believed in God.

"Lord, I thank you for these good people who risk their lives to help us. Make the enemy blind and grant us Your protection. Let no harm come to our friends for the help they are giving us. I pray in Jesus' name, Amen."

Oliver didn't know how long they slept. They were awakened by a pounding on the door of the room above them. Oliver reached out and grasped his daughter's hand in the darkness, holding it tightly. There were angry voices and the sound of furniture being knocked over. A man cried out in pain as someone shouted questions.

"Who is here with you? We know you are hiding someone. Tell us or you will be shot."

"Who is telling you these things? As you can see, my wife and I are alone."

Another voice spoke out. "We have checked the rooms and the storeroom. There is no sign of anyone here."

"Very well. We will go, but be sure you will be watched, closely. Let this be a lesson to you. If any strangers are seen coming to your house, you will be punished. Do you understand?"

There was a thud and the sound of moaning.

Oliver opened the door to the passageway as quietly as possible, letting the noise above mask any sound. Kim-Anh climbed into the passageway and waited for her father to follow. As Oliver started to climb in beside her, he hesitated. The soldiers were leaving the house.

Torn between fear for his daughter's life if they were caught, and knowing someone was hurt in the room above them, Oliver wrestled with his conscience. Then they heard the frightened weeping of the wife and the scrape of the table being pulled aside. She opened the trapdoor.

Oliver climbed back up the ladder and caught his breath. The chairs lay smashed on the floor; the woman bore a huge red mark on her cheek where she had been struck. She pointed to her husband who lay on the floor, blood pooling by his head. At first he appeared dead, but then they heard a soft moan. Oliver turned him over gently and found a big gash on the side of his head. At least he was alive.

Oliver assured the woman that her husband would be all right. They washed and bandaged the wound with some cloth. The woman put her hands together and began to pray softly. The man struggled painfully to his knees and Oliver helped him to his bed.

He spoke to his wife, consoling her for a moment, then he turned to Oliver and Kim-Amh. "You must go below again. We do not know if the soldiers will come back but if they do, they must find only my wife and me. If they return, do not hesitate, take the passageway at once and get to the cave. You may not be safe here. Go quickly and may God protect you both."

"Can we see the trail?"

"If you can wait until dawn, you can follow the trail."

"Thank you for all you've done. I'm sorry to bring trouble to your house."

The man smiled weakly. "I believe I will have to remain quiet for a while. God is good. The soldiers could have shot me, or my wife. It is a small price to pay for serving our God."

The woman smiled at Kim-Anh and urged her to take a small bag of food. She touched her on the cheek, like a mother would, then pointed towards the trap door, and urged them to go quickly.

Oliver thanked her as Kim-Anh took the food, then they descended the ladder again as the trapdoor was closed.

"Father, I do not think I can sleep. I fear the soldiers will be returning. Could we not try to find the cave?"

"I'm thinking the same thing. Let's take our chances on the outside."

Kim-Anh opened the door to the passageway and once again crawled in. Oliver had to bend and crawl on his knees. It smelled like damp earth. Something scuttled across Oliver's hand and he didn't want to think about what it was. Crawling in the darkness Oliver sensed air blowing at them. He reached the opening just behind Kim-Anh and after crawling out, raised himself gingerly to his feet. They were in a stand of trees. It was too dark to see a trail.

"We might as well get comfortable, it will be a while until there is enough light to see. They settled against the tree, keeping close for warmth. Suddenly Oliver felt the familiar throbbing in his head and the chills. With a grimace he worked the plastic bottle of pills Dr. Jensen had given him out of his bag and took one with a sip of water from his flask. He didn't need this right now. How could he deal with the fever and watch over his daughter?

The reassurance came softly on the wind. *I will watch over you and your child.* Oliver put his head down on his arms. He must have imagined it. He listened to the sounds of the night and sighed, lifting his head to look at his young daughter snoring softly against his shoulder. As the trees moved in the shadowy world between darkness and dawn, they almost seemed alive. For a moment Oliver was a young soldier again, hiding in the forest from the Viet Cong. In spite of the whispered assurance, he suddenly felt vulnerable. For the first time since the war ended, Oliver wished for a gun.

FIFTY-ONE

As the first gray light of day broke through the trees, Oliver looked down at Kim-Anh who had fallen asleep against him, and murmured her name.

She yawned sleepily, stood up and stretched. Oliver stood also trying to get the kinks out of his long legs. The pills had helped his head, but he'd slept fitfully, snapping alert with every unusual sound. The ground was cold and his backside felt numb.

Oliver pressed his hands to his temples and willed the pain and nausea to leave. He had to be strong for Kim-Anh. "Let's go."

The path was discernable, but just barely. It hadn't been used recently and the grass had grown up to cover it. They came to a large rock outcropping and Kim-Anh stopped suddenly.

"Father, it is the rock that looks like a face."

Oliver looked up. The part of the rock that faced them did indeed have the similarity to a face, a woman's face. They stared at the rock a long moment.

The path they were on seemed to go around the rock to the right, but Oliver, remembering the words of the guide, parted some of the brush to the left of the rock and they pushed through.

"Be careful not to break any branches, there must be no sign we passed through here."

They moved slowly, parting the brush gently as they went. After about ten feet, they found the path their guide had indicated. Trees had been marked by the small slash of a knife and they went slowly, watching the trees for each mark. Though it had been some time since the marks were made, they were able to discern the places where the bark was missing and the smooth part of the tree showed.

After two hours, Oliver's head was hurting again from the strain of looking for the marked trees.

He sat down on the ground and leaned against a tree. "Whew.

Running away into the forest isn't easy."

Kim-Anh dropped to the ground also and wiped her face with her sleeve. "I feel as though I have walked all day, Father, even though the sun tells me it isn't even noon yet."

They ate some of the bread and dried meat the wife had packed for them and sipped water from their leather flasks.

"We may need to ration the water, I don't know how long it has to last."

She put the cork back in her flask, then leaned back and closed her eyes for a few moments, Oliver took the opportunity to slip some pills out of the bottle and swallow them. He needed the medication to kick in fast.

Back on the trail, the hours went by as they continued making their way. This time it was Oliver who heard the drone of the plane and drew his daughter into the shadow of the forest.

The plane flew low to the trees and moved on. Oliver waited until it was a distant sound before stepping back out on the path.

"Do they look for us, Father?"

"It's a scout plane of some kind. I don't know if they're looking for us. The detachment of soldiers in the village could have been a coincidence. I'm sure Chau was not pleased to find us gone."

She looked down. "He is no doubt very angry."

Oliver tilted his head to one side. "You know, I understood that the soldiers came unexpectedly for someone, the element of surprise. I've been puzzled as to why Chau just told us to come to the government office."

This time Kim-Anh looked up at him and smiled. "I believe God has protected us, Father. You are right about how the soldiers come. Perhaps my brother felt you had nowhere to go. If you did not show up it would be a simple matter to have you arrested."

Oliver chewed on his lower lip, thinking on that. "Perhaps your God has helped us, but I fear for the families of the village, the old aunt and uncle. The soldiers will search everywhere, looking for us."

"They will not harm the family, because of Chau. He will look other places. It is the church I fear for, Father. They will suspect everyone that had anything to do with us. That is their way. We must pray for those who helped us get away."

"You're right. We must remember our last guide and his wife. They are in danger still."

Oliver didn't feel comfortable praying and left it to Kim-Anh, yet he wondered at the strength his daughter was showing through all of this. She bowed her head and offered a prayer for the safely of her friends in Sa Pa, for the guide and his wife, and for those to come who would help them as they made their way to their unknown destination.

He listened and a prayer formed in his heart, for his parents, that they would still be alive, and that they would bear the news Dr. Jensen was bringing them and respond with welcome.

Just as they began to despair of ever finding the second cave, they rounded a large tree and saw what looked like an indentation in the rocks. The entrance had been carefully hidden, and only because they were looking intently for a cave did they even know it was there.

This one was smaller than the first cave, but once again there were blankets, cushions and a supply of food. This food was not as fresh, but the dried goat meat was edible and there were nuts and a metal container of dried fruit. They took a chance and ate it, drinking again from their flasks. Kim-Anh found another container behind a rock that held water. I t smelled like it was potable and they filled their flasks again.

They spent two days in the cave. Oliver tried to be patient, but his concern was that the guide had not been able to pass the word along about their presence due to his injuries and the soldiers in the village. They could strike out on their own, but which direction could they go? Oliver didn't know the mountains. He could lead them on a wild goose chase, or around in circles. What should he do?

Oliver had nothing to read, and so Kim-Anh read Scriptures to him by the light of a small fire inside the cave. In daylight they ventured out in front of the cave to sit in the sunshine. She had been reading through the Book of John and Oliver was amazed to find that it was Jesus who had been with God in the beginning and had created the world. The words ministered to his spirit and soul as he struggled to understand his daughter's faith.

"--But as many as received Him, to them He gave the right to become the children of God, to those who believe on His name."

Kim-Anh smiled shyly. "Is it not good news, Father, that anyone can become children of God?"

Oliver marveled at John 3:16 that God would give His only begotten son for him, Oliver, in spite of all he'd done. He thought again of his friend, Jake, who must have known he didn't stand a chance, yet was willing to buy time so that Oliver could get away. When Kim-Anh read the verse Dr. Jensen had referred to, in John 15:13, "Greater love has no one than this, than to lay down one's life for his friends," tears came to his eyes and he remembered the doctor's words that Jesus had laid down his life so that Oliver might live, eternally.

They talked late into the evening, discussing the scripture. He marveled at his daughter and her knowledge and with God's grace, humbled himself to learn from his child.

It was their third night in the cave and their food was gone. Oliver knew that if someone didn't come by tomorrow, they were going to have to chance going on their own.

Oliver was awake long after Kim-Anh had fallen asleep, pondering their options. At last weariness overtook him also and he slept.

In the first light of morning, Oliver rolled over and was startled to see an old woman sitting quietly on a small mat watching them.

"Good morning," she said, addressing them in Vietnamese.

Oliver rubbed the back of his neck and sat up. "We were beginning to think that no one knew we were here."

She smiled back, showing the loss of several teeth. "Many look for you, Tall One, many soldiers. They question everyone. Others could not come, so I must come. Who pays attention to an old woman going into the forest to gather sticks for her fire?"

Hearing the voices, Kim-Anh sat up and rubbed her eyes. She looked hopefully at their visitor. "Do you have anything to eat?"

"Ah…a growing child is never full. Yes, I have brought you food. Come, I will show you." She unrolled her bundle and laid out cooked rice and a container of soup, with bits of chicken in it. There were fresh bread rolls and Oliver's mouth watered at their fragrance. He remembered the fresh baguettes that Thuan used to buy in the marketplace. Hungry for the taste of the fruit they had known in Sa Pa, both father and daughter were delighted that the old woman had brought a small container of pineapple.

As they were reaching for the bread, she put her hands together and bowed her head. Oliver winced and quickly bowed his head. He was learning who their true provider was.

They packed up the remaining food but left the blankets and cushions as before.

"How far can you take us, Old Mother?"

"I will show you the way to the border of Lao. Someone from the mountain people of the north will come for you. Then you must go through the mountains to the great river. From there others will take you on your way."

"The great river, the Mekong?"

"Yes. You must cross this river into Thailand. You are not safe in Laos."

"Can we travel by road?"

"Many places you can go by road, other places, bad roads, there are many bandits. It is best to go by the river."

Kim-Anh had been quietly appeasing her hunger, but now she looked up. "We can be like the tourists that came to Sa Pa, Father."

Oliver grinned ruefully. "True, we can pass for tourists, until they ask us for our passports."

The old woman shook her head. "You are dressed like Hmong. You would not be like the foreign tourists. Many would see you. You must go by boat."

He frowned. "Will they stop the boats?"

The old woman shook her head. "There are many boats on the river, many tourists, too many for the soldiers to stop."

The old woman gave Oliver the pack with the bamboo food containers in it that she had carried, hidden in her heavy shawl. They left the cave and she trotted ahead of them, showing them the trail. In many places only her practiced eye discerned the direction they were to go. She appeared to be following familiar markers, but as hard as Oliver tried, he couldn't spot them. Maybe it was just as well. The soldiers couldn't see them either.

After two hours of hiking, Oliver heard the sounds of children playing. They were near a village. A dog barked from somewhere below them. If she was taking them to her village, he was wary. "Are there soldiers in your village, Old Mother?"

"I do not know. They come and go. Many months ago, soldiers came and found the missionary teacher. They took him away and we have not seen or heard from him. He told us about the God of the heavens who came to earth to make a way for us. He read to us from the black book about his God. I listened and I knew in my heart that his words were true. I believed and received his God. Now my heart knows peace. Always the God of the heavens is with me."

Oliver nodded pensively.

"Your daughter has found Him. I see it in her face."

Kim-Anh smiled at her. "My mother was a believer also. One day, when I see the God of heaven face to face, I shall see her again."

"She has gone to be with God?"

"Yes. She was very sick and died." She looked down at the ground, remembering.

"How long ago?"

"About a week "

"Aieee...and now you travel so far? The time of mourning is not the time for a daughter to leave the grave of her mother."

Kim-Anh shook her head. "We had no choice."

"Ah, it is the same for all who travel our secret paths through the mountains. Many have come before you and many will come after you. We will help all that we can."

A thought occurred to Oliver. "Have any of those you have guided not made it?

Have the soldiers found them?"

She was silent a long moment. Oliver was ready to repeat the question, thinking she had not heard him.

The old woman looked at the Kim-Anh as she nodded her head slowly. "Yes, some have not made it to the place of safety. Once we had a brother who needed money. He was willing to take the bribes of the soldiers."

"What happened?"

"A family of believers was captured, a father, mother and two children. They tortured the father and then killed him. I do not know what happened to the wife and children, but I can guess."

Oliver knew of the women and children who were taken across the border and sold as slaves. Even in a modern age, man's inhumanity to man never ceased to amaze him. It was the fate Chau had planned for Kim-Anh.

"And the man who informed on them?

"He did not profit from his evil act. When he asked for his money the soldiers laughed at him. I think he was sorry for what he did. He took his own life."

Oliver and Kim-Anh exchanged sober glances.

Knowing the village was nearby, Oliver picked up the bag with their food as they began walking again. Kim-Anh was silent, glancing behind them from time to time.

"We will not stay in the village, Old Mother. It is too dangerous. If you leave us here, can we find the trail?"

"You are wise. I think you will go safely. Come closer, I will show you the marks to look for."

She went closer to a tree and pointed. "What do you see, Tall One?"

Oliver scratched his head. "I don't see anything different. No marks of a knife."

She cackled. "The eyes of an old woman are sharper than yours, Tall One. Look again at the tree."

He followed her eyes and she showed him the nearly invisible marks. If one did not know to look for it, it would have appeared part of the tree and easily passed by.

When she saw that he found the mark, the old woman grinned, a broad toothless smile. "You have good eyes, Tall One, but you must also use your ears and listen for any sound that is unusual. You must always be aware of a place to step into the shadows out of sight. Right now you have more to fear from four legs than two."

"Four legs?" Kim-Anh stepped closer to her father. "An animal?"

"These high mountains are home to bears and the leopard. You must be aware."

"And me with no weapon." Oliver looked around him for something he could used to defend the two of them if necessary.

He turned to the old woman. "How is it that you are not afraid to walk through these mountains alone?"

She shrugged. "The shining ones go with me. I am not alone."

Oliver wheeled suddenly back to her, his eyebrows raised. "Shining ones? What do you mean?"

"Only once, the first time I came alone, when I was afraid, did I see them. After that, I only know that I sense their presence. They are here with us now."

Oliver was tempted to put it down to the ramblings of an old woman, but there was something in her face when she spoke of them. There was no doubt that she'd seen something. She had not only eluded soldiers, but had walked alone for two hours to get to their cave and bring them food. He didn't want to sound ungrateful for all she had done, but he wasn't sure he was ready to contemplate angels. For that was what he was sure she was referring to.

Kim-Anh was more open. "You have guardian angels, Old Mother. If that is so, then they will go with us also." She squared her shoulders and looking more confident than she had in several days, indicated that she was ready to go.

"I must leave you here. It will take you two days to reach the Black River. There is a small village. Hmong. They are wary of strangers for they grow the flower that makes men lose their will."

"Opium," Oliver murmured.

"Yes, but you have come from the high trail and they will know why you have come. You are safe in their village. The soldiers do not come there. Too far away, too hidden. They will help you."

After admonishing them to look carefully for the signs on the trees to follow the path, the old woman left them and disappeared into the woods in the direction of the village. Her last words were,"Go with God."

As they walked along, carefully following the marks that showed them the trail, Oliver was tense. If they missed a marked tree they could get off the trail and be hopelessly lost in the forest.

Suddenly they were startled by the sound of a scream, an animal's scream. It was the cry of a big cat and it was close by.

FIFTY-TWO

Allison paused with the dishtowel in her hand. "Are you all right with going to my grandparents for Thanksgiving?"

Jason had taken Joshua to see a neighbor's new baby chicks. Allison had cleared the table as Kathryn loaded the dishwasher and began washing the pots and pans.

With her hands in the sudsy water, Kathryn paused. "Oh, I'm sure it will be fine, just fine. I have prayed about it. The miracle that God accomplished in the lives of your grandparents will certainly make a difference."

Allison gave her mother a hug. "You'll really like Thea, Mother. She's got a delightful sense of humor that's much more apparent since God has healed the many hurts she was carrying. They're both different from the people you met so long ago."

Kathryn turned so Allison couldn't see her face. "I'm sure you are right. It will be refreshing to go under different circumstances." She'd offered to bring something, but was assured that it was not necessary.

The back door opened and Allison heard Joshua babbling to his father as they entered the kitchen. Jason put him down and Allison knelt and held out her arms as her small son toddled happily into them. He smelled of pine and dirt. Kathryn smiled indulgently at this precious addition to their family. His dark hair and eyes were so like his father.

Little dirty prints followed each footstep and while Kathryn was tempted to say something, it didn't matter. She could always mop the floor.

Allison picked Joshua up. "Time for a clean-up and a nap, my little friend."

Joshua promptly stuffed a grubby thumb in his mouth and allowed himself to be carried upstairs.

A little later when Allison came downstairs she found her mother engrossed in a book she had started, and Jason sprawled in an overstuffed chair with his eyes closed. From his deep breathing, she realized he was asleep.

Kathryn patted the cushion next to her. "I think we've lost Jason. Come sit down and tell me what you've been up to this week."

Her daughter settled herself with a sigh.

"You know, I didn't realize that one little boy could take so much energy. He is a good child, but just into everything! At least I took your advice and when he goes down for a nap, I try to take one too! I just can't seem to get anything done when he is up and around."

Kathryn looked off into space for a moment. "The years pass too quickly. One day he'll start kindergarten and you'll wonder where the years went. I do hope you'll have other children, Allison. I think you were a bit lonely sometimes as an only child."

"Oh, I don't know that I missed having siblings. I had your wonderful paints to play with, and books to read. And I could have my friends over any time I wanted to." Allison smiled at her. "You were a great mom."

Kathryn beamed. "I'm glad you thought so."

"Not changing the subject--" They laughed at the familiar phrase, knowing that's exactly what Allison always said, and did.

"Mother, you never had Christmas with my father, did you?"

Kathryn raised her eyebrows. "Now what made you think of that?"

"I don't know, maybe because we were talking about his parents."

She stared at the carpet a long time as memories crowded her thoughts.

Allison waited, and at last Kathryn looked up, feeling her eyes moist. "No, we were married after Christmas and then of course you know the rest with his parents after our short honeymoon."

Allison nodded, encouraging her to go on. "You had a really short honeymoon, didn't you?"

"Yes, but that precious little guest house has been a special memory."

Allison's eyes were moist now too. "Just a few short days and then you never saw him again."

"I have my memories."

"You loved my father very much."

"More than life. At least I have you to remember him by. He would have been so proud of you, and of his precious grandson."

"Well, we don't know that he doesn't know, Mother. Maybe he's looking down on us even now from heaven."

"I've liked to think that he is. I've felt close to him all these years and in my heart he lives still."

"Remember the balsa wood airplanes?"

The shift in topics again caught Kathryn by surprise. "The airplanes?"

"Hanging from the ceiling of his room."

"Oh, those, you must remember I only slept in his room one night, but I do remember looking up at them. Oliver talked about how he and Cully glued them together."

"I convinced my grandmother to keep them for Joshua, and his sketchbook."

"His sketchbook? Oh. Well I'm glad you did. I'd like to see it again."

"My father never got his wish to be an architect, but then his father never got his wish for my father to be a lawyer either."

The two women were silent a moment, then Kathryn finished rinsing down the sink. "Enough of this sad talk, we have a lovely Thanksgiving to look forward to and much to be thankful for."

"You're right. So, what's your latest book illustration assignment?"

"A darling children's book about flowers that talk and it's in rhyme, very clever. Would you like to see some of the illustrations I've done so far?"

Allison nodded, and with a loving glance at her husband who was still sleeping in his chair, they went upstairs arm in arm, to Kathryn's studio.

As they entered, Allison saw that the picture her mother carried in her Bible for so long had been framed.

FIFTY-THREE

"With all the equipment needed for the baby, and the car seat, wouldn't it be better if we took two cars?"

Allison raised her eyebrows. "We have plenty of room, Mother, or are you planning an early escape from the Thornwells?"

Kathryn cringed a little. "I just thought, well, in case..."

"In case you felt uncomfortable and wanted to leave sooner?"

"Something like that."

"Mother, you'll have a wonderful time. My grandmother is not the woman you met so many years ago."

"Oh, I know that, Darling. My head knows that. It's just that I'm experiencing some feelings I thought were buried."

Allison gave her mother a hug. "I think that's natural, given the circumstances of your last meeting, but you don't have to worry, really. Just go with us."

Joshua squatted down, hands on his knees, intently watching a lizard which appeared frozen to a small rock. He reached out a hand and the lizard was gone in a flash. Joshua sat down abruptly on the gravel driveway, his lower lip protruding. Before he could let out a wail, Jason scooped him up in his arms.

"I don't think the lizard wants to play, son, and its car seat time."

Joshua's countenance brightened, he loved to go with his father. "Ah ah..." he chattered happily.

Allison watched them. "You know, Honey, I think ah-ah is his name for car."

Jason backed out of the car. "Are we ready to go?"

"Yes, if Mother is." She turned towards the house where her mother had dragged a large suitcase out onto the porch. Jason went to pick it up.

"Whoa, Mom, we're only staying for three days. What did you put in here?"

Kathryn spread her hands. "One never knows what one will need."

Jason shook his head as he hefted the suitcase into the car.

On the ride to the Bay Area, Kathryn was quiet, lost in memories of her last visit there. As she lay in Oliver's arms in his room that night after a 'friendly' family dinner, she had listened to him talk about their future and how his parents would take care of her. He'd be home for a brief leave when he finished boot camp, but in the meantime, she could write to him and he would write to her. She'd nodded and re-assured him of her love, feeling the comfort of his lean body next to her. She'd always believed that Allison was conceived that night. She slept little, wanting to talk and savor every last moment together before the morning when he would have to leave her.

"I'll come back, Darling. Don't worry about me."

She knew he was referring to Vietnam. Two of the friends he'd known in college had joined up and one had been killed. She thought then that if anything happened to Oliver she'd want to die too. Instinctively she moved closer and he wrapped his long arms around her, kissing her on the forehead.

"Oh Oliver, nothing must happen t you. I don't want you to go. Why in the world did you have to join the army?"

"Bad impulse, Darling, just mad at my folks and figured that it was the one way I could get away. If I'd thought it through, maybe I would have made a different decision. I wanted us to be together. I didn't get the idea of getting married that day until later. Guess I really made a mess of it. You're not sorry we married, are you?"

"You did what you did, Oliver, but I'm not sorry, about the wedding, I mean. I just can't bear to think of you going overseas to that horrible war."

"I'll be back before you know it. When my folks get to know you, I know they'll love you as much as I do."

"So, where were you?" Allison's voice pierced her consciousness.

Kathryn looked at her daughter. "Hmm? Oh, years back. I was thinking of when Oliver brought me home to meet his parents. I know this time will be different, but I can't seem to shake this uneasiness.

Maybe I shouldn't have come."

"You always worry about things that never happen."

"Oh, I don't know, maybe worrying about them keeps them from happening."

Kathryn was silent for a few moments, watching the cars ahead of them. "You know what has always bothered me most?"

"What's that?"

"There were no personal effects, no dog tags or anything. You said Thea told you that there was nothing of Oliver's returned from Vietnam."

"Mom, maybe there wasn't anything, to find, He might have carried his personal things in his backpack or whatever he carried. They would have been destroyed when the helicopter exploded"

She sighed heavily. "Yes, I've thought of that a thousand times. I've even dreamed of an explosion, of Oliver calling out to me. There were flames all around him and he was hurt. When Oliver died before I could even tell him we were going to have a baby, I wanted to die, too. I think I might have done something foolish, but I kept thinking I had to take care of myself for your sake. It was the thought of having you to at least remember him by that kept me going."

She remembered how Alma's faith and quiet strength had seen her through those dark days after the news of Oliver's death. Then she and her sister Ruth had to face the tragedy of the Miller's death three years later.

"After Alma and Fred were killed I didn't know what to do. I thought I needed to get away. If your Aunt Ruth hadn't given me her share of the house proceeds and the furnishings, I couldn't have bought the lovely old house we live in now."

"What did Aunt Ruth say about this Thanksgiving?"

"Oh, I've kept her posted on all fronts. She can hardly believe, not only the change in your grandmother, but the fact that she'd invited me for Thanksgiving!"

Allison laughed. "What are she and Uncle Matt doing for the holiday?"

"They're going to his brother's house in Santa Maria. He has a big family and she feels comfortable with them. She sent her love."

As they entered Oakland and drove into the Piedmont area, Allison asked, "Do you remember any of this?"

Kathryn shook her head. "No, I was engrossed in Oliver and feeling uneasy about meeting his parents. I couldn't have found the house again if my life depended on it."

Now, as they pulled into the gravel driveway, Kathryn felt the same sense of apprehension she'd felt the first time they'd arrived here. She looked at the huge Georgian style house and felt panic rise that threatened to overwhelm her.

FIFTY-FOUR

As Jason turned off the motor, the front door of the house opened and a tall, lean man came out. Kathryn gasped. Mr. Culpepper! Then a small dignified-looking woman followed him out onto the porch. Oliver's mother had changed little in all these years. Kathryn put a smile on her face and prepared to get out of the car. "Help, Lord," she whispered under her breath.

She watched Thea welcome Allison and Jason warmly and felt a little encouraged.

Thea turned to Jason. "Are you going to keep my great-grandson in the car all day?"

Jason grinned, got Joshua out of the car seat and brought him to her.

The little boy looked at Thea with wide eyes and she beamed at him. "Hello, Joshua. I'm glad to have you at my house. Would you like to come in and have some cookies?"

Joshua understood the word 'cookies'. He leaned towards Thea's outstretched arms and she gathered him in a warm hug. Then, looking over Joshua' shoulder Thea suddenly saw Kathryn standing alone by the car.

"Jason, I think Gordon is anxious to see his great-grandson, and Martha has the cookies waiting in the kitchen."

He took the baby and gave Kathryn an encouraging smile.

"Let's go, Cully, I never liked to let good cookies go to waste." The two men went into the house.

Thea watched them go a moment and then turned back and smiled tentatively at Kathryn.

"Welcome my dear." She held out her hand as she came down the steps.

Kathryn hesitated a moment and then moved forward to grasp Thea's hand.

"Kathryn, when you agreed to come, I rehearsed so many things that I wanted to say to you. Mostly to tell you how sorry I am for the grief we caused you. 'I'm sorry' seems grossly inadequate."

Kathryn gave her a tentative smile. "Thank you for the phone call. After I hung up, I guess I spent a lot of time thinking of what I might say also."

"Will you forgive us, Kathryn? We thought we were doing the right thing. We thought we were doing what was best for Oliver."

"I forgave you both a long time ago, Thea. It's just that as we were coming here, my emotions were in a bit of a tumble. Perhaps it's best to just say we've forgiven each other, and what is past is past."

Overcome with emotion, Thea could only nod and hold out her arms.

The two women embraced as Allison watched with tears in her eyes.

She snapped pictures of the two of them together. It was a historic family moment.

As the women moved towards the porch, Allison turned to her grandmother.

"How is Grandfather doing? Is he all right?"

"He's about the same, Allison. He's waiting in the library."

They went into the house and entered the library. Jason had put Joshua in Gordon's lap and the little boy was watching his great-grandfather with curiosity. With one small hand he reached out and touched Gordon's face. "Bah, bah, bah" he warbled.

Gordon's face was a picture of delight. Absorbed in the little boy, he suddenly became aware others had entered the room. His eyes lit up when he saw Allison and she gave him a hug and kissed him on top of the head. Then he looked past Allison to the other woman with his wife.

"Grandfather, you remember my mother, Kathryn?"

As Kathryn neared, her face softened. Putting out her hand, she hesitated, but only for a moment. "Mr. Thornwell?"

"Gordon."

"Gordon, then."

Emotions came too easily after the stroke and at her tone of compassion, two tears rolled down his cheek.

"Dear girl," he rasped, clasping her hand warmly.

Joshua looked from one to the other and then patted Kathryn on the face and smiled at Gordon. Then he put his arms out for his Grandma Kathryn to pick him up. She hugged him as he played with her earrings.

Jason slid his arm around Allison as they enjoyed the moment.

Just then Cully interrupted, retuning with the housekeeper.

"Noreen, will you show Mrs. Thornwell to the blue room? I'm sure she'd like to freshen up and get her things settled."

"Of course, madam."

She smiled at them all, a marvelous change in the dour woman they had met the first night she and Jason stayed with her grandparents.

Kathryn followed Noreen out of the room and started up the stairs as Jason and Cully brought in the luggage. About half-way up, Kathryn paused, her eyes wide as realization dawned on her. *Mrs. Thornwell?* She turned and looked back at Thea, who had come to the foot of the stairs.

"Thank you," she whispered.

Thea gave her an almost imperceptible nod.

After she got settled, Kathryn crossed the hall to Oliver's room. The door was part way open and she saw Allison taking some things to the closet. Oliver's clothes were gone.

Allison waved at the empty closet. "It was a big step for grandmother, but she finally had the courage to do it."

"They were still there when you were here last?"

Her daughter nodded.

As they worked together to set up the portable crib, Allison sighed. "I wish I'd kept just one item of clothing as a memento."

"Perhaps its best, to let the past be the past, I'm surprised Thea kept them so long."

Allison changed Joshua who'd been playing on the floor and wrestled the squirming little boy into some clean clothes. Pacifying him with his favorite toy, a white teddy bear, Kathryn carried him back downstairs. Thea was alone in the living room laying out family albums. She looked up and beamed at them.

"I thought perhaps you might like to see some of the pictures of Oliver, when he was growing up, Kathryn."

"Yes, thank you, I would."

Allison looked at the albums. "I just hope Joshua doesn't tear anything. He's a little hard on paper things."

"We'll just keep them out of reach." She held out an animal cracker. "How about a little something to nibble on, Joshua?"

Allison put him down and he promptly crawled over to his great-grandmother and pulled himself up by her lap, eagerly reaching for the treat.

"I believe he takes after his father in quite a few ways, Allison."

"If you mean cookies, you're right. I can see myself in the years to come, chained to the kitchen stove, baking batch after batch to keep the cookie jar full!"

Thea chuckled and picked up a velvet bag from the couch. As she opened it and pulled out several ropes of brightly colored glass beads, she kept an eye on Joshua for his reaction. Leaning over, she piled them on the floor. Joshua was fascinated. He sat down and ran his hands over the smooth beads and began to examine them.

"That should occupy him for a little while." Thea looked pleased that he liked them. "Oliver used to play with these when he was a baby,"

Kathryn was soon perusing albums as Thea identified various times and places. Thea had guessed right. Kathryn wanted to see anything that had to do with Oliver. Once Kathryn glanced up and saw Thea watching her face as she looked through the photographs, and realized that at last Thea could share the love of her son and her grief with one who understood.

Joshua was rubbing his eyes and Allison picked him up and

cuddled him. "I think he needs another nap." In spite of her best efforts, she yawned.

Kathryn smiled. "Why don't you take a nap while Joshua is down? He does take a lot of your energy."

"I think I will, Mother. I'm so tired these days. Guess I do chase him around a lot."

She took Joshua back upstairs.

Thea turned to Kathryn and gave her a tentative smile. They needed to talk but neither seemed to know how to begin.

As Kathryn gathered up the glass beads for something to do, Thea took the opening gambit.

"Kathryn, do you mind if I ask you a question?"

She sat back, her face wary. "What did you want to ask?"

Thea took a deep breath. "How did you hear the news about Oliver? We were notified by an Army telegram."

Kathryn looked down at her lap for a moment and sighed. "One letter got through to me before he left for Vietnam. He hadn't been able to reach me and had not heard from me either."

Thea shook her head slightly in anguish. Kathryn realized it was hard for her to hear.

"You got a letter from Oliver?"

"Yes." She looked Thea full in the face and saw her wince at the words, "Oliver was heartbroken and thought I'd taken your check. It was so sad and he didn't seem to care about anything anymore. My godfather, Edwin Miller, got his military address for me and I wrote to him right away. I wanted to tell him we were going to have a baby, that I loved him with all my heart, and that I didn't take the check. The letter came back marked "deceased, return to sender." That's how I knew that he was gone."

Thea's eyebrows went up. "You wrote a letter to Oliver in Vietnam that came back marked "deceased"? Can you remember when this was?"

Kathryn thought for a moment. "Well, a couple of weeks or so after I mailed it. Just long enough for it to get there and then be returned. Sometime in late September, I think. I guess he was, I mean, he died shortly after he got there, didn't he?"

Kathryn hesitated for there was a strange look on Thea's face. "When did you and Gordon hear that Oliver had died?"

"The telegram didn't come until January, four months later."

Kathryn wrinkled her brow. "Four months? It wouldn't take the Army that long to notify you. I don't understand."

"Oliver didn't answer our letters those first few months, but neither were they returned." Thea signed heavily. "I imagine that he was very angry with us. He had a right to be. It was a terrible thing that we did, and yet we thought it was the best thing for Oliver. We did love him, Kathryn."

Kathryn put a comforting hand on Thea's arm. "I know you did. Oliver loved you too. You just weren't communicating on the same level." Kathryn was silent a moment, and her face took on a puzzled look. "You know, this seems strange. Why would my letter be returned right away and your letters not be? They would have returned your letters too."

Thea remained silent, watching the realization dawn on the younger woman's face. Hot tears stung Kathryn's eyes. She put her hand over her mouth and the words were only a whisper,

"Unless he was..."

Thea bravely finished the sentence for her. "Unless he was angry, and hurt, and thought the letter contained something he didn't want to see."

Kathryn stared at her for a moment of disbelief. Putting her face in her hands she let out a cry of anguish. "Oh no! Oh Oliver!"

Thea hesitated and then impulsively reached out and put her arms around her daughter-in-law. Kathryn's shoulders shook with sobs and pain.

When her tears subsided, Thea handed her some tissues from a box on the table and wiped her own eyes with a handkerchief from her pocket. "I'm so sorry, I didn't realize--"

"How could you know. We were miles apart and had no contact

with each other."

"Kathryn, that is not like Oliver at all. Did you check the handwriting?"

"I was too numb with grief. It didn't occur to me Then a thought struck Kathryn, "Did the telegram say how Oliver died?"

"Only that he had been killed in action. Then I got a follow up letter from Oliver's commanding officer who told me that the helicopter Oliver was riding in was shot down by enemy fire and there were no survivors."

"Oh my goodness, it's just like my dream. An explosion and Oliver calling out to me, and fire--"

"Perhaps you had a premonition."

"It was very real. I had the same dream several times, then friends at church prayed for me and it stopped."

"Well, I'm sure if Oliver had survived his commanding officer would not have written me what he did."

"No, of course not. Did he say where Oliver's helicopter went down?"

"I don't know, dear, I didn't think to ask. I was so caught up in my grief all I could think of was that my son was dead."

"I can understand that." She thought a moment, "I imagine the helicopter was taking Oliver and some other soldiers to a new camp or something."

"That's the heartbreaking part. They were going to be sent home. There were peace talks in January in Paris, and a cease fire had just been signed. The US was pulling our boys out of Vietnam."

It was almost too much to take in. Kathryn took a deep breath to compose herself and put her hand on Thea's arm. "It has been hard talking about Oliver, and especially to learn what he did. What he did was cruel, but I think I understand why he did it and how he was feeling at the time. I believe I can forgive him."

"We must think of the good memories, Kathryn."

"Yes, and I need to get on with my life and let Oliver go. I do have some very special memories that I have treasured over the years."

"I need to let go also, Kathryn. I have carried so much guilt and anguish. Not a day goes by that I don't wish I could turn the clock back and do it all differently."

Kathryn gave her a watery smile. "I think we would all like to have "overs" in some way or another, but we have to live in today."

"Yes, you're right, my dear. The most important thing is what God has done in our family. We can meet again under different circumstances and forgive one another. That means a great deal to me, Kathryn."

"And to me too."

Kathryn reached out and put her arms around her mother-in-law and Thea returned the hug."

"If you don't mind, Thea, I think I'll rest a while before dinner."

"That's fine, dear. This has been an emotional time for both of us."

At the top of the stairs she met Allison coming out of Oliver's room.

Kathryn hesitated, looking past Allison to the bedroom.

Seeing the expression on her mother's face, Allison stepped aside.

"The baby is still sleeping but you're welcome to come in."

Kathryn hung back and then slowly entered Oliver's room.

The women spent a long moment looking down at the child they doted on so much. With his rosy cheeks and long lashes, he looked like a sleeping angel.

Kathryn glanced up at the ceiling at the model airplanes.

"I was surprised they were still here." Then she glanced at the large mahogany bed. Voices from the past seemed to whisper to her.

"Oliver, if anything happened to you I'd want to die too."

"Darling, I'm going to be all right. I'll come back to you."

But it wasn't to be. In those first few weeks after learning of Oliver's death she remembered how her godmother sat up the first night with her listening to the heartbreaking sobs, and praying.

Kathryn's thoughts were interrupted as Allison put a hand on her arm, her face a picture of concern.

"Are you all right, Mother?"

She looked about the room, seemingly distracted. "Oh, of course, I'm just going to lie down awhile before dinner."

As Kathryn turned to leave the room, she gave Allison a reassuring hug. "I'm all right. I just need a little rest."

Once the door to her room was closed, Kathryn put her fist to her mouth as the anguish rose up again.

"Oh Oliver, how could you?" and she let the tears fall.

FIFTY- FIVE

Oliver and Kim-Anh stood very still. Oliver's heart was pounding. Which direction was it coming from? He cocked his head, listening, as the strange growling came again.

"Something's wrong, Kim-Anh."

"It is coming from that direction, Father." She pointed to their right.

Oliver saw a large narrow branch lying on the ground that had broken off a nearby tree. He pulled the leaves from it and gripped it firmly. At least he had some kind of a weapon.

"Stay behind me, we don't know what we're going to find." Cautiously they started in the direction they'd heard the cry come from.

The forest was deadly silent and Oliver felt the hairs on his neck rise. This may be foolish, but he felt it was better to confront the animal than have it stalk them.

Suddenly the animal growled again right in front of them and Oliver stopped so suddenly, Kim-Anh crashed into him. Remembering his jungle training years ago, Oliver moved forward slowly, watching where he put each step. Kim-Anh stayed close behind. If the big cat had not cried out again, they would have fallen right into a pit that had been dug and carefully concealed with branches. Judging from the hole in the center, the animal had fallen in. Oliver leaned over and peered into the pit. Two yellow eyes blazed at him and with a snarl, the leopard leaped at the side of the pit right at them. Fortunately for Oliver, the sides were too steep. Sharp pieces of branch were arranged around the sides of the pit to discourage the animal from climbing out even if it leaped up high enough.

Relieved to find the animal in a pit and not on the trail with them, they gave the pit a wide berth. It was growing late and the shadows made strange shapes on the trail. Looking over their shoulders they hurried on their way. They needed a safe place to spend the night.

"Father, the men who dug that pit cannot be far away. Perhaps we are close to the village the old woman spoke of."

"I hope you're right After an hour, they came through the trees and saw the village. Small children watched their approach with wide eyes, more curious than fearful. A dog barked at them but kept its distance. Women looked up from their cooking fires and observed them quietly.

The Headman of the village came out of one of the stilt-houses and slowly climbed down the ladder. He paused and walked toward them.

"Welcome to our village. Where have you come from?" He spoke in the dialect of the Hmong.

Oliver paused, "We were told we were safe in your village."

"Are you people of the Black Book?"

Kim-Anh whispered, "Believers."

Oliver indicated his daughter. "Honored Sir, my daughter, Kim-Anh is of the Black Book and I am, "he sought for the right word, "listening. My name is Oliver."

The Headman studied them. It was clear to Oliver that their appearance was startling to them, a tall man who was dressed as Hmong but obviously not Vietnamese. His daughter's appearance was different also from anyone the villagers had seen before.

Oliver answered, "I am from a country called America across the great sea. I have lived in Vietnam since the close of the war. We are on our way to return to my home. We need to get across the Black River and into Lao to the Mekong. From there we go to Thailand. Do you have a boat that can take us across the river?"

The Headman studied Oliver a moment. "We take many of the Black Book across. We have boats, but," he eyed Oliver's embroidered clothes, "it is not good that you wear those clothes so far from the mountains."

Oliver saw the wisdom in the Headman's words. In the native clothes of Thuan's people with its bright embroidery, he would certainly stand out among the simple villagers along the river.

Before Oliver could answer, the Headman turned to a young man behind him and spoke a few words. The young man hurried off instantly.

In a few minutes the young man was back with another man. He was tall for Lao but a few inches shorter than Oliver. He carried some clothing, loose pants and a couple of shirts. He smiled broadly.

"You are welcome to these."

He handed the clothing to Oliver and pointed towards his stilted house.

"Thank you." Oliver shrugged. "You are welcome to our present clothes, we need to travel lightly." Perhaps the villager could sell them in the marketplace.

The man obviously admired the intricate beadwork on the vest that Oliver wore and grinned, realizing he was getting the better of the bargain. Oliver was in no position to barter, so they climbed the ladder to the man's house and changed, Oliver turning his back to give Kim-Anh a little privacy.

When they came back down the ladder, the women tittered and smiled. The pants were a little short but the shirts seemed comfortable enough.

The Headman grinned widely, revealing his missing teeth. "It is good. You will eat with us and sleep in our village. Tomorrow you will cross the river."

The women brought cooked rice with bits of fish in it and banana pancakes. Kim-Anh relished everything she ate but Oliver ate sparingly of the banana pancakes. They were doughy and not cooked all the way through. He knew they were common among the Vietnamese and Lao, but he'd never gotten used to them. With a smile he ate heartily, letting the village women see that he enjoyed the food. He would deal with his stomach later.

They sat with the Headman and some of the men of the village, talking as the dusk gathered around them.

"Your daughter knows the God of the Black Book. It is in her face.

Oliver glanced at Kim-Anh. Yes, it was true. He had seen her faith and the strength she'd showed so far. Not a word of complaint had he heard since they left Sa Pa.

The Headman studied Oliver. "You will know Him soon, Tall One." He gave them a toothless smile.

Oliver thought about the doctors coming to Sa Pa. Even as he recalled the words of Doctor Jensen, he suddenly knew the hand of God was on his life. Events like pieces of a puzzle had been moved into place one by one. How could he have been so stubborn.

He told the men about their journey and how grateful they were for all the help they'd been given.

The man who brought the clothes was Ling Ta. He nodded with understanding as he listened to Oliver, then he spoke. "A missionary came to our village. Many took the God of the black book for their own. My family and I believe, and many others in the village believe. We are glad to help you return to your family. You have much to share with them. We will pray that your journey is good and that you will be soon in your own land."

Oliver nodded thoughtfully. "Thank you, my friend. We will need your prayers."

Kim-Anh watched his face as they sat in Ling Ta's house where two pallets had been placed on the floor. "You have many thoughts tonight, Father."

He gave her a rueful smile. "I'm thinking what a stubborn fool I've been. God has taken care of us in so many ways. I'm sorry I have put Him off for so long." He felt a little sheepish, but the question had to be asked. He could not rest until he knew.

As his daughter smiled slowly with understanding, she put her hand in his. "Yes, Father?"

"How do you become a believer?"

The words, "and a little child shall lead them," came to mind as he bowed his head. He repeated the words haltingly as Kim-Anh spoke them, and with growing joy, Oliver entered the kingdom of God.

FIFTY-SIX

With a strange sense of lightness, Oliver knew he was changed forever. Later, as he looked down on the face of his sleeping daughter, he bowed his head and murmured softly, "Lord, I'm new at this and I don't know what lies ahead, but I'm going to trust You with our lives. I believe You will see us safely home. Give us a safe journey, Lord, and favor us with help when we arrive in Thailand. Thank you for your care so far. We are in Your hands. Amen."

In the morning two of the villagers took them in a long wooden boat that had a covered bamboo canopy towards the stern. One man poled the boat through the current with a long pole as two others paddled. Fortunately the Black River was not in flood stage and the ride across with the current was fairly easy.

The villagers deposited them on the other side at a specific place where a trail began and wished them well on their journey. The women had given them some packets of food, cooked rice, some fruit, dried meat and two loaves of bread. It was enough food to last several days. After thanking the men for their help, Oliver listened to the careful instructions of Ling Ta that would take them to the border of Laos.

They traveled almost two days, spending the night in a secluded place off the trail among the trees where Oliver felt it would be safe. He took the first watch, urging his daughter to get some rest. Towards morning, Oliver woke her and after making sure she was alert, caught a short nap for himself.

As they continued along the trail, they noted with some apprehension that they were nearly out of food and water. If he had seen the maps and understood the vast distance they were to travel from the mountains of Vietnam bordering China, to the border of Laos, a distance of over three hundred and fifty miles, he would have felt even more apprehensive. Oliver had been looking for the next guide but no one had appeared. They walked steadily all the next day, pausing only briefly to rest and eat, driven by an urgency they both seemed to sense. They must get to their destination as quickly as possible.

The late afternoon shadows grew longer, and they began to look for another safe place to spend the night. As they sat on a fallen log discussing their limited options, Oliver gave an involuntary shudder, something was wrong. Kim-Anh sat quietly, munching on the last of the bread. She didn't appear to be aware of any danger. Oliver began to glance slowly around, not wanting to alarm her. Had another leopard decided to stalk them? He'd kept the walking stick he'd picked up when they first found the leopard in the pit. The hair on the back of his neck stood up and his hand tightened on the stick. His muscles tensed, ready to spring into action. Before he could move, men materialized from among the trees.

They were surrounded and there was no chance of escape.

FIFTY-SEVEN

Though dinner was pleasant and friendly, Kathryn still felt a touch of reserve in the conversation. Martha, preparing for their Thanksgiving feast the next day, kept dinner fairly simple with lamb chops, rice, asparagus and a salad. Kathryn had an aversion to lamb but didn't want to say anything. She slathered on lots of mint jelly and washed it down with iced tea. Feeling rather proud of herself for being so unobtrusive, she glanced up to see Allison suppressing a smile. She knew her mother's feelings for lamb.

They adjourned to the library with Joshua after dinner and the entire family delighted in entertaining him. Joshua gleefully waddled from one to the other gleaning hugs and loving words of encouragement.

Thea bent down and put the ropes of glass beads on the floor and once again Joshua was fascinated by their sparkling colors.

"Bah, bah," he chortled happily.

Kathryn's eyes were on Joshua, but unseeing. She finally looked up to see Allison watching her with a puzzled expression on her face, and Kathryn realized she'd been brooding. She glanced at Thea who was also watching her with concern. Kathryn couldn't seem to shake what she and Thea had talked about earlier in the day.

As Cully came to get Gordon to take him to his room and prepare him for bed, Allison gave her grandfather a warm hug and kiss. Joshua was lifted up to give his grandfather a wet kiss on the cheek and with the 'goodnights' from the assembled family echoing in his ears, he was wheeled from the room.

Kathryn also bid Thea goodnight, but as she went to hug her daughter, Allison whispered, "I need to talk to you."

Kathryn nodded.

Allison yawned in spite of her valiant efforts to stifle it. "Guess I'd better call it a night too. Joshua has been up later than he is used to and he'll be up early tomorrow."

Thea gave her a hug and accepted a kiss from Joshua. "Get your sleep, dear, we have a big day tomorrow."

"Jason?"

"I'm not ready to come up yet, Sweetheart, I'll stay down here for a while. If Thea gets tired of me, I'll do some reading."

Thea waved a hand at him. "You can help me put all these albums away, young man."

"My pleasure."

Kathryn went to the guest room and was taking off her jewelry when Allison stuck her head in the door. "Mother?"

She kissed her grandson goodnight and smiled at Allison.

"Why don't you put Joshua down to sleep and then come over?"

"All right."

From across the hall Kathryn could hear the faint sounds of Allison singing Joshua's favorite song, "You Are My Sunshine."

Then Allison came across the hall.

"Is Joshua asleep already?"

"Out like a light. All the attention and activity got to him."

She closed the door behind her and they went across the room and sat in the two chairs by the window.

"What did you want to talk to me about?"

"You seemed pre-occupied all evening. I was wondering if you were all right. Did Grandmother say anything to upset you?"

Kathryn stared at the carpet and sighed. "No. Not deliberately. It was just some information she shared with me that was a little difficult."

"Do you feel like telling me about it?"

Kathryn was silent a moment and then shrugged. "It was finding out the difference in time between when I got the letter with 'deceased' written on it and the time your grandmother was notified of your father's death."

She told Allison what she had just learned. Allison went down on her knees and hugged her tightly. When at last Kathryn spoke again, she held Allison away from her by the shoulders. "Don't blame your father, Allison. He was deeply hurt and convinced that I'd left him and taken the money from his parents. He just reacted out of his own pain."

"But to let you think he was dead. That was so cruel."

"And not like your father at all. He was a kind man who would never deliberately hurt anyone. I believe his heart was broken over what he felt I had done to him. I'm sure he regretted his action many times over."

"Then he was killed before he could come back and make it right."

"Had he lived, I'm sure he would have come back and looked me up, or tried to find out the truth."

Allison got up off her knees and sat back in the chair. They both stared out into the darkness and listened to the wind fling the rain against the windowpane.

"No wonder you were so silent this evening. You had a lot of things to think about, didn't you?"

"I guess I did." Kathryn shook her head. "This is too much emotion for one day. I'm exhausted, time to get some sleep." She stood up and gave Allison another hug.

"You are a comfort. I feel better getting it off my chest. Good night, dear."

"Good night, Mom."

Kathryn returned to the room and prepared for bed but her mind was busy with thoughts of Oliver. She pictured him getting her letter, holding it in his hand, his temptation to open it and then maybe flinging it down on his bunk. She could see him with the pen, angrily writing 'deceased' on the outside. Had he lain on his bunk as she laid in bed now, thinking of the letter he'd returned and wondering what it contained? The letter was so full of love for him. The letter told the truth about the check she'd never taken. A letter that told him he was going to be a father. He'd never read it and never knew that his anguish was unfounded.

FIFTY-EIGHT

Joshua is as reliable as a barnyard rooster, Kathryn thought to herself as she lay in bed and listened to her small grandson across the hall. She could imagine him dancing in his crib, beaming and cooing at his sleepy parents.

"Hi, hi..." She could hear him saying, over and over.

There was a murmur of voices. Allison and Jason were up.

Suddenly there was thump from Oliver's room and after a few moments Kathryn could hear the cries of her small grandson. She put on her robe and went to tap lightly on the door.

"Is everything okay?"

Jason scratched his head and with a rueful smile beckoned her to come in. "Sorry if we woke you up. We had a small catastrophe. I wish he could learn the difference between a work day and a holiday."

Kathryn laughed. "If you can teach him that you'll make history."

She looked past him to where Allison was sitting on the bed with a teary-eyed little boy who was holding a black and white velour rabbit. Its ears were about six inches long and the black button eyes were intact. Though a little worn in places, it seemed in good condition.

Joshua held his arms out to his grandmother, his lower lip quivering. She went to him and picked him up.

Allison sighed. "He's not hurt. He just got into a box in the closet of my father's old toys. He found this rabbit and has taken possession. I hope it will be okay with my grandmother. I don't know what the box of toys was there for."

Jason disappeared into the bathroom to shave and shower as Allison got out some clothes for Joshua and changed his diaper.

"What happened to his bear?" Joshua was never parted from his bear.

"He's fascinated with this rabbit, Mom. It looked like I was going to start a small war to try to take it away from him. The bear seems to have gone by the wayside, at least for now."

"Let me get dressed, dear, and I'll take Joshua downstairs for his breakfast and give you time by yourself to get ready."

"That would be fantastic. Thanks, Mom." Allison gave her a hug.

Kathryn dressed quickly and put on some light make-up. Her beauty routine never took long for as each day began she was always anxious to get going. She went back, picked up Joshua who was chattering away at his rabbit, and took him downstairs.

Joshua hung on to his toy with one arm and put his other arm around Kathryn's neck. When they reached the kitchen, Noreen was waiting and beamed. The little boy had brought out all her maternal instincts and she looked forward to feeding him his meals.

"Joshua got into the closet and dumped a box over. I think Thea was saving some of Oliver's childhood things. Now that Joshua's found the bunny he doesn't want to let go of it."

"Well," she said, nuzzling her nose against Joshua's cheek, "I don't think it'll be a problem."

"Bye, Bye." Joshua waved over Noreen's shoulder as she settled him in his high chair with a bib. She placed the rabbit on the table just out of the little boy's reach and bribed him with pancakes to occupy his fingers. She assured him he could have his rabbit back when he didn't have sticky fingers. Joshua seemed to understand that his new toy had to wait until after breakfast. It was going to be hard on Noreen when they all had to leave. She'd become so attached to Joshua.

As she turned towards the dining room she nearly ran into Thea, standing in the doorway.

"Good morning, dear, how did you sleep?"

"A little restless, I think."

Thea nodded. "I see Joshua found the stuffed rabbit. He's welcome to keep it. It was Oliver's. As I recall, he carried it everywhere when he was a little boy. I just couldn't bring myself to send those things with the charity truck. When Allison asked me to keep the model planes hanging from the ceiling, I thought, well, maybe one day Joshua might enjoy the toys too. He's too young for the toy soldiers and games but I'd forgotten about the rabbit. I'm glad he likes it."

After breakfast the weather had improved and Jason and Allison took Joshua for a walk. Left to herself, Kathryn went into the library, to look for a book to read. She found an old favorite by Gladys Tabor, a well-known author on Americana in the sixties, and settled down by the small fireplace in an easy chair.

She'd been reading about a half an hour when there was the sound of the front door bursting open and laughter as Allison and Jason dashed in out of the sudden rainfall with Joshua.

She went to meet them. "My goodness, you weren't trying to go for a walk in that, were you?" Her eyes took in the drops of water on the entry floor.

Allison sighed. "Well, it wasn't raining when we started out. We've all been cooped up in the house. It seemed like a good idea at the time."

"Well, you didn't get too wet, but you better get some dry clothes on. We have some time. I think Thea said we were going to eat around four o'clock."

As Joshua rubbed his eyes and reached out towards his mother, Jason ruffled his son's hair. "You go with Mommy, big boy, and have a good nap. We have big day ahead."

They watched Allison go upstairs with Joshua, his new bunny dangling over her shoulder.

Kathryn had taken a short afternoon nap and then sat in the window seat reading the book she'd found in the library until dinner time.

She slipped on a soft blue wool dress with a squared neckline and three-quarter length sleeves.

Once again she went to get Joshua who waved his bunny up and down, looking from one smiling face to another. He was dressed in a little pair of boy's slacks with a short-sleeved white shirt and a clip-on tie. Kathryn thought he looked adorable. Jason slipped an arm around her waist and gave her a quick hug. "You look nice, Mom."

Joshua babbled, and banged his rabbit on Kathryn's shoulder.

"I think he approves too, Mom."

Kathryn beamed at them. "Well, now that I have the approval of the two most special men in my life, I'd better take him downstairs."

As they came into the dining room, Cully was placing bowls and platters on the table. The fruit and nut gelatin salad sparkled on fresh lettuce leaves, the garlic in the mashed potatoes gave a pungent smell, the orange slices glistened on the candied yams, and the fresh green beans lent more color to the table. The turkey, beautifully browned, was served on a silver platter. A large bowl of cornbread stuffing looked tempting. Dessert was on the sideboard; pumpkin and minced pies along with the pumpkin pecan cheesecake. It was almost too pretty to spoil by eating.

Cully had earlier murmured a few pointers in Jason's ear on carving the turkey with the gleaming silver carving knife and fork, and with a grin, Jason assured him he was up to the job.

Joshua was allowed to join them and with a small plastic tablecloth placed under his chair, was seated between Allison and Jason. Thea had made it plain that since Noreen had no family she was part of the Thornwell family now and would join them at the table.

Cully fed Gordon earlier and now wheeled him in to take his place at the table. He would just sip his coffee from a special container during dinner.

"Jason, would you ask the blessing?"

"Be glad to, Thea."

Joining hearts and hands, the family bowed their heads and Jason returned thanks to their Lord and Savior; for the family gathered there, for the bounty of the food placed before them and for the hands that prepared it. Just as he came to the end of the prayer, he squeezed Gordon's hand. "Sir?"

Gordon understood and sat a little taller in his chair. With dignity he closed the prayer with a firm, "Ahhmehennn..."

Kathryn turned to Thea. "The whole table looks lovely; you must have spent a lot of time planning this."

Warmed by Kathryn's genuine enthusiasm, Thea acknowledged her comment with a slight wave of her hand and a smile. "It was my pleasure. I haven't had so much fun planning a dinner in a long time."

Kathry realized the family scene after Thanksgiving dinner could have been repeated in households all over the country. Quiet conversations, Thea knitting an afghan, she, Allison and Jason playing a game of Scrabble, Gordon cheering them on when someone made an especially good word. Noreen entertained Joshua with some story books and some of Oliver's old blocks.

After an hour or so, Gordon's strength gave out and Thea rang for Cully to wheel him out and prepare him for bed. It was easier for Cully now, for with the advice of Gordon's doctor, they had rented a hoist that would lift Gordon from his chair to the bed, which saved Cully's back considerable strain.

Thea told them that after the holidays she was going to bring in a day care person for Gordon. "Edward is just doing too much. We're all getting on in years and none of us can handle him alone."

Kathryn glanced over at Joshua who was rubbing his eyes. Noreen brought him to Allison and he put an arm out to her, hugging his bunny with the other.

"My little man is sleepy? Time to tell everyone goodnight." She took Joshua to his great-grandmother and daddy for a kiss before taking him up to bed.

Jason kissed Allison good-night and picked up a book he'd been reading off and on. "I'll be up in a while, Sweetheart."

Thea went down the hall to check on Gordon and the light went out in the kitchen. The Culpeppers were finished for the day.

Kathryn went back to the library. It was too early for her to go to bed and she absorbed herself in her book. In time, she got up and stretched and went to the window, looking out at the darkness.

The rain appeared to have stopped and it was quiet, yet there was something moving in the air. A light dusting of snow covered the windowsill outside. She pressed her face to the window and saw the yard covered with a soft coating of white. The first snowfall of the season had finally come. She thought of the things that the fresh white snow covered, making everything seem so fresh and new. It was like the fresh start that she and Thea had found after all these years. Perhaps, now, she could finally let Oliver go. She stared out at the snow for a long time.

FIFTY-NINE

As the sun rose the day after Thanksgiving, Kathryn awakened and lay quietly, listening to a bird trilling its song outside her window. At least it was not raining. Then, seeing the touch of white on the windowsill, she remembered it had snowed. The house was peacefully silent. In her mind she went over the events of the last two days. It had been an emotional time, but she marveled at the work God had done in all their lives. She thought of Allison contacting her grandparents, the Thornwell's acceptance of her as their granddaughter, the invitation for Thanksgiving, and most of all, the amazing reconciliation between her and the Thornwells. If anyone had told her a year ago where she'd be for this Thanksgiving, she would not have believed it.

Kathryn went over to stare out the window. The snow covered the yard, marred only by the tiny footprints of the birds. The sun went behind a cloud and all was suddenly gray and overcast. As she watched, the rain started again, spoiling the picture perfect scene she had enjoyed only moments before. It was washing away the snow.

Gordon joined them at the breakfast table. He was surprisingly silent, listening to each of them intently.

"House will be quiet now," he finally garbled.

Allison reached out and patted his hand. "We'll come back soon, Grandfather."

When breakfast was over, Kathryn went up to finish packing but since Noreen had Joshua in the kitchen, Jason and Allison remained at the table talking to her grandparents for a while.

When Kathryn came downstairs, Edward was carrying Kathryn's bags.

"Call me to let me know you're home safe, will you?" Thea looked up at the gray clouds that threatened another storm.

It had been a tearful farewell for Thea and Kathryn, bonded

finally by the one they both loved. Bundled up against the chill, even Gordon had insisted on being wheeled out on the front porch to say goodbye.

"Will you be all right, Kathryn?"

"I'll be all right. It's time to let Oliver go and get on with my life. This time here has helped me do that. Thank you, Thea."

Thea hugged her, and then turned to Allison.

"I wish you didn't have to leave so soon."

"Bye, bye-bye" crowed Joshua as he waved to his great-grandparents. Kathleen and Martha came out to say goodbye as Cully helped Jason put the luggage and folding crib in the car.

Jason rubbed his chin and looked the car over. I think we have everything."

As Allison carried Joshua towards the car Thea noticed that the little boy was hugging his white bear again. The velour bunny was nowhere in sight. "What happened to the you-know-what?"

Allison spread her hands. "That is the strangest thing. He picked up his bear this morning and hasn't looked at the you-know-what at all. I put it back in the toy box."

Thea just shook her head and then waved as Jason started the car. She waved until they were out of sight.

Kathryn settled herself in the back seat to amuse her small grandson on the long trip home. When he dozed off with the motion of the car, she was aware of a profound silence. Each digesting their thoughts of an amazing weekend.

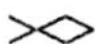

When the car was out of sight, Thea turned and looked up at the house. It had been a shelter that had embraced her new family and given them comfort in times of great change. It had seen anger, betrayal and sorrow, yet it had also seen love, reconciliation and restoration. A spirit of love flowed through the house and the presence of God seemed to permeate its walls. She went in and closed the door behind her.

SIXTY

Gordon and Thea sat in the library by the fire, talking about how well the holiday had gone. Thea looked up as someone rang their front door bell. She wondered if the children had left something behind. Cully entered the library with a puzzled look on his face.

'There is a gentleman at the front door who says he is a missionary doctor recently returned from Vietnam. He wishes to speak with you and Mr. Thornwell. He says it concerns young Oliver." He handed Thea a business card with the name of a medical missionary organization on it.

"Oliver?" Startled, she turned to Gordon, showing him the card.

"Send him in, Edward," Gordon garbled, his face hard.

In a moment a distinguished-looking man followed Cully into the room.

"Mr. and Mrs. Thornwell, Dr. Ralph Jensen."

Thea looked the man over and recognized the quality of his clothing. Whoever he was, he was, he didn't appear to be here as a solicitor.

The doctor took in Gordon's condition and the wheelchair. He also noted Gordon's stern perusal. "I assure you, sir, madam, my mission here is honorable." He reached out and shook Gordon's good hand.

Thea remembered her duties as a hostess. "Would you like some coffee, Doctor?"

He smiled. "Yes, thank you. That would be wonderful."

The butler hurried out with the man's hat and overcoat.

"Won't you sit down? What can we do for you, Doctor Jensen? You said something about our son? He's been dead for many years. What information can you possibly bring us?"

The doctor lowered himself slowly in a wing-back chair. "I

wanted to phone first but it seems the number is unlisted. I needed to speak to you as soon as I returned from Vietnam. It is a matter of extreme importance."

Thea was puzzled. "Is it about where Oliver is buried?'

Dr. Jensen's face was kind as he looked down at her. "It's more than that, Mrs. Thornwell. There is no grave."

Thea sat as still as a statue with her back against the straight back chair next to Gordon's, his good left hand gripping hers.

Thea opened her mouth to speak again but Gordon interrupted.

"Yourr newws? Owiverrr?"

The doctor understood perfectly. "Yes, Mr. Thornwell, you want to know why I came. I came in person," He paused, but only for a moment. "Because there is no easy way to say this." He looked at their anxious faces and dropped the bombshell.

"Your son, Mr. and Mrs. Thornwell, is not dead. He is alive in Northern Vietnam."

"Oh my God! Oliver's alive?" Thea gasped and her fist went to her mouth. Gordon's eyes were wide and his mouth worked but no words came out.

Thea stared open-mouthed at the doctor, her eyes pooling with tears. "My son is alive?"

The doctor nodded emphatically. "Yes."

Thea faced the doctor with tears streaming down her face. "The helicopter crashed. How can he be alive after all these years? Was he a prisoner of war?"

The doctor gazed steadily back at her, his face filled with compassion. "No, Mrs. Thornwell. That is why I needed to come in person, to tell Oliver's story."

Gordon hung his head and murmured to himself. Two large tears slid down his cheeks.

The doctor continued. "Oliver survived the crash, but he was badly wounded. When he recovered the war was over. It was difficult to get out of Vietnam because of the communists," the doctor paused momentarily. "And he didn't believe he had a family to come home to."

Thea caught her breath and slowly shook her head, grasping the implications.

"He believed that his wife had left him and filed for an annulment."

Anguish filled Thea's heart. Their well-meaning actions had cost them what was dearest to their hearts and the repercussions were still overwhelming.

The butler returned and placed the coffee tray on the table in front of Thea. Seeing his mistress upset, he poured coffee for the doctor and handed him the cup. He had heard enough to wait quietly in the background to hear more.

Dr. Jensen then related the story of the helicopter crash and how Oliver got away with Jake's help.

When he finished, Thea wiped her eyes with a handkerchief and murmured, "My poor son. He had no food or water?"

"That's right. He would have had what the army calls "Lurp rations" in his rucksack, but those were lost."

Thea frowned. "Lurp rations?"

"L.R.R.P., long range reconnaissance patrol rations."

Gordon spoke up again. "Go awn, Dotorrr."

Dr. Jensen nodded. "He was able to drink a little rain water, but went four days with no food. His injuries were serious and he became delirious and finally fainted just off the trail."

"Was he in Vietnam?"

"Laos. We weren't supposed to be in Laos but then neither were the Vietnamese."

Dr. Jensen leaned forward. "I know you're wondering if the Viet Cong found him. No, the resistance fighters did. During the war the Hmong and many of the mountain tribes worked against the Viet Cong. They saved many pilots who were shot down." He went on to tell how the resistance fighters carried Oliver to a cave, about Thuan, and finally Oliver's following her to Sa Pa.

Thea raised her eyebrows. "And after he went to her village?"

The doctor gave her a steady look. "He married her."

Thea's eyes widened. "Married? Oliver married a Vietnamese woman?"

"You must remember, Mrs. Thornwell, that Oliver was under the impression that he no longer had a wife in the States." The doctor's face was full of compassion.

"This is hard for you, I know, but Oliver was angry with you both for what you did. It wasn't until we met in the village, and Thuan had died..."

"Thuan. Was that his wife?"

"Yes, Mrs. Thornwell. I treated her for cancer, but it was in the advanced stages and all I could do was give her morphine for the pain. She died a few days later. He took it very hard."

"How fortunate though, Doctor, that you came at that time."

Jensen smiled. "I also very carefully contact members of the underground church and share greetings from their brothers and sisters in America. As you know, Vietnam is a communist country and our religion is not welcomed. It is the people of that church, the believers, who are helping Oliver and his daughter escape."

Thea's eyes grew wide. "A daughter? Oliver has a daughter?" She swallowed and took a breath. "By the Vietnamese wife?"

"Yes. Kim-Anh is fifteen. A beautiful young girl and a believer, as was her mother. It is because of them that they are being helped out of Vietnam."

"They were Christians?"

"Yes."

"And they are being helped out of Vietnam? How, doctor?"

Gordon listened stoically, shaking his head slowly from side to side as he gripped Thea's hand.

The doctor continued. "When Thuan died, I received word that Oliver and Kim-Anh were in danger. Oliver's stepson, Chau, is very involved in the communist party. He evidently had been harboring ill feelings towards his stepfather and had an interrogation planned."

"I take it this interrogation was not going to just be questions?"

"You have assumed correctly, Mrs. Thornwell. Oliver was to report to the government office the next morning, supposedly to answer some questions in spite of the fact that Oliver was in his mourning period. That's what made us suspicious. We learned Chau had plans to send his half-sister down to Hanoi with some soldiers. It would have been a horrible fate for her. He'd been jealous of Kim-Anh, and it would have been a cruel way to get even."

Thea suddenly understood. "By sending her to Hanoi, you mean she would have been—"

"Yes."

"And you told Oliver about this?"

"Yes, I believe you understand the situation correctly."

"What did Oliver have to say?"

"We talked at great length and he realized that in order to save Kim-Anh, they would have to leave the village that night. It was the quarter moon and the heaviest darkness. It was not an easy decision, but the only one he could make. Kim-Anh understood what they had to do. She has great faith for one so young."

Thea glanced at Gordon and then stoically faced the doctor. "This news has been overwhelming for us, yet when Oliver returns he will have some difficult news to face himself. He has another daughter, Allison. His wife, Kathryn, never remarried, and believes she is a widow. We discovered she didn't take the check after all, but that's a long story in itself. She gave birth seven and a half months after Oliver left for Vietnam."

Dr. Jensen stared at her. "How did you find out about Kathryn's child?"

"I didn't know about my granddaughter until several months ago when she wrote to me. It seems Kathryn, due to our actions, kept her a secret from us and raised her in a small mountain community. After Allison married and had a small son, Joshua, Kathryn told her about us and she felt led to write to us, revealing who she was. To make a long story short, Oliver has a wife, daughter, son-in-law and grandson. My granddaughter's dear husband led me to the Lord and there has been a wonderful time of reconciliation."

It was a long speech for Thea, and the doctor listened with a startled expression on his face. "Well," he said finally, as he considered the information, "This is wonderful news. We truly serve a loving God. I'm delighted that things are not as I'd expected from talking with Oliver."

Thea leaned forward. "You said the underground church would help Oliver and his daughter out of Vietnam. How?"

"Two of the believers in Sa Pa were going to lead Oliver and his daughter out of the village into the mountains. They planned to get them out of North Vietnam, through the mountains of Laos into Thailand."

Thea frowned. "Isn't there an embassy they could get to?"

"Not a good idea, Ma'am. The mountain people or Black Tai as they are called, don't trust the U.S. Embassy. It is better to get them to Thailand. The royal family of Thailand has contacts throughout Southeast Asia. Oliver and Kim-Anh will be placed in the hands of the King's men."

"The King's men?"

"It is a term which refers to the men who exclusively serve the King of Thailand. The army officers and police know who they are and will not interfere with their actions."

"How will Oliver meet with these men?"

"The mountain people have their contacts. The King's men will know when Oliver and Kim-Anh are in the country. Nothing escapes their notice or information network."

Thea shook her head, trying to process all this information. "They arrive in Thailand, the King's men are notified and then what happens?"

The doctor took another sip of his coffee. "They will be taken to a safe place until arrangements can be made to get them out of the country."

Thea became aware that Edward was still in the room, but seeing the expression on his face as he understood the news about Oliver, she didn't dismiss him. Their eyes met for a moment of understanding and then she turned back to Dr. Jensen.

"Couldn't the American government just fly them home?"

"It's not as easy as that, Mrs. Thornwell, there are many factors to consider. Most of which I cannot go into at this time."

"Then how will they get out of Thailand?"

The doctor smile reassuringly. "Paperwork will be obtained for them and they will either leave via Thai Airlines or there are other transportation avenues that can be used."

"What other transportation avenues?"

"Unfortunately, ma'am, I cannot go into that matter either."

Thea shook her head. "It sounds like some sort of cloak and dagger thing."

Dr. Jensen laughed. "Yes, perhaps it does sound like that." Then his face became sober again. "I can't give you the details because there are thousands of people involved in the underground church. Their lives and their integrity would be compromised. I'm afraid you will have to take my word for it that your loved ones are in good hands and will somehow be brought out of Thailand to the United States. We will let you know the time and place as soon as we have that information."

Thea had been trying to assimilate the doctor's words. Finally she looked him in the eye. "Are there difficulties in getting my son home, Doctor? Will he need money?"

He smiled, obviously anticipating the question. "We will not need funds from you, Mrs. Thornwell, their paperwork and the arrangements will be taken care of by the King's men. When we know where and when Oliver and his daughter will arrive in the States, you can plan to have someone meet them and bring them here. I assume that is where you want them to come."

Thea nodded emphatically. "Of course. This is Oliver's home." She looked the doctor in the eye. "Forgive me, Doctor Jensen, but you must realize that this news of our son is extremely shocking to us. I feel that you're truly who you say you are, but to think that two weeks ago you spoke with Oliver is, well, hard to believe at this point."

"My dear lady, I understand your reluctance. What I've told you would be a shock for any family. Oliver told me you might be skeptical, considering the circumstances. I asked him if there was anything I could tell you that would convince you that he is indeed alive and that I've spoken to him."

The doctor fingered his mustache. "I have no idea who this is, but Oliver just grinned at me and told me to remember him to a Mr. Salty."

Thea gasped and put her hand on her heart. "Mr. Salty? Oh my goodness, I had forgotten that was his name."

Gordon looked at her and frowned, "Mrrr. Sahlty?"

Thea looked at her husband with tears trickling down her cheeks.

"Oh my dear, it was the black and white rabbit Joshua played with. Don't you remember? We gave it to Oliver for his second birthday. He carried it everywhere."

SIXTY-ONE

Gordon appeared agitated, glancing between his wife and the doctor several times, "Owiver--where?"

Thea squeezed her husband's hand. "Yes, Gordon, you want to know more about Oliver." She faced the doctor. "How much time do you feel it will take for Oliver and his daughter to get to the Mekong River and over to Thailand?"

He studied his coffee cup a moment and then looked up. "I'm not sure, Mrs. Thornwell. I don't know how long it will take to get through the mountains. They will have to be cautious. Not only are there bandits, but there are animals to contend with, large animals."

Her eyes widened. "What sort of animals?"

"Bears, leopards, tigers. Just like in our wilderness areas in the States, they usually won't bother a traveler unless wounded or startled. They would just as soon go the other way from humans."

"What can we do, Doctor Jensen? How can we help my son come home?"

"Basically there is little you can do until they reach the States, in whatever way His Majesty chooses to send them."

The doctor put his coffee cup on the tray. "I can understand that my news is a mixed blessing, Mrs. Thornwell. I sought to find a way to cushion the impact of Oliver's survival, but," he emphasized his words, "it has been my experience as a doctor that people want to know the truth, no matter how difficult it may seem. Oliver has lived another lifetime across the world from you, and bringing a half-Vietnamese daughter into your world, will take courage. Your acceptance of Kim-Anh will go a long way in bringing healing to Oliver. He won't come without her."

Thea nodded slowly, appreciating the doctor's words. She wiped her cheek with her fingers, but when she looked at him he had to feel her love and determination. She glanced at Gordon and his eyes shared that determination.

"We'll face Oliver's homecoming together, Doctor." Thea added. "God has not brought us this far without good reason. He will see Oliver home and as we put this all in His hands, I know He'll show us the way."

Gordon gave a sharp nod of his head.

Dr. Jensen appeared relieved. "Good. I've put out feelers and as soon as I hear any feedback on their progress I'll call you. Until then, the most you can do for them is pray."

As Thea wrote their phone number for the doctor, she had another thought. "Will there be a problem with the Army when Oliver returns to his country?"

"The military will eventually want to talk with Oliver. He was wounded just before the war ended. There is a Center for Prisoner of War Studies in Pensacola, Florida at the Naval Air Station. They may send him there eventually to share his story. They will want any information he can give them about the helicopter crash and those on board. They'll also give him a physical examination."

"And what about Kim-Anh?"

"She is the daughter of an American citizen. I don't believe there will be a problem, especially when there is a family of some prominence."

Thea looked at the doctor hopefully. "Should we meet Oliver when he arrives here?"

Dr. Jensen paused a moment, choosing his words carefully. "Mrs. Thornwell, if you would permit me to state an opinion, that would be a little overwhelming. May I suggest a family friend? Give him time to prepare to meet his parents again. A wife he doesn't know he still has, and a child who is grown and married along with a grandson are a lot to take in all at once. I suggest you move with discretion, and prayer."

Thea acknowledged his words with a nod. "That's a good point, Dr. Jensen." She sighed. "I'm going to have to call Kathryn and relate all this to her. She's on her way home with my granddaughter and her husband. They left just before you got here. I wish we'd known you were coming."

"I'm sorry" He looked down at the piece of paper Thea handed him and nodded his thanks. "As you are aware, the number is unlisted and I had no choice but to go by the address Oliver gave me."

Thea rose. "This will be no simple task, Dr. Jensen, but with God's help I will make that call and share what you've told us today."

"God will give you the right words. Kim-Anh is going to have to face meeting a new family and another woman who is her father's wife. Remember, she just lost her mother to cancer a short time ago. She'll have a lot to adjust to also."

He gave Thea a searching look. "How do you feel about a granddaughter who is half-Vietnamese? Can you accept this child into your family? It will mean a big adjustment for you."

Thea looked at her husband and he gave her his crooked smile, nodding his head in affirmation. She turned back to the doctor.

"She will be welcome here, Dr. Jensen."

Thea was contemplative for a moment. "I'll contact our attorney immediately. He's an old friend of the family. Perhaps he could be the one to meet Oliver."

"That sounds like a very good idea." The doctor stood up. My number is on my card. You can contact my office anytime. And now, if you will excuse me, I need to return to my daughter's. They're expecting me for lunch and to return their car. I'm leaving this afternoon on a three o'clock flight."

Edward, who had been standing by the French door listening in stunned amazement, quickly slipped out and returned with the doctor's hat and coat.

"We'll keep in touch, Mrs. Thornwell. You can count on that."

"Thank you, Doctor Jensen."

"If I may, I'd like to pray before I go."

She nodded, "I was going to suggest that."

The doctor bowed his head. "Father God, we thank you for Your mercy and goodness to these parents. A prodigal son has chosen to come home and like the father in the scriptures, the family eagerly longs for his return. You have taken them thus far,Lord, and brought about healing and restoration. You have prepared them for this day and for what is ahead. We commit Oliver, Kim-Anh, the Thornwells and each of Oliver's family to you, Lord. We trust you to complete this journey, and restore this son, husband and father to his family. Heal the heart of the young daughter who has lost her mother. Give them all Your strength to face any valleys that lie ahead. We place this all in Your capable hands, Lord, and praise You for what you are about to do. We ask these things in the name of Your Son and our Lord, Jesus Christ, Amen."

Thea saw him to the door and for the second time that day, watched a car turn out of their driveway.

Edward wheeled Gordon out of the library. Thea touched his cheek. "Have a good rest, dear. There has been about as much excitement as two people our age can bear."

Gordon nodded. Thea could see he was attempting to hold his emotions in check but tears coursed down his cheeks. She watched Cully wheel him down the hall, then turned back to the library. She had an important phone call to make.

SIXTY-TWO

Oliver's heart was in his throat. Instinctively he moved in front of his daughter holding the staff with both hands. They may kill him, but he would go down giving it all he had.

Kim-Anh's eyes were wide with fear. "Father, what shall we do?"

"I'm not sure, maybe we can talk to them."

One of the fiercest of the men stepped forward and though he wasn't Hmong, Oliver was able to understand his dialect. "You are the people of the Black Book? What are your names?"

Oliver paused. Maybe he could reason with them. Tell them he and Kim-Anh were not a threat, that he was an American.

"I was known as Ahn Cao Qua in Sa Pa. My true name is Oliver Thornwell and I am an American. This is my, ah, son." They must not know she was a girl.

"You are the Jesus people from Sa Pa?"

Still wary, Oliver faced him. "Yes, we are believers." If he died for his new faith, he could at least set an example of courage for his daughter.

The leader scrutinized Oliver's face. "We were told there was a daughter."

Hope rose as Oliver realized they might not be taken prisoner. The men knew who they were. "I ask forgiveness. We thought you to be bandits, and I was protecting her. She is called Kim-Anh."

The leader considered Oliver's words and finally, satisfied that he was telling him the truth, nodded slowly and gave a signal to the rest of his men.

"I am Truong Le. Follow us, we have been told to watch for you and your daughter. You will sleep in our camp tonight."

The rest of the men seemed to relax.

Oliver was almost weak with relief. They were resistance fighters, but not the enemy. He thanked God silently for protecting them.

Truong Le led the way with Kim-Anh behind him. Oliver followed Kim-Anh and the rest of the men followed them single file as they made their way through an almost invisible trail through the forest. Oliver turned to the man behind him. "Where are we?"

"Near Lao, Savannakhet Mountains."

"Are we anywhere near the Mekong?"

The man smiled, "You are a long way yet, Brother. There is still much forest to pass through. Truong Le will tell you more when we reach the camp. It is best to keep moving."

It was almost dark when they reached a clearing and entered the guerilla camp.

Small cooking fires burned and three women watched them warily. There was no sign of children. The camp was made up of crude tents and temporary wooden shelters. It was a camp that was designed to move at a moment's notice. Oliver thought of the Indian tribes he had read about on the plains of America that moved constantly, following the buffalo herds. This group couldn't move in an open plain, they would be targets for their enemies. The mountain range they moved in was dense and vast. There were miles of forest to hide in.

As Oliver and Kim-Anh sat around a small fire, they ate venison that had been cooked on long sticks. It was the first meat they'd had in a while and they both ate heartily.

The leader, Truong Le, addressed Oliver. "You have been traveling many days?"

It was more a statement than a question.

"Yes, many days. We were taken across the Black River by villagers, and have crossed many small rivers on bridges. We've slept in caves, in a village and in the forest. It seems we're still far from the Mekong. Tell me, who told you to look for us?"

Truong Le shook his head. "We have ways of learning many things, but one hand must not know what the other hand is doing. It is dangerous, always."

Oliver persisted. "Do you know of a Doctor Jensen?"

The black eyes registered a flicker of recognition. "He is one of many who come to help those of the Black Book."

"You are not Hmong."

"I am Rhade. We are hill people. Some of my men are Black Tai, Vietnamese, and some are Bru...Lao. We share a common goal, to fight against the enemies of our country, the communists."

"I am very thankful you are also brothers in Christ."

Truong Le laughed out loud. "You were prepared to fight us, even though we outnumbered you. I like that. We could use such a brother in our camp." Then he became serious again. "Yes, my friend, it is good that we are brothers in Christ and also follow the Black Book."

Truong Le pulled the last piece of meat off the stick with his teeth and wiped his hands on his pants. Then he reached into the front of his jacket and pulled out a small black book. Oliver recognized it as a New Testament.

Kim-Anh, having been respectfully silent, suddenly spoke up softly. "I have a Black book also."

Truong Le nodded. "A missionary brought us these. It is in the language of my tribe. Now I can read the words of God for myself."

Oliver moved closer to Kim-Anh so he could follow the words. As the fire crackled and produced a warm glow, a guerilla leader, an ex-American soldier, and a young girl, followed the ancient and healing words of the Scriptures.

><>

Truong Le bid them goodbye the next morning. "I have another direction I must go. My men will take you safely to the Mekong and arrange for you to cross. There is a village across the river in Thailand. You will be taken to a place of safety. Do not look too closely at how you get there and do not ask too many questions. It is best not to know too many things. There are those who would prevent you from leaving Laos. If you are caught it means prison or death, not only for you and your child, but for those who have helped you. The communist government does not tolerate believers."

"I understand. Thank you for your help. I will pray for your safety, my brother."

Throng Le smiled. "And I will pray for you and your daughter. You will reach your home far across the water." They clasped each other on the shoulders and Throng Le smiled. "Go with God."

"Go with God."

Four men were assigned to accompany them to the Mekong and see that they got across. Their four guides were heavily armed with long knives, rifles and grenades.

The men moved with an alertness born of years eluding the enemy, two walked in front of Oliver and Kim-Anh and two walked behind them. They all listened for every sound as they made a way through the dense forest. Confident in their care, Oliver and Kim-Anh moved along quickly, not stopping until the men stopped. They slept in caves and one night in the forest and on the fourth day, the leader of the group stopped them with his hand.

"We approach the big river. We will stay here in the forest and cross when night comes."

Kim-Anh looked around. "You have a boat?"

The men laughed heartily and the leader looked closely at Kim-Anh. "Ah, young one, how is your strength? You are a good swimmer?"

She balked. "I do not know how to swim at all."

Oliver realized they were joking with her and was thankful he'd kept his own foolish question to himself.

They ate dried venison and some nuts. The bread that was left was beginning to harden.

One of the men went ahead to scout and they waited, as silent as if they were part of the forest. They heard no footfalls, yet suddenly he returned and they gathered around him.

"There is no sign of the enemy. No patrols. The boat is safe and still covered."

The leader was pleased. "Good. We will leave as soon as darkness falls."

Later, crouched in the center of the long wooden boat, Oliver and

Kim-Anh watched as the men skillfully took the craft down river to the landing area that would put them in Thailand. As they approached the bank and signs of a village, one of the men told them to close their eyes. To their surprise, they were both blindfolded.

"It is for your safety and ours, my brother. Do not fear. You must not be able to identify the way."

Knowing they had no other choice but to trust these men of the mountains at this point, Oliver only nodded. His head began to throb. It had been several days since he took his last pills from Dr. Jensen, and he had struggled against the headaches and chills that would come and go. He would not complain, lest his daughter become fearful for him but it had taken great will power. Now he hoped that wherever they were being taken, someone knew a doctor. He couldn't hold out much longer.

They were put on horseback and it seemed as though they rode for hours, winding up a trail of some kind. At last they were allowed to dismount and heard the sound of heavy doors being opened. The blindfolds were removed and to their astonishment, they found themselves in what appeared to be a Buddhist monastery.

A monk approached them and bowed slightly. "Welcome. You may come with me."

The four men who had accompanied them on their journey each bowed and wished them well. They nodded to the monk and Oliver caught a look that passed between them. The men were familiar to the monk. They had done this before.

Thanking their protectors for all they had done, father and daughter followed the monk to a narrow room with a small window in the wall. It was sparsely furnished with two sleeping mats and a low table with a small oil lamp. On the table were two bowls of savory soup.

"Strengthen yourself and rest for the night. In the morning we will speak more. You are safe here." He closed the door behind them, but Oliver heard no lock click into place.

"Father, do you think this is a good place? Are we prisoners?"

"No, I don't think so, and I'm going to have to believe it's a good place. A lot of people have taken risks to bring us here."

"Those men knew that monk, didn't they?"

"It looks as though we are not the only travelers they have brought this way. Until we know differently, we will have to trust them."

They gave thanks for those who had helped them, and blessed the food. They picked up their bowls of soup and ate hungrily to the last drop. Oliver realized how hungry he too had been, and felt strengthened after the nourishment. They lay down on the mats, pulled rough blankets over themselves and in moments Kim-Anh was asleep. For Oliver, sleep was elusive despite his fatigue. He lay staring up at the ceiling for a long time, listening to the faint chanting within the temple and the sounds of the night. The sweet, poignant song of a Nightingale drifted through the window and in spite of his throbbing head, Oliver felt a sense of peace.

SIXTY-THREE

Kathryn answered the phone, she was startled to realize it was Thea's voice and she sounded upset.

"Oh Kathryn, I've waited an eternity for you to get home."

"Thea? Yes, we got back about twenty minutes ago. Is something wrong?

"Kathryn, I think you'd better sit down. I've had shocking news and I needed to tell you right away. A man came to the house just after you left. His name is Dr. Ralph Jensen. He is a missionary doctor who works for an organization that sends medical teams into Vietnam."

"Vietnam?" Kathryn slowly sank down on the stairs.

"Yes, and as he said, there is no way to break this news but to come out with it." Thea paused, her voice breaking. "Kathryn, Oliver is alive."

"Oh, dear, oh God, Oliver is alive?" Her heart began to thud in her chest and she felt lightheaded. Her voice came out in a whisper. "How does he know Oliver is alive?"

"Dr. Jensen and his team found Oliver in a small mountain village in Northern Vietnam when they came to set up a clinic. He recognized that he was an American."

A sob escaped as Kathryn tried to comprehend the overwhelming reality of Thea's words. "What did the doctor say?"

Thea broke the news about Oliver's Vietnamese family as carefully as she could, and then waited. The line was quiet. "Kathryn, are you still there?"

"Yes, I'm here. I'm just trying to take this all in. He had a Vietnamese wife who is now dead and he's bringing a fifteen-year-old daughter home?"

"Yes. They will be brought here, but I don't know exactly when they will arrive. We just have to pray and wait."

"I have to know. Was he a prisoner of war or was he living in this village of his own will?"

"He was living there, not as a prisoner, but it was next to impossible for him to try to leave. He was watched by the communists very closely."

"Oh Thea, I can hardly believe it. After all these years he's alive. He's alive."

She could hardly think as a mixture of emotions vied for a place in her mind.

"I don't know how long their trip will take or what the process is. We just have to pray they will make it safely to Thailand and from there, home. I'll leave it to you, Kathryn, to tell Allison and Jason. The one thing we must all hang on to as we face this together is that God has worked a miracle in our family. A work He needed to do before we were ready for this news of Oliver. We'll just take it one step at a time. I'll keep you apprised of any additional news."

"Thank you, Thea. I know this was hard for you too. You're very brave to make this phone call. This is such a miracle."

"We will all have emotions we will have to deal with in regards to the past and Oliver. I know you will sort it out."

They encouraged one another and before hanging up, agreed to keep one another in prayer.

Kathryn slowly went upstairs where Allison was unpacking and changing Joshua. Her face was radiant as she opened the door of the bedroom.

"Allison, I have something to tell you."

SIXTY-FOUR

Kathryn felt strangely like she had left part of herself back with the Thornwells. As the days passed, she had a myriad of thoughts running around in her head; wondering what Oliver had to face trying to get to Thailand. Who was helping them and how?

According to Thea, Dr. Jensen seemed to feel they would be taken care of when they got to Thailand "They may even be there now. I'll be interested in finding out how they get to the States," Kathryn told Allison one day. "They're going to need a passport to enter the country. Oliver may have his old military identification, but I wonder how much good that is after all these years."

She'd read in the paper once about organizations that were trying to get MIAs and POW out of Vietnam. It seemed strange to think there might be men like Oliver, left behind in the country.

Why would there still be POW's after all these years? Then other thoughts assailed her mind and a startling reality haunted her. How would she ever accept the fact he had married another woman and fathered a child?

That was the part that was so hard to bear. Kathryn had remained true to his memory, thinking he was killed. And now, to find out that all those years he'd been married to another woman. And would he want to see her again, and meet Allison? Surely he would, but people change.

After Thea's earthshaking call, Kathryn buried herself in her latest art project, working far into the night. Jason had been spending Christmas vacation working on plans and permits for the home they were building, but went into town to the library and brought home photocopies of some maps of Vietnam, Laos and Thailand. At least they could mark on these and figure Oliver and Kim-Anh's progress to get to Thailand. He also shared another bit of interesting information.

"Mom, the King of Thailand was born in the U.S, at Harvard University Hospital."

"Really? That would sure account for his country being favorable to Americans."

Every time the phone rang, Kathryn jumped, and this time it was no different. She almost hated to answer it, her instant anticipation usually deflated by a telemarketer wanting to sell her something.

She picked up the phone. "Hello?" She listened a moment and put her hand to her heart. "Oh thank God, Thea, that's wonderful news. The what? Yes, I'll tell Allison. Take care, Thea. We've been praying too." She hung up the phone and turned to Allison who was feeding Joshua in the kitchen.

"Oliver and Kim-Anh have made it to Thailand! They're in good health and safe. They are under the protection of the King's Men."

"The King's men. The military?"

"No Dr. Jensen said they were men who did special things for the King. They are trusted men. That's all Thea knows, other than they are safe."

Finally, releasing the emotions she'd bottled up, this time Kathryn gathered Allison in her arms and wept for joy.

SIXTY-FIVE

Oliver woke early to the sound of the monks chanting early morning prayers. It was soothing to him. His headache had subsided to a faint dull ache. He prayed he could handle things, at least for now. He had no doubt the malaria would return with a vengeance. In the village of Sa Pa there had been those who used herbs and the healing arts. Surely there was someone who tended the Buddhist Monks when they were ill. He turned over and looked across at Kim-Anh, still deep in slumber. This trip had been hard on her, yet to her credit, she had stoically covered mile after mile without a word of complaint.

Perhaps sensing her father's gaze, Kim-Anh opened her eyes and looked cautiously around, remembering where they were.

"What do you suppose is going to happen to us next?"

"I have no idea. I do know that we are at last in Thailand and we should be safe here. According to Truong Le, the King is favorable to Americans and we are now under his protection."

Kim-Anh moved to sit cross-legged on her mat. "I hope that monk returns soon."

Oliver sensed her discomfort. In the forest they could step behind a tree. In this temple or monastery or wherever they were, it posed a problem.

As though in answer to their thoughts, the door was opened quietly and they were greeted by the same monk who had met them the previous evening.

"Greetings, you will wish to refresh yourselves. Please come this way." He beckoned with his hand.

As Oliver approached, the monk looked at him kindly. "You are not well. It is the fever? Malaria?"

Oliver grimaced, so much for keeping things a secret.

Oliver glanced at his daughter who paused and waited for his answer, concern written on her face.

"I believe so. The symptoms began a couple of months ago. I've used quinine from a friend, and then was given some tablets by an American doctor. I ran out of the tablets a couple of days ago. Can you get me quinine??"

The monk nodded. "We have one who can help you. I will send him to you after the morning meal."

"Thank you. I'd appreciate that."

"The headaches and fever are getting worse, Father?"

"I can handle it. I'm sure the monks have someone who knows herbs and has something that will help."

"I know when you took the last of the pills Dr. Jensen gave you"

"So you knew about those?"

"I have watched closely. You have suffered for several weeks."

Oliver shook his head. Kim-Anh was not a child. Why did he think she didn't notice the blinding headaches that devastated him from time to time? He smiled ruefully. "Guess I'm not as good covering up as I thought I was."

Kim-Anh looked earnestly at him. "I have known when each one came."

"Well let's hope I get something to keep them at bay until we finish this odyssey and reach the States."

The monk walked quietly down the stone corridor and showed them a room used to wash and take care of other needs. There were two large tubs. A small screen had been place around one tub and Oliver noted the grateful look on Kim-Anh's face. She was growing into a young woman.

A pitcher of warm water had been placed by each tub. Oliver and Kim-Anh removed their clothes and got in the tubs, soaping down and then pouring the water over their heads to rinse. Oliver found a straight razor that the monks used to shave their heads. He soaped his face and shaved using a crude mirror placed against a shelf. They found Buddhist robes laid out for them to put on. Their own clothing was taken away. Oliver chuckled to himself. The monks would probably burn them. After a couple of weeks on the trail, they were in pretty bad shape. Fortunately, he and Kim-Anh still had the pouches with their personal things.

"I feel human again. I wonder what kind of a wild man I looked like when we came here?"

Kim-Anh smiled shyly. "I'm sure they found your beard very interesting, Father."

"But were too polite to mention it?"

Kim-Anh giggled.

When they were ready, the monk took them back to their small room where a simple meal had been prepared and again placed on the table. According to custom, a third bowl of rice and chopsticks was placed on the table for the dead.

"It would be best, my friends, if you remained here until we receive word from those who are to help you. There are arrangements to be made. You understand?" He put his hands together and bowed.

Oliver and Kim-Anh did the same. They would have time on their hands, but they still had a Bible and they would make good use of their period of waiting.

The monk left them but in a few minutes there was a firm knock on the wooden door and Oliver opened it to face another monk. He was rotund and built like a wrestler. His size made Oliver step back for a moment.

The monk did not speak, but entered the room with a small leather bag clutched in his hand. He pointed to Oliver's head and the bag. Oliver understood that this was the monk who dealt with herbs and healing. The monk put his hands together in salutation and then opened his bag. After crushing certain herbs, the monk mixed them with a small vial of liquid. When he was satisfied that it was ready, he indicated that Oliver was to drink the mixture. Glancing at the man's bulk, Oliver decided he'd better do just that.

Making a face at the bitter taste of the potion, Oliver nonetheless finished it to the last drop. The monk nodded in satisfaction and indicated Oliver should lie down for a while. Oliver sank down slowly on his mat, barely making it before the world became fuzzy. He struggled to maintain consciousness. What was happening? Had he been drugged?

"Kim-Anh...." He managed to mumble, and reached out for her before the darkness closed in.

Oliver woke from a deep sleep, the best he'd had in a long time. His head was not hurting either. When he could focus, he looked around the room. Kim-Anh was gone. Oliver sat up, almost too quickly and tried to collect his wits. He found the door to their room unlocked and looked both ways wondering which way to go first. The monk who had first met them appeared suddenly at his elbow.

"You are feeling better now?"

"Where is my daughter?"

The monk smiled and indicated Oliver was to follow him. "She is very wise for one so young."

As they entered a private area in the back of the temple, Oliver was astonished to find Kim-Anh talking with several Buddhist monks. She had her Bible open and was speaking to them. When she saw her father, she gave him a radiant smile.

"Father, I was just sharing the wonderful news of our Savior with our friends."

Oliver struggled to contain his emotions, relief that Kim-Anh had not been spirited away, and pride that she was boldly sharing the word of God with the monks.

He bowed to the monks, and then turned to Kim-Anh.

"I was only concerned that you were gone. How long have I been sleeping?"

"Almost a day, Father. You are feeling better now?"

"Yes, I feel much better. I will have to thank our friend with the herbs. Maybe I can find out from him what he used."

"He cannot speak, Father."

"He is mute?"

"Not by choice, Father." She waved at the man behind her father. "His name is Sang Le. He told me the big monk was captured years ago in Laos. He has no tongue." The implication was clear. Oliver nodded in understanding and dropped the subject.

Sang Le spoke up. "My friends, there is one coming who would speak with you both. It is urgent. Let us return to your quarters."

Kim-Anh put her hands together and thanked the group for listening and then obediently followed her father and the monk back to their room.

The official who was waiting for them had the look of a man on a mission.

He didn't waste any time. He bowed politely and Oliver and Kim-Anh returned his greeting.

"I bring you greetings from His Majesty, the King of Thailand. I am one of the King's men. I shall be in charge of this last part of your journey to the United States."

He glanced at their robes. "We have been told of your arrival here by our sources and we are willing to make arrangements for you and your daughter. We will need to ask you some questions. You and your daughter are to come with me."

SIXTY-SIX

Oliver and Kim-Anh thanked Sang Le for his kindness and left the temple. They were driven to a building in the city. Oliver could not tell where they were from any of the signs they passed.

Once inside, they were taken to an office. Kim-Anh was asked to remain outside and she made herself comfortable on a small couch. Her eyes held questions, but Oliver understood that some things they might ask him were not for Kim-Anh's ears.

"It's okay, just some things they may wish to know that may be classified."

That seemed to satisfy Kim-Anh, and she picked up a Thai magazine to glance through.

The official in front of him smiled benevolently. "We wish to know your reasons for staying in Vietnam after the war."

Oliver settled himself. "Because I thought at the time that I didn't have anything to go home to."

"No family?"

"My wife had left me and I was angry with my parents for their part in that."

"So you chose not to go home."

"I was in a small village in Northern Vietnam, a communist country, I had just healed from my wounds and had I wanted to go home, I had no idea how to do it. The war was over shortly after I was wounded and the U.S. had pulled out of Vietnam."

"You married a Vietnamese woman?"

"She was Hmong. She took care of my wounds for two months and saved my life."

"Why did she not come with you?"

Oliver took a deep breath, the memory of Thuan was still painful. "She died of cancer, about three weeks ago."

Oliver told them about the helicopter crash, how he managed to get away and how the mountain guerrilla fighters found him. He told them of Chau, his stepson, and the threat he faced."

"You have had a long journey through the mountains. It is good that you had help. It can be very dangerous passing through Laos."

Oliver rubbed his newly shaved chin. There was still stubble. "I found that out."

"We have been told that you wish to return to your family in the United States."

"Yes, a friend was going to make contact with them for me."

The official smiled and put his fingers together. "He did so, for he has good contacts in our country. We have been given permission to help you."

"You'll take me to the United States Embassy?"

The man paused. "No, we will make arrangements for you and your daughter to fly home on one of our planes. We of course will notify your government, in due time, that we have done this." He spread his hands. "We have done this for many of your country. It is the King's pleasure to help those he can to return to their homes."

"I see. Well I'm grateful to His Majesty for his help. I will be happy to get back to the States any way I can."

The man studied Oliver. "You were ill. Our sources say you are suffering from the effects of malaria. You were treated by the monks. How are you feeling now?"

"I feel all right. I ran out of the medication Dr. Jensen gave me."

"We will give you a small prescription to take until you can see your own doctor in the States."

"Thank you."

They were given towels and shown where they could shower. The tub bath had helped but Oliver was delighted to be able to take a hot shower. They took their personal things and their Bibles with them, but the monks robes were taken away and disposed of.

When they had showered, they found an American Air Force flight suit laid out for Oliver and a woman's uniform of the Royal Thai Armed Forces Parachute Riggers for Kim-Anh. Someone judged her size for it fit her well.

No sooner had they dressed when Oliver was shown to a chair and a Thai barber gave him a standard military haircut. To Oliver's chagrin, the barber shook his head in disapproval and completed Oliver's shaving job. Kim-Anh's hair was wound in a bun at the back of her head When he finally looked in a mirror, Oliver felt more American than he had in years. The tall man that looked back at him was older, thinner. There were streaks of gray at his temples. Oliver had paid little attention to looking at himself in Vietnam. A barber in Sa Pa took care of his shaving needs and life had been full with Thuan. There had been no need to look in mirrors.

A small, dapper man appeared with a camera and told Kim-Anh to stand against a white backdrop to have her picture taken. In a short time an identification card had been created for her as a member of the Thai military. Oliver had showed the man his old military identification card and after a cursory look, the man took it and bobbed his head. "It shall be brought up to date."

Since he was still in possession of his original dog tags and they were still in good condition, there was no need to duplicate those. He was glad that Thuan kept them for him and even more thankful his stepson would have only found the empty box since Oliver had taken them to Thuan's grave.

Food was brought in for them from a Thai market and as Oliver and Kim-Anh ate, they were filled in on the remainder of their trip.

"You will leave in two hours for the airport. There is a Thai C-130 leaving for California for equipment upgrades and combined military exercises. You and your daughter will be on the manifest of the plane, she as part of the crew, and you as a military passenger. There will, of necessity, be several stops for fuel, but I believe your final destination is Travis Air Force Base, on the West Coast of the United States."

Oliver's jaw dropped in surprise. "Travis Air Force Base? That's only an hour or so from San Francisco. You're getting us that close to home?" He was overwhelmed.

The man shrugged. "It would appear so."

"What happens then?"

"You will leave the base with Thai personnel and will be met outside the base by a representative of your family who will take you to your home."

"My home." Oliver murmured softly, savoring the words on his tongue. Then he looked up at the other man.

"My parents are alive? They are expecting me?" Emotions rose to the surface and Oliver had to turn away to gain control again. After a moment he turned back to the King's official. "Do my parents, ah, know about my daughter?"

The other man smiled. "The message we received was, 'The family of Oliver Thornwell await the arrival of their son and his daughter with open hearts.'"

Oliver and Kim-Anh looked at each other and Oliver enfolded her in his arms. "Thank God," he murmured, "thank God."

SIXTY-SEVEN

Thea kept the staff busy. She had the house cleaned from top to bottom in preparation for Oliver's arrival. She called Nordstrom's department store with a description of Oliver's height, only guessing at his current weight. She had purchased clothing for him when he was in college and supposed his arm and leg length hadn't changed.

"Two or three pairs of pants, matching shirts, underwear, make those boxers, socks, a sports jacket and a suit will be sufficient for now. Oh, add pajamas, two pair."

Oliver could choose additional clothing of his own after he was home. Pleased with her selection, she was ready to end the order and hang up when she suddenly remembered Kim-Anh.

"Oh dear, I forgot my granddaughter. She's fifteen. No, I don't know what size she wears. I, ah, haven't seen her in a long time. I'm sure she's tall, like her father. Oh, heavens, I haven't the faintest idea what fifteen-year-old girls wear right now. Yes, yes, I'll leave it to your judgment, but be conservative. Thank you. Please send them directly to the house; I want the clothes waiting when they arrive."

Thea hung up the phone to find Noreen waiting patiently for her next instructions. "Oh Noreen, do you think that's the right thing to do?"

"It was thoughtful," Noreen replied, "They will need those things. We have no idea of the circumstances they are traveling under."

"If only I hadn't gotten rid of Oliver's clothes--"

"How could you know? You did what seemed the right thing to do at the time."

Thea shook her head. "Oh, I know you're right. I just want things to be welcoming for him. To let him know, he's--"

"That he's loved?"

Thea caught her breath. "Yes."

"I'm sure he will know that. Now is there anything else you wish me to do?"

Thea sank to a nearby chair. "I've been a bit difficult lately haven't I?"

"Under the circumstances you've held up very well. I think I would be doing the same thing if it were my son. We are all so happy for you and Mr. Thornwell. Martha is planning his favorite foods. I caught Edward checking over the model planes hanging from the ceiling in Oliver's room."

Thea chuckled. "I think he built most of them himself, with a little help from Oliver, of course."

Noreen consulted her notes. "The Christmas decorations?"

"Oh yes, tell Edward to get the boxes of Christmas decorations out. We need to start on that right away."

"I believe he's already anticipated that. The boxes are down from the attic and have been placed in the back of the entry. You need to let him know which items you wish to use."

"Everything, Noreen, everything, I want the house to look as festive as possible for whenever they arrive."

The two women hurried to the pile of storage boxes and with a delight she hadn't felt in a long time, Thea pulled open the first box.

SIXTY-EIGHT

Jacob Tingley sat in his favorite leather chair in the study, contemplating the crackling fire. His wife, Charlotte, a small slender woman of sixty-five, sat down in a nearby chair.

"Have you heard any more on the Thornwell's son and his daughter?"

"No, not since the phone call asking me to meet them when they arrive."

A serene woman, rarely ruffled, Charlotte never complained. Though soft-spoken, she ran their household with a firm hand. She studied her husband and frowned.

"Do you feel well enough to go, Jacob? Your cough has gotten worse and the weather has not let up."

He smiled indulgently at her. "I wouldn't miss this for the world, my dear. I'm happy for the Thornwells and Oliver." He sighed heavily and turned wistfully back to the fire.

"Does it seem like John is returning home, Jacob?"

After over forty years of marriage, she knew him well. He sighed again.

Their son John had been killed in Vietnam but they knew without a shadow of doubt that he was dead. His body was sent home and they'd buried him on a rainy spring day. It seemed like so long ago. Now, here was the shocking return of a young man they thought had also been killed in action. He'd been reported dead, yet no body had come home to bring closure to the family. When Jacob received Thea's call, he was speechless and amazed. It was a miracle. Even more than a miracle had been Thea Thornwell's attitude on the phone. Her former imperialistic manner was gone and the woman he spoke to was different somehow, more soft-spoken, courteous instead of bombastic. What had brought about the change? It had caused him a great deal of thought.

"Charlotte, when you took the phone call from Thea Thornwell, did she sound, different in any way to you?"

Charlotte considered a moment. "Now that you mention it, she did sound different. As I recall, she even asked how I was and inquired about our daughter and grandchildren. She's never been interested before."

Jacob rubbed his chin thoughtfully. "I can't say I understand what's happened in that household, but I would like to. Hopefully I can see for myself when I deliver young Oliver to his home."

His wife laughed softly. "He's not young Oliver now, Jacob. He must be at least, let me see, forty-five?

He leaned back in his chair. "Am I getting old? Yesterday and today seem so alike these days."

She got up and came over to put a hand on his shoulder. "We can't stop time, Jacob."

He covered her hand with his own.

"Jacob, did Thea say how Oliver and his daughter were getting to the United States? Through our consulate or something like that? Imagine having a former soldier walk in and say he wants to go home. It probably happens more than we know."

"Thea didn't elaborate. All I know is that I will get a phone call telling me what time to be there. I'm to park just a block outside the base and wait in the car. Sounds a little like a spy novel. I feel like 007."

He chuckled. "You know what is really interesting? It's the girl. Oliver is bringing a fifteen-year-old half-Vietnamese daughter home with him. I'm surprised the Thornwell's accepted her. As I recall, young Oliver married a girl, someone he met at college, eloped with her and then brought her home to the family. That didn't go over."

He chuckled to himself, remembering the storm that incident raised. "I was instructed to draw up annulment papers immediately. Somehow the girl never agreed, or didn't sign, or whatever, and they couldn't get any response from Oliver in Vietnam and the papers were put on hold. Then they got the news he was killed and that was the end of that. Now they have a granddaughter they didn't know they had. They instructed me to change their will, and more recently, to set up a college fund for a great-grandson as well as arrange a surprise gift to help their granddaughter build a house. I tell you, Charlotte, it's a complicated business. Don't pretend to understand how the Almighty works, but it's more than a series of coincidences."

"Well, I must confess that in our Guild there is a lot of talk about how Thea has changed. She says she found God."

"You don't say." He rubbed his chin again. "That would explain a lot of things, wouldn't it?"

"It would indeed."

He began to cough violently. Charlotte rubbed his shoulders and waited for the spasm to subside.

"Jacob, are you sure you must go? You aren't well at all. Isn't there someone you could send?'

He straightened his shoulders. "Charlotte, if I can have even one small part in bringing a lost son home from that war, I will do it. I'm doing it for John, and for all the other young men who didn't make it. I told Thea I'd go if I had to go in a wheelchair. Oliver needs to be prepared for his father's condition and what to expect." He waggled a finger at her. "I'll stay warm and be careful. Don't you worry about me, I'll be fine."

She started to speak, but the look on his face was determined. He would not be maneuvered this time, no matter how gently.

"I'll make you a hot toddy. Would you like that?"

He smiled his gratitude and she rose to start for the kitchen when the phone rang. Jacob picked it up right away. "Tingley here. Yes? How soon? Right. Thank you. I'm on my way."

He rose quickly and straightened his shoulders. "This is it, Charlotte. Their plane is due to land in about one hour. That should give me time to get there."

"Who is driving you?"

"I have young Monroe on call, but ..."

"Jacob, I've met Mr. Monroe. He has all the compassion of a piece of granite. Oliver is bringing a young daughter that is half-Vietnamese. Surely the girl doesn't need someone looking down his nose at her."

"I see." A smile twitched the corners of his mouth. He looked at her anxious face a moment and then nodded. "You are perceptive as usual, my dear. Do you have another driver in mind?"

She nodded and waited.

Jacob Tingley chuckled out loud. "You are a persistent woman, Charlotte."

His wife touched his face with her hand. "I'll get our coats."

SIXTY-NINE

Oliver looked out the small window as they touched down for yet another fueling stop. He and Kim-Anh got out to stretch their legs but stayed close to the crew. To his relief, no one looked too closely at him or asked any questions. There was a small bathroom in the back of the plane but it was cramped for one of Oliver's height.

Once back in the air, Oliver talked with members of the Thai crew. One, Paradorn, even spoke some English. They were indulgent of Kim-Anh, and thought she was very brave.

The plane neared its destination at Travis Air Force Base and Oliver felt the knot in his stomach growing.

He turned to the Thai officer nearest him. "Paradorn, will they question my traveling with you, an American with a Thai crew?"

Paradorn grinned. "The customs officer will check our manifest. You are just an American crewman who has, how do you say it, 'caught a hop' on our plane."

Oliver shrugged. "Well, I guess I did, didn't I?"

"You have done nothing wrong, my friend. You are only returning home. That is why we help."

"It's more than I hoped for."

The Thai officer held out a pack of cigarettes but Oliver shook his head.

There was a sudden shifting in the pitch of the engines as the plane began its decent into Travis Air Force Base. The crew readjusted their safety harnesses in preparation for landing.

Paradorn noticed Oliver's restlessness. "How long since you have seen your family?"

"Almost twenty-five years."

"Do you have a wife or children in the States?"

"No, no other family."

"They have a granddaughter now." The officer looked

thoughtfully at Kim-Anh.

"Yes, and I'm told she will be welcomed. I'm glad of that."

Paradorn took a puff on his cigarette. "What will you do in the States?"

"You mean after I'm settled in?"

"Yes."

"I hope to be able to go back to college. I want to be an architect. You know, design houses and buildings."

"Ah, that is good. This is the occupation of your father?"

Oliver laughed. "No, my father is an attorney."

"You do not wish to follow the law?"

Oliver shook his head firmly. "There are enough attorneys in the United States."

Just then the plane touched down on the runway and began to brake. Oliver and Kim-Anh hung on to their straps and Kim-Anh almost came off her seat with excitement. Oliver checked his pocket for the pills the doctor in Thailand had given him.

"Father, we are in the States. We've made it. God has brought you home, Father, and I am here with you. There is so much I want to see and do."

"There'll be time enough to do some sightseeing, but right now, we need to get off this plane and the base and get home. There are some people you need to meet."

"Ah, my new grandparents, I am anxious to meet them."

"No more than I am, Kim-Anh, no more than I am." The words of the message from his parents had both touched and puzzled Oliver. He and his daughter would be welcomed with open hearts. What did that mean? Were they so glad to get him back that they would allow him to bring Kim-Anh? Had they changed?

He hadn't thought of Kathryn since his time with Dr. Jensen. He still felt the pain of what his parents and even he himself had done to Kathryn. Had she remarried? She probably had four kids and lived in someplace like Peoria. He made a face. If only he hadn't been so bull-headed. It was water under the bridge now. He'd just have to make the best of things, reconcile with his parents and figure out what in the world he was going to do. At his age, he would probably be the oldest student in college. If his parents wouldn't help him, he'd find a way. He'd face that obstacle when the time came. No doubt when the Thai officials notified the American government that they had helped him get home, he would be contacted in short order, something else to face when the time came.

As the plane taxied to a standstill, Oliver felt the dull throb of another headache coming on. He'd been somehow free of them since the potion the Buddhist monk had made him drink. He'd taken the Thai doctor's prescription right away and followed faithfully every 4 hours. He squeezed his eyes closed and prayed silently for the Lord to help him. He couldn't even think and he still had to get home and make things right with his parents. For his sake and for Kim-Anh's, he needed the Lord to help him and take away the pain for now.

To Oliver's astonishment, the throbbing ache receded to a level he could manage. He sighed with gratefulness.

When the door of the plane was opened, a customs officer came up the steps and examined their manifest.

Kim-Anh had been listed under her mother's name Le. The officer went down the list and noted Oliver's name. He prayed silently, watching the officer.

Kim-Anh remained in the back of the plane, half hidden by two of the crew members. The officer glanced their way, saw the uniforms and didn't look farther.

Oliver grinned at him. "Good to be home for Christmas, any way I can get here."

The officer shrugged. "Yeah, you're lucky. I've got the duty Christmas. Have a good holiday." He turned and left the plane.

Oliver almost went weak with relief. With everyone cleared, the Thai officer and crew headed for a waiting car motioning for Oliver and Kim-Anh to follow. Moments later their car passed through the gates of the base. They drove a short distance and slowed down as they approached a black Lincoln Town Car parked by the side of the road.

Paradorn turned to Oliver. "This is where we leave you, my American friend. I wish you and your daughter well." They shook hands all around.

"On behalf of Kim-Anh and myself, thanks for all your help." They got out of the car and stood a moment waving as the crew drove away. Then, as they turned towards the town car, an older man got out of the passenger side and stood by the car.

"Well, Oliver my boy, it's been a long time. I hope you remember me."

Oliver stared a moment and then with a grin moved forward to be enveloped in a strong, warm bear hug. "Uncle Jacob."

Kim-Anh hung back. Oliver reached out and put an arm around his daughter's shoulders, pulling her forward.

"Kim-Anh, this is Jacob Tingley, an old family friend."

She bowed, her eyes bright with excitement. Jacob looked at her and smiled. "Happy to meet you, Kim-Anh."

Jacob gestured for Kim-Anh to get in the front seat then climbed into the back with Oliver. As they got in, Jacob indicated their driver. "You remember my wife Charlotte, don't you, Oliver? She just wouldn't be left out of this."

Charlotte turned and smiled, her eyes moist. "Oh Oliver, we are so glad to see you home." She turned to Kim-Anh. "We wanted to be the first to welcome you to the United States."

Kim-Anh smiled shyly and shook her hand. "I am very happy to be here."

"You speak excellent English," Charlotte commented.

"Students learn it in school in Vietnam. She has spoken it since she was small," said Oliver.

"Such a bright girl. Like your father," Charlotte replied.

"All right, Charlotte, let's get these people home,"

As they turned on to the freeway that would take them across the Oakland Bridge to his home, Oliver leaned back. "It is wonderful to be in the States again. I wasn't sure who was going to meet us, Jacob. I'm glad you're the one they chose."

"Dr. Jensen and your parents both agreed it might be better to have me meet you and let the reunion take place at home. These things can be emotional and stressful."

"I guess that makes sense, considering the past." He put aside any negative thoughts. Was there some reason his father chose not to come?

He turned to the older man. "How have you been? And your family, they're well? It will be good to see John again."

Jacob pursed his lips. "We lost John, Oliver. He was killed in Vietnam."

Oliver closed his eyes. John. Red-headed, full of fun… How many of his friends met the same fate in that war? He wasn't sure he wanted to find out. He looked at Jacob with understanding. "I'm sorry to hear that."

Jacob looked out the window for a long moment. "When we lost him it was a hard time for Charlotte and me." He turned back to Oliver with a wry smile. "At least we've been comforted by the fact that we have our daughter, Marilyn. She's presented us with three grandchildren to keep us busy."

There was silence again for a moment.

"How is the firm? I take it you're still with them."

"Well, Oliver, there have been a lot of changes since your father retired."

"My father retired? I figured he'd hang in there until they carried him away."

Jacob took a deep breath. "They almost did, son. Your father had a massive stroke. He is in a wheelchair and doesn't have the use of his right side. He can still speak, but one side of his mouth droops and you have to listen closely to his words. I thought you ought to be prepared when you see him."

Oliver stared at the older man, absorbing what he'd just been told. "I'm sorry. When did it happen?"

"About two years ago."

Oliver shook his head slowly and glanced at Kim-Anh who was

more occupied with looking out the window at the sights and the sparkling lights of the Christmas decorations than listening to their conversation. "That's a shock. I thought he'd keep going forever." He paused, "How is my mother then?"

"She's fine, Oliver, but there's a change in her as well. I'm not sure I understand what has happened but my wife tells me she's found God. Perhaps that is a comfort in dealing with your father through this time."

"My mother has become religious?" Oliver contemplated that thought a moment. That might account for the words of the message he was given in Thailand. If it was true, he thanked God. It would make his homecoming easier than expected.

"So, tell me how you managed to get out of Vietnam. I understand it was quite a journey through the mountains."

For the rest of the trip Oliver shared what things he felt he could share without exposing anyone who helped him.

As they drove over the bridge into the city, Oliver looked out the window at the signs of the Christmas season. It had been a long time since he celebrated Christmas. He thought of the Christ child, born to make all things new for those who would believe. Maybe it was an appropriate time of the year for him to be returning home. He was made new in Christ. He wasn't the same person who had angrily joined the Army to show his independence. His rash act had separated him from the girl he loved and changed his life forever, but Christ had redeemed him. God had found a man who was surely lost and struggling and given him new life and a hope.

He was brought out of his reflections by Kim-Anh's exclamation of surprise and excitement as Charlotte skillfully brought the big car to a stop in front of Oliver's home.

"Father, this is where my grandparents live? It is a palace. Never did I consider such a house!"

Oliver grinned. "Better get used to it, daughter, it's going to be your home, too, at least for a while."

The huge Georgian house blazed with lights in every window.

Tiny lights twinkled on the bushes and trees outside. A great wreath with red bows hung on the front door and across the front of the house was a banner with the words, "Welcome home, Oliver and Kim-Anh."

The front door opened and to Oliver's surprise and delight, a familiar figure stood in the light of the entry.

Oliver jumped out of the car, "Cully! You old rascal. You're still here. I never would have believed it." They shook hands and Oliver clapped him on the back.

Cully was doing his best to keep his emotions under control. His eyes were moist. "It is so good to see you, also, Sir, welcome home,"

He stepped aside and nodded towards the entry where Thea stood clasping her hands. Tears streamed down her cheeks as she struggled to speak.

"Oliver…oh Oliver…" She held out her arms.

With two swift steps he was at her side and lifting her off her feet as he held her tight. "Merry Christmas, Mother, Merry Christmas."

When Oliver finally set his mother down, Thea reached up and put her hand on his cheek.

"In my mind you hadn't changed. It seems so strange to see you with gray hair, Oliver."

"We all get older, Mother, hopefully I've also grown wiser."

Kim-Anh stood in the doorway, hiding behind Cully and the Tingleys. Oliver walked over and gently brought her to stand in front of Thea.

"Kim-Anh." Thea looked at the girl's face. "She is lovely, Oliver," and held out her hand. "Welcome, child."

Kim-Anh smiled her shy smile and placed her hand in Thea's. "I am glad to meet you, Grandmother."

Jacob Tingley stepped forward, "We're happy for you, Thea, that you and Gordon have Oliver home. We'll be going on our way."

"Won't you stay for a while?"

Charlotte embraced Thea. "Thank you, Thea, but Jacob is not well. I need to get him home. This is your night, but I wouldn't have missed this"

Oliver shook hands with Jacob and hugged Charlotte. "Thanks again for being the ones to meet me, it made my homecoming easier. We'll see you both soon."

Cully closed the front door behind them, went to the library door and waited, clearing his throat.

Thea put a hand to her chest. "Oh dear, your father is waiting in the library. He'll be getting impatient."

She turned to Oliver. "Did Jacob tell you--?"

He took a deep breath. "Yes, I know about the stroke."

Cully coughed discreetly and opened the door to the library, stepping back as Oliver and Kim-Anh entered the room.

Even though he was prepared, Oliver was shocked by his father's condition. The old man sat straight as possible in his wheelchair with a light lap robe covering his legs. The frail old man with white hair and the obvious droop to the right side of his face was a glaring contrast to the vigorous, powerful man, Oliver had left behind twenty-five years before. With a lump in his throat, Oliver struggled to control his emotions as he approached his father.

Gordon held out his good left hand. His eyes were moist and his lower lip quivered. "Ohliverrrr."

Oliver took his father's trembling hand. "I guess I'm a little late getting home, Sir."

As they gripped each other's hands, Gordon kept nodding with tears streaming down his cheeks. He struggled to speak and shook his head in frustration.

Oliver felt his own eyes watering. "I understand, Father. I'm glad to see you too."

Thea nudged Kim-Anh. "Gordon, this is your granddaughter, Kim-Anh."

Gordon looked from his son to his granddaughter. He released Oliver's hand and beckoned Kim-Anh forward.

Nodding his head in approval, Gordon held his good left hand out, grasping Kim-Anh's slender hand in his. "Owiver's girl."

Hearing a sniff behind him, Oliver turned and saw Martha Culpepper standing in the doorway of the library wiping her eyes with a corner of her apron.

"Martha!" Oliver strode quickly to her side and enveloped her in a warm hug. "I can't wait to taste your wonderful meals again."

Thea rolled her eyes and smiled. "She's been cooking for days, Oliver."

"Dear boy. It is a miracle. We couldn't believe you were alive. "

She turned to go back to the kitchen and glanced at her waiting husband. Cully bowed out and closed the doors to the library, leaving the family alone.

Thea indicated the wing chair for Kim-Anh and sat beside Oliver on the love seat.

"Oh, I have so many questions; I don't know where to start." She shook her head. "How did they manage to get you home?"

Oliver rubbed the back of his neck, "It's always best to start at the beginning. I'm sure you were told about the helicopter crash."

"Yes, Doctor Jensen filled us in on what you told him, how you were rescued by the mountain guerillas, and about the woman who nursed you back to health."

He looked out the window a moment, "Thuan."

Thea turned to Kim-Anh. "I'm so sorry about the death of your mother, yet with what Doctor Jensen told us of her faith, and yours, I'm sure it is some comfort to know she is with our Savior."

"Yes, Grandmother, I miss her very much, yet I know she is no longer in pain."

Thea fixed them both with a solemn gaze. "It occurs to me that if you hadn't lost Thuan you wouldn't be here. God in His infinite wisdom went before you."

Oliver nodded slightly. "Perhaps that's true. Thuan urged me to go home and take Kim-Anh. But it seemed impossible. Until I became aware of the underground church the route home was closed to me. I thank God for the brave people who helped Kim-Anh and me."

"Thank God indeed. Can you tell us anything?"

Oliver settled back against the couch. "I can tell you that we slept in caves, in a hut, and in the open and traveled, with the help of other believers, over three hundred miles through thick forest and over rivers. A lot of people risked their lives to help us. They have quite an underground message system." He gave Kim-Anh a questioning look to join in.

Kim-Anh leaned forward eagerly. "Those of the Black Book, other believers, met us each leg of the journey with food and places to sleep. When we reached Thailand, we knew we were safe."

Oliver shook his head slowly. "I had no idea how they were going to get us to the States from there, but it was all arranged."

Thea smiled at Gordon, including him. "We only knew that you were flown on a Thai plane."

Oliver smiled ruefully. "We owe these military flight suits to the kindness to His Majesty, the King of Thailand. Without his sanction and the help of men who work for him, we wouldn't be here."

"I'll remember him in our prayers with thankfulness."

Gordon was eagerly following every word. "Frighttt okay?"

"Yes, Father, lots of stops but quite uneventful."

Thea hesitated a little and then, "Would you like to tell us about Thuan?"

Oliver looked at his daughter whose countenance had fallen. "Go ahead, Kim-Anh, I think you could describe her.'

Kim-Anh looked down at her lap. "My mother was a very good person, gentle and kind. She liked to make things beautiful. She loved flowers..."

Oliver leaned forward, his elbows on his knees. "She was very artistic, Mother. She did beautiful beadwork and embroidery. The garments of the Hmong were very colorful."

Kim-Anh reached inside her flight suit and produced the picture of her mother the European tourist had taken at the marketplace and given her. She shyly held it out to Thea.

"Thank you, Kim-Anh." She studied the picture a moment and then showed it to Gordon. "She was very beautiful, Oliver, I can see why you loved her."

There was a knock on the library door and the butler stepped into the room.

"Dinner will be ready in about a half an hour, Madam, I was wondering if Master Oliver and his daughter would wish to refresh themselves."

"Thank you, Edward."

Oliver shrugged. "We'll have to get some clothes tomorrow. What we have on is all we have."

Thea smiled at both of them. "I ordered some clothes for both of you, Oliver, and I was sure you hadn't changed sizes." She lifted her shoulders apologetically. "Kim-Anh, I had to guess at your size, so if the things don't fit, we'll just order some new clothes for you tomorrow."

Oliver chuckled. "My practical mother, you were always a great organizer." He turned to Kim-Anh. "All right, let's go check out our new wardrobe."

Thea impulsively gave Oliver a hug, which surprised him. He remembered her social hugs, gripping the shoulders and kissing the air. He returned it appreciatively.

Kim-Anh also hugged her new grandmother and solemnly shook hands with her grandfather before following Edward up the stairs. She was taken to the Blue Room, where clothes had been laid out on the bed for her.

As they entered the room, Noreen came out of the bathroom with a big smile. "Oh, Mister Oliver, we are so glad you are home. Welcome, both of you. I've put some fresh towels in the bathroom for your daughter."

Remembering the dour woman he'd known twenty-five years ago, Oliver was amazed. What had happened to this household? At dinner he'd have to ask his mother what miracle had taken place.

"Thank you, Noreen, as usual you are well prepared. Let me show Kim-Anh a few things, if you don't mind."

Oliver took Kim-Anh into the blue and white bathroom and

showed her the intricacies of American plumbing. In a few minutes an awed young girl was shaking her head.

"I have much to learn here in America." She fingered the blouse and skirt laid out on the bed along with underwear, socks and shoes. Kim-Anh fingered the bra and looked up at her father, puzzled.

Oliver scratched his ear. "Ah, that is for your, ah, breasts, to cover them." He glanced at his daughter's small chest. Perhaps it would fit, but he wasn't going to help her put it on. "It hooks in the back. I'm sure you'll figure it out."

She studied the garment and then brightened. "I think I understand."

"Well, Kim-Anh. You'd better shed that flight suit and see how these things fit you. I'll be in the room across the hall.

He showed her how the faucets on the tub worked and left her to the luxury of a bath after their long flight. As he crossed the hall and reached for the handle of the door of his old room, a gamut of emotions assailed him. The last time he'd been in his room was with Kathryn. Oliver opened the door and gazed around the room, half-expecting to see it remodeled. Everything appeared the same as the day he left and he had to stifle the sudden rush of tears that stung his eyes.

Oliver looked up to see the balsa wood planes he and Cully had meticulously built so many years ago. He shook his head in wonder. His mother and father hadn't thrown them away. By some miracle they still hung from the ceiling. A scene came unbidden to mind and he was once again lying in bed with Kathryn that one night, looking up at the model planes and promising her he'd return to her from Vietnam. *My beautiful girl, my wife, what happened to you? Where did you go?* He brushed the memory away and turned towards the closet. Opening the door he saw clothing hanging, but it was only the few new things his mother had bought. All his old clothing was gone. He chewed on his lower lip. That was to be expected. Why should she keep his old clothes all these years?

He glanced up at a box on the top shelf and in curiosity lifted it down. Sprawled on the top was a black and white velour rabbit. He set the box down on the floor of the closet and picked up the bunny. Mr. Salty. Oliver stared at the rabbit and tears rolled down his cheeks. For a brief moment he closed his eyes and saw a lonely little boy, hugging his rabbit, his most prized possession, for dear life as the thunder rolled and the lightening flashed outside his bedroom window. He knew the nanny wouldn't come. She didn't like to be disturbed after hours. His parents weren't home either. They had gone out for the evening. He crept quietly down the stairs, terrified with each clap of thunder, and holding his rabbit, knocked on the door of the Culpeppers quarters off the kitchen.

Martha heard the sound, and as she opened the door and saw the small tearful face looking up at her, she gathered him to her.

"Ah, my poor wee boy." She'd picked him up and settled in one of the kitchen chairs to rock. Comforted and safe, he'd snuggled against her ample chest and fallen asleep. The next morning he'd awakened in his own bed.

Oliver tenderly laid Mr. Salty in the box and put it back up on the shelf. He got himself under control and turned back to the bedroom.

Clothing had been laid out on his bed and he smiled to himself. He could imagine his mother calling the store and deciding what should be delivered. She always had impeccable taste.

He took a quick shower and dressed in a pair of tan slacks and light cream shirt. Fortunately, like riding a bike, he still remembered how to tie a tie. Just as he was tightening it up, there was a timid knock on the door and he opened it to see Kim-Anh dressed in a soft plum-colored skirt and cream silk blouse. She had washed her hair and it hung down in damp, shimmering waves. It was a young woman, not a little girl that stood on the threshold.

He stepped back and she came in slowly, looking around the room with wonder at the ornate furniture. She looked up and laughed with delight when she saw the model planes.

"You made these, Father?"

"Cully, the man who opened the door when we came, did. Well, I helped him a little."

She held her arms out to the sides, waiting for his approval.

"You look very nice, Kim-Anh"

Her eyes danced as she went to the tall mirror on the closet door and turned several ways. The skirt was a little too short, but fit well otherwise.

Oliver grinned. "How do you feel?"

"Like a princess, Father. Never have I had such clothes. I feel like there is more I should put on."

"I understand. The beaded vest and leggings and tunic of your tribe are a bit different, but you look beautiful. Your grandmother was very thoughtful to provide these for you."

"I will thank her for her kindness."

Oliver folded the flight suit and put it on a shelf in the closet. A good souvenir of all he'd been through.

Kim-Anh wandered over to the window, looked down at the sketchbook and picked it up. When Oliver saw what Kim-Anh was looking at, he was further amazed. Why would his parents keep his sketchbook? They didn't encourage his drawings when he was home. Oliver and Kim-Anh looked through a few of the drawings and she was full of admiration for her father's artwork. Oliver pushed his sleeve back to look at his watch and realized he didn't have one. He'd have to start a list of things he needed.

As Kim-Anh walked ahead of him and started towards the stairs for dinner, Oliver realized he had hurried through the first of the sketches and stopped short of the last few. There was a sketch of a girl with laughing eyes and he wasn't sure he wanted to look at her, at least not right now.

SEVENTY

As Oliver and Kim-Anh entered the dining room, her eyes grew large with wonder. The table held a crimson poinsettia arrangement and beautiful china and silver had been laid out. The silver serving dishes gleamed in the soft light and the aroma of Martha's dinner filled the air Thea noted the girl's astonishment and appeared pleased that all her efforts had the desired effect on her son and granddaughter. She indicated two places at the table for them.

"Thank you, Grandmother for my clothes, they are very nice."

"I'm amazed they fit so well. If there is anything you don't like, we can take them back to the store." She eyed the hem of her skirt. "We'll have that let down." She turned to Oliver. "Are your things all right?"

"As usual, you have wonderful taste Mother. They're fine."

"Father, I believe we should have come home long ago..." Kim-Anh fingered her beautiful blouse and then suddenly realized what she was saying and hung her head contritely, "except for my mother--"

Thea signaled the butler to begin serving. First came the cream of asparagus soup, then the Waldorf salad, followed by Oliver's favorite chicken dish, curried chicken and rice. Martha had suggested it, due to the diet she felt Oliver and Kim-Anh might have eaten in Vietnam.

Kim-Anh ate everything Cully placed in front of her with relish. She furrowed her brows at the salad, but after a couple of tentative bites, smiled broadly and downed that too. Thea watched her anxiously.

"American cooking is different, Grandmother," and she hastened to add, "but very good. I think I will like it very much."

From Oliver's place he could see the kitchen doorway, and knew that Cully would report his daughter's appreciative comments to Martha. He felt a twinge of headache and willed it away, but he knew what it signaled and felt his apprehension grow. Was the medication he was given not working or was something else wrong?

Oliver looked around. "Is Dad going to join us for dinner?"

"He'll join us shortly, dear, he has his dinner separately in the kitchen."

"It's difficult for him to eat?"

"Yes."

There was a sudden commotion from the kitchen and they could hear Gordon calling for Cully. The butler hastened to the kitchen and appeared a moment later pushing Oliver's father into the dining room to join them.

As the adults talked, Kim-Anh occupied herself by unobtrusively finishing the last of the vanilla ice cream with warm chocolate sauce.

Oliver gave his parents a grateful look. "Thank you for letting us stay here for now. I won't be any burden to you and Mother. I want to go back to college, but can work that out for myself. There are grants, loans, things like that."

Thea snorted. "Don't be ridiculous, Oliver, you're not a burden to us. You aren't working yet and have no income. We want to help you achieve your dream. It is the least we can do to make up for," she stopped and drew a handkerchief from her pocket to wipe her eyes.

Oliver got up and put an arm around his mother. "The past is forgotten, Mother. It was a long time ago. Let's note talk about it. Forget it happened, okay?" He caught a quick look between his parents. Something was up, but what?

He paused a moment, as a slight wave of dizziness assailed him, but he got himself together and returned to his chair. He caught Kim-Anh's anxious look and gave a brief smile as he sat back down again, to reassure her.

Thea's eyes widened. "Are you all right, Oliver?"

He picked up his napkin and then turned to his mother again.

Forcing himself to remain casual, he waved a hand. "Just a long trip. I think I'll sleep like a log tonight. There have sure been a lot of changes in this household since I left. Noreen is positively beaming and that's not the Noreen I remember. Then I hear that you have made a radical change in your life. You've found God. What brought all this about, if I might ask?"

Thea glanced at her husband who gave her a slight shake of the head. Perhaps she needed to let Oliver settle in before she shocked him with her information.

Taking a deep breath, she faced Oliver. "I was led to the Lord by a very dear and precious young man. Certain events had taken place that forced me to consider the direction my life was going. God gave me a new heart and a new appreciation of our marriage."

She gave the butler a warm glance as he began collecting the dessert dishes. "Edward and Martha have been praying for us for a long time. It certainly explained why they are still with us after some very difficult years."

Oliver raised his eyebrows. "I'd like to meet the young man that brought all this about. How do you know him?"

Thea chewed on her lip, apparently considering how to proceed, especially with Kim-Anh following their conversation with interest.

"Oh, there's time enough to go into all that when you've recovered from your long trip." She turned to Kim-Anh who was finishing her ice cream. "Tell me, what do you think of America so far?"

Kim Anh looked up shyly. "It is very wonderful, Grandmother. There are many beautiful lights everywhere. It is the time you celebrate the birth of our Savior, is that not true?"

"Yes, Kim-anh, that is true. I am glad you are a believer also." Thea looked at Oliver. She wasn't sure where he stood.

Kim anh spoke up. "Father is of the Black Book also." She smiled her sweet shy smile. "Our God was kind to let me say the words of new faith with him."

Oliver listened to this exchange and rubbed the back of his neck. "It took me a little longer to realize what or rather Who I needed."

Gordon's hand came down on the table for emphasis and they all jumped. "God iss Goooood"

Oliver laughed, relieved. "Yes, Dad, God is good." Then, suddenly, without warning, the room began to move before his eyes and he felt hot. The spoon he'd been holding in his hand clattered against the dish before landing on the tablecloth as the headache that had been in abeyance began to throb in his head and he shivered with the first chill. He put a hand over his eyes and willed it away, but this time it returned with a vengeance. The last thing he remembered was Kim-Anh's voice calling, "Father!" as the world went dark.

SEVENTY-ONE

Christmas Eve Kathryn was sitting in her studio. She was staring out the window when Allison knocked on the doorway.

"Am I interrupting anything?"

Kathryn turned from her reverie. "Oh, no dear, I was just thinking..."

"About my father returning for Christmas?"

"Yes. Thea only had a few moments while they were getting cleaned up and changing clothes upstairs. At least we don't have to worry about your grandparents being alone for Christmas. I know the Carradines are delighted to have us for Christmas dinner tomorrow, but I was just wondering how everything was going..."

"And if he knows about us yet?"

"Something like that."

Allison put her arms around her mother' shoulders. "I know it's hard. We just have to be patient. Are you anxious about meeting my father again?"

"Yes, and no. I don't know if I'm ready to face your father. We're both older. It is so much easier to cherish a memory than face him in person."

"I suppose so."

"Oh, I know Thea will call again just as soon as she can. I imagine they want him to themselves for a little while."

"What do you suppose he looks like now?

"Probably still handsome, maybe a little gray in his hair, and maybe a little thinner."

Allison looked at the photograph of her father on the table. "I've tried to picture him older with graying hair. I guess you're right. It's easier to live with a memory than face the real person after so many years."

Kathryn nodded.

Allison's next question voiced what Kathryn herself had been wondering.

"What do you think Kim-Anh looks like?"

She shrugged. "I don't know. Maybe Oliver's freckles, long legs, I don't know." She thought a moment. "Her mother was Vietnamese, so she would probably have her eyes."

"Oh, that's true." Allison sank onto the settee. "It's a little exciting and a little scary, isn't it?"

"Yes."

"Mother, you're still beautiful. You haven't changed that much in all these years. I'm sure he'll be thrilled to see you. Grandmother will explain about the check. He'll know you didn't take it and leave him."

"I know. Yet, how will he feel, knowing what he did? Will he want to face me after all these years?"

"After all you've told me about him, and what the doctor told us about him, the one thing my father isn't is a coward."

Kathryn sighed. "No, he isn't. He'll see me. I just don't know what will come of it after we meet. He may have no feelings left for me. He was in love with someone else for years, and had a child with her."

"Maybe you are worrying unnecessarily. At the worst, you could just be friends."

"Friends--" Kathryn dragged out the word. He was the love of her life.

She picked up a paintbrush and sat back down on the stool by her drawing board. "I guess I'd better get back to work."

Allison gave her another hug. "I guess I'd better check on Joshua. Jason is reading him a story down in the living room.."

After her daughter left, Kathryn put the brush down. How was Thea going to broach the subject of his first wife—and the only legal one? How will Oliver react to that, and his American daughter? Did having Kim-Anh make a difference? And how would she react to a new sister? The questions raced around in her head.

She needed to stop brooding.

Allison was struggling to put pajamas on the squirming toddler on the couch as Kathryn came in. "Snack, Gama?" He'd learned the right word early.

Kathryn gave him a hug and went into the kitchen to bring him an animal cracker and his small cup with some milk.

Joshua clapped his hands. "Cookies" he said gleefully.

Kathryn looked down at her small grandson and chuckled. Like father, like son, cookie monsters. When he'd finished his treat, Kathryn kissed him goodnight and stood at the bottom of the stairs waving as Allison took him up to bed.

Suddenly the phone rang and Kathryn picked it up quickly.

"Hello."

"Kathryn!" The word was uttered with a sob.

"Thea, what's wrong? Is it Gordon? What's happened?"

"It's Oliver. He collapsed at the dinner table tonight. He's very ill. Kim-Anh told me her father has had these blinding headaches and fever for a long time. It's malaria, with complications. Kim-Anh says he ran out of the pills Dr. Jensen and the Thai doctor gave him. Kathryn, we had to call the paramedics. He's in the hospital. I'm sitting in the hallway here with Noreen and Kim-Anh waiting for the doctor to tell us how he is."

"Oh, Thea, the hospital? What do you want me to do?"

"For now, please pray. The doctors are taking x-rays and examining him as we speak."

"Thea, I'm sure the doctors are doing their best. How soon will you know of his condition?"

"We don't know. Your grandfather is beside himself. I'm afraid it will bring on another stroke. Oh, Kathryn, we just got him back and now this."

"Where is he?"

"Alameda Medical Center was the closest. I don't think there is anything you can do as yet, at least until he is stabilized. I'll call again as soon as I know more."

Kathryn hung up the phone as Jason came in from the kitchen.

"Mom? What's up?"

She bit her lip and motioned for Jason to follow her upstairs to Joshua's room.

When they suddenly came in the door, Allison took one look at Kathryn's face and her hand went to her mouth. "What's wrong? It's my father, isn't it? I've felt strange all afternoon, like something was happening."

Kathryn waited while Jason kissed Joshua goodnight and he and Allison tiptoed out and closed the door. Jason led Kathryn into their room and they sat down on the edge of the bed.

"Mother?"

"Your father is in the hospital." She repeated what Thea had told her.

Allison's eyes were bright with tears. "But he just got home."

"They're running some tests on him. Kim-Anh told your grandmother that her father has been suffering from this for months and trying to hide it from her because her mother was so ill and he didn't want her to worry."

Jason put his arms around both their shoulders. "This looks like a good time to pray."

"Dear God, we come to you with fearful hearts. Lord, we place Oliver in Your care. You made it possible for him to return to his home and bring his daughter safely out of danger. We know that there is a purpose and plan in all of this and while we don't understand, we trust You for what You wish to accomplish through all of this. Give us courage and strength, Lord, and wisdom to know how to proceed. There is more restoration to be done and we don't believe you would bring Oliver this close without completing the job You've begun. We thank you, Lord, for Your hand in this and we commit Oliver to You. In Jesus' name we pray, amen."

The two women murmured a soft "amen."

Kathryn shook her head. "I can't remember when I've shed so many tears."

"You have bottled up your emotions for so many years, never

talking about it, but hurting," said Allison. "I know. I've watched you, but never knew the complete story of why you seemed so sad at times. If you can find some release in tears, then I say, cry your eyes out."

Kathryn gripped her daughter's hand.

"I suppose." Kathryn stood up. "I wonder just how soon Thea will be able to call us back with a report on your father. Malaria is not as dangerous as it was years ago, but I've heard there can be serious complications, and you never really get rid of it."

"Grandmother will call as soon as she can, Mother, you know that."

Kathryn felt in her heart that she should be at the hospital with Oliver. After all, she *was* still legally his wife. Never mind some silly law about seven years of separation that dissolved a marriage. Yet she did not want to intrude, either. She bid Allison and Jason good night and went to her room, her mind churning with all the possibilities of Oliver's illness.

The winter night was crisp and cold with a blanket of new fallen snow. She opened her window and there were frosty wisps of air as she breathed.

The moon had come up and she looked up at the silvery glow against the trees.

"Get well, my love. Please, get well."

SEVENTY-TWO

Thea sat on the leather chair in the waiting room, her back ramrod straight and her hands in her lap. Noreen glanced at her from time to time. Kim-Anh's face, pinched and pale, reflected her anxiety as she watched the doorway of the waiting room for someone to bring word of her father's condition.

Thea had promised to call Edward and Kathryn as soon as she heard anything for she knew they all waited as anxiously as she.

"Oh Noreen, I wish they would tell me what's happening. When the paramedics came for Oliver he was sweating and feverish. He's very ill."

Noreen turned to Thea. "You know, I didn't think Oliver looked well when he came upstairs but he seemed in good spirits so I didn't think more about it. I thought maybe he was just tired from the journey."

Thea looked down at her hands. "I was so overjoyed to see him I didn't think about anything else."

She smiled sadly at Kim-Anh. "All that trouble and traveling and now this." Noreen glanced again at the hallway. "Surely they know something by now they can tell us."

Just then a man in a white medical coat strode briskly into the waiting room. "Mrs. Thornwell?"

Thea rose quickly. "Yes?"

"I'm Dr. Samuels. Your son is resting. We are doing some lab tests to affirm the strain, but he definitely has malaria. I understand he's recently returned from Asia, is that correct?"

"Yes, he came out of Vietnam through the forests of Laos to Thailand and flown home from there." Thea looked up at the doctor's face. "I know little about Malaria, can it be cured?"

"I don't believe there is anything serious to worry about right now. We have excellent anti-malarial drugs now, such as chloroquine.

Most strains can be treated and cured with that."

"You said *most* strains?

"Yes, Mrs. Thornwell., there is one strain, falciparum malaria, which is very severe and can be resistant to chloroquine. Should the lab tests indicate this strain, we will have to alter the medication. We have some other options available." He studied Kim-Anh for a moment. "This is his daughter?"

Kim-Anh rose to shake hands with the doctor.

"Yes, Sir."

"Well I'm glad to meet you. I'm going to recommend that you have a lab test done to be sure that you are not carrying the malarial virus yourself. It takes six to twelve hours to confirm the disease. It wouldn't be a bad idea to start you on some medication just as a precaution."

"I will do what you say, Doctor." Kim-Anh seemed small in the sterile hallway.

"Mrs. Thornwell, you need to sign a release for the lab tests. Her father is incapable at this time. Are you the next of kin?"

"Yes, Kim-Anh's mother died in Vietnam. I will sign the forms."

Dr. Samuels handed the clipboard to Thea and indicated where she must sign. As she did, she looked up wistfully at the doctor. "This is not how I anticipated spending Christmas Eve, or Christmas. I'm sure it isn't what you would prefer either. I'm sorry."

The doctor's eyes twinkled and he shrugged. "I appreciate your concern, but I generally work over Christmas. Since I don't celebrate that particular holiday, it frees up others to be home with their families."

Thea put a hand to her cheek. "You said your name is Samuels. You're Jewish?" When he nodded, she smiled up at him. "How kind of you to be so generous, Dr. Samuels. We're fortunate you're here to see to Oliver's care."

"Perhaps more than a coincidence, dear lady, my specialty in residency was in parasitic diseases."

The doctor stroked his beard. "With all that your son has been through, I would say he's been in greater hands than mine."

Thea nodded slowly. "God is with him, Dr. Samuels, I'm sure of that. So many pieces have fit into place that one cannot attribute to coincidence." She bit her lip and looked up into the doctor's face. "When can Oliver come home?"

"I'm not sure yet, Mrs. Thornwell. Probably a week or more. If the results of the blood slides don't indicate the falciparum malaria, he'll recover. I'm anticipating that we will have good news and the malaria will be one of the other more treatable forms. It's just important that all bacterial parasites are cleared from his system."

Kim-Anh spoke up. "Father was taking some pills. I'm not sure what they were."

"Ah, yes. Well, evidently this medication helped, but it wasn't enough nor was it taken over a long enough period of time. It kept the virus at bay for a while but it has attacked his system again."

Thea interrupted. "Can I see my son, Doctor?"

"He's sleeping, due to the medication, but I'm sure there is no harm in seeing him for a few minutes."

Kim-Anh's eyes questioned and the doctor inclined his head toward the hallway. "You need to come with me first and have that blood test. Then you can join your father and grandmother in room 563."

The doctor beckoned to a nurse and gave her orders to call the lab technician. Kim-Anh would be shown to a nearby alcove to wait. Thea called home from the nurse's station.

As she hung up the phone Thea saw Kim-Anh looking forlorn as she waited in the alcove for the lab technician. Thea walked over and quietly sat down next to her. Kim-Anh gave her a grateful smile and looked up tentatively at her grandmother.

"Your father is going to be fine, Kim-Anh, don't worry. When you're finished there you come down and join me."

Noreen went to sit by the frightened girl. Kim-Anh appeared visibly reassured by her words and presence. She clasped her hands in her lap and waited.

Thea thanked the nurse for the use of the phone and glanced up at the directional sign on the wall turning towards room 563. Like a dying person, her life passed before her eyes and she thought of the times when a small Oliver was sick and called for her. His face was so wistful when she left him with Edward and Martha for yet another social engagement. Martha brought him chicken soup when he had the flu and Martha and Edward nursed him through the chicken pox.

It struck her to the core as she thought of the number of times she wasn't there for Oliver. She thought of her young grandson, Joshua, hugging Mr. Salty the rabbit and lugging him around the house, but then, in her mind, the little boy with the rabbit became Oliver. She willed the tears back and looked heavenward and murmured,

"Lord, I wasn't a good mother when Oliver needed me. So many times over the years I failed him. Yet You are a God of second chances. Thank you for bringing Oliver home to us. Thank you for showing me Your love when I was so unlovable. You have done so much for all of us. I give You praise, Lord, and my eternal gratitude. Help me to be what Oliver needs right now. Let Your love shine through me to my dear son."

Thea wiped her eyes with a handkerchief, straightened her shoulders and with firm steps, approached Oliver's room. She took a deep breath and pushed open the door.

This time, my son, I won't fail you.

><>

Oliver opened his eyes and tried to blink away the haze in his mind. Where was he? White sheets, a hospital bed. How did he get here? He moved his head slowly and saw a figure nearby. He blinked again and his mother came into focus. Her knitting needles clicked softly in the quiet room.

"How long have I been here?"

Thea looked up and smiled with joy. "Oliver! You're awake."

She put the knitting down and hurried to the bedside, taking his hand. "You've been sleeping almost fourteen hours."

"How did I get here?" He tried to move but his body felt like lead weight.

"I called the paramedics when you collapsed at the dinner table. You gave us all quite a scare. The doctor said you didn't have enough medication over a long enough period of time. The malaria returned."

He gave her a rueful smile. "I didn't mean to bring more trouble home with me."

"Oliver, you're no trouble. You're on excellent medication and the doctor says you can be cured."

"Malaria has a way of coming back, Mother. I may have to deal with this the rest of my life."

Thea smiled. "No, you won't. There are new drugs available that can rid your system of the parasite permanently."

He raised one eyebrow. "Really?"

"Yes, really." Thea leaned down and kissed him on the cheek. "We're going to take care of you and make sure you get well."

Oliver studied her face a moment and his eyes twinkled. "I think I like this new mother I've got."

"Oh, Oliver, I have so much to regret, yet the past is gone, covered with the blood of my Savior. I only hope you can forgive me, and your father, for what we did. I carried the guilt of that for all these years, feeling our actions put you in harm's way."

He moved his hand to cover hers. "I forgave you when I realized what I'd done, Mother. I'm in no position to point fingers."

She sighed. "We can't change the past, Oliver, but we can trust God with our future."

Thea pulled her chair over and sat down next to the bed. "Kim-Anh is in good hands at home. She stayed here at the hospital last night for a long time. The doctor gave her a blood test to check for malaria. We'll get the results this afternoon. We have to wait six to twelve hours for the test results, but Dr. Samuels doesn't seem to feel Kim-Anh is infected. From what Dr. Samuels tells me, there are four types of malaria. One is very serious but the other three are easily treatable. You have a treatable strain."

"That's good to know."

A nurse entered abruptly to take Oliver's pulse and temperature. She gave him his next dose of medication and left without a word.

Thea looked towards the departing nurse. "They are overworked and short-staffed. Most are exhausted at the end of their shift." When he raised his eyebrows, she gave a slight shrug, "I talked to some of them at the nurse's station."

"How long will I be here?"

"A week or so, at least until you get strong and they are sure the parasite is out of your system."

"Guess I made a whale of an impact on your Christmas."

"Oliver, we're just glad to have you home." She looked at her watch. "I have to return home and give a report to your father. He's beside himself with worry and I have to keep reassuring him you are still going to be with us."

He smiled wanly, feeling the weariness in his body. Talking suddenly exhausted him again.

Thea kissed him on the forehead. "Get well, Oliver. We've so much to talk about but now isn't the time."

His eyes closed slowly as her retreating footsteps echoed on the tile floor.

SEVENTY-THREE

After she returned home from church, the phone rang several times that evening, but none of the calls were from Thea. Kathryn gave up trying to work in her studio and came downstairs to join Allison in the kitchen. Allison stirred a pot on the stove, keeping an eye on Joshua who was playing on his special rug in the corner of the large kitchen.

Kathryn heaved a big sigh. "Have you made the salad yet? I need something else to do"

"No. Go ahead. Take your time. The chicken isn't quite done yet."

When the phone rang Kathryn jumped up and hurried to the hallway before Allison could move.

It was Thea, finally, and she filled Kathryn in on all the doctor had to say.

Kathryn put her hand on her heart. "Oh, that is wonderful news. Yes, that would be a wise precaution."

She hung put the phone back in its cradle slowly. Allison waited in the kitchen doorway.

"Mother? Are you all right? What did grandmother have to say?"

Kathryn looked at her daughter's anxious face and smiled. "It looks like your father doesn't have the more serious form of malaria. He's going to be fine." She filled them in on the specifics of Oliver's illness and his treatment. "Oliver is sleeping right now. They've given him some antibiotics to rid his system of the parasite.

"Thea will know more tomorrow." She told them about the blood test for Kim-Anh to make sure she was not carrying the virus. "Your grandfather is doing well, especially now that she's assured him Oliver will get better." She stared at the tablecloth for a moment. "She hasn't told him."

"About you and me?"

"Yes, she felt it was better to let him recover before she broke that kind of news. He doesn't know I never got the annulment or that he has a daughter, or should I say, *another* daughter."

"Is there a statute of limitations or something, on a marriage after twenty-five years?" Allison wondered.

Kathryn said, "Technically, after a spouse is missing for seven years a marriage is dissolved, but legally, we are still married. I just thought I was a widow."

Allison put her arm around Kathryn's shoulders. "Did Grandmother say when we could see my father?"

"She didn't say. I don't know if I can stand this, knowing he's only a few hours away."

She jumped up and flung her hands in the air. "It's this waiting. If there was only something I could do." She turned to her daughter, "and don't tell me to just pray. I am doing that, but I want to do more!" She sank back down on the chair. Allison reached sympathetically for her mother's hand, sharing her anguish.

When Jason and Allison had gone to bed and the house was quiet, Kathryn crept into the small guest room that had been turned into a nursery for Joshua until the new house was finished. She looked down at the angelic face, his one hand clutching his blanket and the other arm around his treasured white bear. Her heart overflowed with love for him.

Then the thought came. She knew what she had to do.

SEVENTY-FOUR

It was evening by the time she walked down the long corridor. There were few visitors. She approached the nurses' station.

"Oliver Thornwell?" She asked tentatively.

The nurse didn't look up. She checked her chart, murmured, "Room 563", and returned to what she was doing. She expected to be told to wait until visiting hours, but the nurse seemed too busy to care.

She followed the signs, feeling her heart beating erratically in her chest. She gripped her purse as she neared his room number.

A nurse smiled at her as she left Oliver's room with a medication tray, but didn't comment.

His eyes were closed as she walked in quietly and stood by the side of the bed. It was not official visiting hours, so no one else was with him. Her first sight of him, after all these years, stirred stronger feelings inside than she thought possible. He was thinner, probably due to the illness. His hair was still auburn, with streaks of gray at his temples. She wanted to touch him but waited, torn between wanting him to wake up and wanting to flee.

He opened his eyes slowly as if sensing her presence.

She took a deep breath. "Hello, Oliver."

His eyes opened wider. "Kathryn?"

"Yes, Oliver."

He tried to move, to reach towards her, but couldn't.

She wanted to touch him too, but didn't.

"You gave us all quite a scare."

He looked stunned. "Us all? You've been talking to my mother?"

She smiled. "We have, shall we say, reconciled our differences?"

"Reconciled your-- and how did this come about?"

"She called and invited us for Thanksgiving." A smile twitched the corner of her mouth.

Oliver felt his mouth go dry. "She just called and you spent Thanksgiving with my parents? You and your husband?"

"No, the rest of my family."

"No husband?"

"I've never remarried."

He sighed. "I think you had better explain. I'm a little confused right now."

"You have a daughter, Oliver."

He frowned, not understanding. "Yes, I know that. Evidently Mother's told you about Kim-Anh."

"Yes. She told me you were married to another woman and had a child. That was harder to take than finding out that you were dead."

"I was angry, Kathryn, at what you did. I just didn't want to come home. There wasn't any way to get home anyway."

"You had no reason to be angry, Oliver. How could you believe I'd leave you, for anything? I left the check in your room. Someone found it and forged my signature. It's a long story, and I'll tell you about it when you are better. My son-in-law proved it and cleared my name, and that's why your parents have accepted me again."

Son-in-law? He'd lifted his head and now dropped it back against the pillow. "

"Kathryn, if that is really true, I have so much to regret. I only hope one day you can forgive me for what I did."

"It is true Oliver, and I forgave you, even when I found out you returned my letter and made me believe you had died."

He scrunched up his face."I was devastated and hurt, and pretty immature."

"I figured it out when your mother and I compared notes as to when we heard of your death."

"I am so sorry, Kathryn."

She sighed. "We can't change the past, Oliver, but we can trust God with our future."

He wrinkled his forehead. "You said you were at my parent's house for Thanksgiving with your family. Did you say son-in-law?"

"You have another daughter besides Kim-Anh, Oliver. She's a beautiful girl and her name is Allison. She looks very much like her father."

He took a quick intake of breath. "We had a daughter?"

"Born nine months after our honeymoon. That was what was in the letter I wrote you, that and a lot of other things, including the fact that I hadn't taken your parent's check."

Oliver looked stricken. "I really messed things up, didn't I?"

"It's in the past."

Oliver stared at a speck on the wall for a long moment. "Another daughter. What did you say her name was?"

"Allison"

"I like her name." He frowned. "Who else should I know about?"

"Well, you have a grandson, Joshua. He's a Darling little boy, almost a year old."

"I'm a grandfather." He looked amazed. "How did you happen to reconcile with my folks?'

"Allison grew up in a small mountain community, Lewiston, which is where we still live. I supported us by doing illustrations for children's books. I'd been pretty secretive through the years and I didn't want your parents to know about her. I was afraid somehow they'd get custody, as they had so many resources and I didn't. After she was grown and Joshua was born, I realized she was safe and I could tell her about her grandparents. She then decided to contact them."

"I can imagine what a shock that was."

"Oh yes." Kathryn decided to hold back on any more information. She'd already shared more than she intended to.

He was silent a while, contemplating what she'd told him. She waited. The old feelings of love and attraction were growing in her again, but she didn't want to open herself to the pain of rejection if he didn't feel the same.

"Do you think Allison will want to meet me? I'm a pretty poor excuse for a father. I guess as far as she's concerned, I wasn't one at all."

"She doesn't hold any hard feelings against you, Oliver. As a matter of fact I think she's most anxious to meet you."

Oliver rubbed his temples. It was a lot to digest.

He closed his eyes. "So I'm home with a daughter you didn't know I had, and you have a daughter I didn't know I had." His eyes began to water and he covered them with his hand. He was completely exhausted again, physically and emotionally.

"What a royal mess I made," he whispered.

"God works in mysterious ways, Oliver. Somehow His hand was in all of this and some good things have come out of it."

He looked up at her. "It's good to see you again, Kathryn, I wondered what had happened to you—" He paused, his emotions getting the better of him.

"You need to rest and get well, Oliver. We'll talk again when you feel stronger. I'm sure you have a lot of other questions."

The medication was beginning to take effect. "I want to, Kathryn." His voice faded and his eyes began to close.

She watched his face a long time and then leaning down, kissed his forehead lightly. She did not see a young, pretty, part Asian girl standing in the doorway staring at her. No one had told Kim Anh about Kathryn---or Allison.

The girl's eyes widened and suddenly she turned and ran down the hallway, so light she hardly made a sound on the linoleum.

SEVENTY-FIVE

Oliver learned that the doctor had asked his family not to visit him for a few days so he could completely rest. The visits exhausted him. He thought of Kathryn and wondered if it was just a dream brought on by the medication. Had she really been there, in his room?

Where is Kathryn now? He couldn't help but wonder. He thought it best not to speak of the dream either to his mother or the doctor, at least for now.

Dr. Samuels studied the final test results again as he stood by Oliver's bed. "Well, my friend, it looks like you are getting a handle on this virus. You don't have the plasmodium falciparum, which is the one we were concerned about. I think with strict attention to the medication and plenty of bed rest, you'll overcome this. I'm continuing you on the Doxycycline." He rattled off continued instructions.

Oliver raised an eyebrow and glanced at his mother, "Got all that?"

Dr. Samuels reached into his pocket for a pad of paper. "Don't worry, I'll write it out for you just as a precaution."

"Does this mean you are releasing Oliver, Dr. Samuels?"

"Yes, Mrs. Thornwell, he should be able to go home today. I'll notify the nurse. He can get dressed now. Mrs. Thornwell, if you will come with me, we'll get the paperwork taken care of. Nurse Adamson is on duty today. I'll send him in to finish up things here and assist Oliver if he needs it. Hospital policy says Oliver must be taken to your car in a wheelchair, so Nurse Adamson can bring him out when he's ready."

Oliver gave the doctor a grateful look as Thea turned to gather her knitting "Very well, Doctor, I'll bring the car out front."

Later, loaded with the anti-malarial medication, Oliver was placed in the front seat of the Lincoln that had been tilted back for his comfort.

Oliver noted the size of the car and the diminutive size of his mother and suppressed a grin. She could barely see over the steering wheel. He leaned his head back and closed his eyes a moment. He had another problem to face at home, how to tell Kim-Anh about Kathryn. Since he was still married to Kathryn, even though he didn't know it at the time, his marriage to Thuan was not legitimate. That would make Kim-Anh illegitimate. He would have to choose his words very carefully when he spoke to her.

On the way home he prayed silently, *Lord, here's another hurdle for you. I really need Your help when I talk to Kim-Anh. This whole thing has gotten complicated, but I guess You already know that. I don't know what is going to happen here, but I trust you for whatever the outcome. Please give me the words to say so I don't make it worse.*

They rode in silence for quite a while and finally Thea glanced over. "You're awfully quiet, Oliver, how are you feeling?"

"I'm fine, just a little tired. I've been trying to work things out in my mind. Has Kim-Anh asked any questions?"

"No, not that I know of, she's been concerned about you and how sick you were. Rather stoic actually, but I imagine she's just keeping her emotions under control. She reads her Bible a lot I'm told, and the household has been praying for both of you."

He occupied himself with looking out the window as they passed through the city. His mind kept drifting back to Kathryn, even as he made small talk with his mother.

"Kids sure dress differently now."

"Yes, they do, especially the girls. I don't suppose they think anything of it, they wear whatever the latest fad is, but I do wish they would have a little more modesty."

"Well, we probably shocked the older generation with what we wore. I think each older generation looks back on the younger with the same thoughts."

"I suppose so. It's just that some of these young women are so attractive and they dress like--"

"I get your drift."

They finally pulled up in front of the house and Cully was there to meet them.

Where is Kathryn? She probably despises me, deep down, for what I have done to her life.

"Welcome home again, Master Oliver." He saw Oliver into the house and settled into a comfortable chair by the fire in the library. Then he went to put the big car in the garage.

Kim-Anh came rushing into the room. "Father, you are home. I am so glad you are home. I missed you."

She studied her father's face. "Are you feeling better, Father? I was very worried."

Thea stood in the doorway a moment, caught Oliver's eye and backed quietly out the door to give them time alone.

"I'll need to lie down in a little while but the medication is already working. I feel a lot better." He chewed on his lower lip a moment and considered how to begin.

"Kim-Anh, there's some things we need to talk about. I'm sure you've heard enough to cause you some questions. I'd like to clarify things, if I may."

"I know that you used to love someone else before you met my mother. That is all I know. Mr. Culpepper told me that when you came home you would explain. I do not feel that he thought it right to talk about family."

"He is a good man, and wise. This is something I need to tell you about myself."

Kim-Anh sat down on the sofa, her hands in her lap, her face apprehensive.

"Many years ago, when I was in college, I met a girl. She was beautiful and we fell in love. My parents at the time did not want us to get married. They felt it was not the right time. We argued over this and I left the house and in my anger I joined the Army. I also eloped with the girl I loved and married her. Her name was Kathryn."

Kim-Anh nodded her head slowly. "She was your first wife?"

"Yes, my parents didn't like her, and I thought she had taken money from them and left me."

"That must have made you very sad."

"Sad, yes, and very angry. I couldn't understand how she could do this if she loved me. It all turned out to be a misunderstanding, but I did not know that until just recently."

"I do not think she would take the money, Father. You are a good person. A wife you would choose could not be a bad person."

Oliver leaned forward and put a hand on Kim-Anh's shoulder. "I appreciate the vote of confidence, but I'm not sure I deserve your kind words." He leaned back, feeling the weariness steal over him again. "When the chopper crashed I was still thinking that my wife had left me. The rebels your mother was working with found me, and she nursed me back to health. I fell in love with her and feeling like I had nothing to return home for, stayed in Sa Pa. The rest you know."

"This first wife did not leave you?"

He hung his head and shook it slowly. "No."

Kim-Anh sat silently for several moments staring at her hands. Oliver waited, letting her process what he'd told her.

Finally Kim-Anh looked up and there were tears in her eyes. "When you married my mother, you had this first wife still?"

"Yes, but I didn't know that. I thought I was free to marry again."

"Did this first wife come to your hospital?"

Oliver frowned. "You saw her?"

"I finished my food in the cafeteria and came back to the room. She kissed you on the forehead. I did not know what to say, so I ran away. She did not see me."

"I see."

"Will she--wish me to--go away?"

Oliver saw where Kim-Anh's thoughts were going and pulled himself up out of the chair. He reached out and caught his daughter in a bear hug.

"You are my daughter, Kim-Anh and I love you with all my heart.

Your mother and I also loved each other and you were born as a result of our love. No one will separate us, no one."

The girl's shoulders shook with silent tears as she clung to Oliver with all her might. "I have been afraid, Father, ever since I saw that woman with you. I prayed so hard. I did not want you to send me away."

Oliver wiped his own eyes with the back of his hand. "No one will send you away, Kim-Anh, that is, not until the day you go to college."

Kim-Anh backed off and gave her father a startled look. Oliver grinned at her and watched his daughter's face go from pinched anxiety to a smile.

"You make a joke, Father, but I am glad it will be much time until I go away to college."

Oliver tapped his daughter's chin lightly with a playful fist. "You just remember that, okay?"

The verbal exchange had worn him out and Oliver sank back down in the chair.

"Father, you must rest, you are tired."

"I think that's a great idea. Why don't you get Mr. Culpepper? I may need some help getting upstairs."

As if on cue, the doors to the library opened and Cully appeared, pushing his father in his wheelchair.

"Owiver…"

"Sorry to cause everyone so much concern, Father."

Gordon waved his good hand in the air. "More conshern to think you were dead!"

Oliver swallowed. "Well, I have to agree with you there." If they had lived with the thought of his death all these years, a little sickness was certainly a better alternative.

Gordon turned to Cully. "Son upstairs. Needs rest. I'm okay. You help him upstairs."

The words were clear enough. Cully settled Gordon by the fire and turned to Oliver who was standing, holding on to the chair. "If you'll just give me your arm, Master Oliver, I believe we can help you."

Kim-Anh came on Oliver's other side. The two of them managed to get Oliver upstairs to his bed. When he was settled, Thea came in and brought him some hot soup in a large mug. Kim-Anh stood anxiously at the foot of the bed.

"Kim-Anh your father will be all right. He just needs to sleep."

"Go ahead, your grandmother's right."

The girl reluctantly obeyed and left the room.

Thea sat on the edge of the bed and helped Oliver slowly drink the soup.

"Save your strength, Oliver, God will work all this out."

He yawned. "You're right, Mother, as usual. I can't even think about what to do next at this point." She set the empty mug of soup on the tray and took his hand. "I remember a very famous minister who used to say, "More things are wrought by prayer than this world dreams of." We just have to trust Him."

"I do, Mother. God has given me a new life and brought me through a lot of things in the past month. I feel His presence with me."

The medication and the warm soup had done its work and his eyelids slowly closed. Thea left the room and he listened to the sound of rain outside his window. It seemed to form words in his mind, over and over.

Where's Kathryn?

SEVENTY-SIX

It had been a week since Oliver returned home from the hospital and Thea, true to her word, kept Kathryn appraised of his progress.

She was waiting, longing for Oliver to invite her to visit. Was Oliver waiting for her to ask to come?

Finally, the phone rang that morning.

"Kathryn?"

"Oliver!" It was the voice she had longed to hear on the other end of the phone for so long and her heart leaped.

"My mind has been going crazy since that night at the hospital when you came. Would you consider—that is, would you be willing to come here to talk some more?"

She took a breath to calm herself. "Yes, Oliver, I'll come if you want me to. When?"

"As soon as it works for you, how about tomorrow?"

"I'll can be there by early afternoon, depending on traffic."

"Thank you, Kathryn. It will be good to see you."

"And you, too, Oliver."

Her heart beat harder as she hung up the phone and stood quietly. No problem, just drive to the house and confront your prodigal husband after twenty-five years. There was so much more to tell than she had said in the hospital, and she still had some unresolved feelings. What would she say? What would Oliver say? She sank down on the stairs and put her face in her hands. The ticking of the grandfather clock seemed to echo loudly in the silence.

The next morning Kathryn kissed Allison goodbye and hugged Jason and Joshua. She knew their thoughts and prayers were with her. She suggested Allison come, but her daughter wisely decided to wait. She and Oliver needed to be by themselves. She shook her head, realizing what a level-headed young woman her daughter had grown up to be.

She drove steadily toward the Bay Area praying for traveling mercies, for her mind wasn't on the road ahead of her. Had she been wrong to come to the hospital? Thea hadn't mentioned the incident at all. Maybe Oliver had kept it to himself. And what about Kim Anh? What did she know? She felt like a sixteen-year-old getting ready for her first big date. Before she left nearly every outfit she had was pulled out of the closet and spread on the bed.

Allison came into the room and watched Kathryn a moment and then giggled. "You can't decide what to wear?"

"Nothing looks right."

"Mother, I don't think my father is even going to notice what you are wearing. You're going to have a lot to talk about."

Kathryn slowly returned to the closet the dresses she felt were not right.

"I think you look best in those wonderful earth colors that accent your hair." She got up and moved over to the bed, reaching into the pile and pulled out a dress of soft, pale green wool with a square neck and three quarter length sleeves. "Now this dress looks terrific on you. It has slimming lines too." She held the dress out.

"How did I miss that one? Thank you, dear, it is pretty. You think this is the one?" It suddenly dawned on Kathryn that it was similar to the dress she'd worn on her wedding day. Was that the reason she'd liked the dress so much, and bought it?

"Definitely, he won't be able to take his eyes off you."

"Oliver said he was feeling stronger and wanted to talk to me."

"Then I don't know which of you is probably more nervous." Allison put an arm around her mother's shoulders. "It will be fine. So what's the worst-case scenario? That you just remain friends?"

"I suppose, and that would be all right. I'm not expecting anything."

Allison raised one eyebrow. "Really?"

"Oh, I don't know what I'm expecting." She put her hand under Allison's chin. "You should be going with me. I know you are anxious to finally meet your father."

"That's true, but there will be time enough for us to meet, soon. This trip is about you and my father. As anxious as I am to meet him, you need to go this time by yourself."

"Do you suppose she'll like me?"

"Who?"

"Kim-Anh."

"Of course she'll like you, unless you plan to ride in on a broom."

Now as the hours and miles passed, Kathryn hardly noticed the long drive. Her mind was filled with memories of past years with Oliver. Scenes passed through her mind of the beautiful wedding at the Presidio with all the flowers and she remembered that precious little guest house in Sausalito, their wonderful hostess, Margaret, and four wonderful days together. She thought of the times she and Oliver met secretly and how the hours flew as they talked and shared their hearts. She tried to picture Oliver wounded, struggling through the jungle and finally to imagine the face of an Asian woman who cared for Oliver and saved him, and later became his wife.

Oliver had been her soul mate. It was if she always knew him. They had been so perfect for each other. How could things get so mixed up? If she had not written that last letter to him, if his mother had not opened it and precipitated the row that caused Oliver to join the Army. Her mind was filled with all the 'what ifs' and finally she sighed and looked up at the sky that was clearing from the rain.

Aloud she murmured, "Even when there is a gray sky and clouds, somewhere above them is a blue sky. You're always there, Lord, aren't You? You know I need Your help desperately. You know in my heart I'm hoping for a blue sky after all the grey clouds of the past twenty-five years. Only You know what the outcome of this meeting will be. We're both older, Oliver and I, and yet in my heart-- " Tears began to run down her cheeks. "I just have to trust You, Lord. I put all my expectations in Your hands."

As she finally drove through the now familiar gateway into the circle drive of the Thornwell home, she felt like she couldn't breathe.

She looked at her reflection in the rearview mirror, combed her hair, then took a couple of deep breaths as she shut off the ignition and slowly got out of the car.

Cully opened the door. "It is good to see you again, Madam." He took her raincoat and small suitcase. As he stepped aside, Kathryn saw Thea waiting in the entry.

"Kathryn, dear," Thea embraced her. "He's in the library. I've filled him in on a few things." Obviously Oliver had not mentioned her visit that night.

Cully set her case down, and with her coat over one arm, opened one of the doors to the library. As she stepped into the room, he quietly shut the door behind her.

Her heart pounded as she saw him rise from an easy chair by the fire. He was so tall and still handsome.

"Kathryn?"

"Oliver."

He stood hesitantly, unsure of himself. He was older, definitely, but he was still Oliver.

"I'm glad you could come." He said quietly.

"I wanted to see, ah, how you were--"

"I'm doing well, thanks to modern medicine. Won't you sit down?"

He sat down again, perched on the edge of the chair and she lowered herself on the chair across from him.

"Would you like something? Coffee?"

"No, not right now, thank you. How are you feeling?"

"A little like my old self."

They sat staring at each other for a long moment. Finally he smiled, the smile she knew and remembered, that crinkled the tiny lines by his eyes.

"You haven't changed, Kathryn, you're still beautiful. I like the dress."

"Thank you." She didn't want to talk about the dress.

The conversation was inane, foolish.

He studied his hands for a moment. "I wanted to say how sorry I am for the mess I caused. There's no excuse for what I did to you. I was so angry--"

The hurtful thoughts burst out, "I believed that when you came home, you'd find me, you'd learn the truth, make things right between us. You didn't come back. When your mother and I compared stories, of when you died, I knew what you'd done."

"You should hate me."

"No, Oliver, even after I knew, I didn't hate you. I was angry with you and cried a lot, but I forgave you." She studied his face. "What you did brought you to the Lord. For that I'm deeply grateful. Your daughter is a wise young woman. She said that all these things had to happen for you to see your need for God."

"She's right. Even before I went to Vietnam, I had no time for God. I hated church."

She stood up, nervous as a schoolgirl, and walked over to the window, looking out at the gathering dusk.

"I also had to find Christ in my own way. God had to work in the lives of your mother and father before a reunion could take place. There has been a lot of healing in this house."

She heard him get up and move to join her at the window. "It never ceases to amaze me to see the change in this household from what it was when I left. And all because our daughter had the courage to contact my parents."

She did not miss the 'our daughter' although she wondered if Oliver realized he'd said it.

"What will you do now," she asked, so aware of him near her and the pounding of her heart.

"I'm returning to school. I may be the oldest guy in the class, but I'm going to get my degree."

"Law?"

"No. I had it out with my father. I'm studying architecture."

She turned to face him then, her eyes alight. "You are? Oh, Oliver, you're going to follow your dream. I'm glad for you."

"I can't, don't want to do it alone. It was your idea, Kathryn, remember?"

"Yes. I remember." Hesitantly she turned back to the window. "Will Kim-Anh go to school here?"

"She'll go to school wherever I live. She's a wonderful girl, Kathryn. You'll like her."

She wrapped her arms around herself, "What was she like?"

He knew she wasn't talking about Kim-Anh.

"She was gentle and kind, like you. She was strong. She lost her husband in the war. He fought with the rebel forces."

"That was harder to take than hearing that you were dead."

"That I married her? I guess I can understand that. I know how I felt when I thought you'd left me and taken my parent's check."

"So much has happened, Oliver, so many years. What's to be done with them?"

He stood behind her and she felt the warmth of him, so close and yet seemingly so far away.

He turned her to face him, his hands gently gripping her shoulders. "We can let those years go, Kathryn. We can thank God for the lessons we learned, for a future that wasn't there before."

Her voice was soft, in the way of women as her eyes searched his face. "Is there a future, Oliver?"

Then she saw in his eyes what she had waited for, dreamed of, hoped for. Still there, flickering with warmth like the fire that crackled in the fireplace behind them.

She smiled at him, and all of her soul was in her face.

He reached out and pulled her close, murmuring in her hair. "My beautiful Kathryn, my precious girl, and miracle of miracles, still my wife."

She lifted herself up for his kiss and the years melted away as though they'd never been. The heaviness she'd carried in her heart for so long slipped away into the shadows of the past. Both of them had crossed mountains that had loomed as barriers between them, and what was to come, they would face together. There were still relationships to forge and nourish, but now, leaning against him, she sighed. She was in Oliver's arms again, at last.

Epilogue

April, 1999

Kathryn paused to study her painting and added a few brushstrokes to the ear of a little mouse. It was a charming story and she looked forward to reading it to Joshua when the book was published.

A robin perched on the branch outside her window and trilled his heart out in the spring afternoon. To Kathryn, it reflected the joy she felt. She smiled to herself, the happiness inside spilling out like the sunshine that poured into the upstairs studio.

She and Oliver had renewed their vows with Kim-Anh and Allison as bridesmaids. Jason and Cully were the groomsmen.

Kathryn glanced at her watch. Kim-Anh and Oliver would be home soon. Oliver had applied for the fall semester at the Academy of Art Institute in San Francisco, her old alma mater, and to their delight, was accepted right away. He was studying architecture at long last and with one semester under his belt, hurried to classes like an eager schoolboy.

Tears still came readily to her eyes whenever she thought of the moment Oliver and Allison faced each other for the first time. He'd shaken hands with Jason and then stood awkwardly gazing at the daughter he'd never seen, not sure what to do. Then that slow grin began to spread over his face and seeing the longing in her eyes, opened his arms. Allison rushed into them and with tears rolling down both their faces, Allison murmured against his chest, the one word she hadn't been able to say to anyone in her entire life, "Daddy."

It was a difficult moment for Kim-Anh, but Oliver reached out for her too and enfolded both daughters in his arms. It was both a relief and a blessing to see how, after the initial tentative meeting, the half-sisters had taken to one other. Kim-Anh and Allison kept in touch by e-mail almost daily. Kim-Anh relished the idea of having an older sister and Allison seemed eager to share with Kim-Anh the ways of girls her age in America.

Kathryn and Allison wondered how Joshua would react to Oliver since Jason's dad was the only grandfather he knew, but Joshua had seen his daddy shake hands with this tall, friendly man and watched speculatively as his mama hugged Oliver. In the guileless way of small children, he decided this was a good person and wrapped his arms around Oliver's leg. Oliver picked him up and Joshua patted Oliver's face. "Gampa?" he questioned.

"Yes, Joshua," Oliver said softly, "I'm your gampa." Joshua beamed and his little chest swelled. "Gampa," he announced to everybody. Now they couldn't get enough of each other.

Oliver and Allison talked two to three times a week and Joshua always seemed to know when his mama was talking to Oliver. He would demand the phone to chatter away at his new "gampa."

She remembered the day up at the house in Lewiston when she and Oliver were trying to decide how to go about finding a place to live while Oliver was in school. That very afternoon Thea called with her news.

"Kathryn, tell Oliver a dear friend of mine, Elsie Dugan, will be moving into an assisted living residence next month. Her family mentioned they were going to rent out her place, so I told them about you and Oliver. They are willing to let you rent her home while Oliver is in school. It's an older condominium but in a nice area, not too many miles from downtown San Francisco. Oh Kathryn, I do feel that God is in this. Will you talk to Oliver?"

"He's off at the park with Joshua, Thea, but I'll talk to him as soon as he gets home. It sounds wonderful. When can we see it?"

"Why don't you come this weekend? You can stay with us and I'll make arrangements to meet someone from Elsie's family at the condo Saturday afternoon."

"Sounds great. We'll do that."

Kathryn and Oliver were delighted with the condo. It was perfect for their needs. Elsie had been a quilter and used the top floor bedroom with its many windows for a workroom. It became a studio for Kathryn's easel and art equipment, with half the room for Oliver's drawing board and computer. The master bedroom was comfortable with a fireplace they'd already made use of.

The second bedroom belonged to Kim-Anh who was enrolled in a private school not too far away where she was rapidly catching up on what she needed to reach her proper grade level. Once indoctrinated into the intricacies of the transportation system, Kim-Anh made her own way to school and home again. She was absorbing her education like a flower drinking in the morning dew.

As she looked around their comfortable new home, Kathryn remembered a few awkward moments in the condo when Thea insisted she and Gordon would pay the monthly rent while Oliver was in school.

"Oliver, you can't put your mind to your studies and work at the same time. Let us help you. It means so much to your father. We discussed it and he wants to do this for you."

Oliver was prepared to be stubborn and object, but when he saw how much it meant to them, he finally nodded his head and agreed. He had to consider his father who seemed to grow frailer each time they saw him and the possibility Gordon wouldn't be with them very much longer. For now he and his father were getting to know one another on different terms.

"At least my father is alive and was here for me when I returned from Vietnam," Oliver commented to Kathryn on the way home from looking at the condo.

Then the house in Lewiston was unexpectedly rented to a middle-aged couple who'd lost their home in a fire and decided not to rebuild. They were happy to have the house which was still partially furnished, since all her furniture wouldn't fit in the condo. They agreed to a lease of three years. After that they'd rent on a month to month basis, as the husband would be retiring and they wanted to move closer to their son and his family in Oregon. Kathryn marveled at how God had drawn all the loose ends together for this new phase of their life together.

The front door suddenly opened and closed and Kathryn heard quick footsteps on the stairs. Kim-Anh burst into the room, her eyes alight with pleasure.

"Mother, I made an A on my math and history tests today. I was worried I would not do well."

Kathryn smiled at her new Vietnamese daughter who was fast becoming a typical American teenager. "I'm proud of you, Kim-Anh. You'll be up to grade level very soon, I'm sure."

Kim-Anh came over to the easel. "Oh, a little mouse. You are so good, Mother. I love your paintings."

Kathryn gave her a hug. "I think I'd better stop for now. Why don't you put your things away and we'll start dinner."

"May I tell Allison about my tests?"

Kathryn waved a hand, "I'm sure she'll be glad to hear your news. Don't take too long though, your father will be home in an hour and he'll want to eat and get to work on his studies."

"Yes, Mother, I'll be very quick."

"Give my love to Allison--" Kathryn called after the slender figure, racing out of the room again, and shook her head. So much had happened in a few short months. She could never have imagined, a year ago, that once again she'd be dealing with a teenage girl in the house.

She cleaned her brush and put it away. As she left the room and started for the kitchen, she glanced down at the framed picture of Oliver on her work table. Kissing two of her fingers, she touched them to the photograph and hurried downstairs to prepare dinner for her family.

More titles by Diana Wells Taylor

Biblical Fiction books:

Journey to the Well (the woman of Samaria)

In the fourth chapter of John's Gospel, Jesus tells His surprised disciples that they must go through Samaria. Most Jews went out of their way to avoid that land because of animosity between the Jews and Samaritans. Though apprehensive, they didn't question the Master, and after a long journey, they arrived at Jacob's Well. Jesus stopped to rest of there while the disciples went into the town of Shechem to buy food. As he waited, a lone Samaritan woman came to draw water. Since Samaria had many springs, she could have gone to the local well. Instead she went a mile out of her way in the hottest part of the day to draw water. Who was she? Why did Jesus choose this woman as the first person to whom he would reveal himself as the Messiah? Was there more to her than we have supposed?

Journey to the Well is a compassionate and riveting portrayal of a woman who has historically been maligned. This surprisingly fresh look at the woman of Samaria reveals an inner strength and courage that helped her face the joys and heartbreaks that shaped her life. One by one, the pieces fall into place that draw her at last to Jacob's Well, and a life-changing confrontation with Jesus.

Mary Magdalene

One woman desperate for hope. One Savior with the power to heal.

A beautiful girl blossoming into womanhood, Mary has high hopes for a life filled with learning, family, and young love. In one dreadful night, all of that changes. The nightmares come first, then the waking visions of unspeakable terror, until Mary hardly remembers her dreams for the future.

Can the Most High deliver her from this torment? How long must she wait for healing?

This vivid portrait of the enigmatic Mary of Magdala comes to life in the hands of an imaginative master story-teller. Diana Wallis Taylor introduces you to a Mary who is both utterly original and respectful of the biblical account, opening your eyes to a redemption that knows no bounds.

Martha: A Novel

Perhaps one of the most misunderstood and misrepresented characters of the New Testament is Martha. Often painted in the colors of reproach, Martha seems to be the poster child for how not to be a follower of Jesus. From the mind of Diana Wallis Taylor comes this touching, well-researched portrayal of Martha of Bethany, sister of Mary and Lazarus. Through Taylor's lush descriptions and inspired combination of imagined and recorded dialogue, Martha's world–her trials, triumphs, and loves–vibrantly comes to life. Follow Martha as she is jilted by her betrothed, falls in love with a Roman soldier, grieves the death of her father, cares for her siblings, and serves her Lord with dignity and grace. Readers will never read the biblical story of Martha the same way again.

Claudia, Wife of Pontius Pilate

Claudia's life did not start easily. The illegitimate daughter of Julia, reviled and exiled daughter of Caesar Augustus, Claudia spends her childhood in a guarded villa with her mother and grandmother. When Tiberius, who hates Julia, takes the throne, Claudia is wrenched away from her mother to be brought up in the palace in Rome. The young woman is adrift–until she meets Lucius Pontius Pilate and becomes his wife. When Pilate is appointed Prefect of the troublesome territory of Judea, Claudia does what she has always done: she makes the best of it. But unrest is brewing on the outskirts of the Roman Empire, and Claudia will soon find herself and her beloved husband embroiled in controversy and rebellion. Might she find peace and rest in the teaching of the mysterious Jewish Rabbi everyone seems to be talking about?

Readers will be whisked through marbled palaces, dusty marketplaces, and idyllic Italian villas as they follow the unlikely path of a woman who warrants only a passing mention in one of the Gospel accounts. Diana Wallis Taylor combines her impeccable research with her flair for drama and romance to craft a tale worthy of legend.

House of the Forest

It was fun setting my romantic suspense story, "House of the Forest" in Big Bear in the San Bernardino mountains of California. I have an 81 year-old house there and it made a great setting: a motley crew of people trying to find almost a million dollars in stolen bank money and a romance thrown in.

A young woman must face her own heart as she deals with the death of her favorite aunt, her precarious engagement to an ambitious young pastor, and her sudden embroilment in the search for long lost bank funds stolen by her estranged uncle years before.

Smoke Before the Wind

He was every girl's dream...

Carrie Dickson can hardly believe her good fortune-engaged to the handsome and rich Andrew Van Zant, she returns home to her beloved mountain community and to her family to make final preparations for her fast-approaching wedding.

While there, she renews her friendship with Scott Spencer, a young man she had a secret crush on in high school. Scott's strong Christian commitment causes Carrie to examine her own faith-and her fiancé's-and her growing awareness triggers in her troubled feelings and jeopardizes her happiness. But with the wedding only weeks away, Carrie resolves to make the best of the future she willingly chose with the man she has promised to marry.

However, when Andrew finally arrives in the mountain town to meet Carrie's parents, things don't go as planned. Her cousin Linda, who has always considered Carrie's boyfriends fair game, exposes Andrew's true motives and Carrie is faced with the reality of the direction she is going.

Confused over the pressure from Andrew for a hasty marriage, as well as her burgeoning feelings for Scott, Carrie realizes that only God's strength and wisdom can help her choose the right path. She feels she needs more time. But, before she and Andrew can talk, a raging forest fire erupts and threatens all she holds dear.

Carrie has only moments to make the decision that will forever change her life...